CAMMIE & ALEX'S
adventures in the
ICY PARK

CAMMIE & ALEX'S
adventures in the
ICY PARK

OLGA JAFFAE

TATE PUBLISHING *& Enterprises*

Published by Tate Publishing & Enterprises, LLC
127 E. Trade Center Terrace | Mustang, Oklahoma 73064 USA
1.888.361.9473 | www.tatepublishing.com

Tate Publishing is committed to excellence in the publishing industry. The company reflects the philosophy established by the founders, based on Psalm 68:11,
"The Lord gave the word and great was the company of those who published it."

Book design copyright © 2011 by Tate Publishing, LLC. All rights reserved.
Cover design by Brandon Wood
Interior design by Nathan Harmony

Published in the United States of America

ISBN: 978-1-61346-226-3
Juvenile Fiction / Fantasy
11.08.01

ACKNOWLEDGMENTS

I would like to thank my wonderful husband, Gary Jaffae, for believing in me and the book and for his neverending help and encouragement.

My deepest appreciations go to the physical therapists and staff of the Lancaster Orthopedic Group for helping me with rehabilitation after my injury.

Special thanks go to the talented young ice dancer Alexander Petrov for his interesting and creative ideas.

Table of Contents

DOUBLE AXEL

"No, no, no!" Coach Ferguson slapped Cammie's green skate guard against the boards. The sound ricocheted against the glass walls of the rink, startling the rest of the skaters. They stopped in the middle of what they were doing to look at Cammie, who had just clumsily gotten back on her feet after another failed attempt at the double axel. Panting, Cammie skated up to her coach.

"You need more height," Coach Ferguson said sternly. "Have you been doing your ankle strengthening exercises?"

"Sure." Cammie brushed the ice off her gloves. Too late. Her hands were already wet, and the cold air of the rink was causing them to stiffen.

"Well, I don't see it. Okay, let's try another double axel. And pull in tighter."

The coach's suggestion reached Cammie's ears when she was already gliding across the rink trying to pick up enough speed for a two-and-a-half revolution jump. Woohoo! The wind whistled in her ears. The green walls of the rink whooshed by; the skaters in green skating clothes blended in a foggy mist. Cammie got on her forward outside edge and bent her left knee, waiting for the right moment to spring up.

Faster, faster, she told herself. She swung her arm and her free leg trying to jump outside the circle and then quickly pulled in. Yes! For a split second, she believed she had done it. Her right toe brushed against the ice; she opened up to check her landing, but no, it was too late. Cammie fell hard, but the pain in her right thigh was familiar. She picked herself up from the pale green surface without a wince.

"That's it!" Coach Ferguson had skated up to Cammie, and there was determination in the woman's gray eyes. "We'll lay off the double axel for a while. You aren't ready for it."

"No, please! I have actually landed it four...no, three times. You saw me." Cammie pressed both hands against her heart as though the gesture could help her to make her point. Wishful thinking. Coach Ferguson was well known for her toughness.

"A jump needs to be consistent before you put it in a program. So you'll do a single axel instead."

"But—"

"Don't argue with me, Cammie! Sometimes a well-executed single looks better than a forced double."

"But … I can't win with just a single axel!" Feeling her eyes moisten, Cammie scanned the rink.

As though overhearing her, Dana, a pretty blonde girl from Cammie's dorm, flew up in the air in a beautiful double axel.

"Liz can do it too. I, I know," Cammie stammered as she pointed to a petite Asian girl who was doing split jumps in the opposite corner.

"And I even saw those four try double axels." Cammie nodded in the direction of younger girls who were practicing their group number on the other side of the rink. The girls kept messing up, but the mistakes didn't seem to discourage them. One moment they would fall on the ice in a green heap; in another second, they would laugh at the top of their lungs.

"You can't compare yourself with other skaters," Coach Ferguson said impassively.

That was the silliest thing Cammie had ever heard. In spite of her distress, she couldn't suppress a smirk. "Yeah, right. What are competitions for, then?"

Cammie had said *competitions*, though in reality, she was thinking of one particular event: Skateland Annual Competition that was supposed to start as early as the next morning. It was one of the biggest events in the country. Top finishers usually got passes to Junior Nationals and Grand Prix events.

So far, Cammie had never been able to medal at a Skateland Annual Competition, except of course, three years ago when she had gotten a gold medal. But it didn't count because back then Cammie had competed in a no-test event, and that wasn't a high enough level to place Cammie among the best skaters in the country. This time, however—

"So that's it for today." Coach Ferguson skated away from Cammie. Their private lesson was over.

Cammie took a deep breath then let the air out slowly, trying to control her anger. How could her coach not understand that it was important for Cammie to win this time? She was thirteen years old already, and at that age, most top skaters had already landed one or more triple jumps. And Cammie had been stuck with the elusive double axel for almost a year without much progress.

Well…perhaps things weren't that bad. Cammie hadn't lied to Coach Ferguson when she had told her that she had landed the double axel several times. Now all she needed was consistency. And every skater knew that consistency came with practice. Which meant that Cammie needed more practice. As simple as that.

Cammie took a big gulp of water from her bottle and put it back on the board. She rubbed her frozen hands and skated back to the middle of the rink. She went into backward crossovers, preparing herself for another attack at the double axel. *There, get up higher*, she told herself. No, she landed on both feet. Well, it wasn't acceptable, but at least she hadn't fallen.

"Cammie, come back here!"

Startled, Cammie looked at the exit where Coach Ferguson stood, her eyes narrowed in anger.

"I almost did it this time!" Cammie said excitedly.

"When I told you *that's it*, I meant it," Coach Ferguson said. "No more skating today."

"Why not?"

"Freestyle session is over."

"So what? I can stay for the public session." Cammie looked around. Her skating friends had already left the ice, but the arena was quickly filling up with families, young couples, and plump women in tracksuits.

"No public session. You need rest before tomorrow." Coach Ferguson turned away from Cammie, signaling that the conversation was over.

"But, Coach Ferguson, please—"

"Did you hear what I said?" The coach stopped abruptly, and this time, her gray eyes looked almost black with anger. "Your program is strong enough, and you are going to the dorm now. Is that understood?"

Cammie blinked, trying her best not to cry. "I will never win without a double axel! I—"

"See you tomorrow. Excuse me!" The coach's last sentence was not for Cammie but for a formally dressed man who was placing his skate guards on the boards.

The man winked at Cammie. She realized that he had heard everything and looked away.

"Try to get a good night rest," Coach Ferguson said calmly.

Cammie waited until the woman disappeared in the coaches' room, then pulled on her skate guards and waddled away. Tears clouded her eyes; she walked into somebody, blurted out a quick apology, and slammed the locker room door hard behind her. Luckily, the locker room was empty; the skaters from Cammie's freestyle group were gone.

Cammie plopped herself on the bench and pulled her backpack closer to her.

"That's not fair!" She jerked the zipper on her skating dress. It moved about half an inch then got stuck in the green polyester fabric. Cammie pulled it hard, but the zipper refused to move.

"Just great. Now it's broken," Cammie mumbled, trying to free her dress from the metal clutch. It didn't work. Now the zipper was less than half open, and it was all Coach Ferguson's fault.

"She is evil, evil!" Sobbing, Cammie squirmed her way out of the dress and got into jeans and a sweatshirt. She quickly stuffed her dress into her backpack and ran out of the locker room. She pulled the heavy exit door and walked outside.

Cold winter air brushed her flashing cheeks and wiped the tears off her eyes. Cammie stopped on the porch and sighed. Though it was just after six o'clock, it was already dark. Light snow was falling, and it seemed to Cammie that every snowflake was executing a perfect double axel. Cammie sniveled, feeling her eyes fill up with tears again.

What was the point of competing tomorrow if she was going to lose anyway? Perhaps it would be better to merely withdraw from the competition. *Yes, that would be great*, Cammie thought to herself.

Tomorrow everybody would skate their programs, and she would sit in her dorm room all alone and cry. Perhaps she could even leave Skateland for good, return to her home, and forget about figure skating altogether. Or maybe, she could—

"You skated well today. I like your program," a throaty voice spoke up.

As Cammie turned around, she found herself face-to-face with a tall, slightly overweight woman. The lady's dark-brown hair was pulled up in an elegant chignon, and her eyes were covered by dimmed glasses in gold frames. The woman wore a silvery mink coat that flowed down to her feet clad in custom-made skating boots.

She must be one of the judges, Cammie thought. Did she say she liked my program? How cool! Yes, but...

"I'm still struggling with my double axel," she said, feeling strangely guilty.

"I saw your double axel. It's this close." The woman brought her thumb and index finger together. Cammie thought there was a silver monogram on the judge's black leather glove, but she couldn't read the letters.

"Just work on it a little more, and you'll land it at the competition. But what a program! Strength, grace, and poise—you have it all, girl. I believe I'm talking to our next intermediate national champion." The lady's full lips twisted in a smile. Her impeccable teeth appeared even whiter against hot-pink lipstick.

For a moment, Cammie had a fleeting thought that she had seen the woman somewhere. But before the idea could register, the lady handed Cammie a huge bouquet.

"Here is something for good luck tomorrow, charming skater!"

"Roses! My favorite." Cammie wrapped her fingers around the long stems and buried her face in the soft petals. Squinting with delight, she breathed in the flowers' delicate fragrance, she tightened her grasp...

"Ouch!" Sharp pain shot through Cammie's hand. As she looked at her left middle finger, she saw a drop of blood.

"Oh, not before the competition!" She picked a handful of snow and pressed it against the tiny wound.

"I forgot that roses have thorns," she said nervously, unwilling to look like a baby in front of the generous judge. Yet when she looked at the spot where the woman had just stood, she saw nothing except for a swirl of dancing snowflakes. The lady was gone.

Cammie shrugged. Surely, she couldn't expect the busy judge to hang out with her too long. The good thing was that she was in a much better mood now. So what if Coach Ferguson thought that Cammie Wester wasn't up to a double axel? There was somebody who really believed in her.

Suddenly Cammie had an idea—simple yet brilliant. Her double axel was almost there–even the judge had just confirmed it. All she needed was consistency. And consistency came with practice. Which only meant that Cammie had to use the few hours she still had before the competition to work on her double axel some more. Where, though?

Cammie looked around. The small square adjacent to the Green Rink looked busy. More people were coming to the public session. It meant that the ice would be jam-packed, so landing doubles would be a real problem. Besides, Cammie wasn't sure Coach Ferguson had left the rink. What if the coach decided to stay in her office longer and found out that Cammie had disobeyed her? No, Cammie wasn't ready to face Coach Ferguson's fury, thank you very much! Which left Cammie with only one option: an outdoor rink. Cammie pulled down her wool hat to cover her ears better and skated in the direction of the dorm, weighing her options as she moved ahead.

There were quite a few outdoor rinks in Skateland, but Cammie didn't have to think about which of them suited her purpose best. She didn't want to go to the Main Square Rink. Even though it was big and the ice was fast and smooth, the surrounding area was filled with quite a few shops and restaurants. Someone would notice Cammie's effort at landing the double axel right away and tell her to go to an official practice rink.

And of course, Cammie couldn't go to any of the private rinks that many Skateland residents had in their backyards. That would mean trespassing, and Cammie didn't look forward to facing Skateland police. She could practice her jumps on one of the countless ice paths that people used to skate to their destinations. Yet that wouldn't be a good idea because the ice on sidewalks was too hard and didn't hold the edge well. No, for her double axel, Cammie needed the best ice—and that left the Icy Park, a huge recreational area that gradually merged into a forest.

The section of the Icy Park that was closest to the residential area looked nice, all trimmed and polished with beautiful paths, ice sculptures, and gazebos. Several frozen ponds had been turned into rinks with ice of different colors. Skateland residents enjoyed spending their free time in the park skating among bright evergreen trees with the sun caressing their faces. But if an excited visitor skated too far into the depth of the park, he could see the trees become taller and darker. The upper branches of the trees swirled and intertwined, letting in very little light; thick, gnarled roots weaved across the ice paths, blocking the skater's way, impeding his progress.

But what made the Icy Park particularly creepy was the fact that it was the place where Skateland witches lived. The exact location was unknown, but the witches' homes had to be somewhere far in the woods; at least that was where Cammie and her friend Alex had met the witches on several occasions.

Skating witches were quite unusual characters. All of them had been skaters at some point, but because they had been unsuccessful in their athletic careers, they had become bitter and decided to dedicate the rest of their lives to revenge and destruction. The witches had their hearts firmly set on jeopardizing other people's skating careers, and they were particularly good at that.

More than once had Cammie seen her friends getting attacked by witches, and she too had only narrowly escaped the evil women's clutches several times. Even though most of Skateland residents didn't really believe in witches, people still preferred to stay away from the dark paths of the Icy Park. Parents and coaches had warned their children against taking shortcuts through the park. Some kids took the advice seriously; others chose to ignore it.

A year ago, after Cammie's roommate, Sonia, had been abducted by the gang of witches, what once had been a mere caution turned into an official Skateland rule. Skaters had been absolutely forbidden to practice in the park, and as far as Cammie knew, everybody had complied. That is, everybody except Cammie. Even after the official order had been released, Cammie had visited the Icy Park several times.

Cammie stopped in the middle of the street about a hundred feet away from her dorm. The trees of the Icy Park towered on her left. If she had taken the shortcut from the rink through the park, she would have reached her dorm in fifteen minutes instead of forty. But that wasn't the issue now. Cammie looked around, making sure no one could see her. Every window of the dorm building was lit; the skaters were probably putting final touches on their costumes or merely relaxing before tomorrow's competition. There was not a living soul outside.

Cammie quickly stepped off the sidewalk into the snow and then onto a winding path that led into the depths of the Icy Park. Immediately she found herself in thick darkness; the chunky limbs blocked the light coming from the lampposts completely. Yet Cammie wouldn't let that little detail intimidate her. She skated fast without looking around, and before she knew it, she reached a miniature rink that was ensconced between old snow-covered trees.

Cammie had come across the small circular pond a year ago, when she was also desperate for extra ice time. The ice on the pond was good—solid and smooth—and Cammie could practice her jumps there without being afraid of getting hurt. But the best thing about the rink was its location. It was only half a mile from Cammie's dorm, yet the bulky trees around the pond kept it well hidden from view. Cammie was sure nobody else, including the witches, knew about the pond. She didn't go there very often, only when she needed to work on some move that Coach Ferguson had discouraged her from trying. It was there that Cammie had finally managed to get her double lutz consistent a year ago. After that, she nicknamed the pond *my lucky rink*. Perhaps it would bring her luck again, and she would finally land her double axel.

Cammie put her backpack and her flowers on the snow and jumped onto the ice. She could swear she heard it sing under her feet. The ice was pleasant to skate on, neither too hard nor too soft. Even though light snow was still falling, the trees provided perfect protection from snowflakes, keeping the ice smooth.

Cammie set herself in preparation for her double axel, bent her knee, and jumped. Miraculously, she landed the jump on the first try—a good, solid double axel.

"Wow!" she cried but forbade herself to get too excited. She had to try another one to make sure the first successful attempt wasn't a fluke.

She sped forward and shot herself in the air again. She rode out on a secure backward outside edge.

"Yes!" Cammie threw her fist in the air but didn't stop. Instead, she picked up more speed. She absolutely had to land another double axel so her body would remember how to do it right. She bent her knee; the ice scraped under her blade. *What if I miss this one?* she suddenly thought. But she was already spinning in the air faster and faster. She landed solidly and clapped her hands, unable to hide her excitement anymore.

"I did it! I did it!" she sang.

A snowflake fell on her hot upper lip. She licked it off impatiently and looked around.

"Gosh, and nobody has seen me land those double axels," Cammie grumbled. Well, what did it matter? She could do it; that was important. Humming

"If You're Happy and You Know It," Cammie raced around the pond, landing one double axel after another. Boy, why had she had so much trouble with this jump in the first place? Double axels were easy; they were wonderful!

Well, perhaps the generous judge had managed to instill some confidence into her—and that was exactly what she needed. Coach Ferguson had been putting her down for the last couple of weeks; surely she had been unable to land the difficult jump cleanly. Now as Cammie kept replaying the judge's nice words in her mind staring at the roses, she felt almost like an Olympian.

Cammie completely lost track of time. She jumped and jumped, feeling like one of the snowflakes that still swirled in the air.

"Ye-e-e-e!"

Hey, what is that? Something howled. Is it an animal? Panting, Cammie stopped before she could try another double axel and listened in. The park was eerily quiet. She peered into the thicket. She could see nothing but solid darkness. Her heart pounded heavily in her chest. For the first time tonight, she thought it might be late. And she had an important competition tomorrow. Perhaps it would be best to get back to the dorm.

Cammie stepped off the ice into the snow and bent down to pick up her backpack and her flowers. And then it happened. The peaceful silence was ripped by another blood-curdling shrill, and the thicket on Cammie's left spread like a curtain on a stage. A solitary candle flickered, and a hooded figure dressed in white stepped out onto the ice.

"No!" Cammie tried to scream, but the sound got stuck in her throat. Her knees gave way; she slid down onto the snow.

"We meet again," a creepy voice said. A gaunt hand lifted the hood, and Cammie saw the familiar bloodshot eyes that belonged to the Witch of Fear.

"No!" Cammie stepped back, her knees banging against each other.

"You aren't going to escape this time, girl!" the Witch of Fear said calmly.

The darkness behind her stirred, and out walked five more figures, equally menacing looking. The witches were closing around Cammie, and there was absolutely nothing she could do.

"Help!" she screamed and squeezed her eyelids tight to escape the reddish glow coming from the Witch of Fear's eyes. She was sure that if she kept looking into those demonic eyes, she would die on the spot. Of all the witches, it was the Witch of Fear Cammie hated the most. She was sure she could fight pride or injuries—anything. But what could she do against the cold feeling of horror that crept into her joints, weakening her limbs, almost paralyzing her? Cammie's eyelids twitched. No, she wouldn't open her eyes. But even without looking, she knew that the witch was getting closer. Cammie gagged at the pungent smell of sulfur coming from the witch's mouth, shuddered, tried to step away, and fell backward.

"Cammie! Cammie!"

What was it? Another witch? No, it was a human voice. Of course, it didn't belong to any of the witches; the voice sounded familiar. Somebody had come to rescue Cammie.

She opened her eyes. The Witch of Fear still stood bent over Cammie, but the woman's posture telegraphed uncertainty.

"Cammie, where are you? Do you hear me?"

Finally, Cammie recognized the voice. It belonged to Mrs. Page, her dorm supervisor.

"Over here!" Cammie shouted so loudly that the Witch of Fear squirmed and recoiled.

"So you think your dumpy dorm supervisor can scare me away?" the witch hissed. "How naïve!"

"Get away from me!" Cammie slid backward unto the ice.

"You're coming with me!" The witch definitely wasn't going to give up.

There came a cracking of limbs. "Skateland police!"

This time, Cammie heard two male voices shouting almost in unison.

"I'll be darned!" one of the witches who stood behind the Witch of Fear spat out; Cammie could swear it was the Witch of Injuries, also known as Winja.

"Let's get out of here!" the Witch of Fear said quickly.

More cracking and scraping followed, and a split second later the witches were gone. But before Cammie could sigh with relief, the darkness rippled, and two policemen materialized in front of her. Cammie recognized the familiar gray uniforms with Skateland logo on the front pockets picturing a skater in the attitude position who held a flower. Each of the petals of the flower represented one of Skateland's official practice rinks.

"There she is. Oh, thank God!" a female voice exclaimed, and Cammie saw that the policemen were closely followed by Mrs. Page.

"You are under arrest for breaking Skateland law!" the younger of the two policemen said haughtily. As he approached Cammie, she recognized the long nose and full lips belonging to Lieutenant Turner. Cammie had met the young man before and hadn't liked him, thinking the guy was too full of himself.

"Let me handle it, officers!" Mrs. Page carefully stepped onto the ice and stretched her hand toward Cammie.

Cammie grabbed the woman's hand and jumped to her feet.

"Are you all right?" The woman looked at Cammie's hands and feet, probably fearing she might be injured.

Cammie hopped several times. "I'm fine. Thank you." She was still trembling, but the presence of other people had pushed the memory of the Witch of Fear's terrifying eyes to the back of her mind.

"Oh, you're fine!" Now that Mrs. Page didn't have to worry about Cammie's health, she looked as though she wasn't going to contain herself any longer.

"Cammie, what were you thinking? Do you realize what time it is? I was worried sick about you. I called the rink, but Coach Ferguson had already left, and the night guard said he hadn't seen you."

Oh, so Coach Ferguson didn't know about Cammie's secret practice. Good.

"I had to call the police so they could help me find you!" Mrs. Page shouted.

"Oh, no!" Only now did Cammie realize that Mrs. Page wasn't kidding. Boy, had she really called the police? But why? Why hadn't she just waited for Cammie to come to the dorm? Although, if Mrs. Page hadn't called the police, the witches would have jinxed Cammie for sure.

"What were you doing out in the park so late anyway?" Mrs. Page yelled.

"It's not that late," Cammie said feebly.

"It's eleven forty!" Lieutenant Turner said nastily.

"What?" Cammie couldn't believe what she had heard. How could it be? In all the excitement of landing her double axel, Cammie had completely lost track of time. She had thought it was seven, maybe eight o'clock. And surely, she hadn't expected Mrs. Page to call the rink or go to the park looking for her.

"Mrs. Page, I'm sorry I got you worried, but I absolutely had to land my double axel before the competition, so—"

Before Cammie could even finish her speech, Mrs. Page's face contorted with fury. "Double axel? And you went to the park to practice it? As far as I know, you have freestyle practices to work on your jumps."

"Well, Coach Ferguson wouldn't let me practice anymore and … ah!" Cammie stopped midsentence, realizing she had made a terrible blunder. Now everybody knew she had been working on her jump against her coach's orders.

"Well, this will be something for Coach Ferguson to find out, then," Mrs. Page said. She was still breathing hard. Apparently, a half-mile run across the park was too much for the plump middle-aged woman.

Cammie gasped in horror. "Oh no, Mrs. Page, you can't tell Coach Ferguson about it. Please, anything but that. I—"

"I think we're missing the point here," the older policeman spoke up. "Cammie, do you realize that going to the Icy Park alone at night is a serious offense? Don't you even understand that you could be hurt?"

"But I was only practicing!" Cammie knew the older policeman too; his name was Captain Greenfield. Last year, when Cammie, Alex, and Sonia had found themselves surrounded by the whole gang of witches, Captain Greenfield had scared the evil women away. And now he had helped Cammie again.

"Thank you for your help, Captain Greenfield," Cammie mumbled. She liked the man. He was nice and fair, unlike Lieutenant Turner, who always tried to use a skater's weakness to his advantage. Lieutenant Turner had once been a competitive skater but hadn't gone too far. He still couldn't get over the bitterness of never making it to the top, so he vented his fury on young lawbreakers.

Lieutenant Turner could probably become a perfect skating witch, Cammie thought. She pictured the young man in a white gown, long hair falling down his shoulders. The image was so ludicrous that Cammie couldn't suppress a giggle.

Immediately she realized she had made another big mistake, for Lieutenant Turner jerked his chin up in an expression of utter disgust. "See? She thinks breaking the law is funny. She has absolutely no respect for authority. Captain Greenfield, I would suggest disqualification, probably for a year. And of course from tomorrow's competition."

Cammie stopped laughing immediately. "What?"

"You heard me!" Lieutenant Turner said maliciously.

Cammie felt dizzy. Fearing she was going to faint, she staggered to a nearby tree and leaned against the trunk. No, it couldn't be true. They couldn't disqualify her. For what? Just because she had been practicing too hard? The cops' faces blurred; Cammie swallowed hard to drive the tears away.

"Well," Captain Greenfield said uncertainly, "I think disqualifying Cammie would be too harsh a punishment. Personally, I would vote for a regular disciplinary action that can be well handled by her coach."

"Yes, I can take care of it," Mrs. Page said glumly. "What I'll do is, I'll let Coach Ferguson know what happened tonight, and I assure you Cammie will be punished."

"Mrs. Page, please!" Cammie raised both arms, but the dorm supervisor interrupted her.

"I'd better take her to the dorm, Officers. She needs to be in bed," Mrs. Page said firmly.

"Well, in that case..." Captain Greenfield took an official-looking notepad out of his pocket. "I need to make a report. Here, Mrs. Page, I want you to sign here and here. Yes, right where it says that Cammie Wester has been released to your authority."

They make me look like a criminal, Cammie thought angrily. Her joy of landing her double axel and then getting rescued from the witches was slowly beginning to evaporate.

"Let's go!" Mrs. Page grabbed Cammie by her hand unceremoniously and pulled her in the direction of the dorm. Reluctantly, Cammie obeyed. She heard the scraping of the policemen's blades behind her, so she kept her mouth shut until they reached the dorm building. Cammie watched the cops get into a silver ice mobile with "Skateland Police" lettered on the side.

Mrs. Page still wouldn't let go of Cammie's hand. She pulled Cammie up on the porch and unlocked the front door.

When the door lock was secured after her, Mrs. Page finally released Cammie from her firm grip and brought her reddened face closer to Cammie's. "Now I need an explanation from you, girl. And you'd better be quiet. You don't want to wake up the rest of the girls."

"But, Mrs. Page, honestly—"

"Is landing one jump worth ruining your skating career for good?"

"No, but—"

"I thought you of all the skaters didn't have to be reminded of the witches."

"Sometimes you have to forget about the witches. There are more important things in life."

"Oh, really?" Mrs. Page stomped her skate guard against the wood floor. Then she grimaced at the loud banging sound and looked up surreptitiously, apparently fearing that the sound would wake up everybody in the dorm.

"If I'm not mistaken, I heard you out there crying for help." Now Mrs. Page was almost whispering.

"Uh, yeah, I mean thank you!" As Cammie thought of the Witch of Fear's menacing glare, she shuddered again.

"Whom did you see there?" Mrs. Page asked softly.

Cammie averted the supervisor's eye. "It was the Witch of Fear who approached me. But there were several other witches behind her."

"My goodness, they could have cursed you! If we hadn't come in time … Oh!" Mrs. Page quickly covered her mouth and looked up, yet the dorm was quiet.

Cammie sighed deeply as she thought of the cold fear rising in her chest when the evil witch bent over her. The worst thing about curses was the effect on a person's skating career. Several years ago, Sonia, Cammie's friend and roommate, had been viciously attacked by the Witch of Fear. As the result, Sonia had developed supernatural fear of ice, and she couldn't skate for almost two years. No, Cammie definitely didn't want the same to happen to her.

Cammie knew that Mrs. Page was still waiting for an apology.

"I'm sorry," Cammie said humbly.

Mrs. Page let the air out, and Cammie knew that the woman's anger was ebbing away.

"Well, it's too late to call Coach Ferguson now," Mrs. Page said uncertainly. "But I'll inform her of your misdemeanor first thing in the morning."

"But you can't do that. Coach Ferguson will be busy at the competition," Cammie said sweetly. Now she hoped things would be all right. Her dorm supervisor was well known for her leniency.

"I'm sure your coach will want to know what happened," Mrs. Page said stubbornly. "And it will be up to her to decide whether you will be competing or not."

"Mrs. Page, come on!"

The dorm supervisor cut Cammie short. "Look, it's past midnight, and I'm tired. I want you to go to bed *now*."

Mrs. Page waited for Cammie to walk up to the third floor; then there was a click of the light switch, and the front lobby turned dark.

Cammie sprinted along the long hallway lit up with sconces on both sides and turned the door handle to her room.

A head covered with red tangled locks rose from one of the beds. "Gosh, Cammie, where were you? I was so worried. I couldn't sleep. And it's so important to get a good night's rest before the competition."

Cammie sat down on the edge of Sonia's bed and smiled right into her roommate's sour face. "You know what? I landed my double axel. And not just once but maybe fifteen times. And tomorrow I'll do it in my program. That's it!"

SKATELAND ANNUAL COMPETITION

When Cammie woke up the next morning, the joy of landing her double axel still hadn't worn off. She felt strong and rested, even though she had only gotten six hours of sleep. Cammie opened her eyes and stared at the ceiling, enjoying the feeling of excitement welling up inside her. Even the thought of today's competition didn't put her on edge; somehow she knew she was going to have a great day. Cammie stretched like a cat, grinned, and jumped out of bed.

"Aren't you nervous at all?" Sonia asked as she watched Cammie pull on her tights.

Cammie, who had been humming her program music, smiled. "Perhaps a little. But you know what? I really think a have a shot at winning this time. Can you believe it? Last night Coach Ferguson took the double axel out of my program. I was so ticked. I thought of giving up skating altogether. And then, I landed it."

Cammie figured it would be better not to tell Sonia about her trip to the Icy Park. Let her friend think Cammie had landed her double axel at the public session. Sonia was such a stickler for rules, and after being viciously attacked by the witches twice, Cammie's roommate turned into a nervous wreck each time someone said the word *witch* close to her. So what was the point of making Sonia worry? And who cared where exactly Cammie had landed her double axel?

She had the jump, and that was it.

Sonia's hand holding a hairbrush froze in the air. "What? Coach Ferguson told you not to do the double axel?"

"That's right. Can you imagine? *Do a single!*" Cammie mimicked her coach's almost expressionless drawl and grunted.

"But…" Sonia put down the hairbrush and started twisting her wavy red hair in a bun. "Coach Ferguson may still want you to do a single axel in the program. Your double axel can't be consistent enough."

"Oh stop it! I don't want to hear it again!" Cammie slid her hands through the sleeves of her sweatshirt and stood up. "Last night I landed every double axel I tried."

"Well, it's not the same as doing it in the program at high speed."

Cammie smirked. "Yeah, like you can pull off a double axel from a standstill."

"You know what I mean," Sonia said calmly. "And anyway, you can't put a jump in your program without the coach's permission."

Cammie scowled. Of course, she wasn't going to do anything behind Coach Ferguson's back, but… "She'll let me do it. I know."

Sonia replaced her soakers with skate guards. "Just make sure you talk to her about it, okay?"

"Of course!" Cammie dismissed her friend with a casual wave of her hand. "Do you think Coach Ferguson doesn't want me to win?"

"Sure, but sometimes skating a clean program is more important than trying difficult jumps."

Yes, that's a nice thing to hear from someone who can land triples! Cammie pressed her lips tight but preferred to remain silent.

As she started combing her hair, one of the bristles of the hairbrush opened up the wound on her finger. "Ouch!"

"What's wrong? Let me look at it." Sonia was by her side, examining Cammie's finger.

With a grunt, Cammie put the finger in her mouth. "It's just a stupid thorn. I forgot that all roses have those."

Sonia's blue eyes narrowed. "What roses?"

"Ah!" Cammie waved her healthy hand. "Someone gave me roses last night. And…oops, I must have left the bouquet in the Icy…uh, at the rink. " Gosh, she had almost said *in the Icy Park*.

"Here!" Sonia handed Cammie a Band-Aid.

"Thanks." Cammie put the Band-Aid on her bleeding finger.

"Those fans!" Sonia shook her head angrily. "Haven't they heards of wraps? You can't handle roses with bare hands."

"Well, actually, it wasn't a fan. It was a judge."

Immediately, Cammie regretted having said those words. If Sonia had looked edgy a minute ago, now she was all a bundle of nerves. "Now wait a minute. I'm not sure I heard you right. Did you just say that a judge gave you flowers?"

"That's exactly what I said," Cammie said haughtily. "And for your information, it was she who suggested that I go for my double axel at the competition. She just told me to practice a little longer, and that's what I did last night in the par…uh…at the rink. So now my double axels are consistent."

"But Cammie, something is wrong here." Sonia appeared to be thinking hard. "Judges normally don't give gifts to skaters."

"That lady did!" Cammie barked. Sonia's piercing look was beginning to make her uncomfortable. "Shouldn't we get going? You're the first one who wouldn't want to be late."

As the two of them went down for breakfast, Sonia went on and on about the importance of obeying the coach and how the skater should put a new jump in the program at least two weeks before the competition, or else…

At some point, Cammie's mind blocked out Sonia's monologue and focused on more exciting things. With her double axel, Cammie could definitely take one of the top four spots in her category. And then she would go to the national competition. The nationals! That was something she had dreamed of ever since she took her first skating lesson five years ago.

"Cammie, are you listening to me?" Sonia asked sharply. "I was saying that perhaps focusing on that double axel wouldn't be too wise, because—"

"Oh, sure!" Cammie said, faking seriousness, although she really wanted to laugh. Sonia always thought she knew everything. Cammie and Sonia were of the same age, both thirteen and in the eighth grade. And yet Sonia often acted as though she were Cammie's mother. Or at least, her older sister. Well, of course, as a skater, Sonia was much more advanced than Cammie.

Sonia was born in Skateland, where her parents, both former skating champions, had lived and worked as coaches. Sonia's parents had put their daughter on skates when she was two. At four, the girl already won her first gold medal. Now Sonia was a junior skater, and she could land all triple jumps. Cammie, of course, still competed at the intermediate level. She couldn't wait to get her double axel out of the way and start working on triple jumps. But…the double axel proved to be much more challenging than she had anticipated. Cammie's thighs were still blue from all the hard falls she had taken. And then finally, last night, she had had a breakthrough. So if Sonia thought anything could ruin Cammie's festive mood, she was surely mistaken.

When Cammie and Sonia entered the dining room, Mrs. Page smiled at them from behind a big bowl of oatmeal that sat on the counter. "Good morning, my beautiful skaters. Good luck at the competition, Sonia!"

"Thank you!" Sonia said politely. She glanced at Cammie and then at Mrs. Page. Surely, the fact that the dorm supervisor hadn't included Cammie into her good wishes hadn't escaped Sonia's ears.

"I'll skate well today too, Mrs. Page," Cammie said cheerfully. She straightened her back, raised her chin, and put one foot slightly behind the other. As she glanced at Mrs. Page, Cammie was sure she looked just like a star ballerina.

"You! It's still not definite that you'll compete at all. I haven't spoken to Coach Ferguson yet." Mrs. Page grabbed a plate from the shelf. As she ladled some oatmeal into the plate, her hand shook slightly.

"Come on, Mrs. Page. You don't have to tell Coach Ferguson anything," Cammie said softly so no one else could hear.

"You bet I will." The woman added butter and brown sugar to the oatmeal and handed the plate to Cammie.

"Mrs. Page, please!" Cammie accepted the plate from the dorm supervisor, put it on the counter, and enclosed the woman in a bear hug.

"Mrs. Page, I'm really, really sorry I got you worried last night," Cammie whispered ardently. "This competition is so important to me. You see, I may qualify for the nationals!"

Mrs. Page's light-brown eyes darkened. "So? Does it give you the right to break the law? Now let's end this discussion, Cammie. I'm only doing what I have to do."

"But could you at least talk to Coach Ferguson after the competition? Please!" Cammie looked the dorm supervisor straight in the eye.

The woman's forehead creased, and Cammie could tell that Mrs. Page was really considering the possibility.

"Oh all right. Now get out of my sight and eat. You're not the only skater here, you know." Mrs. Page grunted.

"Thank you! Oh, thank you so much!" Cammie grabbed her plate and carried it to the table where Sonia and she normally sat. Everything was great. Mrs. Page wasn't going to mention Cammie's disobe-

dience to Coach Ferguson at least before the competition, and then, who knew what would happen?
If Cammie won a medal, her coach would definitely
forgive her. And if Cammie lost…Cammie's heart
hit hard against her ribcage, causing her to fidget.
Well, if she lost, nothing would matter anymore.

Cammie put her plate on the table and sat down.
The other two seats were already occupied by Dana
and Liz. They also skated at the Green Rink, and
they were going to compete in the intermediate category. Just like Cammie.

"I don't know how I'm going to last through my
program. I feel so jittery." Liz, a small Chinese girl,
warmed her hands against her cup and pushed her
unfinished oatmeal away.

"You'd better eat; you'll need your strength
today," Sonia, who had just approached the table,
told Liz.

Liz scowled but picked up her spoon and dug into
her oatmeal. "It's easy for you to eat. You don't have
to worry about the competition at all. You're going
to win anyway."

Sonia's blue eyes widened. "I can't be sure of that."

Dana, a pretty blonde, sneered. "Don't give us that,
Sonia. Like you could get anything short of gold!"

"Yeah, by the way," Dana said before Sonia could
interrupt her, "I heard there would be a special prize
for the most charming skater. And…I probably have
a shot at winning that one." Dana ran her fingers
through her long, straight hair and smiled confidently.

Cammie put down her spoon. "A special prize? And what will that be?"

Dana studied her reflection in the metal sugar bowl. "No idea. But I'm sure it'll be something terrific. They say Mr. Reed made it."

Melvin Reed! Cammie's heartbeat increased. Melvin Reed was Skateland's best skate sharpener, but his skills and qualifications went far beyond making blades sharp. A tall, gray-haired man, Melvin Reed had once been a competitive skater himself. After retiring from the sport, he became an engineer and built a beautiful skating museum in Skateland.

But what was even more important, Melvin Reed had magical powers. He usually skated at an outdoor skating rink with purple ice that miraculously revealed skaters' strengths and weaknesses. Evil witches were afraid of the purple ice, for they couldn't skate on it without getting burns all over their bodies. And then two years ago, Cammie and her best friend, Alex, had had an opportunity to try on Mr. Reed's self-spinning boots that helped a skater to perform multi-revolution jumps. Yes, Mr. Reed was really cool. So if he had taken the time to make a special prize for the most charming skater, his new invention was bound to be something incredibly good. Cammie wondered if she could win the special prize. Well, with her double axel she really had a good chance.

"Time to go!" Sonia said nervously, and as though confirming her words, the grandfather clock in the corner of the dining room chimed nine. Actually, nine o'clock in the morning was a late start for young skaters. Normally their morning practices began at six o'clock. But today was Saturday and a competition day. Still Cammie had spent half the night dreaming about her winning program. But she was too excited to feel tired.

As they walked outside, Cammie squinted at the brightness of the snow that glittered in the bright morning sun. Dana and Liz skated away immediately, apparently trying to make it to the Sport Center in record time.

Cammie was going to rush after the girls, but Sonia stopped her.

"Are you crazy? You'll need all that energy for your program. Skate slowly and breathe through your nose."

No wonder Cammie often called her roommate *Momma Sonia*. Cammie opened her mouth to tease Sonia some more but decided against it. Instead, as she pressed deep into her edges skating forward, she did a mental run-through of her program. Okay, so she would start with two three turns and then do four forward crossovers and a Mohawk. Once she was on her left forward outside edge, she would bend her knee and do an axel. A double axel, of course, not a single.

"Cammie, aren't you listening to me?"

Oh! Cammie hadn't even realized Sonia was saying something.

"I'm just asking if you ever tried to do a double axel in your program," Sonia said.

Cammie shrugged nonchalantly. "Nope. But we'll have a practice before our competition starts, so—"

Sonia shook her head, looking grim. "Cammie, I wouldn't take that risk. Why can't you save the double axel for your next competition?"

"It's *this* competition that matters!" Cammie hadn't realized that she had shouted the last words out loud.

Two little girls holding their mother's hands jumped away, looking scared.

"Excuse me!" the girls' mother said irritably.

Cammie saw that the woman was pulling a big, heavy bag on wheels. Apparently, the bag contained the girls' skating dresses. No surprises there; everybody was on the way to the competition.

The woman pulled the bag hard; its wheels skidded on the ice and careened to the right.

"Oh, for goodness' sake!" the woman snapped and glared at her daughters. "Cindy, you'd better let go of my hand. Hold on to Sandy's hand, okay?"

"I want to skate next to you, Mommy!" the blonde, pink-cheeked Cindy wailed.

"But I don't have an extra hand to pull this bag," the woman said, sounding desperate. "Look, Cindy, why don't you show me your forward swizzles!"

"Ah, okay." Immediately, Cindy let go of her mother's hand and glided forward, doing one swizzle after another.

"I can do swizzles too!" Sandy, who looked exactly like her sister, pulled her hand out of her mother's grip and rushed in the direction of the Sport Center. One swizzle, then another ...

"That's better." The woman sighed with obvious relief and picked up speed.

Cammie and Sonia looked at each other and giggled simultaneously.

"They must be competing in Tots," Sonia said softly so the girls' mother wouldn't hear her. "I still remember my first competition. I was four. Can you believe it? I wasn't nervous at all!"

Cammie did a quick swizzle, imitating the little girls. "I wouldn't know. I never competed in the Tots' category. I only started skating at eight."

They crossed Axel Avenue and approached the octagonal glass building of the Sport Center. A built-in computer monitor on the front door greeted them with familiar words: *Welcome to Skateland Annual Competition! Please enter your name.*

Cammie and Sonia put on their skate guards and took turns typing in their names using the built-in keyboard. Ten seconds later, the computer screen lit up again. *Welcome, Cammie Wester and Sonia Harrison!* The door opened with a click, and the girls stepped into the brightly lit lobby.

"Wow, I can't believe there are so many competitors!" Cammie groaned as they pushed through a thick crowd. There were skaters everywhere: little girls and older girls, tots and adults, nervous-looking boys and confident guys who carried themselves as first-class skaters. Singles, pairs skaters, and dancers—everybody looked incredibly focused. The spaces closest to the walls were occupied by vendors, who sold skating clothes and jewelry, skates, books, and toys. Cammie knew there would be plenty of time to look at all the things after she skated, so she walked past the brightly decorated tables without as much as a casual look.

Cammie and Sonia were about to turn right and head for the girls' locker room when Sonia grabbed Cammie's hand. "Look!"

But Cammie already stood glued to her spot, staring at the huge sign that hung directly across from the podium positioned in the middle of the lobby. The sign said "Special Prize for the Most Charming Skater." Cammie rose on her toes to check out the prize, but it was completely blocked from view. Instead, she saw Melvin Reed looking dignified in a black tuxedo. Next to the skate sharpener stood a woman with short brown hair, probably a reporter. She held a microphone next to Mr. Reed's mouth. The man was saying something with an expression of both excitement and mischief. Cammie walked around a giggling dancing couple and approached Mr. Reed. Sonia trailed behind.

"Yes, I designed this skating bag three months ago," Mr. Reed said. "Unfortunately, I still haven't managed to sell it."

"But what gave you the idea of a new bag?" the reporter asked. "As far as I know, there are plenty of skating bags in the market."

The corners of Mr. Reed's lips twitched. "Not like mine. As you may have noticed, all the existing skating bags ride on wheels and are therefore poorly suited for Skateland streets. You see, Skateland residents don't walk anywhere; they skate to their destinations. And the icy paths we have here make it very difficult, if not impossible, to navigate the traditional skating bags."

Cammie nodded as she thought of the mother of two little girls. The woman definitely had had hard time pulling her bag-on-wheels along the icy paths.

"My bag, however, is equipped with blades so you can easily pull it behind you as you skate," Mr. Reed said.

"Well, that sounds terrific!" the reporter said enthusiastically. "But if the bag is as good as you say, why hasn't anybody bought it yet?"

The man rubbed the bridge of his long nose, looking somewhat sheepish. "I hate to admit it, but my excessive creativity kind of got away from me. When I finished attaching the blades to the bag, I thought the whole thing looked too simple. Nothing special. So I added an alarm clock and a media player."

"Wow!" The reporter shook her head, looking positively impressed.

"The skating bag is also equipped with a navigator that helps the owner get to any location in Skateland," Mr. Reed said brightly. "And another thing. You will no longer have to pull the bag behind. If you wear this pendant, the bag will glide right next to you."

Out of his pocket, Mr. Reed produced a silver skate hanging from a chain.

"I can't believe it!" The reporter glanced at the crowd as though inviting everybody to join her in admiring Mr. Reed's invention. The skaters clapped eagerly; Cammie brought her hands together too. Wow, wouldn't it be awesome to own such a state-of-the-art skating bag?

"And the name of the bag is…" the reporter asked.

"Kanga bag!" With a theatrical wave of his hand, Mr. Reed stepped to the side of a small table.

Cammie and Sonia gasped in unison. Seated on the table was what looked like a three-foot kangaroo. It had soft light-brown fur; long, pointed ears; and a rather sour facial expression. Just like Mr. Reed had said, the animal's back legs rested on blades. Cammie could even discern the toe-picks. The kangaroo's long tail trailed behind, and—Cammie liked it the most—the animal held a bottle of water in its clawed front paws.

"Oh, I see Kanga will also carry your water bottle for you!" the reporter exclaimed.

Mr. Reed chuckled. "Oh, yes, I forgot to mention the cooler that is hidden inside Kanga's pouch."

The man took the bottle out of the animal's paws and slid it inside the pocket on Kanga's belly. "See? The cooler will keep your water nice and cold."

"Yes, the bag is truly amazing." Now the reporter's voice sounded quite sincere. "But if it's so great, I still don't understand why nobody wanted to buy it."

Mr. Reed spread his arms. "The problem is the money. What do you expect? With all the functions included, I had to set the price of the bag at two thousand dollars."

"Two thousand dollars for a skating bag!" Cammie actually saw the reporter drop her microphone, though she managed to catch it just before it hit the hard floor.

"Yes, I know it's pricy, but unfortunately, I had no choice," the man said sadly. "So there I was, stuck with the beautiful bag I had made. I couldn't sell it, but I hated the idea of this masterpiece sitting in my shop, collecting dust. That's when I had a thought. *Why don't I present the bag to the most charming skater at Skateland Annual Competition? A well-deserved price that would be and a perfect reward for the skater's wonderful achievements.*"

"But who will pick out the most charming skater?" the reporter asked with obvious interest.

Mr. Reed looked at the woman with surprise. "Me, of course. Who else? It was I who designed Kanga bag."

"Well…" The reporter looked as though she were debating whether to share her thoughts or keep her mouth shut. "Mr. Reed, don't you think your approach to what makes a skater charming can be a little subjective? Wouldn't it be fairer to let the judges pick out the winner?"

"No!" Mr. Reed said firmly. "The decision will be mine. And believe me: my choice won't be affected by any personal preferences or the skater's previous achievements. My decision will be based solely on the skater's performance at this competition."

"But what will you use as the criterion?" the reporter insisted. "Will the technical ability be taken into consideration at all, or are you going to reward a skater for his or her physical attractiveness?"

"What kind of a question is that? Of course, there can be no charm without proper technique. You may have forgotten, but I was once a skater myself. So I can tell whether a performer is up to high technical standards or not."

"Okay, but there are quite a few skaters with good technique." Apparently, the reporter wasn't going to leave Mr. Reed alone until she got every piece of information out of him.

Mr. Reed looked up for a second; then his pale blue eyes scanned the silent crowd. He must have recognized Cammie and Sonia, for he smiled and greeted them with a wave of his hand. The girls mouthed a quick *hello*.

"The most charming skater will be a boy or a girl who will be able to portray the true beauty of skating," Mr. Reed said slowly. "We all understand that technique is important, and skaters spend hours and hours perfecting their spins or throwing their bodies into multi-revolution jumps. But how often do we forget about what matters the most in hot pursuit of technical perfection!"

Mr. Reed stopped for a moment, letting his words sink in. With bated breath, Cammie waited for the man to go on, but Mr. Reed was quiet.

"So what is it?" the reporter asked impatiently. "What's the important thing that really counts?"

"This is something that keeps our sport alive, something that makes you want to go on and on." Mr. Reed was now speaking very softly, so Cammie stepped closer not to miss anything.

"This thing makes us get up after we took a painful fall. It wakes us early in the morning when our bodies are still sore from yesterday's practice and our whole selves scream for rest. It helps us not to get discouraged when we get beaten by other skaters. Yes, this is what keeps us on the ice, not medals."

"But what is it?" The reporter stomped her foot clad in a brown shoe with a spiky heel. The microphone shook in her hand; the woman looked as though she was eager to finish that interview as soon as possible and move on.

"Come on, Mr. Reed. You've got to be more specific!" the woman said.

The older man glanced at the reporter. With his six-foot-three frame, he looked like a father disciplining his little girl.

"The important thing is love," Mr. Reed said calmly. "Pure, unadulterated love for skating."

There was a deep silence followed by a shuffling of feet, whispers, and sighs. The reporter's face was twisted in surprise bordering on disgust. "Love? Is that it? I really thought you would tell us something new, Mr. Reed!"

Someone pulled Cammie on the sleeve of her parka. Cammie looked around and straight into Sonia's wide-open eyes.

"Cammie, we need to go. The practice, remember?" Sonia whispered.

The girls started walking in the direction of the locker rooms, when Mr. Reed's deep voice reached Cammie's ears again. "Yes, and one more thing. If you truly love skating, even the most wicked witches can't destroy you."

Cammie stopped short. "Wow, Sonia, did you hear that?"

"What? Cammie, the practice starts in six minutes, and we still need to change."

"Ah sure!" Without giving Mr. Reed's words another thought, Cammie followed her friend.

In the locker room, Cammie quickly changed into her new skating dress. It was fantastic—light green with silver sequins in the front, and it went well with Cammie's eyes. Now it was time for makeup. Just yesterday, Dana had given Cammie some tips. Appearance really mattered, and today Cammie wanted to look her best.

Cammie closed her left eye and gently rubbed some pink eye shadow over the right lid. She did the same on the other side and studied the effect. Not bad. She added some mascara and looked at her reflection again. How cool!

"Practice for intermediate girls starts right now!" a voice boomed from the speaker.

"Oh, Cammie, that's you!" Sonia squeaked from the corner.

Cammie quickly applied some pink lipgloss and stuffed her makeup kit into her backpack.

"Cammie, you'll be late!" Sonia's voice trembled as though it was she who was wasting the precious practice time.

"Relax. There's still plenty of time!" Cammie gave her friend a cheerful wave and walked out of the locker room. She moved with deliberate slowness just to tease Sonia. Yet when she was out of her roommate's sight, Cammie broke into a run.

"There she is!" Someone grabbed Cammie by the hand, causing her to stop.

"Alex!" Cammie beamed at the sight of her best friend, who looked gorgeous in his black skating outfit. "When are you competing?"

"Right now, actually. Are you coming to cheer for me?"

Cammie gasped. "Now? Gosh, I can't. My practice has just started. Boy, how stupid!"

"Ah, it's okay. You'd better go." Alex gently pushed her in the direction of the White Rink.

"But how can I miss your winning performance?" Cammie pouted.

Alex grinned. "I'll show you the video."

"Okay. Hey, you know what? I landed my double axel yesterday. And I'm going to do it in my program today." As much in a rush as Cammie was, she had to share the good news with Alex; she knew he would be really happy for her.

Alex clapped his hands. "That a girl! So triples are next, huh?"

"Naturally!" Cammie shifted her feet and cast a nervous look at the clock hanging on the wall across from the locker rooms. "Look, I really need to run."

"Yeah, me too. Good luck out there!"

Cammie wished Alex to skate his best and ran up the steps to the second floor. Her practice was scheduled at the White Rink, where the ice shimmered like fresh snow and the white carpet around the arena was dotted with squashy couches and armchairs. The cozy, relaxed atmosphere of the White Rink always attracted a lot of spectators. The White Rink was the official training arena of pairs skaters and dancers, and when they skated their programs, the audience often broke into loud applause. Sandra Newman, a pretty dancer who trained at the White Rink, had once told Cammie that for her every practice felt like a show.

Cammie's competitors were already on the ice, fervently trying to put final touches on their programs. Cammie quickly removed her skate guards and flew around the rink. She couldn't wait to try her double axel again, but she knew rushing her warm-up wouldn't be wise. Skaters were known to take bad falls and even get injured if they didn't warm up their muscles properly. Therefore, Cammie did two quick laps around the rink followed by backward cross-overs. She went into a well-centered change-foot spin and finally moved on to jumps.

She started with three delayed waltz jumps then did a single axel, which turned out perfect, and now her body was ready for doubles. Everything went well. Cammie moved across the rink with good speed, and her jumps appeared effortless. Okay, now it was time for her double axel. She closed her eyes for a moment, remembering the snowflakes dancing in the air and the dark surface of the pond in the Icy Park. She had been perfect then; she hadn't missed one jump. The wild beauty of the park had worked magic in her technique, and she had become a better skater overnight. Okay, now! Cammie jumped as high as she could, pulled in … Yes! She flew up into another double axel.

"Intermediate girls, your practice is now over. Please leave the ice," the familiar voice said from the speaker.

"Oh no, not yet!" Next to Cammie, Liz dropped her arms, looking upset.

"Liz, come up here! I didn't like that camel spin of yours," Liz's coach shouted from the boards.

Cammie knew Coach Yvette too well. The slightly overweight, dark-haired woman was as demanding as Coach Ferguson. Yet unlike Cammie's coach, Yvette never stayed calm when she wasn't happy with her skater's performance. She would yell the instructions and criticisms so loudly that the whole rink knew exactly what Liz had done wrong.

By the way, where was Coach Ferguson? Despite her festive mood, Cammie couldn't help feeling a little ill at ease. Perhaps she needed to tell her coach that she was planning to do a double axel in her program after all? Cammie scanned the boards. There were several coaches talking to their skaters, but no matter how hard Cammie looked, she couldn't see Coach Ferguson's small frame anywhere at the rink.

She's probably watching some of her students skate, Cammie thought. Well, perhaps it was better that way. Cammie felt very confident about her double axel, and that was all that mattered.

Cammie spent the rest of the time before her competition walking around the lobby, looking at the skating dresses, and talking to her friends. When she saw her parents, who had come all the way from Clarenceville to watch their daughter compete, Cammie ran to hug them.

"Oh, sweetheart, we miss you so much!" Cammie's mother kissed her daughter. "Oh, wait, now you have my lipstick smeared all over your cheeks." Cammie's mother took a tissue and started wiping Cammie's face. "Hmm, I can't take all of it off. It's okay though; now your face looks a little brighter and actually healthier. By the way, don't you think you went too heavy on the makeup? And the pink eye shadow looks a little eccentric to me."

"It's fine. Dana showed me how to apply makeup properly, and she knows the latest styles," Cammie said.

"So is our champion ready to show the world what real skating is like?" Cammie's father winked at her.

Cammie straightened out and nodded. "Absolutely."

"Well, we'd better go and get the best seats. All right, sweetie?" Cammie's mother smoothed the tiny creases on Cammie's dress, her father gave Cammie another cheerful wave, and both of her parents walked through the entrance to the Silver Rink, the official Skateland competition arena.

Cammie thought of following them but decided to stay in the lobby until the beginning of her warm-up. The rink was way too cold.

"There you are! So how did your practice go?" Coach Ferguson seemed to have materialized out of thin air.

"It was great!" Cammie looked her coach right in the eye and smiled.

"Okay, remember: the beginning is very important. I think it's great that you're starting with an easy jump. After you land that axel, you'll feel a lot of confidence to ace the rest of the program."

Aha! Cammie couldn't help but notice that Coach Ferguson had said *axel*, not *double axel*. She thought for a moment. If she was going to tell Coach Ferguson about her double axel, now was the best time to do it.

If Coach Ferguson forbade her to go for the jump in the program but Cammie tried it anyway, it would be considered a very disrespectful thing to do. But if Cammie landed her double axel, it would be too late for Coach Ferguson to rebuke her for disobedience. Cammie could always pretend she had forgotten about the latest changes in the program.

"There. They've just announced your warm-up. Do each jump once, and you'll be all right. Go!" Coach Ferguson walked Cammie up to the entrance to the rink and took Cammie's skate guards away from her.

Cammie joined the other five girls who were gliding across the rink. She went through the most difficult elements of her program again, happy that her body felt light, and even her knees weren't shaking. Of course, she only did a single axel in the warm-up. Cammie stepped off the ice feeling pleasantly warm.

Coach Ferguson gave her an approving nod. "Good. Just stay focused, and you'll do fine."

Cammie was scheduled to skate third in her group. She decided not to watch the first two girls who were going to do their programs before her. Instead, she listened to her program music on her iPod and visualized herself doing every move properly.

And there was the second girl walking off the rink, and Coach Ferguson nudged Cammie in the direction of the ice.

"Representing Skateland, here is Cammie Wester!" the announcer said.

Cammie straightened up, smiled, and glided to the middle of the rink. She took her starting position. The last couple of seconds before her music began were the worst. That was the time when doubts started creeping in, and fear tried to grab a hold of the skater's mind. A nasty thought flashed through Cammie's mind. *What if I mess up the whole thing?*

Before Cammie could rebuke herself for even giving in to that idea, the beginning chords of her *Romeo and Juliet* music started. And that was all she needed. Cammie went into her first three turn, and from that moment on she was fine. She didn't even have to fight the fear of not landing her double axel, because there was no fear. She went right into the jump strongly, confidently.

"Perfect," the wind whispered in her ear. And in agreement with the wind, the stands broke into a loud applause. Cammie flashed a huge smile in the direction of the judges' panel and picked up more speed. There was no time to rejoice. She still had the rest of the program ahead of her. Her double lutz-double toe combination came next, and Cammie landed both jumps with ease. The audience roared.

Cammie arched her back and glided around the rink on her forward outside edge in a graceful spiral position. She bent forward, almost touching the ice with her hand. The rink tilted to the left; the spectators gasped, but Cammie didn't fall. She did a quick Mohawk and went into a combination spin, her favorite move. She spun and spun, watching the walls of rink and the people turn into a silvery mist. She didn't remember ever spinning so fast, but today she felt she could do absolutely anything.

The crowd cheered for her, but Cammie was barely paying attention. She felt light like a butterfly flying through the air, barely skimming the surface of the ice. And there it was, her final change foot spin, and Cammie finished her program in a flash, one foot slightly behind the other, her arms up in the air. There was ringing in her ears, but eventually she began to hear the clapping of the dozens of hands around her, and the sound was getting louder. Cammie curtsied to the panel of judges, turned around, and bowed to the audience. The cheers intensified.

"Cammie! Cammie!" her friends yelled.

Cammie could recognize Alex's and Jeff's voices. She saw her parents sitting in the third row, and her father held a sign that he had probably made himself: "North or South, East or West, Cammie Wester Is the Best!"

Cammie laughed.

"Thanks, Dad!" she shouted, waved at the audience again, and skated to the exit where Coach Ferguson stood looking strangely nonexcited.

"Well..." That was all the coach said as Cammie started telling her about her performance, stammering, leaving out articles and prepositions.

"I...can't believe it was...ah, awesome!" Breathing hard, Cammie bent over to put on her skate guards. Her coach was still silent.

After dropping her skate guards twice, Cammie finally managed to cover her blades, and she turned her sweaty face to Coach Ferguson. "Did you see that double-double? And the double axel! I was so high in the air... What?"

Cammie stopped talking as she peered into her coach's pale face. For some reason, Coach Ferguson didn't look happy. As though Cammie hadn't just pulled off the performance of her life. As though the audience hadn't rewarded her with loud cheers.

"Ah!" a collective gasp came from the stands.

Cammie quickly looked at the arena. Dana was clumsily getting on her feet. Apparently, the girl had just fallen from her double axel.

"Oh, it's a shame!" Cammie said sincerely. She had seen Dana land her double axels in practice consistently. But competitions were different. The nerves could really get in a skater's way. *But I did it!* Cammie thought, feeling elated.

She turned to Coach Ferguson. "Did the first two girls land their double axels?"

"The first one went for it, but the jump came out two footed. The second girl only did a single," Coach Ferguson said dryly.

"Wow!" Cammie's mouth opened wide, and she hurried to cover it with her hand. "It means I can actually medal here," Cammie said slowly.

"It doesn't mean anything," Coach Ferguson snapped. "Megan Ligovski from New York has a solid double axel and a triple salchow."

"Oh!" Cammie frowned. "But I—"

Before she could say another word, her coach's eyes turned into two angry slits. "Cammie, is there something I don't understand, or are you really missing the point?"

"What?" Cammie gasped, surprised at Coach Ferguson's sudden outburst. What had Cammie done? She had skated beautifully.

The coach didn't say anything more, eyeing Cammie with obvious contempt. Cammie furrowed her eyebrows, trying to look like someone who had just been unfairly hurt. But she couldn't act sad; the joy over her outstanding performance was too strong. Against her will, Cammie smiled widely, and her heart leaped in her chest in anticipation. She was definitely going to get a medal.

Coach Ferguson pressed her lips tight; the fine lines in the corners of her mouth deepened. "I don't think you're in the condition to talk. So we'll have to deal with it later. Go celebrate."

Of all the things Coach Ferguson had said, Cammie's mind only registered the last words: *go celebrate*. So she gave her coach another bright smile and waited for the woman to grin back. When it didn't happen, Cammie mumbled a quick, "Bye," and ran out into the lobby.

THE MOST CHARMING SKATER

"**Y**ou were fantastic!" Someone slapped Cammie on the shoulder.

She turned around and looked right into Alex's green eyes. "Alex!"

He grinned. "Congratulations! That was your strongest performance ever."

"Thanks." Cammie looked around, making sure no one could hear them. "You know, I only got that double axel consistent last night."

Alex whistled. "And you went for it in the program. That's pretty impressive."

Cammie smiled coyly. "True, and I didn't even tell Coach Ferguson that I was going to try it."

Alex's widened eyes looked like two green ponds. "Are you saying that you did a double axel without your coach's permission?"

"Yup."

"Cammie, you are…" Alex shook his head, his face showing a mixture of awe and disapproval. "But what if you had missed it? You were taking a big risk."

"Well, I landed it, and that's all that matters." Cammie took off her Green Rink warm-up jacket. "I'm sure it will be enough for a medal. The girls who have skated so far made mistakes."

"Did your coach say anything to you after you were finished?"

"No," Cammie said lightly. She thought for a moment. "Coach Ferguson acted kind of funny, though."

So could my double axel be the reason Coach Ferguson hadn't shown any joy over my stellar performance? Cammie grimaced and put the unpleasant thought to the back of her mind. "Hey, how did you skate? Did you get the gold?"

Alex's face darkened; he looked away. "Hmm, no, actually, I didn't."

"What?" Cammie thought she had misunderstood her friend. "But you always end up with the gold. Just like Sonia—always at the top."

"Well, not this time." Alex grinned, although Cammie could tell that he was upset. "I fell on my triple flip and doubled the first jump in my triple-triple combination."

"Oh!"

"Well, there was probably still hope, but I got discouraged, so my footwork was slow, and I traveled on my sit spin like crazy, and then…" Alex snorted and made a nasty face. "I finished way after the music."

"Oh, I'm so sorry!"

"It's okay."

Cammie could see how hard her friend was trying to show that his poor performance was nothing, that he wasn't disappointed in the least. But she knew better than to believe him. Not only was Alex ambitious; he had also been working very hard. And everybody from judges and coaches to their friends always said that Alex Bernard had real talent, that one day he might go to nationals, the worlds, and … Hey, wait a minute. The nationals!

"But you're still going to the nationals, aren't you?" Cammie asked gingerly.

Alex hung his head. "No, actually, I came in fifth."

"Fifth!" Cammie's heart sank. The fifth position was the worst. Only the top four finishers made it to nationals. For that reason, most skaters believed finishing the competition in sixth, seventh, or eighth place was better than coming in just one place short of the coveted fourth. Perhaps even the tenth spot was better than the fifth, as long as it wasn't the last place, of course. Coming in last was also a disaster.

It had happened to Cammie once when a girl, whom Cammie had considered her best friend, had slipped her a magical pin. The pin had brought a curse upon Cammie, and she still remembered how devastated she had felt back then.

"Oh, Alex, I'm so, so sorry!" Cammie whispered.

Alex's jaw tightened, but his lips spread in a smile. "It's okay. Big deal. There's always next year."

"Who's in first?" Cammie asked softly.

"Kyle Lyons. He's the best."

Cammie nodded, remembering a tall, graceful skater with powerful jumps. "How about Jeff?"

"He's in second place. He skated great."

"Yeah, he always does."

Cammie and Alex had met Jeff, a short dark-haired boy, three years ago when he had been viciously attacked by the Witch of Injuries. Cammie and Alex had broken the evil curse, and Jeff had developed into a very solid skater.

"So Jeff is going to the nationals," Cammie said slowly. She was happy for Jeff, but she couldn't stop grieving over Alex's fifth-place finish.

"How did Sonia do?" Alex asked.

"She competes in juniors. She's probably skating now." Cammie looked at the clock. "We'll probably be able to see her if we go in."

But they were late. As soon as Cammie and Alex approached the entrance to the Silver Rink, the door swung open and out ran Sonia, her cheeks flushing.

"Oh, I can't believe it!" Sonia ran up to Cammie and kissed her. Then she whirled around and hugged Alex.

"Hey, what's the fuss about? Everybody knows you're the best," Cammie said.

"Yeah, tell us something new for a change." Alex winked at Cammie.

"I landed a triple-triple combination!" Sonia breathed out. Her eyes sparkled like two huge sapphires.

"She was incredible." Jeff appeared from behind Sonia, looking equally excited. "Uh, Cammie, I saw you skate. Congratulations!"

Sonia slapped herself on the forehead. "Oh, I completely forgot. How did it go, Cammie? Did you try that double axel?"

Cammie laughed. "Not only tried, I landed it."

"Oh, Cammie, congratulations!" With a loud shriek, Sonia enclosed Cammie in her arms.

"You always say *next time*. I hate those words!" somebody whined on Cammie's right.

Cammie looked around and saw Dana's tear-stricken face. The girl was crying openly, ignoring the mascara that ran down her cheeks leaving dark streaks.

A tall blonde woman, who had to be Dana's mother, was hurriedly wiping the smears off the girl's face. "It's okay, sweetheart. Stand still now. That's a good girl."

"What's wrong?" Cammie asked.

Liz materialized from behind Dana's shoulder and pulled Cammie away. "She came in fifth!"

"Ah!" Cammie nodded sadly. "How about you?"

Liz's mouth twitched. "Sixth."

"Oh…" All of a sudden Cammie got panicky. Dana and Liz had competed in her group. It meant the results were up, and Cammie still hadn't seen them.

Immediately forgetting everything else, Cammie ran toward the notice board. There was a big crowd in front of it. Skaters jostled one another, trying to get closer to the sheets of paper where their results were posted.

"Excuse me! Excuse me!" Cammie mumbled as she tried to break through the crowd.

She rose on her toes looking for the right sheet of paper. *Intermediate Girls' Free Skate*—that was it, and in first place…

"Yes!" Cammie screamed at the top of her lungs.

Someone coughed near her; then there was a hiss followed by a giggle. She didn't care.

"I won. I won! Oh, I can't believe it." Cammie could actually feel everybody's eyes fixed on her. Megan Ligovski from New York actually snorted and looked away. Cammie scanned the results again. Megan's name was in the second spot. Wow! Cammie knew that Megan had been everybody's favorite to win. She had a double axel and a triple salchow in the program.

Isn't it great that I went for that double axel? Cammie thought. *But I'd better get that triple salchow soon.*

"Here is the champion!"

Cammie swirled and found herself in her father's arms. "Daddy!"

"You were terrific, honey. I never saw you skate like that." Cammie's mother hugged her too. "Now would you like something from the vendors' stands? A nice piece of jewelry, perhaps? Or a new teddy bear? I bet your Mr. Skate is getting old."

Mom was talking of Cammie's bear, who had sat on her bed ever since she first started skating five years ago.

Cammie laughed and shook her head. "Mr. Skate will never be too old for me. Look, Mom, can I get a new skating dress?"

Cammie's mother's brown eyes opened wide. "But I thought you liked your green dress."

"Sure I do. But you can't have too many skating dresses. Besides..." Cammie lowered her voice. "I've just qualified for the nationals. So I absolutely have to look my best."

"That's right. It was a qualifying competition." Cammie's father raised his finger in the air. "My daughter will be a national champion soon."

"Awards ceremony is starting in two minutes!" the familiar announcer's voice blasted from the speakers.

"Let's go!" Cammie smoothed her skirt, grabbed her father's hand, and pulled him in the direction of the podium. Her mother followed, grinning widely.

As Cammie stood on the top of the podium, she pictured herself in a different place—at the worlds or even at the Olympics. And it might really happen one day. Now Cammie had absolutely no doubt about that. As she closed her eyes, she almost heard the national anthem playing in her honor, and she heard the clicking of cameras.

"Look at me, champion!"

Startled, Cammie opened her eyes. So she hadn't imagined the photographers; her father really stood in front of her with a camera in his hand.

"I want to see that gold medal well... Yes, here you go!" her father mumbled.

"You look so good with that medal around your neck!" Cammie's mother patted her on the head after Cammie stepped down from the podium. "Now let's all go and eat."

The three of them started walking in the directions of the exit, but before they left the building they heard the announcer's voice again. "Attention, everybody. Mr. Reed is now going to present his special award, the Kanga bag, to the most charming skater."

"Oh!" Cammie stopped short. How could she forget? So who would Mr. Reed give his terrific skating bag to? It would probably be Sonia. Not only could Cammie's roommate land multi-revolution jumps with amazing ease, but she poured her whole soul into skating. When on ice, Sonia could turn into a butterfly, a gazelle, or a snow fairy. Cammie often wished she could be as light and fluid as Sonia, but sometimes she admitted sadly that she probably never would.

"I wonder who it will be," a girl's voice said somewhere behind Cammie.

Cammie turned to see who it was, but there were too many people in the lobby, and more skaters were running in from the arena and the snack bar to hear the news.

Mr. Reed stepped forward, tall and solemn, his white hair looking especially bright next to his black tuxedo. "It's my honor to announce that this magical Kanga bag is awarded to…" Mr. Reed made a meaningful pause, during which Cammie could hear the beating of her heart.

"Come on!" she whispered.

"Cammie Wester!"

Cammie and her parents had dinner at the restaurant called Skater's Finest Food. It was located just a block away from Main Square. Cammie wore her gold medal all the time. From time to time, she ran her finger against the cold, smooth surface, feeling her lips spread in a smile. The waitress and even some customers congratulated her and wished her many more medals. All residents of Skateland had either skated in the past or still worked on their technique. Therefore, they took competitions very seriously.

Everybody was also anxious to take a look at Cammie's new Kanga bag. Cammie had to explain that she didn't have the bag with her. She had asked Sonia to take Kanga to the dorm, fearing the bag might be too cumbersome to be carried into the restaurant. In fact, Cammie hadn't even had a chance to take a closer look at her wonderful prize.

"I'm sure it will be great not to carry a backpack around," the waitress said as she put a steaming plate of pasta in front of Cammie.

Cammie nodded happily. "I know. In fact, Mr. Reed added the Bluetooth function, so I won't even have to pull Kanga behind me. It will glide beside me on its own."

"Amazing!" The waitress poured more Sprite into Cammie's glass. "You need to stop by sometime and let me take a look at your bag. Who knows? Maybe one day Kangas will go on sale, and I'll be able to afford one."

The evening rolled by, filled with the aroma of delicious food and the sounds of lovely Italian music that poured out from the speakers. Cammie felt both elated and relaxed; she wished the night would never end.

After they finished their dessert, Cammie's father checked his watch and clicked his tongue. "Oops! It's eight thirty. I think we'd better hit the road, Linda."

"Do you want to come home for a couple of days, sweetie?" Cammie's mother asked. "You could use some rest, and we miss you so much."

Cammie swirled the spoon in her half-melted ice cream. Of course, going home for a few days would be cool. She could show her gold medals to the girls at her home rink. She could even see Coach Louise. But...weren't some things more important?

Cammie didn't want to disappoint her parents, but she shook her head. "I wish I could come with you guys, but I really can't miss practices. The national competition is only two months away, so I'd better work hard."

"True." Cammie's mother folded her napkin, looking sad. "But couldn't you come with us now? Dad would bring you back on Monday morning. You would only miss one morning practice. And we could have a nice party; you could invite Margie and Susie—whoever you want."

The party! Cammie slapped herself on the forehead. "Oh, my gosh! I completely forgot. The winners' party is tomorrow! I have to be there."

Her father raised his head from the bill he had been studying. "The winners' party?"

"Yes!" Cammie couldn't believe she could forget such an important thing. "Wilhelmina—you know, our president—always throws a party after an annual competition. Only medalists are invited, so I never had a chance to attend. But people who did say it's amazing."

"Oh, well." Cammie's father signed the bill and stood up. "I think we need to let this young lady go to bed. But, honey, you've got to promise us that you'll never forget your old mom and dad once you're a big star."

"Oh, come on!" Cammie laughed and kissed her father on the cheek. "I love you both so much!"

Cammie hugged her mother too and smiled brightly. She still couldn't think of herself as a champion of Skateland. But she'd better believe that from that moment on, her life would never be the same.

THE WINNERS' PARTY

From the moment she woke up on Sunday morning, Cammie couldn't think of anything but the winners' party. The celebration was going to start with a dinner in the reception hall of the Sport Center. For this occasion, all the guests were expected to dress up; yet, they also had to bring their skating clothes for the night dance at the Main Square Rink.

Cammie rummaged through her closet and took out the dress that her mother had bought her for her thirteenth birthday. It was made of white, shimmering silk with a mini skirt and a tight bodice held by two narrow straps. Cammie didn't use a lot of makeup. After all, she wasn't going to a competition.

She only put a touch of pale-pink lipgloss and let her hair down.

She looked in the mirror. Perfect! With her white shoes and brown hair streaming almost down to her waist, Cammie looked like a snow princess. Cammie raised her arms above her head, spread her fingers gracefully, and rose on her toes. "Hey, Sonia, how do I look?"

Sonia, who looked positively cute in her short blue dress and matching shoes, ran her fingers through her red locks and clapped her hands. "Wow, Cammie, you're gorgeous! Wait. Let me take your picture!" She took a camera from the top shelf of the closet, pointed it at Cammie, and clicked several times. "There, you can look at yourself."

Cammie glanced at the monitor. Amazing! She couldn't even recognize the poised, confident girl. The girl's eyes were wide and bright, and the light smile playing on her lips said *champion*.

Cammie swirled around. "I'm a champion, a real champion, and I look so great and cool!"

Sonia stifled a giggle. "By the way, how is your finger?"

"My finger?" For a moment, Cammie couldn't understand what Sonia was talking about. Then she vaguely remembered being pricked by a thorn. Big deal! She glanced at her left middle finger. A small scab had already formed over the wound.

"It doesn't hurt anymore."

"You know what? I've been thinking of something," Sonia said pensively as she took off her blue shoes and started putting on her skates. Party or not, the champions were expected to skate to the Sport Center like on any other day.

"What's that?" Cammie asked absentmindedly.

Sonia stopped lacing her boot. "I don't think the woman who gave you those roses was a judge."

"Well, she didn't exactly say she was a judge." Cammie put a white wool sweater over her dress and reached for her skates. "I just thought she was because she looked really classy, and she wore a mink coat. That's what judges usually wear, unless she's a coach, of course. But as we know all coaches in Skateland, she couldn't be … Sonia, what's wrong with you?"

Cammie was shocked to see how dark Sonia's freckles appeared against her paled face.

"Why would a judge want to give you flowers?" Sonia asked in a strangely calm voice.

"Perhaps she loved my skating." Cammie felt herself getting angry. Why did Sonia want to ruin her joy?

"Judges may give you high scores for a good performance, but I've never heard of any judge giving material rewards to skaters. At least, no judge has ever presented *me* with a bouquet."

Cammie dropped her boot on the floor with a deliberately loud clank. "So now you're jealous. Great. Some friend you are!"

Sonia's already huge eyes appeared even bigger. "Jealous? Why would I be jealous? I got a gold medal too."

"Sure, but no one called *your* performance outstanding. No one gave *you* flowers. And you didn't get the Most Charming Skater award either. You just can't stand the fact that for once I am a better skater than you!" Cammie shouted.

For a moment, she wished she hadn't said those words. Sonia's trembling lips and dropping shoulders meant that the girl was deeply hurt. Perhaps Cammie should have been more sensitive to Sonia's feelings. After all, her roommate had always been nice to her. But as Cammie thought more about her friend's behavior, she shook her head. Sonia was definitely wrong. She should have congratulated Cammie, not criticized her.

"Cammie," Sonia said, looking away. Her voice was slightly husky as though she was trying hard to fight tears. "I really didn't want to rain on your parade—"

"Well, you just did."

"I'm sorry if I did, but... doesn't it even occur to you that the woman who gave you those roses may be a witch?"

"What?" Cammie leaned back in her chair.

"I mean it, Cammie." Sonia put her boot away and moved closer to Cammie. "Do you remember how Jeff got injured last year?"

"Well, sure." When Sonia had been abducted by the witches last year, Jeff had thought of joining

Cammie and Alex in their rescue mission. But just the day before the three of them were about to travel to the past using the president of Skateland's magical book of skating history, Jeff had sprained his ankle.

"Don't you remember that before Jeff fell and got hurt, Winja hit him with her crutch?"

"Well…" Now that Sonia had mentioned it, Cammie could vaguely recollect that the Witch of Injuries had really attacked Jeff. But what did it have to do with Cammie?

"I didn't even see Winja today," Cammie said defensively.

"The judge who gave you the flowers could be a witch."

"No, she couldn't!" Cammie said confidently.

"And why not?"

"Why not?" Cammie didn't really have the answer to that question. "Because… because she didn't look like any of the witches I know."

Sonia smirked. "Like you know all the witches. There are dozens of them, remember?"

"But still… she looked so classy, so… polished."

"Isn't that how the Witch of Pride appeared to you and Alex last year? You told me."

The Witch of Pride. Hmm. Could Sonia be right, and the woman in designer clothes was really the Witch of Pride? Cammie closed her eyes for a moment remembering the president of Skateland's calm voice. "Pride comes in all forms," Wilhelmina had said. *And when the Witch of Pride attacked Alex last year, none of us recognized her either*, Cammie thought. The witch had dyed her auburn hair blond, and Cammie and Alex had thought…

Cammie gasped. They had both believed they were talking to a judge!

"The Witch of Pride gave Alex a drink," Cammie said slowly. "It was called P.E.P.—Pride Enhancing Potion. And after that, Alex acted funny all the way to the past. He did a triple salchow at the 1910 worlds, and they almost named it Bernard jump after Alex's last name. Well, I told you all about it."

"Sure you did." Sonia's blue eyes were firmly fixed on Cammie. "So don't you see the similarity? The witch gave Alex a drink. That was the magical connection, and he became proud. Now she gave you roses, your finger got pricked, and—"

"And what?" Cammie snapped. "Nothing happened to me. I'm not proud."

Cammie looked down at her feet, moved her fingers. Had she changed? She touched her sides and her knees, raised her arms, and turned her head to the right and to the left. No, she felt perfectly normal. Were there any proud feelings in her heart? Cammie closed her eyes and tried to listen to her thoughts. Well, of course, she was happy that she had won the competition. So? Did it make her proud? Hardly. Being excited about winning the gold was natural; there was nothing wrong with it.

Cammie opened her eyes and met Sonia's unblinking look. "What? Are you trying to tell me something?"

"Well, you do act kind of funny," Sonia said softly.

Cammie folded her arms. "What do you mean?"

"You keep calling yourself a champion and—"

Cammie hit the floor with a skate guard. "I *am* a champion, for crying out loud!"

"Okay, forget it." Sonia stood up. "We'd better go."

"No, wait." Cammie leaped forward, blocking Sonia's way. "You still can't put up with the fact that I won a gold medal, that you're not the only champion in this dorm, right?"

"Cammie, stop being ridiculous! I'm only worried about you."

"So *I* am being ridiculous now? You know what? The truth is that you're much more proud than I am, and you don't want to share your glory with anyone else." Cammie threw her skating clothes into her backpack, grabbed her parka, and headed for the door.

"Cammie, wait! You have it all wrong."

"*You* are wrong. By the way, if you want to see the Witch of Pride, look in the mirror!" Cammie ran out of the room and slammed the door as hard as she could.

The door to the room across the hallway opened, and Dana peeked out. Cammie noticed that the girl's eyes were swollen; she must have cried the whole night.

"What's wrong? I heard you yelling," Diana asked.

"You'd better ask the top skater. What do the rest of us know, anyway?" Cammie nodded in the direction of her room and clomped away in her skate guards. She felt Dana's startled look on her back until she turned around the corner and started walking down the steps.

"All set?" Mrs. Page looked out of the kitchen.

"Uh-huh. Bye." Cammie waved at the dorm supervisor.

"Where's Sonia?"

"She's coming. Sorry, Mrs. Page. I don't want to be late." Without waiting for the woman's response, Cammie ran out of the building.

Outside, she took off her skate guards and shoved them into her backpack. She remembered her new Kanga bag. Perhaps she could put her stuff there; it would be a great opportunity to break in her prize. But going back would mean facing Sonia again. Cammie thought for a moment and shook her head angrily. She would carry her things in her backpack one more time. Everybody at the party would be too busy to look at her new bag anyway.

In her excitement, Cammie covered the distance to the Sport Center in record time. When she reached the porch, she put on her skate guards and walked inside.

"Wow!" The moment Cammie found herself in the spacious lobby, she felt she was in a different world. The whole area was ablaze with lights, and the walls were decorated with multicolored signs and banners.

"Congratulations on the Silver, Megan Ligovski!" one of the signs declared in blue and silver letters.

"Way to Go, Sonia Harrison!" another sign said in different shades of red and green.

"Jeff Patterson, You Are the Best!" a sign hanging to the right of Cammie proudly announced.

Cammie walked by several more signs congratulating the top four finishers in every division until she came across the sign where her own name stood written in pink and gold: "All the Best to Cammie Wester, Our Golden Beauty!"

"I like that!" Cammie clapped her hands and moved closer to get a better look at the magnificent sign.

"How about a picture for *Skateland Sensations*, champion?" someone said from behind Cammie.

As she looked back, she saw a heavyset, middle-aged man with a camera. The man was staring straight at her.

"Wanda is writing a big story about this year's champions." The man nodded in the direction of a short, brown-haired woman. Cammie recognized her from yesterday; the woman had interviewed Mel Reed about his Kanga bag.

"Wanda!" the man called.

"In a minute, Frank!" The woman didn't bother to give them a look.

Cammie saw that the reporter was interviewing Megan Ligovski, the girl from New York who had won the silver medal in Cammie's category. Megan, a gangly fourteen-year-old, didn't even glance in Cammie's direction.

"Okay, Cammie, why don't you approach the sign…No, move slightly to the left…that a girl!" Frank clicked his camera several times, making Cammie squint at the bright flashes.

"Now turn your head a little bit…No, don't raise it. Yeah, that's good!" Frank took several more pictures, making Cammie move, change her posture, smile, toss her hair to the side, fold her arms, let them hang loose, point to the sign…

Toward the end of the photo shoot, Cammie couldn't wait to get away from Frank and join the rest of the skaters who were milling around the lobby chatting excitedly.

"Not until you've talked to Wanda, sweetie," Frank said as he took another picture of Cammie, this time with her hands clasped behind her.

Cammie sighed and furrowed her eyebrows slightly.

"No, no, give me a nice smile!" Another click. Frank looked at the picture. "Not bad. Now how about—"

"Franky, Sonia Harrison has just walked in." A very busy-looking Wanda pushed the photographer away and approached Cammie. The woman's high heels clicked loudly against the hardwood floor.

Wanda pushed the microphone in Cammie's face; if Cammie hadn't ducked, she might have gotten hit. "Okay, Cammie Wester, how does it feel to be a champion for the first time?"

"Huh?" Cammie didn't really know what to say. How could she feel? Happy, of course. What else?

"And the whole atmosphere of glory..." Wanda waved her arm, pointing at the balloons streaming from the ceiling.

At that same time, music erupted from the speakers. Cammie recognized the piece. It was "Georgia."

"Does all the attention inspire you to greater skating endeavors?" Wanda asked briskly.

"I...I don't know." Cammie faltered.

"Well, of course, it does." Wanda's lips spread, revealing the woman's perfectly straight teeth.

Cammie thought the conversation was rather funny.

"Doesn't every skater always have greater and more challenging goals?" This time, Wanda didn't even sound as though she expected an answer from Cammie.

From the corner of her eye, Cammie saw Jeff with two balloons. The red balloon said, "Jeff, the Champion"; the blue one declared, "Sonia, the Best Skater." Jeff stopped about three feet away from Frank, who was taking pictures of the pink-cheeked Sonia, and shook the balloons in front of her. Sonia giggled.

"Yes, that was the smile I needed!" Frank clicked his camera again.

Cammie sighed. She wished Alex were at the party too. They would surely have fun together. Now who was she going to hang out with? Frank and Wanda?

"Cammie, I believe becoming a champion has given you a lot of confidence for the forthcoming nationals," Wanda said.

The words *champion* and *nationals* revived Cammie instantly. She straightened up. "I'm definitely counting on getting the gold at the nationals. Now that I won my Skateland competition, the top award at the nationals is really within my reach!" Cammie said with determination.

"That's better." With a nod of approval, Wanda brought her microphone closer to Cammie's face. "Keep going."

"The Kanga bag, airhead! You forgot about her Charming Skater Prize!" Frank hissed at Wanda. He had already dismissed Sonia and was now pointing his camera at Kyle Lyons, the gold medalist in the men's junior competition.

Wanda brushed the bangs off her forehead. "Oh, how could I forget? Sorry, Cammie. Please, tell me how does it feel to be the most charming skater in Skateland?"

Cammie caught Kyle's wink and smiled one of her best smiles. "Oh, it's just great. I never thought it would be possible, but now that I have my Kanga bag, I can surely beat anybody."

Cammie felt confidence rush through her. Of course, now everything was possible. She would go to the nationals and get the gold. Next year, she would become a novice. Hey, why not skip a level? Of course she could do it. If Sonia was a junior, why shouldn't Cammie skate in the junior division? She wasn't much worse than Sonia—hey, she was better. After all, who had just won the Most Charming Skater Award?

"So I believe triple jumps are your next goal?" Wanda asked.

Cammie felt her head spin a little, but the sensation was pleasant. "Well, sure. I don't think it will be particularly difficult once I have my double axel."

"Oh, yes, I heard the double axel is even more difficult than triple jumps," Wanda said.

That was true! Cammie had definitely heard Alex say once that he had found the triple salchow less challenging than the double axel.

"Have you tried any triples yet?" Wanda asked.

"Hmm, sure. In fact, I almost have my triple salchow." Cammie felt blood rush to her cheeks. That was a lie. She hadn't started working on the triple salchow yet. *But I can try it on Monday*, she said to herself. *Sure, why not? I'll ask Coach Ferguson to start working on it with me.*

"How about the triple toe loop?" Wanda asked. The reporter's excitement was contagious.

"Uh, it's almost there," Cammie lied. She felt the tips of her ears turn hot. She surely hoped she could get that jump soon too. Why not? The triples couldn't be that hard. Cammie's double toe loop was excellent, so one extra revolution couldn't be a problem.

"And the triple loop?" Wanda's brown eyes shone in anticipation.

Cammie coughed. "Well, actually I—"

"Wanda, cut it, okay? We don't have all night. Go talk to Jessica McNeil and Peter Deveraux while I take pictures of the juvenile skaters!" Frank yelled.

"True." Wanda moved her microphone away from Cammie. "My best wishes to you, champion! And good luck on your triple flip and triple lutz."

"No, wait! I—"

"Bye, Cammie!" With a casual wave of her hand, Wanda walked away in the direction of the dancing couple who were sipping Perier and chatting in the corner.

"Oh, no!" Cammie shook her head in desperation. Wanda had definitely misunderstood her. Why had the woman been talking about the triple flip and the triple lutz? Cammie surely wasn't ready.

"Does the most charming skater care for a drink?" Cammie turned to the sound of a male voice and gasped as she saw Kyle Lyons smiling at her. Kyle, a tall, slender, dark-haired boy, was one of the most popular guys in Skateland. As much as Cammie rooted for Alex, she knew that her friend couldn't beat Kyle.

Kyle's jumps were incredibly consistent, and he was a born performer too. Gliding on ice, Kyle looked like a big sleek panther with musical talent. Cammie also knew that a lot of older girls had a crush on Kyle, so the very idea that the handsome fifteen-year-old would take an interest in little Cammie Wester was ludicrous.

"So? Are you a charming skater or a sleeping beauty? Hey, I asked you if you were thirsty!" Kyle's teeth looked big and healthy.

"Uh, sure." Cammie wished she could say something more sophisticated.

"A graceful skater like you surely deserves a glass of champagne, but as we are still in Skateland, not at the Olympics, we'll have to settle for ginger ale." With a graceful bow, Kyle handed Cammie a tall glass.

Her hand trembled as she accepted her drink. Cubes of ice clanged against the glass. Cammie sipped the cold drink and whispered a quick, "Thank you."

"The dinner is about to start. So we'd better move on." Kyle pointed in the direction of the banquet hall. The invisible band was now playing "Arthur's Theme."

"We?" Cammie thought she was in a dream.

"Hey, do you still have your skates on? You'd better change fast. You want your feet rested before the big dance at Main Square." Kyle winked at her.

"Ah, sure." Only now did Cammie realize that everybody around her wore shoes. She quickly changed into her white high-heel shoes and stuffed her skates into her backpack.

As she tried to get into the locker room, she realized that the door was locked.

"Here, I got the key from Coach Ferguson. But she wants the door locked again."

Cammie turned around. Sonia stood behind her with a big shiny key in her hand. Cammie expected her roommate to be upset, but Sonia looked her usual calm self.

"Why have they locked the door?" Cammie thought out loud.

Sonia clicked her tongue. "Isn't it obvious? They don't want anybody tampering with our skates."

"Come on. There can't be any witches at the party!" Cammie had already thrown her backpack and parka inside and was hastily locking the door.

"You can't be too careful," Sonia said impassively. "And anyway, what were you doing there with Kyle Lyons?"

Cammie's hand froze. "What do you mean?"

"You're not in his league; he dates older girls," Sonia said firmly.

Cammie jerked her chin up. "I'm a champion, so we have a lot in common."

"Cammie, I don't think—"

"Yeah, right, now tell me Kyle is a witch too. You know what, Sonia? You have a big case of…yeah, witch-phobia!" Cammie stuck her tongue out at Sonia and walked into the lobby.

Kyle was still there waiting for her. Cammie put her hand on his elbow, and together they walked into the banquet hall. Cammie could feel Sonia's eyes on her back, but she couldn't care less.

The dinner was wonderful. After big servings of Caesar salad, the champions were offered a choice of steak or salmon with rice or baked potatoes. But the biggest hit was, of course, the trophy treat—a three-foot-high chocolate trophy decorated with gumdrops of all possible colors and flavors. The chocolate trophy had three layers. The first layer contained delicious medals made of candy and different kinds of chocolate. Cakes, pies, and fruit tarts were piled inside the second layer. The third layer also had medals, only those were made of ice cream.

Wilhelmina stood up, calling for attention. Today, the elderly lady looked particularly festive in her long, silvery gray dress. "Congratulations on your wonderful achievements and on the start of a new period in your lives. As you celebrate your victory, remember that tomorrow is another day. New goals, new challenges, more hard work, and more difficulties."

Wilhelmina made a short pause and looked at the skaters with her bright, gray eyes. Everybody was silent, slightly surprised. Why on earth was the president talking of some difficulties?

"All I'm trying to say, my beloved skaters, is that every day is different. You may be happy today, but tomorrow you may get disappointed. And yet never forget that as you work toward your goal, there is always progress. A slight setback is nothing but a stepping-stone to victory. And therefore, my dear friends, rejoice! Sink your teeth into these delicious treats; savor the rich flavor of chocolate, fruit, and ice cream; and think positively. And if tomorrow brings grief, remember this night, shake off the disappointment, and flow in the excitement and freedom of moving across the ice. And if you feel your practice has been especially hard and tedious, eat something sweet. You have my special permission." Wilhelmina made a dramatic pause.

"Cool!" Jessica McNeil, who was known for her sweet tooth, clapped her hands.

"But don't overdo it!" Wilhelmina looked at Jessica with exaggerated sternness, and everybody laughed.

Just as the president had suggested, Cammie stuffed herself with the trophy treat till she could hardly breathe. She ate four chocolate medals, devoured two fruit tarts and a chocolate chip cookie, feasted on three ice-cream medals—strawberry, pistachio, and butterscotch—and finally ate half of a cherry cheesecake medal. She couldn't finish the whole thing.

"Have another cup of tea. It'll help." Wilhelmina, who had been watching Cammie, gave her an encouraging smile.

Cammie returned the smile but shook her head, refusing to swallow another bite.

"Now if you are all fed, let's head to Main Square for our traditional night dance," Wilhelmina said cheerfully. "Yet, as much as I don't want to ruin your festive mood, I have to give you a warning. Champions or not, you are all expected to report for practice at six in the morning. You are an example for the rest of the skaters here, so we don't want you to be late. Personally, I'll be leaving the rink at nine o'clock sharp, so we will make this your official curfew.

"Before getting into my ice mobile, I will give you a farewell wave. This will be the sign for all of you to head for your dorms and go to bed. I expect maturity from you. Because it's Sunday night, there will be quite a few Skateland residents at Main Square frolicking till the crack of dawn. And after midnight, the witches are likely to show up at the Main Rink to play tricks on careless champions. Do not fall prey of their evil schemes. I believe that you may feel invincible now, but let me remind you that the witches are particularly sensitive to any manifestation of weakness. Therefore, I urge you to exercise extreme caution. Now to finish my speech on a positive note, I want you to glide, run, and have fun!"

Wilhelmina waved at the skaters, sank into her wheelchair, and rode out of the banquet hall. The champions sat quietly for a moment, as though waiting for the president's words to sink in.

Kyle was the first to speak up. "Hey, what are we waiting for? Let's go!"

The skaters stirred up; there was a chuckle, a sound of a broken glass, an *ouch*, a shuffling of feet… Within a moment, everybody was on the way to the locker rooms.

In the crowded locker room, Cammie replaced her shoes with skating boots, slipped her parka over her dress, and ran out into the lobby, where Kyle already stood waiting for her.

MOONLIGHT DANCE

Though it was late, the snow made everything appear lighter. Cammie and Kyle glided past small wood houses, went around a small park whose benches were dug in the snow almost up to their backs, and finally entered Main Square. The gray ice of the Main Rink had just been cleaned. The smooth surface caught the reflections of bright neon signs from the stores and restaurants, making the whole area look like a giant piece of jewelry.

A fast and strong skater, Kyle was the first to step onto the ice. He pulled Cammie by the hand, and together they glided forward faster and faster. Music began to play from the speakers positioned all around the square, and from the corner of her eye, Cammie could see the rest of the champions whoosh by.

After half a dozen laps around the rink, Kyle stopped short. "Well, now that we're warmed up, how about a dance? Can you do a waltz?"

"No! I never took ice dancing." Now that Kyle knew how inexperienced she was, he'd definitely leave her alone in the middle of the ice arena.

"Neither did I. Well, we're not at a competition, so we don't have to think of beating them." Kyle nodded in the direction of junior dancers who were waltzing about fifteen feet from them.

Cammie scanned the rink and saw several more dancing couples. Melvin Reed appeared on the ice, pushing Wilhelmina's wheelchair. Ten seconds later, the two older skaters swirled around the rink in perfect unison.

"Here's my coach dancing with your Coach Ferguson. Not bad." Kyle pointed to the right.

"How come that doesn't surprise me?" Cammie grinned and looked in the other direction, where Sonia and Jeff were doing a decent waltz.

"Where did *they* learn to ice dance?"

Kyle made a funny face. "Isn't it obvious? They don't know the steps; they're just moving with the music. Do you want to try?"

Cammie wasn't sure she could pull off a decent waltz, yet she let Kyle guide her. Before the thought could register in her mind, they were dancing in fast tempo around the rink.

"I can't believe I'm doing it!" Cammie relaxed in Kyle's strong arms, letting him support her and carry her forward and around. She arched her back and looked up at the silvery pattern of stars in the black sky. For a moment, she thought of the sky as a huge skating rink, where each star was a skater. The brighter the star, the better the performance.

So it means there are competitions in the sky too, Cammie thought. She picked out the brightest star, imagining it was her, Cammie Wester. As they bent their knees and turned, Cammie tried to keep the star in the focus of her vision.

Ouch! She tripped over Kyle's boot and would have fallen if he hadn't caught her.

"Oops! I got dizzy." Cammie laughed, holding on to Kyle's hand.

"Yeah, me too. Dancing isn't as easy as I thought. We'd better do what we can."

As though overhearing them, the music changed to fast rock then to hip-hop, and soon the whole rink was dancing. Cammie laughed hard as she watched people do the most incredible moves on the ice.

Mel Reed was moon walking without a trace of a smile. Mr. Walrus, a Zamboni driver, appeared from nowhere performing a Cossack dance. Coach Ferguson did a lunge turn and slid into a split, and Wilhelmina showed the excited audience her famous blurry spin that was only a couple rotations short of her record-setting, hundred-revolution spin.

Cammie didn't remember ever being so happy. She wanted the party to go on and on, but at some moment, the clock on the tower across from where she stood came to life and struck nine times. Right on the last beat, a silver ice mobile appeared from around the corner. The inscription on the side of the vehicle said Skateland President, and next to it was the Skateland logo. Cammie also noticed that there was no driver behind the steering wheel; the ice mobile was moving on its own.

"Have a very peaceful night, skaters!" Wilhelmina raised her small hand clad in a silvery glove and gave everybody at the rink a cheerful wave. Supported by Melvin Reed, the president jumped into the ice mobile and shouted, "Home!" Immediately the silvery sled took off.

"Well, that was your clue, skaters! Time to get back to your dorms." Kyle's coach, a slender gray-haired man, clapped his hands.

"Oh, no!" The two boys who stood next to the coach exchanged sour looks.

"No objections accepted." Coach Ferguson stepped forward, eyeing the boys sternly. "Everybody off the ice!"

Cammie saw Jeff leading Sonia away. The dancers and the pairs followed them, appearing very unhappy. One of the guys slammed the ice with his blade; his partner made a nasty face. Megan Ligovski shrugged and whispered something to a tall girl rising from a back pivot next to her. Within a moment, the two of them were gone. Now the rink was almost empty, except for the coaches.

"Now what are you waiting for?" Coach Ferguson barked at a bulky boy, who was doing one split jump after another. When he wouldn't stop, the coach moved in the boy's direction.

Cammie felt Kyle's raspy breath on her neck. In another moment, the boy grabbed her by the hand, pulling her aside behind a lamppost.

"Hey, we don't have to leave like obedient tots!" Kyle whispered.

Cammie whirled around. "What?"

"Let's wait till the coaches leave, and then we can keep skating."

"Oh!" That was definitely an excellent idea. For never in her life had Cammie been more reluctant to leave the ice. She didn't feel tired in the least. Her body was full of adrenaline; she wanted to jump, to spin, and to have fun. For crying out loud, this was her day! She had just won the gold at Skateland Annual Competition. Hey, not just the gold; she had received the Kanga bag. So now that she was the best skater in Skateland, the stupid rules didn't apply to her.

"So what do you think?" Kyle asked impatiently.

"Of course I'd like to stay. Wait. Are the coaches still here?" Cammie peeked from behind the lamppost.

"Yeah, Coach Darrell is leading Coach Ferguson away. Good," Kyle said happily.

Cammie saw a black-and-yellow Zamboni machine pull out from behind a corner. "Okay, here's Mr. Walrus resurfacing the ice. I know him; he's from my home rink."

"Oh yeah, I liked his Cossack dance," Kyle said.

They watched the ice resurfacing machine move around the rink, leaving long trails of clean ice behind. As the night was cold, they didn't have to wait long for the water from the Zamboni machine to freeze up.

"Let's go!" Kyle rushed back onto the ice, Cammie following shortly.

They skated around again, feeling the cold night wind carry them forward. A loud song erupted from the speakers again.

"So what jump are you working on now?" Kyle shouted on top of the music.

"The triple salchow!" Cammie yelled back.

"That's cool. Wanna try one for me?"

"Sure," Cammie said confidently but had second thoughts right away. The truth was, she couldn't do a triple salchow; in fact, Coach Ferguson had never even shown her the difficult jump.

"Go ahead!" Kyle pushed her forward.

Now she didn't have a choice. She did a quick Mohawk and went into her backward crossovers, gaining speed. *What if I land it?* she thought. *It can't be more difficult than the double axel.* She went into her three turn, bent her knees…She jumped…no! She didn't have enough height and landed hard on her rear end.

"Not cool!" Kyle said.

As though Cammie didn't know!

"Okay, that's the triple salchow. Look at me!" Kyle demonstrated the jump. His posture was perfect in the air, and his landing was soft and noiseless, like a cat's. "Now you try it," Kyle said.

Cammie attempted a couple more triple salchows, and even though she wasn't even close to landing them, she felt encouraged. At least, now she could officially announce to her friends—and the media—that she was working on triples. That in itself was a big deal. And tomorrow she would ask Coach Ferguson to give her some preparation exercises. She would be able to land her triple salchow very, very soon.

Someone pushed Cammie from behind and apologized. Before she could say it was okay, two young women swished by, almost cutting her off.

"What's going on?" Cammie asked angrily. She looked around.

There were people stepping on the ice, approaching the rink from all directions. Apparently, the night public session had just started. Within ten minutes, the rink was jammed. There was no way Cammie could do any of her difficult jumps with the crowd that thick.

"Never mind. We'll just stroke around!" Kyle shouted in Cammie's ear.

She nodded, squeezing his hand. Really, they didn't have to do any fancy moves. It was enough to fly forward, letting the wind cool their flushed faces.

"Hey, buddy! Are you Kyle?"

Cammie stopped at the sound of the voice. Two young men who appeared to be in their late twenties were staring at Kyle.

"Do you guys know me?" Kyle asked, sounding a little surprised.

One of the young men burped loudly. "I've never seen a bigger lutz since Brian Boitano's stellar performance at the Olympics. My dad has the video; you can borrow it if you like."

"Oh, thanks!" Kyle grinned, looking positively delighted.

"Wanna join us as we toast for your success at the nationals? The young lady is invited too." The other guy shook what looked like a bottle of wine.

Cammie felt her eyes widen with horror. "Kyle, no!"

"I'll be right back!" Kyle patted her arm and glided to the edge of the rink to join the young men.

"Oh, no!" Cammie looked around helplessly. Perhaps she should have left with everybody after all.

The rink was now filled with people who zoomed across the ice surface, yelling at one another and singing aloud to the music. Twice Cammie almost got hit, so she had to move closer to the edge of the rink where Kyle was still chatting with his fans.

"Okay, let's show them what real skaters can do." Kyle had rejoined Cammie and was now pointing to the wild crowd.

"Are you sure we won't get hurt?" Cammie asked tentatively.

"Hey, you're with me. Come on!"

They darted forward, going faster and faster. The familiar rhythm of gliding across the rink calmed Cammie down, and soon she found herself laughing again, cheering with Kyle, daring him to pick up even more speed. The stars flew over them, and the night was young.

Cammie completely lost track of time. She didn't know how long they had been skating, but she definitely didn't want the beautiful night to end.

A loud whistle came from Cammie's left followed by an angry voice that sounded familiar. She went into a quick T-stop and looked in the direction of the sound.

"Oh, no!"

"What?" Kyle stopped about fifteen feet away from her.

Next to the rink stood the familiar police ice mobile, and Captain Greenfield was talking harshly to Kyle's drinking buddies.

"The two of you are under arrest for SUI," the policeman said sharply.

"What's SUI?" Cammie whispered to Kyle.

"Skating under the influence," he hissed back.

"You can't come to public sessions drunk," Captain Greenfield said. "Yes, and don't tell me you're not aware of the law."

"Hey, man, two glasses of champagne don't make anyone drunk. It's a holiday, after all. We only

toasted to our champions' success at the nationals,"
one of the guys said dismissively.

Kyle let out a quick *ouch*. "I'm getting out of here.
Gosh, if they find out that I've been drinking too, I
may be disqualified from the nationals. See you!"

Kyle bent over and glided away from the middle
of the rink into one of the side streets.

"Wait! Wait for me!" Cammie rushed after her
friend.

Kyle glanced back, apparently making sure
that they were no longer in plain view of the cops.
"What's your problem? You aren't drunk."

"It's worse. They caught me skating in the Icy
Park two days ago."

Kyle snickered. "So you already have a police
record, huh? Anyway, I need to rush."

"Aren't you going to walk me to my dorm?"
Suddenly, Cammie panicked. She hadn't realized
how late it was. And Skateland at night wasn't a safe
place for a young girl. Cammie picked up speed and
caught up with Kyle again.

"What? Don't you know the way to your dorm?"
he asked angrily.

"Sure I do, but it's dark, and there may be witches
skating around."

Kyle leaned back and guffawed. "What? Witches?
Boy, you're such a baby, Cammie."

"I'm not a baby. And if you only knew … You see,
last year, Alex and I—"

Kyle interrupted her harshly. "Look, it's not a good time for childhood memories, okay? And anyway, I'm not your chaperone. You knew what you were up to when you agreed to skate late. So … I'll see you."

He skated away with smooth, long strides, leaving Cammie alone on the ice-covered sidewalk, her mouth wide open.

"Jerk!" She picked a block of ice and threw it at Kyle. Naturally it didn't reach him. The boy was already far away, and he didn't even look back. So what was Cammie going to do? Stupid question. Of course, she would skate to her dorm and the sooner the better.

She turned around and skated in the opposite direction from what Kyle had taken. She wished she could take a shortcut through the Icy Park, but it would definitely not be wise to take that risk. Either the witches would get her or the cops would catch her and accuse her of breaking the law again. She didn't even know what would be worse: getting her skating career ruined or being expelled from Skateland. No, she'd better spend another half an hour skating to her dorm along the dark, quiet streets.

A heavy hand landed on her shoulder, causing her to scream.

"Hey, what're you doing here so late?"

Oh no, the cops had found her after all. She looked back and sighed with relief. The face of the man who had grabbed her shoulder didn't belong to either of the policemen she knew. Instead, Cammie saw two bright-blue eyes and a long mustache. "Mr. Walrus! What're you doing here?"

"It's me indeed," the man said cheerfully. "And to answer your question, I'm cleaning the streets, of course. It's my job. How about yourself? Don't you know what time it is?"

Cammie shrugged. "I haven't brought my watch to the party."

"It's almost midnight," Mr. Walrus declared.

"Oh, no!" *Mrs. Page will definitely kill me*, Cammie thought.

"You look scared. Are any of the witches chasing you?" Mr. Walrus looked worried.

Cammie hung her head, feeling embarrassed. "Not the witches, the cops."

That was definitely not the answer Mr. Walrus had expected. His thick eyebrows shot up. "The cops?"

"I should be in the dorm. The curfew, remember?"

Mr. Walrus clapped his gloved hands. "Aha! Well, I'd better give you a ride. It's not good for you to skate alone at night. By the way, why isn't your boyfriend with you?"

Cammie snorted. "Kyle isn't my boyfriend. And he's a jerk."

"I see. As rude as the descriptions sounds, it probably suits Kyle the best. Leaving a young lady alone like that..." Mr. Walrus sighed and started humming an unknown tune.

Cammie listened to him singing until she almost fell asleep in the Zamboni machine. She barely remembered the vehicle sliding to a stop and Mr. Walrus's strong hands carrying her up the steps to her dorm.

Looking furious, Mrs. Page thanked Mr. Walrus for bringing Cammie in. She didn't say a word to Cammie, but Cammie thought it was actually for the best. Tripping over her skate guards, she trudged up the steps to her room on the third floor.

Sonia was already in bed in deep sleep. Cammie quickly took off her skates and collapsed on her bed in her skating dress. Within a few seconds, she was asleep.

REALITY STRIKES

Cammie's dreams were full of risky jumps and spins. At some point, she saw herself dancing in the sky, but the ground was dangerously close, and to avoid a nasty fall, she had to keep her eyes shut.

Ding dong dong!

Yes, those were the witches trying to get Cammie to open her eyes. But she wouldn't fall for their stupid tricks; she knew better than that.

"Oh my gosh, it's hilarious!" Sonia laughed somewhere nearby.

Well, perhaps in Sonia's mind getting chased by the whole horde of witches was funny, but Cammie knew better. And she wouldn't open her eyes, no way.

"Cammie, open your eyes, for crying out loud! Look at it."

It was definitely Sonia, not a witch. Well, as much as Cammie hated the idea of opening her eyes, at least she could do it without getting attacked. But, boy, was it hard! Cammie's eyelids felt as though they were glued shut. She put her fingers on her lower eyelashes and forced her eyes open.

Oh no! Seated in front of her was a big brown stuffed animal. It was shaking its head topped with long, pointed ears, and its big eyes flashed yellow.

"Who's that?" Cammie asked, slurring her words.

"Don't you recognize it? It's your Kanga bag!" Sonia almost choked with laughter.

Cammie stared at the weird creature. As though feeling her gaze, Kanga opened its mouth and began to speak in a croaky voice that sounded neither male nor female.

> Wake up right now, sleepy head.
> It's time to leave this cozy bed,
> For it is later than you think.
> Wake up, and hurry to the rink!

"For crying out loud!" Cammie exclaimed.

"Oh, it's so cute!" Sonia fell on the carpet and kicked her legs, shaking with obvious delight.

"Come off it, Sonia!" Cammie said irritably. "I'm going back to sleep." She pulled the covers over her head and closed her eyes.

"It's five o'clock," Sonia said.

"So what?"

"Are you crazy? The practice, remember?"

"I'm too tired. I came home at twelve thirty last night."

"So? It's your fault. Why didn't you leave with Jeff and me? We called your name; we waved at you. Yet you stayed with that Kyle. What did you like about him anyway?" Sonia said, sounding very much like Coach Ferguson.

Cammie grimaced. It wasn't that Sonia was wrong, especially about Kyle. The guy was a jerk after all, but Sonia was the last person Cammie was going to discuss it with. "Sonia, look, I'm beat. Nothing will happen if I miss one practice, okay?"

Before Cammie could say another word, a loud hiss came out from the insides of Kanga bag, and the animal began to speak again.

The practice is about to start.
Pack up your gear and depart.
But if you stay in bed and snooze,
You'll never win; instead you'll lose.

Cammie heard Sonia clap her hands. "Fantastic! Now you don't have an excuse, Cammie. Get up!"

"Yes, I do. I already won the gold, remember?" Cammie said stubbornly. She was really mad. So that was her Charming Skater Prize—a stupid animal that acted as an alarm clock. Like Cammie needed it! She hated waking up early, but she did it because their morning practices started at six o'clock. But today was a special occasion, and surely Cammie deserved a couple extra hours of sleep. Nothing would happen if she took it easy for a day or two. In fact, any professional athlete would agree that practicing when you were tired was really bad for you.

Someone growled next to Cammie, and a moment later, she felt her down quilt pulled off her.

"Sonia, stop that!" She would probably stay in bed anyway, but the morning air felt really uncomfortable. Shivering, Cammie jumped off her bed to get her covers back.

Sonia sat on the floor almost bent in half with laughter. "It's not me!" she breathed out.

Cammie stared at her dully. "Who else but you?"

"It was Kanga."

Cammie looked in the direction of Sonia's hand and saw that the nasty animal really held her quilt in its sharp paws.

"You stupid beast, give it back!" Cammie hollered, trying to reach the quilt. Kanga looked at her with its yellow eyes and, Cammie could swear, shook its head. "I said give it to me!" Cammie roared as she advanced on the animal. Kanga hopped away, its eyes still following Cammie's every move. "Come on!" Cammie leaped ahead, tripped on her skates that sat in the middle of the room, and fell.

Sonia giggled louder.

"Stop it!" Cammie rose from the floor, rubbing her thigh.

"Sorry. I didn't mean to be nasty. But look. Kanga did manage to get you out of bed, after all."

Cammie could see that Sonia was trying to look serious, but the mischievous glint in her eyes was a definite giveaway. Cammie waved her hand dismissively and wobbled to the shower. Contrary to her expectations, the hot water didn't revive her. As she sat down on her bed to put on her tights, she felt light-headed as though she had just come out of a very fast scratch spin. The only thing she wanted now was to get back in bed and pull the covers over her head.

"Why didn't you come home after Wilhelmina left anyway?" Sonia asked.

"Oh, Sonia, please not again!" Cammie groaned. Dull pain was forming behind her eyelids and in her forehead. If it weren't for the nasty Kanga, Cammie would definitely skip the morning practice. She needed rest; she deserved it. After all, she was a star now, and champions weren't supposed to be treated like ordinary skaters. Why did Cammie need two practices a day anyway? One would be just fine.

Cammie barely touched her breakfast. After only four and a half hours of sleep, she felt groggy and nauseated. As Cammie toyed with her food, Mrs. Page gave her a couple spiteful looks but fortunately didn't say a word. That was good, for Cammie wasn't in the mood to talk. She didn't even care whether the dorm supervisor was going to tell Coach Ferguson about Cammie's practice in the Icy Park. It would be too late to do it anyway, for Cammie's extraordinary success at the competition trumped whatever she had done before.

Sonia, who now practiced at the Yellow Rink, was the first to leave the dining room. Cammie forced herself to swallow a slice of toast and downed half a cup of hot tea. Reluctantly, she followed Dana and Liz out of the building. Outside, the cold winter air made Cammie feel a little better, though she still felt drowsy. She could barely keep up with the girls, who skated very fast, deeply involved in their own private conversation.

At the beginning of Axel Avenue, Liz turned back and glared at Cammie trudging gloomily behind. "Cammie, hmm, do you mind if we don't wait for you? We're not champions, so we can't be late for practice."

Cammie wasn't quite sure whether the girl was being sarcastic or not, but she had no strength to think about it. "Fine, go ahead."

When Cammie stepped onto the ice of the Green Rink, the practice was in full swing. Automatically, Cammie looked at the clock. It showed six twenty. Cammie's heart sank. Coach Ferguson hated it when skaters came late, and Cammie was sure the coach wouldn't let her get away with it.

Cammie turned out to be quite right. The moment Coach Ferguson saw her hastily taking off her skate guards, she skated up to Cammie, looking furious. "And what's your excuse for coming late, Miss Champion?"

"Uh, I'm just a little tired from yesterday." Cammie smoothed out her green skating dress nervously.

"Ah, of course, partying till midnight is more important for you than practicing. Yes, Mrs. Page told me everything."

Cammie clenched her fists. Whatever she had done last night was none of Mrs. Page's business. She only wished she could shout those angry words into the face of the dorm supervisor right now.

"And what's the explanation of *this*?" From a pocket of her green down coat, Coach Ferguson pulled out a newspaper folded together.

Cammie glanced at the front page, and her heart sank. It was the last issue of *Skateland Sensations*.

"Was I surprised when I opened it this morning!" Coach Ferguson shoved the newspaper into Cammie's hand.

Cammie gasped at the sight of her own face staring at her from the front page. The caption underneath read: "Skateland Top Intermediate Skater Is about to Make a Big Sensation at the Nationals."

"Go ahead. Read it!" Coach Ferguson said coldly.

Though the story covered two whole pages, it didn't take Cammie a long time to scan the whole thing. Under different circumstances, Cammie might have been happy to see her own pictures in different skating positions scattered across the pages. But Coach Ferguson's furious face expression robbed every ounce of joy from Cammie's heart.

Of course, after Cammie looked through the story, she knew what had made her coach so upset. Not only had the reporter written down everything Cammie had said, but she had taken Cammie's words to the extreme. "The young skater already lands the triple salchow, triple toe loop, and triple loop consistently, and her triple flip and triple lutz are getting better every day," the reporter wrote. The woman also quoted Cammie saying that she was about to skip two levels and try to take senior moves-in-the-field and freestyle tests.

"Look, I…" Cammie tried to say something, but the very first word stuck in her throat. She coughed hard.

"So is that true? Did you really say you could do triple jumps?" Coach Ferguson took the newspaper away from her and stuffed it back in her pocket.

"No, no, of course I didn't!" Cammie raised both hands, feeling her face flush.

"Then where did this scumbag get all the information from?" Coach Ferguson demanded.

"Well…" Cammie shifted her feet. "I only told her that I was working on triples, but—"

Coach Ferguson raised her thin eyebrows. "Oh, is that what you are working on? How come I'm not aware of that?"

"That's not what I meant!" Cammie exclaimed. Angry tears pricked her eyes, but she tried her best to stay calm. Surely the coach would understand why Cammie had exaggerated her achievements a little bit.

"All I told the reporter was that I was about to start working on triple jumps. *Working* on them, not *landing* them," Cammie said, trying to keep her voice down.

Coach Ferguson tilted her head. "And what, may I ask, gave you the idea that you're ready for triple jumps?"

Cammie frowned. "But I just landed my double axel, so I thought—"

"And that's another thing I wanted to talk to you about," Coach Ferguson said harshly. "What right did you have to do the double axel in your program without my permission?"

"But I won, didn't I?" Cammie smiled her best smile. That was something her coach couldn't ignore. Cammie was a champion. "And actually, I was going to ask you to show me how to do the triple salchow today. Okay?" Cammie looked Coach Ferguson in the eyes.

The coach's face expression didn't soften a bit. "Well, I'm flattered that at least you wanted to ask my opinion. Well, the answer is no. You're not ready for triples."

"But, but..." Cammie stammered; she felt blood rushing to her cheeks. Why was Coach Ferguson so unfair? Didn't she want Cammie to succeed? "Coach Ferguson, I absolutely need at least one triple jump to compete at the nationals. Megan Ligovski does have the triple salchow, and if she lands it—"

Cammie grimaced at the sound of the coach's skate guard making a strong contact with the boards.

"I don't care about Megan Ligovski. And while I'm still your coach, the decision about what jumps you're going to work on will be mine."

"Coach Ferguson, please…" Tears streamed down Cammie's face, but she wasn't even making an effort to wipe them off. She had to convince the coach that triple jumps really wouldn't be a problem for her.

"One more word and you're out of here!" Coach Ferguson said firmly.

Cammie clenched her teeth. Her face was wet, and she felt herself shiver in the cold rink.

"It's not fair!" Cammie said shrilly. "You're just upset because I tried that double axel without your permission. But see, I wouldn't have won if I hadn't gone for it. And now I need that triple, and you don't want to help me!"

The moment Cammie closed her mouth she was almost deafened by the silence around her. Even the skaters had stopped in the middle of their practice. Everybody was staring at Cammie with their mouths wide open.

Coach Ferguson's nostrils flared. "Get out of my practice. Now!"

"What?" Cammie stepped back, unable to believe what she had just heard.

"I don't care whether you're a champion or not." The coach's face was completely white. "Unless you're here to learn something and follow the instructions, I can't help you. So I want you to leave the rink and not come back until you have a change of attitude."

"But..." Coach Ferguson's face blurred in front of Cammie; she was afraid she was about to faint.

"Bye, Miss Wester." Coach Ferguson turned around and skated to the middle of the rink.

Cammie stared after the woman. *Miss Wester?* Her coach had never called her anything other than *Cammie* before.

Dana landed a perfect double axel right in front of Cammie and stuck out her tongue at her. Feeling her chin shake, Cammie whirled around and ran into the locker room. She grabbed her parka and her backpack and rushed out of the building sobbing.

Luckily, Mrs. Page didn't ask her any questions. She merely glanced at Cammie's tear-stricken face and stepped away, letting her in. Sniffling, Cammie ran up the steps to her room and closed the door tightly behind her. She threw her parka in the corner and sat down on the floor. As she unlaced her skating boots, her fingers trembled.

"It's not fair, not fair!" Cammie shouted and slammed her fist against the carpeted floor. Everything was over. Not only hadn't Coach Ferguson agreed to work with Cammie on her triples, she had kicked her out of the practice session. So what was Cammie supposed to do now? *Don't come back until you have a change of attitude!* Coach Ferguson's words rang in

Cammie's ears, causing her head to throb. What was wrong with Cammie's attitude? Was it bad to work toward a gold medal at the nationals?

When Cammie thought of the nationals, she cried even harder. Being as furious as she was, Coach Ferguson would probably forbid Cammie to compete at the major competition altogether. Gosh, why had it all happened now, when Cammie had finally had a breakthrough? Now she had a real chance at medaling at the nationals; she just knew it. And instead of supporting her, Coach Ferguson had turned into her worst enemy.

"She's just like a witch," Cammie grumbled. Yes, that was the real witch—Coach Ferguson, not the classy judge who had presented Cammie with roses.

"I wish Sonia had heard what Coach Ferguson said to me!" Cammie said out loud. She got up from the floor, threw her skates into the closet, and plopped on her bed, thinking hard.

What was she going to do? Sonia would probably side with Coach Ferguson and tell Cammie to apologize to the woman. Would that be a good idea? Cammie thought about it and shook her head stubbornly. She didn't feel she had done anything wrong. Besides, even if the coach did forgive her, she still wouldn't help Cammie with triple jumps. Cammie was sure about that. It meant that Cammie still wouldn't have a chance at winning the nationals.

Now wait a minute! Cammie thought. *Why do I need a coach to learn triple jumps? I landed my double axel on my own. And last night, Kyle showed me how to do the triple salchow!*

Cammie rose to her feet slowly, feeling her head spin with excitement. Why couldn't she go to the Icy Park and practice her triple salchow there? And after she mastered it, she would go to Coach Ferguson and apologize; that was no big deal. And once Coach Ferguson allowed her to compete ... Cammie smiled widely. With a solid triple jump, she would definitely win the competition.

There was one thing, however. Cammie frowned slightly. *How about the police?* What if she got caught practicing in the Icy Park again? Then Coach Ferguson would definitely withdraw her name from the nationals. Cammie scratched her head then dismissed the unpleasant thought. Last time, the police had come looking for Cammie because it was late at night. And who said that Cammie couldn't practice her triples in the park during the day? Well, technically, it was still against the law, but who would know about it? Unless Cammie stayed at her lucky rink after the official curfew, no one would even think of looking for her in the park.

For the first time that day, Cammie felt excited. She looked at the clock. It was only seven thirty. She wouldn't go to school today. Instead, she would get into bed and take a nice long nap. She needed rest to be able to land difficult jumps. And when everybody left for their afternoon practice, Cammie would sneak to the Icy Park and work on her triple salchow.

And once she won the nationals, nobody would even remember that she had disobeyed the coach.

Funny how fast things changed. Yesterday and the day before, when Cammie had stood on the top step of the podium with a gold medal around her neck, nobody cared that she had perfected her double axel while breaking a couple of silly rules. After all, it was skating that mattered, not the law.

The decision made, Cammie slipped into bed and pulled the covers over her head. Before she drifted away to sleep, she allowed herself to think of the wonderful feeling of being the best. Again and again, she relived the wonderful memories of landing every difficult jump in her program, of seeing her name at the top of the winners' list. She remembered how the gold medal had felt around her neck. And then a reporter interviewed her.

By the way, she'd better get a copy of *Skateland Sensations* for her scrapbook. Cammie also thought of skating around the Main Rink and of Kyle leading her in a dance pattern. She made an angry face. Kyle was a jerk; she didn't need him. He hadn't even walked her to the dorm. Alex would never do anything like that. Alex … Perhaps the two of them could get together sometime soon. Maybe Alex could give Cammie some tips on landing the triple salchow. Before Cammie could land a decent triple salchow in her dream, her mind went blank; she was asleep.

Cammie barely heard Sonia come in and leave. At some point, it seemed to her that Mrs. Page was by her side, asking her questions. She still didn't open her eyes.

When Cammie finally woke up, the sun stood low in the pale-blue sky. Cammie looked at the clock; it was four o'clock.

Cammie jumped out of her bed. "The afternoon practice! It already started."

Then she remembered that she wasn't going to the Green Rink. Instead she had planned to work on her triple salchow in the Icy Park. Well, that was much better.

Cammie quickly took off her wrinkled green skating dress. Gosh, it was the second time in a row that she had fallen asleep in her street clothes. Well, she didn't need the official Green Rink outfit to practice outside. It would probably be windy in the Icy Park, so she'd better be prepared. Cammie put on a long-sleeved T-shirt over her white cotton one and got into a wool turtleneck. From her closet, she took out a thick, hand-knit sweater that her grandmother had given her when she moved to Skateland. She laced her skates and put on her parka. That had to be enough. In fact, practicing too hard might actually make her hot, but she could always take an extra layer off.

Humming a tango tune from last night's dance, Cammie ran down the steps to the first floor.

"Going to practice?" a familiar voice asked.

"Ouch!" Cammie hadn't expected to see Mrs. Page at that hour. She thought the woman would be in her bedroom reading a romance novel.

"You haven't had lunch," Mrs. Page said grumpily.

"Oh!" The moment the dorm supervisor mentioned food, Cammie realized how hungry she was. She had only eaten a slice of toast at breakfast. And since then, she hadn't swallowed a bite.

"Why couldn't you wake up earlier?" Mrs. Page shook her head. "Wait!"

The woman went back to the kitchen, leaving Cammie in the lobby. Cammie quickly pulled off her white wool hat and unzipped her parka. She was sweating bullets in the warm building.

"I know what happened." Mrs. Page was back in the lobby with a huge package in her hand.

Cammie shrugged and looked away.

"And see, you're late for practice again. At least you've decided to go to the rink; that's good."

Cammie stifled a smirk.

"You're a talented skater, Cammie, but you know nothing about discipline."

So now Cammie had to endure another lecture. She pressed her lips, feeling annoyed.

"When I was your age, I didn't like grown-ups telling me what to do either," Mrs. Page said. "Well, now I understand how right they were. And look; when I called Mrs. Ferguson and told her about your wrong behavior, I didn't do it to hurt you or make you suffer."

I wish you knew how you made me suffer, Cammie thought. *I can't even go to practices anymore. Not that I want to, of course.*

"Was Coach Ferguson really upset?" Mrs. Page asked, this time sounding a little guilty.

Cammie almost giggled. "A bit."

"Of course. She's your coach, and you disobeyed her. But don't worry. I've known Laura—that's her first name in case you don't know—since she was a little girl. She's strict, but she has a kind heart. And when you apologize to her, she'll be really happy."

Cammie didn't say anything.

"Okay, you'd better go. There's a chicken sandwich and a bag of chips in here for you. And there's a bottle of water too." Mrs. Page handed Cammie the package.

"Thank you." Cammie stuffed the package into her backpack.

"Hey, I don't see your new Kanga bag!" Mrs. Page exclaimed. "Why don't you take it with you? It can carry your lunch and keep your water cold."

That was the last thing on Cammie's mind. She didn't really want the pushy animal to yell instructions at her all the way to the Icy Parl. "Uh, I still didn't have time to figure out how to use it."

Mrs. Page smiled. "Well, Kanga surely did an excellent job waking you up this morning."

Cammie wondered how many people Sonia had told about Kanga's alarm clock. "I've got to go, Mrs. Page. Thank you for lunch."

"And come home right after practice, do you hear me?" Mrs. Page unlocked the door to let Cammie out.

"Uh-huh."

The door slammed behind Cammie. She exhaled and stepped on the hard ice path. As she turned the corner, she thought that news surely traveled fast in Skateland. She looked back at the dorm building. She was sure Mrs. Page was looking at her through the window. It meant Cammie couldn't enter the Icy Park immediately; she had to give the dorm supervisor the impression she was on her way to the Green Rink. Cammie skated along Axel Avenue for almost five minutes till the first intersection. There she looked around, making sure no one was watching her. She stepped off the ice path and sprinted along the snow-covered lawn and into the park.

TRIPLE SALCHOW

Cammie reached her lucky rink in record time. She quickly got rid of her backpack and put it on the snow near the edge of the pond. Then she positioned her skate guards next to her backpack and stepped onto the ice. It fell smooth and hard under her blades. Cammie spread her arms and skated forward, gaining speed with every stroke. Cold wind caressed her face; she finally felt strong and rested.

"It's great!" Cammie shouted and went into energetic power pulls. It was wonderful to skate alone, away from Coach Ferguson's sarcastic remarks and from the other girls' sneers. Funny how quickly things changed. Only yesterday Cammie had been in the center of attention; everybody had told her she was the best. And now, only a day later, she had been kicked out of practice. But she wouldn't allow herself to think of bad stuff now. What did it matter anyway? She was about to start working on triple jumps, and she would prove to her enemies that she was really a top skater.

Cammie's face felt hot. Feeling she had warmed up enough, she slipped off her parka and threw it on the snow next to her other things. Immediately she felt lighter. Again she glided around the rink practicing steps, doing crossovers, preparing her body for jumps. She went over the moves she knew well. Everything worked, except for the double axel that Cammie two-footed three times. Well, it didn't matter. After all, she wasn't at a competition.

Finally, Cammie decided she was ready for a triple salchow. She would start with a high double then gradually add an extra revolution. Cammie did a quick three turn, held her edge, and jumped. Good! Her double salchow was solid. Okay, so how was she going to add another rotation? Cammie thought for a moment, trying to remember her transition from singles to doubles. Of course! She would jump into a backspin, and once her flow became natural, she would try a triple. Cammie did several salchows followed by backspins. No problem. She tried a double salchow-loop combination and landed it perfectly.

"That was easy!" she exclaimed and clapped her hands. If Coach Ferguson saw her now, she would probably shake her fist at Cammie and yell that she wasn't ready for triples.

You wait. I'll show you what I can do, Cammie thought as she picked up more speed. This time, she was going to try a triple salchow. She went into a three turn. *Bend your knee more*, she told herself. She took off her toe and swung her arms. One, two, three … No, she wasn't rotating fast enough. The ice rushed toward her, and she landed on her behind.

"Ugh!" Cammie kicked the ice with her toe pick and stood up reluctantly. She had to remember that for a triple, she needed to pull in faster.

"Concentrate, concentrate!" she whispered as she skated around the rink, trying to shake off the effects of her fall.

The wind whistled through the trees. For a moment, Cammie had a weird sensation that she wasn't alone. She quickly scanned the dark row of pine trees. What if Mrs. Page had really suspected something and decided to visit Cammie's lucky rink after all? Or perhaps the policemen were preparing to raid the park?

Cammie stopped in the middle of the pond and listened. No, everything was quiet. *But what if the witches show up again?* she suddenly thought. How come she had completely forgotten that the Witch of Fear had tried to attack her only two days ago?

"But it was late at night!" Cammie said out loud. The sound of her voice chased the fears away immediately. How silly! Of course, there was nothing to worry about. The cops had really scared the witches away last time. Now the evil women would probably never even think of coming so close to the end of the park.

After all, Axel Avenue was only half a mile away. If Cammie cried for help, somebody would surely hear her. But of course Cammie wasn't going to attract any attention. Her goal was the triple salchow.

Cammie turned around and skated in the opposite direction. She knew she was going really fast. She did a three turn, ready to spring up. She wouldn't relax her arms so she would remember to pull in the moment she was up in the air. Now! She lifted herself off the ice.

A dark figure loomed in front of her, blocking her path. Someone else was on the ice skating directly toward Cammie; they were going to clash.

"No!" Cammie screamed. She did her best to change direction, but her body was already going around fast. She felt a strong blow on the shoulder; she went down with a loud thud. Then terrible pain shot through Cammie's body; it was worse than anything she had ever experienced. The pain started in her right ankle, and it went farther up her knee and her thigh. Cammie clenched her teeth, trying not to scream, but the pain climbed up her chest and closed around her throat. Cammie felt she was about to suffocate.

"No!" she tried to yell, but the sound stuck in her throat as though a strong hand were squeezing her neck.

"Well done, Winja! You've earned your reward," a cold voice said somewhere nearby.

There was a scraping sound of something hard brushing against the ice, and a squeaky voice whined, "She collided with me. I think I pulled a muscle. It hurts!"

"Ah, tell us something new! You always hurt somewhere, whiner!" a throaty voice guffawed.

"*You* do it next time, Pride!" the squeaky voice said.

The throaty voice chuckled. "I did my share of the job. I gave her the flowers, didn't I? Now the proud brat is at odds with her coach."

"It's easier to buy someone a bouquet than to risk getting injured yourself. Ugh, can anybody help me? I need some ice for this thigh!"

"There's plenty of ice around you, Winja! Why don't you just sit down? Ha ha!" Several voices broke into laughter around Cammie. A moment later, she was enveloped in a thick fog where there was nothing but ice and snow.

"Cammie, Cammie, wake up! Can you hear me?" A strong voice broke through the heavy cloud of drowsiness and pain. It was loud and persistent, and it was causing Cammie's ears to hurt. Oh, no, not Kanga again!

She groaned without opening her eyes. She was too tired. Why wouldn't the evil animal let her sleep in?

A strong hand grabbed Cammie's shoulder, shaking her hard and liberating her from the fog.

"Leave me alone, stupid Kanga!" Cammie grumbled and rolled on the other side. Immediately, sharp pain shot through her right ankle. The pain was so strong that Cammie cried out and opened her eyes.

A tall, bulky figure stood over her, bent almost in half. As the person crouched next to Cammie and looked her in the face, she recognized the bald head and the long mustache.

"Mr. Walrus!"

"Yeah, it's me, kiddo! What're you doing here?"

She grimaced with pain. "Sleeping, I guess."

"Hey, what happened to your leg?" The man's pink face twisted into a grimace of concern.

"My leg?" Cammie glanced at her right ankle and screamed. It was bent at a wrong angle, as though it weren't even part of her body. As Cammie tried to move her foot, she realized she couldn't do it.

"What…what happened?" Cammie gasped.

"Let me see." Mr. Walrus clasped his strong fingers around her ankle. "Does it hurt here?"

"Ouch!" The pain was excruciating, unbearable. Tears rushed out of Cammie's eyes; her cheeks began to sting.

Mr. Walrus straightened up, looking stern. "Now don't get scared, Cammie, but it looks like you broke your ankle."

"No!" Cammie tried to sit up, but every move sent hot darts of pain into her injured leg.

She grimaced. "It can't be broken. I'm sure it's only a bruise. I just need to rest, and I'll be fine tomorrow."

Felling drowsy, Cammie lowered her body onto the ice again. "I'll just sleep a little, okay?"

Her head spun; she felt as though she were flying though space faster and faster.

"There it is; easy now!" She felt Mr. Walrus pulling her leg; it hurt terribly.

"Please, don't!" She moaned and sat up again. The tops of the pine trees swayed over her as though shaking their heads in silent rebuke.

"Sorry, Cammie, I had to take your boot off. With an injury like this, your leg may swell up. If it happened, we might have to cut your boot in half."

Cammie looked at her ankle and groaned. It was almost twice its normal size, and the swelling seemed to be growing. Even under her tights, Cammie could see that the ankle had a nasty purplish color.

"It's really bruised," she said weakly. "But it's good, right? Because it means it's not broken, right?"

"I wish it were so!" For a split second, Mr. Walrus's penetrating eyes lingered on her face. "Anyway, kiddo, let me take you to the emergency room."

Cammie flinched. She hated doctors. "No, please. Just take me to the dorm, okay? My ankle will be fine by tomorrow. I promise. You know what? Actually, I think I can even skate back myself."

She made a feeble attempt at getting up, but Mr. Walrus's hands squeezed her shoulders, bringing her down. "Don't even think of stepping on this foot. Wait."

Cammie watched Mr. Walrus take off his red scarf and pile some snow onto it.

"What's that for?"

"You need something cold on your ankle; it will keep the swelling down. Here!" Mr. Walrus carefully put the snow-covered fabric on top of Cammie's bruise and wrapped the scarf around the ankle. The combination of the pain from the injury and the burning feeling of the snow was unbearable, and Cammie moaned again.

"Sorry, Cammie, but believe me. It'll help. Now grab my neck, will you?"

As Cammie wrapped her arms around Mr. Walrus's neck, he lifted her off the ice and carried her to his Zamboni machine.

"Mr. Walrus, I still think I can skate on my own," Cammie said, fighting a fit of nausea.

"Be quiet!" Mr. Walrus started putting her down then stopped midway, appearing deep in thought. Cammie watched him pull off his red parka. Underneath was a thick white sweater that the man took off too.

"What's that for?"

Without a word, the man spread the sweater on the rusty floor of the Zamboni machine. He gently lowered Cammie on top of the sweater and covered her with his parka. Now Cammie felt much more comfortable, and the familiar smell of Freon from Mr. Walrus's clothes made her feel better instantly.

"No, really, I'm not that cold!" The minute Cammie said it she felt her teeth chattering. She hadn't even realized how hard her body was shaking.

"Here, take this." Mr. Walrus took the lid off his thermos and poured something thick and brown into the lid.

Cammie smiled gratefully. "Hot chocolate!" She took a sip, feeling warmth rush through her body. "Thank you, Mr. Walrus."

The man grinned through his long mustache. "I'm glad you're feeling better."

The Zamboni machine glided along an icy path away from the pond. Cammie lay cuddled under the warm parka, sipping her chocolate. She only hoped her injury wasn't that bad after all. The snow on her ankle had caused the pain to subside a little. Cammie grasped the lid tighter and managed a weak smile.

"Why did you skate in the park? Isn't there enough room at your rink?" Mr. Walrus asked without taking his eyes off the road.

"I had to land my triple salchow," Cammie said curtly.

"And the coach thought you weren't ready," Mr. Walrus said, sounding as though he knew the answer already.

Cammie yelped. How come the man had got it right away?

Mr. Walrus looked as though he didn't even need her answer. "So what happened? I presume you took a nasty fall from the triple, right? It means your coach was right after all."

"Not really!" Cammie sat up but fell right down, as the pain cut through her ankle again. "It was

Winja; she cut me off. And the rest of the witches were there too. The whole gang." Cammie choked, feeling tears rush down her throat.

"Yes, I thought something like that happened. I wish I had come earlier," Mr. Walrus said without looking back. The Zamboni machine rolled out of the Icy Park onto a brightly illuminated street. The lights of the lampposts blurred in front of Cammie.

"Now don't you cry, Cammie. Hopefully the doctor will fix your ankle."

"Sure." Cammie wiped off the tears with her glove. She would be fine. Mr. Walrus was right. She shouldn't have skated in the Icy Park alone.

"Here we are." Mr. Walrus skidded to a stop in front of a big modern-looking building. A big sign written in multicolored letters flashed over the entrance: Skaters' Restoration and Rehabilitation Center. On both sides of the double doors were figures of skaters, mostly pairs doing huge, risky lifts.

Cammie watched Mr. Walrus get out of the Zamboni machine, skate by the entrance to the right side of the building, and approach a smaller door under the bright neon sign Emergency Entrance for Seriously Injured Skaters. The man pressed a button, and the door opened almost immediately. A young man appeared pushing a wheelchair. As he approached Cammie, she saw that the man was blond and slender. He wore dark-green scrubs and a nametag that said, "Tim Meadows, Orderly." When the man lifted her and put her in the wheelchair, Cammie realized that his skinny arms were surprisingly strong.

"I can walk myself!" Cammie protested. Being carried around like a porcelain doll made her feel like an invalid. But she wasn't handicapped; she was a skater, a champion, for crying out loud!

"Just relax and enjoy the ride!" Tim Meadows winked at her. His toothy smile was contagious, and Cammie grinned back at him. "Why do you look familiar anyway?" Tim stopped for a moment and studied Cammie's face. He clapped himself on the forehead. "Hang on! Cammie Wester, huh?"

"How do you know me?" Cammie had surely never met the young orderly.

The man whistled. "From *Skateland Sensations*, of course. So you're the queen of the triples, right?"

Cammie felt herself blush. "Uh, not really. I just fell from my triple salchow."

"Well, that's pretty unusual. Normally skaters get injured *before* major competitions, not after them. It's been a quiet night so far. Okay, first thing we'll do is take an X-ray of your leg."

Getting a picture of her ankle wasn't an uncomfortable procedure in itself. However, when the technician moved Cammie's foot around, she had hard time fighting tears. She sighed with relief when the ordeal was finally over and she was moved back into the wheelchair. The orderly pushed Cammie's wheelchair into a small cubicle and moved her to a couch. Cammie tried hard not to grimace, but she couldn't stifle a quaint, "Ouch."

"Maybe you could give her something for pain?" Mr. Walrus, who had been following closely, asked.

Tim sighed as he adjusted the pillow under Cammie's head. "Not until the doctor examines her. A painkiller may camouflage her symptoms."

Luckily, Cammie didn't have to wait long. In less than five minutes, the door to her cubicle opened and in walked a tall, slightly heavyset man accompanied by a young woman. The man had thick light-brown hair and warm brown eyes.

"Hi, Cammie! Congratulations on your gold medal. I recognized your name the moment I looked at your chart," the man said.

Immediately, Cammie felt better. Wow, so she was famous in Skateland. How cool!

"My name is Dr. Eislaufer, and this is Vicki, our night nurse," the man said cheerfully. There was something warm and trustworthy in the way he smiled, showing his healthy teeth. "So what are you doing in my emergency room, Cammie? I thought skaters were a healthy bunch." Dr. Eislaufer clipped Cammie's X-ray picture to a light screen on the wall and began to study it.

Cammie squinted at the dark and gray shadows on the screen but couldn't understand a thing. Really, what was wrong with her leg?

"How did you get injured?" Dr. Eislaufer asked.

Cammie noticed that the doctor didn't look very cheerful anymore. That made her nervous. "I was trying to land a triple salchow."

"Was your coach with you when you fell?"

Why was that important? An injury was an injury. But both the doctor and the nurse stared at Cammie, apparently waiting for an answer. For the first time, Cammie looked at the nurse closely. The young woman was slightly on the plump side with very pale gray eyes and platinum hair that she wore in braids wrapped around her head.

"Cammie? Did you practice alone?" The doctor didn't look friendly anymore; his eyes were narrowed.

Well, Cammie didn't have a choice. She took a deep breath. "I practiced in the Icy Park. Alone."

The room became very quiet as both Dr. Eislaufer and Nurse Vicki stared intensely at her.

"Do you know that the ponds in the park are not supposed to be used for practices?" the doctor asked calmly.

"Yes, I know that." What were they going to do? Send her away? Refuse to treat her ankle? She blinked, trying to stanch tears.

Dr. Eislaufer gave Cammie's chart to the nurse.

"I'm afraid I have bad news, Cammie. You have a broken fibula. It's an ankle bone. See, here and … here." He pointed to two dark spots against the white outlines in the picture.

Even though Cammie was prepared to hear something like that, she felt lightheaded. "But … but

I'm a competitive skater. I'm going to the nationals in two months. I can't miss any practices."

The doctor nodded sympathetically. "I understand. However, Cammie, you have a nasty injury here. I'm afraid I'll have to perform surgery to fix the problem."

Surgery? Cammie must have misunderstood the doctor. *What was he talking about anyway? Surgeries are for older people.* Cammie wasn't old; she was still a kid. Oh, no. *No!*

"The surgery is called open reduction internal fixation. I'll put a metal plate with two screws here and...here." Dr. Eislaufer drew circles on the X-ray picture with his index finger. "They will keep your bones together, which will help them to heal nicely."

"No, no!" Cammie said feebly. "I don't want surgery. Please!"

The doctor tapped her on the shoulder. "Now don't you worry, champion! We'll put you to sleep, and you won't feel a thing. You'll be back on the ice in about eight weeks."

In a sharp voice, the doctor gave some instructions to Nurse Vicki and then gave Cammie an encouraging smile and walked out of the cubicle.

"Here, drink this. It'll relax you." Nurse Vicki handed Cammie a plastic cup filled with clear solution.

With a trembling hand, Cammie accepted the drink and emptied the cup in two quick swigs. Only then did she realize how thirsty she was. The liquid had a pleasant lemon taste.

"Now lie down and try to rest, okay? There's nothing to worry about."

The nurse walked away from Cammie, and for a while Cammie lay alone on her back, desperately trying not to cry. How she wished she hadn't gone to the Icy Park alone! She should have invited Alex to come with her. He could have given her tips on the triple salchow too.

If Alex had been with Cammie, the witches wouldn't have attacked her. Really, how many times had Cammie and Alex faced the evil women together! Nothing bad had ever happened to them. Cammie and Alex were strong as a team. Cammie glanced at her ankle wrapped in an ice pack. Really, how long would it take for her leg to heal? The doctor had said *eight weeks*. Maybe he was wrong. Maybe Cammie would be fine in a week? Her ankle didn't hurt that much anymore. Maybe she would still be strong enough to go to the nationals?

Cammie didn't hear the nurse return. She opened her eyes only when she felt something cold against her skin. Nurse Vicki was attaching rubber patches to Cammie's chest.

"These will be connected to the machine that will monitor your heart rate," the nurse explained.

She also put a clip on Cammie's finger. "This will let us check your pulse during surgery. And now, Cammie, I'm going to adjust an IV. Don't get scared. It will hurt for only a moment."

From the corner of her eyes, Cammie saw Vicki put an IV stand next to her couch. A plastic bag filled with clear solution sat on top of the stand. Attached to the bag was a long tube topped with a needle.

The nurse fastened a tourniquet around Cammie's wrist. "I want you to clasp and unclasp your fingers several times."

As Cammie did the exercise, she felt her fingers getting slightly numb.

"Okay, now make a fist. Don't worry; it'll only hurt a second." The nurse rubbed Cammie's wrist with alcohol and quickly inserted the needle.

"Ouch!" Cammie grimaced.

"That's it. Now enjoy your sleep, and when you wake up, you'll be all set."

Cammie wanted to ask more questions, but to her surprise, she didn't care much about what was going to happen to her. Not anymore. For the first time since her nasty fall, she felt warm and relaxed. Her fears were gone. Her eyelids were like lead; she closed her eyes. She felt the couch move under her. It felt great, like riding in an ice mobile.

I wish I had my own ice mobile, Cammie thought.

The ice mobile shot forward, picking up speed, and Cammie felt herself glide into a soft, peaceful darkness.

THE NIGHT VISIT

When Cammie woke up, it was a bright, sunny day.

Oh, no! I missed my practice again. Cammie moaned. Where was Sonia? Why hadn't she woken Cammie up?

"She's awake!" a familiar voice spoke next to her. "Oh, thank God. Howard, she's fine."

Cammie's mother's face appeared in Cammie's field of vision, and a moment later she saw her father staring at her without a smile.

Cammie rubbed her forehead. "What are you guys doing here?"

Her mother frowned slightly. "Visiting you, of course. Don't you remember anything?"

What was she supposed to remember? Cammie turned her head, squinting at the unfamiliar surroundings. Instead of her dorm room, whose bright white walls were decorated with posters of famous skaters, she was in a smaller room with a tile floor and walls painted light blue. Cammie moved her left hand and squinted at the sudden feeling of pressure in her wrist. She tilted her head and saw a plastic tube with a needle stuck right into her vein. Her eyes slid up to an IV stand.

"What's wrong with me? Where am I?" Cammie whispered.

"You're in the hospital, honey. You had a skating accident," her father said softly. "You broke your ankle, so the doctor performed surgery to put the bones in place. But don't you worry. You'll be all right."

Cammie's father stroked her hair. Cammie gasped as the horrible memories of her unfortunate practice came back. Of course! She had been working on her triple salchow; then she felt a hard blow on her chest; she fell … She saw Winja's jubilant face.

"It was Winja!" Cammie blurted out. "It was all her fault. She cut me off."

"What did you say?" her mother bent over her.

Cammie only shook her head. Her parents didn't believe in witches, so it would be pointless to tell them about the attack. She let her eyes travel to her right ankle wrapped in a pink cast.

"The doctor thought you'd like that color," her mother said. "See, the bedding is pink too. Isn't it great?"

Cammie glanced at her pink sheets with small figures of a pink-cheeked doctor wearing glasses. The doctor had skates on, and he was doing a one-foot glide on pale-gray ice. Very appropriate for Skateland hospital!

"When did I get injured?"

"Yesterday," her father said.

Cammie inhaled deeply as she tried to keep her hands steady. She was shaking all over. "When…when will I be able to skate again?"

Her mom and dad exchanged quick glances. Dad crackled his knuckles. Cammie knew he always did it when he was nervous.

"What are you trying to hide from me?" Cammie asked, shifting her eyes from one to the other.

Before her parents could say another word, the door opened, and in walked the doctor Cammie remembered from the previous night. Nurse Vicki was following him closely.

"Okay, it looks like you're awake," the doctor exclaimed cheerfully.

Cammie thought the doctor's joyful attitude was completely out of place. There she was stuck in the hospital with her leg in a cast, and the man was grinning like a clown.

"Do you remember who I am?" The doctor was still smiling.

What does he think I am, an idiot? Cammie thought. Yet she forced herself to smile back. "You're Dr. Eislaufer."

The man clapped his hands. "Great! Well, now I'm sure you're on your way to recovery. Are you in any pain?"

Cammie shook her head. Her ankle didn't hurt anymore, and, but for a slight drowsiness, she felt fine.

"Do you have any questions or concerns?" Dr. Eislaufer pulled up a chair and sat down, his thick thighs against Cammie's bed.

"Will my ankle heal by the nationals?" Cammie asked.

Nurse Vicki's thin lips twitched. Cammie thought she didn't like the young woman too much.

"I'm afraid you'll have to miss the nationals this year," Dr. Eislaufer said. He patted Cammie on her needle-free wrist.

"What?" Cammie whispered. Tears sprung out of her eyes. *What is he talking about? Miss the nationals? But it's impossible.* For the first time in her life, Cammie had qualified for this big competition, and now the doctor was telling her she couldn't go. The man had to be crazy.

"Maybe I could still try. Even if I have to skate in a cast." Cammie looked at the doctor, hoping he would think of something. After all, nowadays doctors could do almost anything. Cammie had heard of many people getting injured and winning major competitions anyway.

"It's not that simple, Cammie." Dr. Eislaufer was speaking kindly, apparently trying to soften the blow. Yet his words stung like dozens of needles pricking

Cammie's skin. She felt herself cringe under their cruel power.

"You'll have to be in cast for the next eight weeks and then—"

Cammie didn't let the doctor finish. "Dr. Eislaufer, you don't understand. I'm a competitive skater. I can't wait that long. I have to stay in shape."

"Don't you worry, Cammie." The doctor's grin was warm, but it only made the whole nightmare worse.

"Eight weeks will pass before you know it. And once the cast is off, you'll do physical therapy. Believe me; you won't be bored."

Cammie felt the room spin around her. *Oh, if only it were a dream,* she thought. *Really, maybe the whole accident is nothing but a nightmare, and then I'll wake up and everything will be back to normal. I'll go to practice, and everybody will congratulate me on my gold medal. And then I'll start working on my triples...*

Cammie closed her eyes tight, as though expecting the nightmare to disappear. She unglued her eyelids. Nothing had changed; her parents still lingered behind the doctor and the nurse, their faces blank. Nurse Vicki smirked nastily, and Dr. Eislaufer eyed her with obvious concern. His pity only made the whole thing worse.

"No!" Cammie turned to the side, ignoring the pulling sensation in her wrist.

"Hey, you'd better be careful with that IV!" Nurse Vicki squeaked.

Cammie felt her arm repositioned.

"Cammie, honey…" her mother's voice came.

Ignoring the sounds around her, Cammie buried her face in the pillow and sobbed. Nothing mattered if she wouldn't be able to skate at the nationals. Nothing. A strong arm raised her head. She sniffled as she looked into Dr. Eislaufer's kind face.

"Here, drink this. You'll feel better. I promise." He handed her a plastic cup.

Automatically, Cammie reached for the cup, but her hand shook too much. Dr. Eislaufer wrapped his fingers around her trembling wrist, supporting it. Cammie took a deep breath and downed the drink. It tasted nice, like a strawberry skate shake. But there had to be something else in the drink, for before Cammie knew it, her eyes started closing by themselves. And then she was sucked into the thicket of the Icy Park until darkness closed around her.

Cammie woke up feeling she couldn't sleep anymore. She glanced at her nightstand, hoping to find out what time it was. For some reason, her alarm clock shaped like a snowman wasn't there. Instead, she saw an empty glass and a lonely orange. Oh, no, she was in the hospital with a broken ankle!

Cammie looked up at the IV stand next to her bed. It was disconnected. Okay, at least something was good. She needed to use the bathroom, and she wasn't sure she would be able to move with a needle in her vein. Cammie shifted her weight to the front and sat up. She felt a little dizzy; she closed her eyes for a few moments. When she opened them again, she saw the pink cast around her right ankle. Gosh, how was she going to walk with that thing on? Well, she didn't have a choice. Gritting her teeth, Cammie pushed against the wall with her right hand then moved to the edge of the bed. She put her left foot down.

The door opened with a loud crack, and the bright light from the hall made Cammie blink. Instinctively, she shielded her eyes. Nurse Vicki walked in, looking crisp and polished as though it wasn't the middle of the night.

"I came to check on you," the nurse said briskly then raised her voice. "Where do you think you're going? Don't you know you aren't supposed to get up?"

"I need to use the bathroom."

"You can't put weight on this leg at least for a month. Didn't you hear what the doctor said?" The nurse pushed Cammie back on her pillow.

Again, Cammie thought she didn't like the young woman. "How am I supposed to go to the bathroom, then?"

"If you need something, you push the button on your nightstand. See?" Nurse Vicki pointed to a big pink button.

Cammie sighed. So she couldn't even go to the bathroom on her own. Great!

"Okay, let's go." Cammie sat up.

Nurse Vicki bent down and picked up something from under Cammie's bed. "Turn around."

"What?"

"Just do as I say. Aren't you used to following your coach's instructions?"

Another stupid question. They weren't at the rink, for crying out loud. Gritting her teeth, Cammie turned on her right side, careful not to disturb her injured leg. Something cold and metal slid under her.

"Ouch! What's that?"

"A bedpan."

"What?" Cammie screamed, probably louder than she had to. She had heard of handicapped people using bedpans. But she was an athlete, a champion.

"Stop acting like a brat!" the nurse said coldly.

"I'm not an invalid!"

The woman simpered. "Oh yes you are."

Feeling crushed and humiliated, Cammie realized she didn't have a choice. After she was done, the nurse pulled the pan from under her and handed Cammie a small blue pill.

"Take this."

Cammie put the pill in her mouth and took a swig of water from the glass. She lowered herself on the pillow again.

"And try not to bother me till morning. I need rest too, you know." The door slammed.

Biting her lip in fury, Cammie stared at the dark ceiling over her and then at the window. It was dark, except for a faint glow of the street lamp. Cammie felt miserable. She thought she wouldn't be able to fall asleep again. But in about five minutes, her thoughts slipped away from her, and she felt tired, very tired.

Clank! The sound of broken glass woke Cammie up. She tried to open her eyes, but they felt heavy.

"You stupid Winja! Can't you even cross the room without breaking something?" someone hissed next to Cammie's bed.

"It's my crutch, stupid Pride!" a very familiar voice screeched on Cammie's right.

Immediately, Cammie felt her body stiffen up. Winja! The evil Witch of Injuries, the one who had cut Cammie off in the Icy Park, causing her to fall, was now in her room. What was she doing in the hospital anyway? Cammie opened her eyes halfway. Four dark silhouettes towered over her.

"Now be quiet all of you! You'll wake up the brat."

Now this is the Witch of Fear, Cammie thought. She squeezed her eyelids tight, fearing she might see the red glow in the witch's colorless eyes. She knew she wouldn't be able to handle that look. Had the witches come to finish her off? If that was the case, they would be able to do it easily. Cammie was alone in the room, and she wasn't allowed to walk. She couldn't run away. But there had to be something she could do. Bingo! The pink button on her nightstand. All she needed to do was press it, and then Nurse Vicki would come to her rescue. Okay, the nurse would probably be upset that Cammie had woken her up, but it was an emergency. Cammie was in grave danger.

Cammie flexed the fingers on her left hand. Okay, now!

"The brat isn't going to wake up. I gave her Soporifex. It's a strong sleeping pill," a calm voice said.

Cammie froze under her blanket. What? The voice belonged to Nurse Vicki, to the woman who was supposed to take care of patients. How come she was with the witches?

"So what are you guys going to do with her anyway? Kill her? Not that I mind, but you've got to make it look like an accident. I don't want to lose my job."

Oh, no! Cammie thought her heart had stopped for a moment as she struggled for breath. She opened her mouth to scream, but no sound came out.

The Witch of Fear laughed next to Cammie. "Kill her? Come on. That isn't our intention at all. We don't care about her soul; it's her skating career we want to destroy."

Cammie exhaled slowly. Okay, at least she wasn't going to die.

"What are the chances that the sucker will skate again?" the Witch of Pride asked.

Vicki cackled. "Very slim, if you want my opinion. Well, she'll probably be able to do Mohawks and three turns, but that's about it."

"Perfect! That was my intention three years ago when I first met her!" the Witch of Pride exclaimed.

"You know what? I'll even bring her to my rink to see her struggle with pre-preliminary moves."

Someone kicked the edge of Cammie's bed. The blow woke up the pain in Cammie's ankle, and she barely suppressed an *ouch*.

"Stay away from her, Fear! She may wake up," Vicki hissed.

"*Witch* of Fear to you, missy. Don't you forget you aren't a witch yet! And I may still decide not to sign your recommendation at the end of your training."

"I'm sorry, Witch of Fear," Nurse Vicki mumbled. "I was just worried—"

"No one cares about your worries. Besides, you gave her a pill, so what's all the fuss about? Anyway, I would like to add the curse of fear to the curse of injury. Because—"

"She also has the curse of pride. Don't you forget that!" the Witch of Pride's angry voice said.

"But when did you manage to curse her, Pr...I beg your pardon, Witch of Pride? I thought Cammie only had Winja's curse." Vicki's voice sounded sycophant.

The Witch of Pride snorted. "Don't underestimate me, kiddo. She took my pride-infested roses; a thorn pricked her finger, and voilà!'

"Brilliant!" Vicki squealed.

"You bet. Don't miss any more of my seminars, and you'll actually learn something," the voice of the Witch of Pride sang.

"Quiet, everybody! I'm about to inflict the curse of fear on her, so don't break my concentration!" the Witch of Fear hissed.

It was now or never. Cammie drew as much air in her lungs as she could.

"*A-a-ah!*" The scream that came out of Cammie's mouth was so loud that she was sure everybody in the hospital building was now awake. Yet she still kept her eyes closed, too scared to look.

"Ah!" the Witch of Fear breathed out.

"Gosh, she's awake." The Witch of Fear spat and cussed loudly.

A door slammed somewhere in the hallway.

"Everybody, out!" Vicki sounded frightened.

"Don't push me. I can't walk fast on my crutches," Winja said angrily.

Someone pushed Cammie's bed again. Sharp pain shot through her ankle, and this time, she yelled openly, "Help me! There are witches in my room!"

"For crying out loud, out!" Vicki's panicky voice shouted.

The door cracked, and as Cammie opened her eyes, she saw three hooded figures slip out of her room.

A phone rang somewhere in the hallway; then a woman's voice called, "Mrs. Somner needs a pain-killer. Nurse?"

"Help!" Cammie shouted again.

Vicki jumped on top of her and pressed her cold hand against Cammie's mouth. "One more word, and I'll break your other leg. Even if it costs me my job."

"Nurse Vicki!" the woman's voice called again, and Cammie could tell that the lady was coming closer to her room.

The door opened again, revealing a bulky silhouette wearing a hospital gown. "I'm sorry, but Mrs. Somner is in a lot of pain."

Vicki moved her hand away from Cammie, but there was an unmistakable warning in the nurse's pale eyes. "Of course, Mrs. Drew. I'll just give Cammie her sleeping pill and be right with you. It's her first night after the surgery, you know."

If Cammie hadn't seen Vicki with the witches, she might have thought that the nurse was really a warm and caring person. The smile on the young woman's lips appeared perfectly sincere, and as she handed Cammie another blue pill, she looked as though she was really concerned about her patient's well-being.

"Oh no, Cammie, you broke your glass!" Vicki chanted, shaking her head. "Mrs. Drew, do you mind getting me one of those plastic cups from the water cooler? Yes, and fill it with cold water, please."

"Oh, it's not a problem at all." The door closed behind the woman.

Immediately the smile slid off Vicki's thin lips. "I repeat: not a word to Dr. Eislaufer or—"

A sliver of light from the hallway fell on the floor as Mrs. Drew reappeared carrying a plastic cup.

"Open your mouth!" Vicki held another blue pill next to Cammie's face.

Cammie shook her head stubbornly. "I don't need it."

Vicki's eyes looked like slits. "Are we going to have a problem here?"

"Sweetie, you need to follow Dr. Eislaufer's orders," Mrs. Drew crooned. "He has your best interests at heart."

"Yes, but *she*'s a witch; she tried to break my other leg!" Cammie snapped.

Vicki rolled her eyes. "That's postoperative delirium, Mrs. Drew. Cammie broke her ankle during practice, you know."

"The witches attacked me!" Cammie shouted.

Mrs. Drew's lips rounded. Cammie could tell the woman didn't believe a word she had said. "Poor thing! But she'll be all right, won't she?"

"Of course, she will!" Before Cammie could protest some more, Vicki forced her mouth open and pushed the pill between her teeth.

Cammie gagged.

"Drink this!" Vicki put the plastic cup next to Cammie's lips. Automatically Cammie took a swig. "That's better." Looking satisfied, Vicki stepped away from Cammie's bed. "Okay, Mrs. Drew, I'll tend to Mrs. Somner now."

"Good night, Cammie," Mrs. Drew said sweetly.

Cammie turned away from the woman. If the lady was going to side with Vicki, Cammie wouldn't talk to her. She tried to think of the witches' unexpected visit, but she couldn't keep her eyes open.

THE WITCH OF PRIDE'S GLOVE

"The witches were here. I swear!" Cammie said angrily. "There were three of them: the Witch of Pride, the Witch of Fear, and the Witch of Injuries. They wanted to curse me and—"

"Cammie, it was just a dream." Dr. Olsen put his big, warm hand on Cammie's shaking wrist.

Dr. Olsen was a specialist in internal diseases who had come to give Cammie a physical examination. So far she had been declared healthy, except, of course, for her injury. But the doctor's kind-hearted attitude had changed since Cammie started talking about her last night's experience. Now the man appeared positively worried.

"It wasn't a dream. Winja, the Witch of Injuries, came in first, and she broke my glass. See, it's no longer here. I have a plastic cup instead."

"But…" Nurse Mary, who worked in the ward during the day, looked at Cammie with surprise. "You broke the glass yourself; that's what Nurse Vicki wrote in her report. You got agitated and knocked the glass down on the floor."

"Which isn't uncommon with patients recuperating from surgeries," Dr. Olsen said quickly.

"I didn't knock down that glass!" Cammie exclaimed. "Why don't you believe me?" She saw the doctor and the nurse exchange quick glances.

"Cammie, we aren't accusing you of lying," Dr. Olsen said seriously. "What we are saying, though, is that you're a very emotional person, obviously a talented skater, so—"

"Can you please get to the point?" Cammie snapped, surprised at her own behavior. She didn't mean to be rude. But the doctor's attitude was getting to her.

She had already spent half of the day desperately trying to convince people that the witches had really sneaked into her room in the middle of the night. And if they had done it once, they could surely enter the hospital again. Allowing the witches to wander freely around the ward was hardly acceptable policy. They could hurt patients; they could destroy people's skating careers. Hurting talented skaters was the witches' only aspiration in life.

Cammie had already talked to the laboratory technician who had showed up at six in the morning to draw blood. She had explained to the cleaning lady who had come to sweep away the pieces of the broken glass that it wasn't her fault. Cammie had also shared the whole story with the lady who had brought her breakfast at eight in the morning. None of those people had taken her seriously.

Finally, Cammie's mother came to visit at ten in the morning. At that point, Cammie thought she had made herself perfectly clear. Her injury wasn't due to a nasty fall; it was an attack. And last night, the witches had paid Cammie a visit to finish her off. Could Cammie's mother please talk to the hospital security personnel?

Cammie's mother's reaction had been completely unpredictable. Instead of looking for a security guard, she had merely sniffled, dabbed her eyes with a tissue, and said that she would talk to Cammie's doctor. Unfortunately, Dr. Eislaufer was busy performing surgery. Cammie's mother had decided to wait for him in the waiting room, so now Cammie was stuck with Dr. Olsen, who apparently didn't believe a word of what she was saying.

"And you would probably be interested to know who let the witches in," Cammie said angrily. "It was Nurse Vicki. Yes, and she is also taking some kind of class with the Witch of Pride."

Cammie saw Nurse Mary put a hand over her mouth and quickly turn around. Cammie could swear she heard the woman stifle a giggle.

"It's no laughing matter!" Cammie said, raising her voice.

"Nurse!" Dr. Olsen said sharply.

"Sorry!" Nurse Mary's blue eyes looked perfectly innocent, but Cammie knew the young woman was trying hard not to laugh.

"Cammie." Dr. Olsen patted Cammie's hand again. She withdrew her hand angrily. "Cammie, let me explain to you what happened. Getting injured was a big shock to you, and I don't blame you. You were scared and upset. Besides, Dr. Eislaufer gave you general anesthesia for your surgery. Perhaps you don't know that sedatives may provoke *hallucinations*. Are you familiar with this word? A hallucination is the image of an object that doesn't exist in real life, so—"

"I know what a hallucination is, thank you very much!" Cammie interrupted him. "But you're wrong. I wasn't imagining things. The witches were right here in my room!"

Dr. Olsen leaned back in his chair and let out an exaggerated sigh. "Cammie, in this case, I think it would be better for you to talk to a psychiatrist."

Cammie clenched her teeth. "I'm not crazy."

"Oh of course, that's not the word I was about to use. You're just a little … hmm … disturbed."

"I'm *not* disturbed!"

The doctor stood up. "I think you need rest now. I'll talk to you later." The door closed behind the doctor and the nurse.

"Ugh!" Cammie grabbed the plastic cup, ready to toss it at the closed door, then put it back on the nightstand. That wasn't going to help. But she had to do something. What if the witches showed up in her room again? Last night, she had managed to scream, and that had scared the evil women away. But now that everybody in the ward thought Cammie was crazy, there was little hope that anybody would come to her rescue even if she made a lot of noise. She had to think of something else.

Feeling tired, Cammie spent the rest of the morning sleeping. When lunch was served—a grilled chicken sandwich with garden salad—Cammie only picked at her food and closed her eyes again. She hadn't got a lot of rest last night, and the effects of her sleeping pills probably hadn't worn off yet. Her parents came to visit, but Cammie barely talked to them.

She was really upset that her mom and dad still didn't believe that the witches had attacked her. *I wish Alex were here*, she thought, swallowing angry tears. She found herself wondering why none of her friends had bothered to come. She even asked her mother to call Sonia and invite her to come. Her mother said that so far only family members were allowed to see Cammie.

"Dr. Olsen thinks you are too weak and shaken by your injury, honey," Mom said.

Not as much by the injury as by the witches, Cammie thought but decided not to say anything. Why bother?

After her parents left, Cammie folded her hands on her chest and closed her eyes again. She had to think of a way to deal with the witches. Now she had no doubt that they would return. Nurse Vicki would definitely tell everybody in the hospital that Cammie had the reputation of a loony. It meant that nobody would come to Cammie's rescue even if she screamed at the top of her lungs.

The door cracked; then there was a shuffling sound. Someone was in Cammie's room. She wondered if the witches had already come. She stiffened up then opened her left eye slightly.

There was a faint outline of a figure leaning on crutches. *Winja!* Cammie thought. Well, all she could do was yell. Cammie drew in as much air as she could and shouted, "Help!"

There was a loud yelp. "Cammie, stop! I'm not going to hurt you."

The voice definitely wasn't Winja's; it sounded too young. Cammie opened both eyes and found herself staring into the frightened face of a girl who looked only a little older than Cammie. The girl wore pink hospital pajamas with the familiar images of a bespectacled doctor doing one-foot glides. She leaned on crutches, keeping her left bandaged leg slightly bent.

"Oops, sorry." Cammie tried to smile, but her lips shook. "I thought you were definitely a witch."

The door opened again and in peeked a slightly ruffled Nurse Mary. "Is everything all right here?

Did I hear you shout, Cammie? What are you doing here, Heather?"

Heather tossed her light-brown braid to her back. "Nurse Mary, we were just talking."

The nurse shook her head. "Heather, Cammie has been under a lot of stress, and she needs rest."

"It's okay. I'm not tired," Cammie said quickly.

Heather smiled at the nurse. "I was just telling Cammie not to worry too much about her leg. It will heal, just like mine did."

The girl put her injured foot down and bounced on it for a couple of seconds. "I can finally put weight on it. And it doesn't hurt anymore. See?"

Nurse Mary's hard face softened. "Well, I guess you girls can chat a little. But don't make it too long."

"Five minutes!" Heather said cheerfully and pulled a chair closer to Cammie's bed.

Nurse Mary nodded and walked out.

Heather plopped on the chair, carefully positioning her crutches on the floor and brought her face closer to Cammie's. "Cammie, I want to tell you something: you aren't crazy. The witches were really here last night. I saw them too. Hmm, I'm Heather by the way."

Cammie felt her mouth get dry. She swallowed hard. "Did you really see the witches?"

"Sure. I was in the hallway and—"

"Wait. What were you doing in the hallway in the middle of the night?" Cammie was puzzled.

Heather's pale cheeks turned slightly pink. "Well, walking, of course. Dr. Eislaufer told me to get as much exercise as I could. You see, after my injury, I needed to learn how to walk again. But there are so many people in the hallway during the day. I feel so stupid not even being able to walk properly. Evil Winja!"

Cammie felt her mouth open. "Did Winja attack you too?"

"Of course. Who else?" Heather stared at her bandaged leg morosely. "You see, I only started skating a year ago. I was thirteen then. It's kind of late, of course."

Cammie nodded sympathetically. She knew what Heather meant. Most skaters began to skate seriously when they were four or five years old. And Sonia had started taking skating lessons at the age of two.

"My mom didn't want me to skate," Heather said. "Can you believe it? She was a competitive skater when she was younger, but she never made it to nationals. So she wanted me to do something else. She never allowed me to go to the rink, even though she's a coach. Can you imagine? But then my friend invited me to the rink a year ago, and I did so well. Coach Darrell was there, and he said I was a natural skater. He suggested I take some lessons, and he even talked my mom into it. Then we all moved to Skateland, and I got all of my single jumps within a year. It's pretty good, isn't it?"

"Sure," Cammie said, but Heather didn't wait for her answer.

"I started working on my axel two months ago. And I was this close." Heather brought her thumb and her index finger close together. "I practiced and practiced, and one day, as I was leaving the locker room, I tripped over a crutch. There was that stupid crutch sitting right next to the entrance to the rink."

Cammie rose on her elbows. "Was it Winja's crutch?"

Heather smiled wryly. "Who else's? So I fell, and I tore a couple of ligaments in my knee and in my ankle."

"Oh, I'm so sorry!" Cammie said. "Winja attacked me too, only I was in the Icy Park."

"I know," Heather said. "Nurse Mary has been telling everybody about a crazy girl who practiced in the park and got scared by a bush or something."

Cammie's face turned hot. "It wasn't a bush; it was Winja! Why doesn't anyone believe me?"

"I believe you. Last night, when I left my room, I saw three weird-looking women. I got so scared, you know." Heather's eyes got big. "I never saw the other two before, but one of the women was Winja."

"The other two were the Witch of Fear and the Witch of Pride," Cammie quickly added.

"Well, I was sure they were witches. Yes, and Nurse Vicki was with them too, and she led them into your room."

"Nurse Vicki is taking some witch course," Cammie said grimly.

Heather gasped. "That's how they all got in!"

"So what happened next?"

"Well, they were in your room for a while, and then you screamed, and the four of them ran out.

And the witches ran to the emergency exit at the end of the hallway, and they were out in a jiffy."

"And they're coming back tonight to finish me off," Cammie said. "Last night they tried to add more curses."

"Ah!" Heather stuffed her fist in her mouth, looking horrified.

"The Witch of Fear said she'd scare me so I'd never skate again," Cammie hastened to add.

"That's about as bad as getting killed," Heather said nervously. "Gosh, we've got to talk to hospital security."

Cammie shook her head. "No one will take me seriously."

"Then I'll talk to them!"

"Then they'll think you're crazy too." Cammie felt a sense of hopelessness close around her. Really, how many times had Alex and she tried to convince the residents of Skateland that skating witches were real! The closer a skater came to achieving her goals, the bigger were her chances of getting injured or scared away from the ice. And how many successful careers had been destroyed because skaters had been lifted up with pride, thinking that they were so superior to other athletes that rules didn't apply to them.

Hang on, isn't that what happened to you? a small voice said inside Cammie's head. That wasn't a pleasant thought.

To take her mind off it, Cammie told Heather how Alex and she had battled the witches several times.

Heather listened with her hands clasped together, her mouth wide open. When Cammie finished telling her about bringing Sonia back from the past, where the witches had left her scared and confused, Heather jumped off her chair. She landed right on her injured leg but only grimaced slightly. "And no one believes you? Even after that?"

Cammie spread her arms. "You can see for yourself."

They were silent for a few moments thinking of the night ahead. If the witches did show up, it would be impossible for Cammie to face them alone. The witches were strong and athletic women, and Cammie was confined to her bed, unable even to walk.

"I wish Alex were here," Cammie said glumly. "But they won't even let my friends visit me."

Heather's face brightened. "Hey, how about me? I can help you."

"How?" Cammie looked at the girl's wrapped leg. "You can barely walk yourself."

Heather put her finger to her mouth. "I have an idea. I'll come to your room at night, and we'll wait for the witches together."

"And then?" Cammie still wasn't sure. Heather was definitely not a match for the witches.

"We'll take them by surprise. I'll use my crutch on them. That will scare them away."

"How about me? You can't defeat them on your own, Heather."

Heather clapped her hands. "I'll get you a cane. There's a storage room right across from mine, and I saw plenty of canes there. All you need to do is pretend that you're asleep, and when the witches come close, you hit them. And I'll attack them from behind."

"Brilliant!" For the first moment since she had gotten injured, Cammie felt excited. So she wasn't completely helpless. And it would be great to have somebody else in the room next to her when the witches arrived. Cammie smiled at Heather and saw the girl wink at her.

"So you'll be here close to midnight, right?" Cammie asked.

Heather picked up her crutches and headed for the door. "It's a deal."

Nurse Vicki came to her night duty at nine o'clock and immediately handed Cammie a blue pill with a glass of water.

"Your medicine," the nurse said curtly.

"Thank you," Cammie said meekly. She put the pill in her mouth and brought the glass to her lips, pretending to swallow the pill.

"Open your mouth!" Nurse Vicki ordered.

No problem. Cammie had hidden the pill under her tongue, so she wasn't afraid to show her mouth to Vicki.

"Good." The nurse turned off the light. "Have a good night."

"Good night." Cammie closed her eyes.

Nurse Vicki left the room. Cammie quickly took the pill out of her mouth and threw it under the bed. When the witches arrived, she would be alert.

Nurse Vicki came to check on Cammie three times, but whenever the young woman entered the room, Cammie lay in bed with her eyes shut, pretending to be in deep sleep. Fortunately, she had slept almost the whole day, so now she felt perfectly rested. Of course, Vicki's pill would have knocked her out, making her an easy target for the witches. But Cammie knew better than to swallow Soporifex.

Still she must have drifted away, for when she opened her eyes to check the time, it was eleven thirty. The moon shined in Cammie's window, leaving two silvery rectangular shapes on the dark floor. Except for the slight buzz of the radiator, everything was quiet.

Ten till twelve. Heather had better come soon. Cammie was sure the witches would show up at midnight.

The door creaked. Cammie felt her body tighten under the blanket. A dark outline of a skinny figure on three crutches slipped inside.

"It's me, Heather, not Winja," a quiet voice said.

"Oh, great." Cammie sat up. "Are you using three crutches now?"

"No, silly. The third crutch is a cane, and it's for you." Heather put the carved black cane on Cammie's bed. "Hey, you'd better cover it with your blanket. You don't want the witches to see it."

Cammie did as Heather had told her. "So where are you going to be?"

"In the corner." Heather stepped away from Cammie's bed to the darkest spot right next to the door.

"The witches will approach your bed, and then I'll attack them from behind," Heather said excitedly.

Cammie grinned. "I like that. But—"

The door opened. Before Cammie squeezed her eyes shut, she caught a glimpse of Heather leaning against the wall as though trying to blend into it. She heard steps.

"Are you asleep, Cammie?" Nurse Vicki's quiet voice asked.

Cammie didn't say anything. Her heart pounded. She only hoped the nurse wouldn't reach for her hand to check the pulse. If she did, she would know right away Cammie wasn't really asleep.

The sound of steps moved in the direction of the door. Before Cammie could sigh with relief, Vicki spoke up again. "Okay, you may come in. Quiet, though."

More steps followed, and this time Cammie was sure the witches had joined the nurse.

"Vicki, you'd better stay in the hallway as a look-out," Winja's voice bleated.

"No, it'll look suspicious," Vicki snapped. "Have you ever seen a nurse standing in the middle of the hallway at night?"

"Just stay with us." That was the Witch of Fear's voice.

Cammie inhaled quietly, trying not to move.

"Now as I count to three, Winja and I will hold the girl, and you Fear cast the spell." That was undoubtedly the Witch of Pride.

Cammie's hand reached for the cane; she closed her fingers around it.

"Okay, one, two—"

Before the Witch of Pride could say three, Cammie sat up abruptly and swung the cane, hitting Winja on the side.

"Argh!"

"What the—"

"Ah, you little…" Vicki was by Cammie's bed. She grabbed the cane, trying to snatch it away from Cammie. Cammie fought hard, but the nurse was stronger. Vicki raised the cane, aiming it at Cammie…

"Freeze! Don't move!" a voice said from the corner of the room.

Vicki dropped the cane. It missed Cammie's left hand by inches and fell to the floor with a loud thud. Heather ran toward Vicki from the shadows and hit her on the back with a crutch. The nurse slumped over in pain. In another moment, however, Vicki whirled around and reached for Heather, missing the girl's arm by inches. Heather swung the crutch again and stubbed Vicki in her stomach.

The nurse doubled over. "Heather? What are you doing here? Ah ah!"

Taking advantage of the nurse's shock, Cammie bent over the side of her bed and retrieved the cane.

Vicki spread her fingers like an angry cat and advanced on Heather. "You little—"

Cammie raised the cane and smacked Winja two more times.

"Help! Murder!" Winja screeched.

"Are you out of your mind?" the Witch of Pride roared. "You'll wake up the whole hospital. Fear, do your job now!"

"I can't concentrate with all this racket," the Witch of Fear said angrily.

The Witch of Pride came closer and grabbed Cammie's cane. Cammie wouldn't let go. "You're dead, girl." The witch pulled harder. "Man, it's hot here."

The Witch of Pride took off her gloves. "I don't think I need to worry about fingerprints too much. Vicki, why do you need two radiators in a small room like this?"

"Help! Somebody help us!" Heather yelled.

"Shut up!" Vicki yelled.

From where Cammie was, she could see Heather wrestling with the nurse. The rest of the witches still encircled Cammie's bed, apparently trying to decide what to do.

"Help us!" Cammie shouted. She couldn't believe the horrible noise they were making could be mistaken for a little girl's nightmare.

Heather, who had somehow managed to set herself free from Vicki's grasp, ran to the door. "Security! We've been attacked. Help us!"

"Be quiet, you idiot!" Vicki rushed after Heather, but the girl was already in the hallway.

"Security!" the girl's voice sounded from outside the room.

Cammie heard several doors slam and scared voices asking what was wrong.

"Gosh, it's not going to work. Not tonight. You've got to leave now." Vicki looked around frantically.

"Ah!" The Witch of Pride spat on the floor, whirled around, and dashed outside.

The Witch of Fear cursed loudly and headed for the door without another look at Cammie.

"Winja, out!" Vicki shouted hysterically.

"You'd better show me some respect, silly girl. I'm the only one here who completed the assignment." Winja nodded at Cammie.

"Security! What's going on here?" a deep male voice came from a distance.

With a loud gasp, Vicki ran out of the room.

"Uh huh!" Winja sprinted to the door, dragging her crutches behind her.

The door closed. Cammie fell on her pillow, trying to catch her breath. She listened in. The security man sounded as though he was asking questions. She heard Vicki's voice too, but there were no more shouts. The witches had probably managed to escape.

Within the next ten minutes, the ward was quiet again. Cammie sighed with relief. At least the Witch of Fear had failed to bewitch her. She suddenly felt tired. She smiled, thinking that the witches' visit had actually worked better than Vicki's sleeping pills.

As Cammie pulled the blanket over her chest, she felt something soft against her hand. She brought the object closer to her eyes. Immediately she recognized it. It was one of the gloves the Witch of Pride had worn—a beautiful, cream-colored glove made of fine leather. Engraved on it were two gold letters: *W* and *P*.

BYE-BYE, SKATELAND

When Cammie opened her eyes, Dr. Eislaufer stood by her side with her file in his hand.

"Dr. Eislaufer!" Cammie sighed with relief. She was happy she didn't have to face Dr. Olsen again. She hated being treated like a loony.

"Good morning, Cammie. You look much better today." As the doctor looked through Cammie's file, she noticed that the man's watch was shaped like a boot with a blade attached to it. The man had to know something about skating.

"What concerns me, Cammie, is the fact that you don't sleep well at night. Is there a problem? Are you still having nightmares?"

Cammie shook her head. "Dr. Eislaufer, there were three witches in my room last night and the night before. They wanted to curse me. You see, the Witch of Injuries has already attacked me. And now the rest—"

Dr. Eislaufer raised his hands. "Whoa, wait a minute. Cammie, everybody here says you've been hallucinating. Yet I was inclined to believe you. I know witches exist, and they can be a big nuisance to promising skaters."

Cammie felt as if a huge burden had been lifted from her. "Oh, so you believe in witches, then?"

"It's not of matter of believing. I *know* they exist. Here!" The doctor rolled up the sleeve of his pale blue robe, and Cammie saw a thin scar running from the man's elbow down to his wrist.

"It's Winja's job," the doctor said grimly.

Cammie rose on her elbows. "So you were a skater too?"

"I'm an adult skater," Dr. Eislaufer said. "See, it's my picture on the bedding and the hospital clothes."

Cammie looked at the image of a smiling doctor doing a one-foot glide on her pink pajamas and grinned. "I thought the skater looked familiar."

Dr. Eislaufer chuckled somewhat sheepishly. "I wish I could have a picture of myself doing a more advanced move. Unfortunately, my body isn't as nimble as yours. You see, I wanted to skate as a child, but my parents couldn't afford figure skating lessons. I took up the sport five years ago, and I got addicted to it. So when I heard of a job opening at Skateland

Orthopedic Center, I applied right away. So now I skate every day. By the way, my last name means *figure skater* in German."

The doctor gave Cammie a big white smile. "I heard about skating witches many times, but I thought it was nothing but superstition. Then a year ago, I skated at the Blue Rink. I had just landed my first loop jump, and I was in seventh heaven. So I kept doing one loop after another even after I got tired. I think I was trying too hard, because at some point I leaned into the edge too much and slipped off. I fell on my elbow, but it wasn't too bad until someone skated right over my arm."

Cammie gasped. "It must have hurt terribly!"

The doctor nodded. "It was Winja who attacked me. There was no collision; she simply targeted me because I had been working hard on my technique, and of course, I was enjoying myself. As you may already know, witches have zero tolerance for skaters' joy."

Cammie nodded sadly.

"My arm was badly cut. I needed thirty stitches, and I still have the scar. So how can I deny the existence of witches after this experience?"

"I'm so happy someone finally believes me!" Cammie sighed.

"However." Dr. Eislaufer raised his finger. "I've never heard of witches attacking skaters outside the rinks. And I've never seen a witch inside the hospital building. Which brings us straight to the point. Cammie, are you sure you weren't dreaming?"

"They were here. I saw them," Cammie said firmly.

"But the hospital security would never let in a stranger in the middle of the night."

"It was Nurse Vicki who opened the door for the witches," Cammie said.

The doctor's face darkened. "Nurse Vicki? Are you sure, Cammie?"

"I'm positive."

Dr. Eislaufer rubbed his forehead. "I don't even know what to say. I did hear some complaints about Vicki being too harsh on patients, but the witches—"

"She's taking some class with them," Cammie said. "And she brought them to the hospital twice. They wanted her to be a lookout while they attacked me. And then…"

Stammering, trying not to leave out an important detail, Cammie described the events of the last two nights. As she was talking, she saw the doctor's brown eyes get wider and wider. And when she told him how Heather and she had hit the witches with a crutch and a cane, the doctor leaned back and laughed openly.

"I didn't realize how brave two little girls could be." The doctor winked at Cammie.

"We are skaters, remember?" Cammie smiled back.

"Sure, the jumps you can do… oh, man! Anyway, Cammie, I don't think you could make up a story like that."

"Wait! There's more." Cammie sat up and reached under her pillow. "I have a proof that the witches came here. Do you see this glove? It belongs to the Witch of Pride."

Cammie put the creamy leather glove into the doctor's big hand. The gold letters *W* and *P* glistened as though confirming her words. Dr. Eislaufer brought the glove up to his nose. "I can smell perfume; it's probably expensive. And the initials, of course … Do you mind if I keep it?"

Cammie nodded. "Sure."

The doctor didn't look cheerful anymore. His high forehead was lined with deep creases Cammie hadn't noticed before.

"Okay, Cammie, I'll talk to you later." The doctor nodded at her and walked out of the room, closing the door slightly behind him.

Cammie lowered herself on her pillow again. Well, it looked as though the man had really believed her. She wondered what the doctor was going to do with the information. Would he have the witches arrested? Send Vicki to prison? The evil nurse surely deserved that.

Cammie waited for Dr. Eislaufer to come back to her room later, but he seemed to have disappeared from the ward. She asked Nurse Mary, who brought her medications, if she could ask Dr. Eislaufer to stop by Cammie's room again. The nurse gave her a look of annoyance and told her that the doctor had more important things to do than listening to little girls' fantasies. Okay, how about Heather? Could the nurse probably tell the girl to visit Cammie again?

Instead of answering, Mary told Cammie to open her mouth, stuck a thermometer in, and only then said nonchalantly that Heather had been discharged.

"So soon? But she didn't tell me anything."

"Because it's none of your business," Nurse Mary said arrogantly and walked out of the room.

Cammie felt sad. What a shame Heather had to leave today! And she hadn't even said good-bye to Cammie. Cammie felt lonely and bored. The day dragged by like a dreary moves-in-the-field practice. When the sky outside began to darken, Cammie wondered what surprises the night held for her. Would the witches come back? With Heather gone, Cammie would have to face the evil women alone.

"Oh man!" Cammie sighed and closed her eyes. How long would it take for her leg to heal? And how many more opportunities would the witches have to finish her off? The door slammed. Cammie opened her eyes. "Mom! Dad!"

Her parents were in her room smiling at her. Cammie's mother bent over and kissed Cammie on the cheek. "We have good news for you, sweetheart. You're going home today."

Cammie's mouth opened wide. "What?"

"That's right. You're being discharged. Isn't that great?" Cammie's father rubbed his hands excitedly.

"We're taking you home right now. And first thing we'll do is have a nice meal together. How about Chinese takeout? I bet you're tired of this hospital food." Cammie's father winked at her.

Cammie pressed her hands against her cheeks, feeling confused. "Wait! How can the doctors discharge me if my leg isn't healed yet? I can't skate. I can't even walk!"

Cammie's mother was hastily packing Cammie's belongings into a small blue suitcase. "Cammie, it takes a while for broken bones to grow back together. But you don't have to stay in the hospital for this. Won't it be nicer to be back at home in your own bed?"

"But, but…" Cammie shifted her eyes to her father and then looked at her mother again. "But how can I leave Skateland? I train here. I belong here. I—"

"Cammie, let's be realistic." Her father took Cammie by the hand. "You have a serious injury, and you're supposed to wear this cast for eight more weeks. Until then, you won't even be able to squeeze your foot into a skating boot."

Cammie cringed. Even though the doctor had told her the same thing, somehow she hoped that she wouldn't need that much time to recuperate.

"And then you'll have to learn to walk again before you step onto the ice," her father said.

Learning to walk? Cammie's heart sank. Somehow she had assumed that once the cast was off, she'd be able to go back to practicing her jumps.

"But maybe I'll be able to skate once they take the cast off," she said stubbornly. "I feel very comfortable on ice."

Her mother zipped up the suitcase. "All done. And, Cammie, it's too early to talk about skating now. Let's cross this bridge when we get to it, okay?"

Cammie grimaced. "Sure."

"Okay, let me help you to get dressed."

Assisted by her mother, Cammie got rid of her hospital johnny and put on terry-cloth pajama pants that her parents had brought. Cammie was sure her mother had chosen the pants because they were wide enough to accommodate the cast. She slipped a thick wool sweater over a long-sleeved T-shirt and reached for her parka.

The door opened again, and in walked Dr. Eislaufer. "Cammie's papers are ready. If you folks don't mind, I'd like to talk to your daughter alone for a few minutes."

Cammie saw her parents exchange puzzled glances. Then her father shrugged. "Sure. Come on, Linda."

He picked up the suitcase with Cammie's things and led her mother out of the room. Cammie sat on the edge of her bed, eyeing the doctor questioningly.

Dr. Eislaufer sat on the chair next to her. "You may be wondering why I'm discharging you so soon."

Cammie shrugged. "I can heal at home, no problem."

"Well, that wasn't the original plan, you see. Here, in Skateland, you could start your physical therapy as early as next week. It might actually speed up your recovery. We have more experience with skating-related injuries than other hospitals and better rehabilitation equipment. However, after what happened to you last night, I see that the risks outweigh the benefits. You are not safe here, Cammie. And neither was Heather. I think you already know that I sent her home this morning."

So that was the reason Heather had left so abruptly! "Yes, Nurse Mary told me," Cammie said.

"Heather's parents live in Skateland, so she'll be able to come here for her physical therapy. You, however, will have to start rehabilitation procedures in your home town."

Cammie frowned. "But I don't want to leave Skateland."

The doctor squeezed her hand. "I know. But we don't have any choice at this moment. The witches are vicious; they realize you're a talented skater, and they're determined to destroy you. You're not safe here, Cammie."

"When will I be able to come back?" she asked in a small voice.

"As soon as you can get back on the ice." The doctor smiled. "It's Skateland, after all." He stood up. "Okay, the orderly will be here with a wheelchair in a minute."

"Wait!" Cammie looked the doctor in the eyes. "What's going to happen to Nurse Vicki?"

"Oh!" The doctor grinned somewhat mischievously. "Vicki is no longer a nurse. She got fired. I mean, letting strangers into the hospital in the middle of the night…I had no problem convincing everybody on staff that Vicki had broken several hospital rules."

"And they believed you? They didn't think I had another nightmare?"

Dr. Eislaufer laughed. "Heather and you did a terrific job on the witches. The noise all of you made was enough to wake up everybody in the ward. All the patients confirmed they had heard several voices. And four patients saw Vicki lead the witches out through the emergency exit. And, of course, the glove you gave me helped too. So I gave Vicki a choice. She could either resign on her own or face criminal charges for lawbreaking. She preferred leaving at once."

Cammie clapped her hands. "Cool!"

"You're a brave girl, Cammie," Dr. Eislaufer said seriously. "And I have no doubt that you will skate again and even better than you did before. Don't let this injury ruin your confidence."

When her parents' car drove past Skateland's main gate, Cammie turned around and looked back. She wanted to remember every little thing about the place she had learned to love so much. Her eyes slid over the grid of the fence decorated with snow-flakes and skating figurines. She whispered a quick good-bye to the statuette of a skater in the attitude position holding a flower. Each of the petals of the flower had a different color, and the petals represented Skateland's eight official practice rinks.

Cammie's eyes rested on the green petal, the one that stood for the Green Rink, Cammie's training ground. The car turned around the corner, and Cammie could no longer see Skateland from the window. But in her mind, she was still gliding along the ice paths, and she saw people passing her on their way to work, to school, or to the Main Rink for a party. Cammie thought of the bakery on Main Square that sold skating-related sweets and the Skating Museum that she had visited last year with Alex. She missed all those places already.

But above all, she missed skating, the excitement of flying across the rink, of swirling and leaping in the air, landing softly on one foot. When she was on ice, she was in a different world filled with exquisite moves, beauty, and music. And now she was leaving the love of her life behind.

Cammie stretched in the backseat and wept silently.

KANGA'S NEW FUNCTION

Cammie sat up in bed and rubbed her eyes. Her room was bathed in the bright morning sun; it had to be late. She looked at the clock and shook her head. It was a quarter till ten. But what did it matter? Cammie didn't have to go anywhere. Almost two months had passed since she left Skateland. Not that much time, but it seemed like eternity to Cammie.

Sometimes as she looked back, she wondered if the girl who had got up at five in the morning every day, who had worked on the ice for hours and hours, had been someone else, not her. Someone other than Cammie had done difficult steps around the rink; someone else had spun like a top; someone else had shot up in the air in strong jumps. It had been so long since Cammie put her skates on that she often wondered if she was still a skater.

Life in Clarenceville was so different. Nobody challenged Cammie about landing a double axel. Nobody fussed about not getting enough revolutions on the sit spin. Nobody was worried about not making it to the nationals. Cammie was in a non-skating world that was governed by different laws. At the beginning, the very feeling of being on the outside had hurt a lot; then the pain had subsided. But Cammie was still sad.

Sometimes when she lay on her back, staring at the pink cast around her ankle, she thought nothing would ever change. Weeks would turn into months, years would pass, and Cammie would still be bed-ridden. She would grow up and become an adult, but she still wouldn't be able to get up. And then she would grow old and die, and nobody would even remember that there had once been a girl who loved skating more than anything else in the world.

Of course, Cammie wasn't alone all the time. Friends from her old school came to visit, and her parents had hired three tutors to help Cammie with her schoolwork.

"Honey, being at home is a wonderful opportunity for you to catch up on your studies," Cammie's mother had said. "When you are back on the ice, you won't have extra time."

Perhaps it was true, but Cammie found it incredibly hard to concentrate on math or the Revolutionary War. So she hardly put any effort into her studies.

"I left my school books in Skateland," Cammie had told her parents so they would leave her alone. "And anyway, we have a completely different curriculum there. We study the history of figure skating, not general history."

"Personally, I never trusted Skateland education," Cammie's mother had said. "There are more things to life than skating."

Cammie had raised her head from her geography book. "Is there?"

Cammie would never forget the look her mother had given her. Cammie yawned and rose on her elbow. She scanned the rows of stuffed animals on the shelves and posters of famous skaters on the walls. With a deep sigh, she stared at the special shelf where her medals and trophies were displayed. The room looked so familiar. It had been her home before she moved to Skateland, and now it almost felt as though she had never left.

Cammie glanced at a pile of books sitting on her desk and made a nasty face. She knew she had to study, but...her schoolbooks were so boring. Although she might as well do some assignments; at least it would take her mind off skating.

Reluctantly, Cammie picked up her biology book from her nightstand where she had left it the night before. She had read exactly one half page. Three get-well cards flew out from between the pages of the book and fluttered to the floor. Holding on to the side of the bed, Cammie reached for the cards. She had read and reread them so many times that the cards now appeared frayed. Yet Cammie knew that the messages from her friends would lift her spirits.

The first card had a picture of a blonde curly-haired girl lying in bed. The message inside read,

> So you are hurt, my friend. It's sad.
> But lighten up. Things aren't too bad.
> Just take it easy, lie and rest,
> And once again, you'll be the best.

The card was signed Sonia. Cammie smiled gratefully. A very sweet card it was and nice—just like her roommate.

Cammie opened Jeff's card next.

> The last few weeks have been quite rough.
> But as a skater, you are tough.
> When things around you go wrong,
> That's when you prove that you are strong.
> I want you to be free from pain,
> To glide, to spin, to jump again.
> Now don't give up; stand up and fight.
> And I believe you'll be all right.

The picture on Jeff's card showed a boy wearing shorts and boxing gloves. The boy skated around the pond with a big smile on his face. As weird as the skater looked, the card had definitely served its purpose. Cammie was grinning widely. The very idea of wearing shorts and boxing gloves to the rink was enough to cast the sad thoughts away.

Yet she knew it was the third card that would send her into a real frenzy, the one Alex had made up for her. Cammie was sure Alex had failed to find the exact message he wanted in Skateland Gift Shop. Apparently, he had written the message himself and typed the whole thing on the computer. With a big smile, Cammie opened the card and read out loud,

> Cammie, I know how you feel.
> But lighten up; your leg will heal.
> Your blades are sharp—just like a spear.
> Kick those witches in the rear!

It wasn't the first time Cammie had read the poem, but she couldn't suppress a squeak of excitement. To think of hitting the evil witches hard with her blades—oh my, oh my! But that wasn't everything. To get his point across, Alex had drawn Cammie doing a big split jump. One of her blades was positioned against the Witch of Fear's bottom; the other aimed right at the massive backside that belonged to the Witch of Pride. Cammie had to admit that Alex was quite a good artist. Cammie looked very much like her real self, and as for the witches... Well, so did they—ugly and stupid.

"That's right. I'll just kick them!" Cammie kicked the edge of the bed with her healthy foot and let out an exaggerated wail, faking the injured witches' likely response. She laughed so hard that she didn't hear her mother open the door.

"Well, I'm glad you're in a good mood. Here's your lunch." Her mother put a tray on the night-stand next to Cammie's bed.

Cammie twisted her face in a grimace of repulsion. "I'm not hungry."

That was true; she wasn't. When she had lived in Skateland practicing four hours a day and skating everywhere, she had devoured everything Mrs. Page had put in front of her and longed for more. Now that she spent most of her time in bed, her body didn't need that many calories.

"Cammie, if you don't eat, you'll have no strength to heal."

Cammie stared morosely at the bowl of chicken soup. Next to the soup sat a plate with two loaves of bread. "Do you expect me to eat all this?"

"Cammie, let's not start this discussion now."

With a long sigh of someone who was being severely tortured, Cammie picked up the spoon and began to eat.

The doorbell rang downstairs, and Cammie's mother left the room to answer it. Cammie took a bite from the loaf of bread and put it back on the plate. No, she was definitely not in the mood to eat.

There was a sound of voices coming from downstairs. Cammie recognized her mother; she sounded excited, but there were more people in the hallway talking all at once. And then Cammie heard the sound of footsteps. Someone was coming up the stairs. The door to Cammie's room burst open, and in ran Sonia wearing blue jeans and a blue Skateland sweatshirt.

Cammie clapped her hands. "Sonia!"

And then she saw that Sonia was closely followed by Jeff, and behind him was Alex, tall and blond, dressed casually in tight black jeans and a matching sweater. Cammie's heart leaped in her chest.

"I don't believe you guys are here!" she shrieked.

Sonia rushed forward and hugged Cammie. Jeff and Alex stood next to her bed.

"We thought it would be a great idea to see you," Alex said, beaming at her.

His smile was so familiar; Cammie felt joy well up within her.

"I've just been rereading your cards," Cammie exclaimed. "They are absolutely terrific."

Alex raised his index finger. "But you can't deny the obvious fact that mine is the best."

"Sure! You made it yourself!" Cammie shouted but then stopped short. She didn't want to offend Sonia and Jeff. After all, they had come up with the best cards they possibly could. "I love everybody's card, really. So how did you guys get here? You don't drive."

"By bus. It took us two hours. I slept all the way." Jeff closed his eyes and snored.

Alex grunted. "By bus, how about that? As though there isn't a better way."

Cammie nodded, signaling that she understood. Alex was referring to Zamboni machines that could take a skater anywhere in the skating world within minutes. Unfortunately, Zamboni machines weren't officially approved as means of public transportation.

Still Cammie and Alex had once managed to travel to Skateland in the back of a Zamboni machine. But that was their secret, and Cammie doubted that Jeff and Sonia would be willing to try it anyway.

"So how are you feeling? Does it hurt?" Sonia pointed to Cammie's right ankle that was still wrapped in a cast.

"Not anymore." It was true. The sharp pain had disappeared within a week after Cammie's surgery. Now she didn't feel any discomfort at all. In fact, she was sure that if the doctors allowed her to step on the injured leg, she would be able to walk easily. And not only walk; of course, she would be able to skate. She would go to Skateland immediately and start doing her doubles. In fact, she practiced them all the time…in her dreams. Unfortunately, her new doctor in Clarenceville didn't share her enthusiasm.

"How did it happen anyway? Your injury, I mean?" Alex asked. He sat cross-legged on the floor next to Cammie's bed. Sonia perched on the edge of her bed, and Jeff had taken the only chair in the room next to Cammie's desk.

"Winja attacked me," Cammie said simply. She hadn't expected her words to have such a strong effect on her friends. Sonia gasped. Alex frowned. Jeff dropped Cammie's math book that he had been perusing.

"I knew it," Jeff said.

"You didn't tell me." Alex looked Cammie straight in the eye.

"Were you at the Green Rink at that time?" Sonia asked, looking concerned.

Cammie sighed. She already knew what was coming. "No, in the Icy Park."

"What?" Sonia shrieked. "But, Cammie, how could you? Don't you know? Oh my!"

"Come on. Tell us about it," Alex said impatiently.

Cammie described her unpleasant experience. She left out nothing; she even told them about the witches' visit to the hospital.

"So that's the reason they discharged you so soon," Jeff said slowly.

"We came to visit you, and the receptionist said you were gone. We wondered why," Sonia said.

Cammie nodded. "The doctor didn't want the witches to attack me again."

There was a deep silence; everybody seemed to be digesting the information.

"But you're coming back, aren't you?" Alex asked.

Cammie shifted in her bed. "Sure, after the cast comes off. I have an appointment with an orthopedic doctor in two days."

"Good!" Alex sighed with relief.

"And I'll come to Skateland right away. And then … Sonia, what's wrong?"

Sonia's eyes were dark with grief. "You'll have to learn to walk first. And then—"

Cammie rolled her eyes. "I'm not a baby."

Sonia stared at her patronizingly, as though Cammie really *was* a baby. "You don't understand. When you don't use your muscles for a long while, they have to be trained to do simple things again. Same with skating."

"I know I will be able to skate."

"You will, but—" Sonia cleared her throat.

"Sonia, that's enough. If Cammie really wants to skate, nothing will stop her. Yes, Cammie. That's what I'm saying, Jeff Patterson, the king of injuries." Jeff stood up and gave Cammie an exaggerated bow.

As distraught as she was, she couldn't help laughing. "I thought Winja had that title."

"Nay, she's nothing but a witch."

The door to Cammie's room opened again, and Cammie's mother wheeled in a tray. "Anyone ready for tea?"

"Thank you, Mrs. Wester," Cammie's friends shouted in unison.

Now that Cammie wasn't alone, she felt she could really have something to eat. Besides, her friends had brought her candy and cookies from Sweet Blades. As she sipped tea and nibbled on chocolate pretzel skate guards, she felt as though she were back in Skateland. She laughed when her friends told her about the latest rumors at the rinks.

"George joined a hockey team. Yeah, without talking to his coach. He cut a couple of practices, and now he's in big trouble," Jeff said. George was his roommate.

"And we're going to the nationals in a week," Sonia blurted out.

"Ah!" Hot tea burnt Cammie's throat; she coughed and put her cup down. Of course, she was happy for her friends, but she couldn't help feeling disappointed too. Right now she too could be practicing hard getting ready for the nationals. *If it only hadn't been for that evil Winja, I would definitely have a shot at winning*, she thought.

Cammie took a deep breath then exhaled slowly. She didn't want to ruin everything for her friends. They deserved to go to the nationals; they had been working hard. So now she was going to rejoice with them.

Cammie wasn't sure her smile looked genuine, but at least she was trying to put up a good front. "Um, I'm so happy for you guys. Yes, you, Sonia, and you, Jeff, and Alex, of course."

Alex sneered. "In case you have forgotten, I'm not going anywhere."

Cammie dropped her spoon. "What?"

Alex put away the copy of *Uncle Tom's Cabin* that Cammie had been reading for her English literature class and folded his arms on his chest. "I came in fifth at Skateland Annual, remember?'

"That's right!" Gosh, how could Cammie forget? Of course, Alex hadn't qualified for the nationals. And she had been so focused on herself that she didn't even realize her best friend had his share of problems. Only now as she thought about Alex's situation did Cammie understand what her friend had been going through the last couple of months.

He had had to watch his friends polishing their tough moves. Surely, he had been going over his poor performance at Skateland Annual Competition, asking himself for the thousandth time what might have happened if he hadn't fallen from his triple flip and doubled his triple salchow. That must have been hard enough, and besides, Alex's coach couldn't have been too happy either. Cammie wondered if she had hurt Alex's feelings by assuming he was going to the competition after all.

"I'm sorry, Alex," Cammie said sadly.

He raised his hand. "No big deal. There's always next year. And the same goes for you, by the way."

"Okay." Somehow Cammie felt encouraged. Alex was right. She would definitely have another chance.

She looked at Sonia and Jeff. "Well, at least the two of you are going. And…who is replacing me?"

Sonia's pale face turned pink. "Dana. She came in fifth, remember?"

Ah! Of course. Cammie made a huge effort to shake a fit of self-pity off. "I only wish they would show the junior events on television. But they never do. I really would like to see you guys compete."

Sonia, Jeff, and Alex exchanged enigmatic glances.

"Actually, you can watch Junior Nationals," Alex said.

Cammie frowned. "What do you mean?"

Without another word, Sonia jumped off Cammie's bed and ran out of the room. She reappeared seconds later, pulling in the familiar brown animal on wheels.

"Wow, it's my Kanga bag!" Cammie reached out and patted the animal. How come she had completely forgotten about her Charming Skater Prize? Having the bag in her room in Clarenceville was like another get-well wish from Skateland.

"Thanks for bringing it, you guys. Unfortunately, I can't use you now, Kanga. You'll have to wait till I start skating again." Cammie patted the animal's ears.

"Actually you can," Jeff said meaningfully.

"How? Obviously, I can't skate, and I don't want Kanga to wake me up at five in the morning. Well, it probably can, but I can't go to the rink anyway. Besides, my parents only get up at seven. I bet they won't be too happy to hear Kanga's wake-up call."

"Don't worry about it," Alex said.

"You don't know my parents."

"Mr. Reed knows about your injury, and he understands you need rest. So he has disabled the alarm function until you get better."

"Well, that's good," Cammie said. "So I'll just keep Kanga in my room as a toy. What else is it good for?"

"Have you even read Kanga's instruction book?" Alex asked, looking amused.

Cammie shrugged. "No, I didn't. Should I have?"

"Tah tah!" Sonia bent down and pressed an invisible button on the animal's belly. There came a whooshing sound. Kanga's paws reached inside its pocket and reappeared holding a big monitor. The screen lit up, and a long list entitled "Current Skating Competitions" appeared in bold print.

Cammie gave Sonia a puzzled look. "I don't understand."

"Kanga has a built-in media player. With its help, you can watch any skating competition in the world," Jeff said excitedly.

"I can't believe it!" Cammie squinted at the screen. "I don't see the nationals on the list, though."

"It's because they haven't started yet." Alex scrolled down the menu, and Cammie saw the name U.S. Figure Skating Championships.

"Wow! So I'll be able to see you guys compete?" Cammie still couldn't believe it.

Jeff chuckled. "You bet. And you'd better cheer for us loudly or—"

Cammie beamed. "I will. I will."

Now she felt positively better. And somehow, being around her friends, she had no doubt that she was going to skate again and very, very soon.

Cammie's cast came off a week later. As the technician cut off the hard pink wrap and Cammie stared at her leg, her heart fluttered in her chest, and she was afraid she might faint. Was it really her leg? The one that had once been so strong and muscular, the one that had taken the impact of so many jumps?

Now Cammie was staring at what looked like a dead chicken leg, white and skinny, with a huge knee cap and protruding ankle bones. When Cammie tried to move it, the leg appeared numb, as though it didn't belong to her. How on earth was Cammie supposed to walk on her leg? And how about skating?

"Don't worry, Cammie. Your leg will get stronger as you go on with your physical therapy." The technician threw the remains of Cammie's cast into a trashcan.

Cammie looked up at the man's cheerful face. "Can I go skating today?"

The technician swallowed hard, apparently shocked at Cammie's question. "Oh, would you like to talk to your doctor about it?"

Cammie's new doctor's name was Dr. Gordon, and she didn't quite like the man. Tall and trim, he always looked aloof, and when he talked about Cammie's injury, he used a lot of scientific terms that Cammie couldn't understand. In fact, she didn't even think she needed all those gory details. All she wanted to know was when she would be able to step on the ice.

"We can't be sure at this point." Dr. Gordon averted his eyes. His hands clasping Cammie's file were pale and skinny, like her injured leg. She was sure the man had never exercised in his whole life. So what could he know about skating anyway?

"It will probably be a year or a little longer before you will be able to skate competitively again," Dr. Gordon said.

What? A year? Cammie had probably misunderstood the man. He had definitely said *a week*; surely that was what he had said, and she was so stupid.

"Of course, I'm not trying to say that you'll never skate again." Dr. Gordon's pale lips spread, revealing small, sharp teeth.

He looks just like a witch, Cammie thought vindictively.

"What does a year matter to a young girl like you?"

A year? So he did say a year *after all.* She straightened up. "I can't wait that long, Dr. Gordon. I'm a competitive skater; I qualified for the nationals this year."

The doctor spread his arms. "Cammie, I'm really sorry."

"No, you aren't!" she cried out. "Because if you were really sorry, you would be trying to do something!"

"No, Cammie, really—"

"I don't want to hear it!" Sobbing, she covered her ears and closed her eyes. It couldn't be true. No no no! There had to be some mistake. Or maybe something was wrong with her ears too. The doctor couldn't have said *a year*. It was too terrible, too unfair.

The room spun around Cammie. From that moment on, everything looked blurred. She remembered her parents walking into the examination room, her mother fumbling with her purse, her father looking grave. The doctor said something; her mother nodded. Of course! Parents always sided with doctors, even if it meant keeping their children away from skating for a year.

The ride home seemed endless. When Cammie finally reached her room, she buried her face in her pillow, refusing to talk. Her parents stood by her side, saying something in hushed tones. Then she heard the door close behind them; they were gone. She bawled louder. Her life was over.

The door to her room opened again, and in walked her father.

"I have good news," he said with a smile that looked a little weird under the circumstances.

Cammie sat up quickly. "What? I can skate again?"

Her father coughed into his fist. "Well, perhaps the news isn't quite that good. Anyway, Cammie, you can start your physical therapy tomorrow."

"And that's it?" She felt disappointed.

"Well, that's the first step toward complete recovery. Listen, honey, physical therapy is a great thing, really. When I was in high school, I injured my shoulder badly playing basketball. It took a while to heal; in fact, I thought I'd always be in pain. Then the doctor recommended physical therapy. And you know what? I felt better right away, and now I barely remember the injury ever happened. Watch me." Cammie's father swung both arms energetically several times. He looked so funny that she couldn't help smiling.

"That's my girl. So shall we make an appointment for tomorrow, then?"

"Wait." Suddenly Cammie remembered what Dr. Eislaufer had said about rehabilitation procedures in Skateland. *We have more experience with skating-related injuries than other hospitals and better rehabilitation equipment.* Those were the doctor's exact words. So what was she waiting for?

"Dad, you know what? I'll be doing my physical therapy in Skateland," Cammie said, feeling somewhat relieved.

Dad's face registered confusion. "In Skateland? But, honey, why would you want to leave home now? You're not strong enough yet."

"But they have the best rehabilitation program in the country." Cammie told her father about Dr. Eislaufer's words.

"But he did send you away," her father said.

"Well…" There was no point in telling her father the real reason why Dr. Eislaufer had wanted Cammie away from Skateland. Her parents didn't believe in witches anyway; they would only think Cammie had an overactive imagination.

"Dr. Eislaufer wanted my cast off before I started physical therapy," Cammie said.

"Well…" Her father looked hesitant. "I think it's possible. Let's talk to your mother, okay?"

Naturally, her mother wasn't too eager to let Cammie return to Skateland so soon. But Cammie was adamant. She needed to get on the ice as soon as possible.

"You wouldn't want me to waste the whole year, would you?" Cammie asked her mother.

"You can hardly call rehabilitation a waste."

What did her mother understand? Cammie was thirteen years old already, and most elite skaters were young. How much time did she really have?

"And who would help you get around in Skateland?" her mother asked. "Here, at home, you have everything done for you."

Cammie shrugged. "There's everything I need in the dorm. And Dr. Eislaufer did say I would get healthy faster in Skateland."

Her mother didn't look too excited, but finally she gave in. Okay, Cammie could go back to Skateland, but she had to make her return official.

"I'll call the Admissions Office and ask them if they can have you back," Cammie's mother said.

"Oh, I can do that," Cammie said quickly. She didn't want her mother telling Skateland authorities that Cammie was still weak, that she needed special attention. Once they heard that, they might have second thoughts about allowing her to take a reha-bilitation course in Skateland.

Cammie's mother raised her arms as though in surrender. "Suit yourself."

Feeling her heart bouncing hard against her rib-cage, Cammie reached for her cell phone that sat on her nightstand. Yes, there was the number for Skateland Admissions Office. She quickly pressed the button. The phone rang three times; then there was a click followed by a cheerful female voice. "Hi, you have reached Skateland Admissions Office. Unfortunately, the office is now closed, but if you leave your name and your number, we will contact you as soon as we can. If you are a skater, press *one*. If you are a coach, press *two*. If you are a parent of a skater, press *three*. If you are a judge, press *four*. If you are a skating fan, press *five*.

Cammie pressed *one*, waited for the beep, and began to speak. "Hi, it's Cammie Wester. I'm in Skateland Skating Program, but I had to leave because of an injury. Now I'm perfectly healthy and ready to come back. Please, call me as soon as possible."

Cammie pressed the off button and sighed with relief. Good. Someone from the office would definitely contact her in the morning and then ... Cammie gave a small squeak of excitement as she thought that she would probably be back in Skateland as early as tomorrow. Or the day after tomorrow. Life was definitely beginning to get better for her.

Cammie looked at her watch. It was six thirty, still a lot of time to kill before tomorrow. She wondered if it would be a good idea to do some schoolwork. No, she definitely didn't feel like it. Besides, there were more exciting things to keep her busy. And what could be more fun for an injured skater than watching skating videos. Cammie owed this privilege to Mr. Reed and his fantastic Kanga bag.

Funny how at the beginning Cammie hadn't been particularly excited about her Charming Skater Prize. Well, of course, the very fact that she had been chosen as the most charming skater had been a good reason to celebrate. But she hadn't found the bag itself particularly nice. She had failed to understand all the fuss about the bag. After all, Cammie could have carried her stuff in a backpack.

And as for the alarm function, the one Mr. Reed was particularly proud of, Cammie had found it more than annoying. Getting up at five in the morning had been hard enough, but it had to be done. Just like everybody else in Skateland, Cammie had jumped out of bed dutifully at five sharp, but it had always taken her at least an hour to wake up completely. Until then, she had always felt drowsy, grouchy, and definitely not in the mood to enjoy Kanga's wakeup poetry.

Now, however, when Cammie was cut off from Skateland and her life as an athlete, the brown animal had somehow become Cammie's best friend. Every day she spent hours watching skating videos on Kanga's monitor. And sometimes, when she felt particularly lonely, she even talked to the brown animal. Of course, she realized how silly it was. Kanga was just a bag, not even a stuffed animal. But when she started complaining to the kangaroo about her situation, the animal's eyes flashed, and it looked as though it sympathized with her. Sometimes she could swear Kanga had a mind of its own.

Cammie positioned her right foot on a stack of pillows to keep the swelling down and reached for a silver pendant that hung from her neck on a chain. Though shaped like a figure skate, the pendant wasn't a mere piece of jewelry but Kanga bag's remote control. As Jeff had explained to Cammie, Mr. Reed had supplied the bag with Bluetooth function. It meant that as soon as Cammie wore the pendant, she could speak to the bag, and it would respond to her commands.

"Come here, Kanga!" Cammie said. The kangaroo's eyes flashed, and the bag rolled up to her. "Media player," Cammie said.

The animal took a monitor out of its belly pocket, and a split second later, a menu listing different competitions appeared on the screen. Cammie touched the words *Junior Nationals* with her finger then clicked on the icon that read "Junior Men's Short Program" and leaned back on her pillow, ready to watch.

A big Olympic-size rink appeared on the screen, and Cammie saw the names of the contestants—twenty all together. Jeff's name was also on the list.

"Jeff's going to win!" Cammie clapped her hands. The stack of pillows collapsed under her foot. Kanga's eyes flickered disapprovingly.

"Oops. Sorry, Kanga. I got too excited. But we want him to win, don't we?" Her eyes fixed on the monitor, Cammie readjusted the pillows.

"Representing Skateland, here is Kyle Lyons!" the announcer said.

"Ugh!" Cammie made a nasty face. Somehow she had forgotten that Kyle was also competing at the Junior Nationals.

Dressed in a black outfit with a bright orange pattern on the sleeves, Kyle skated to the middle of the arena. He didn't appear nervous at all. In fact, his familiar mischievous smile reminded Cammie of the way he had led her around the Main Square Rink.

"Yeah, and then left me alone in the dark." Cammie stuck out her tongue at him. "I hope Jeff beats you!"

But by the time Kyle finished his program, Cammie realized the guy would be hard to defeat. Kyle was simply perfect. He landed his triple axel with ease. Cammie knew Jeff only had a double. Kyle's triple-lutz-double-toe-loop combination was equally flawless, and he finished his program with a flashy combination spin. Cammie sighed as she thought that in addition to being a strong technical skater, Kyle also had tremendous presentation ability. Skating to "Take Five," a quick jazzy piece, the boy never failed to show his flexibility and grace.

Kyle's short program score was 75.8—a tough number to top. Eighteen more boys skated after Kyle, but no one could measure up to the high standard. Finally, Jeff appeared on the ice wearing a light brown outfit.

Cammie rose on her pillows. "Woohoo, Jeff, show them how it's done." She thought it was good that Jeff skated last. She always liked skating after her competitors.

Jeff's music—Rachmaninoff's concerto—began, and Cammie clenched her fists. Jeff went for his double axel and landed it securely. Good. If only he had done a triple like Kyle! The rest of the program went well too, except for a slight misstep on the triple lutz. When the scores were announced, however, Jeff was in fourth place.

"Not good," Cammie said to Kanga. "You see, only the top three finishers will go to Junior Worlds. Well, of course, there's still the long program."

Kanga didn't say anything; apparently, it agreed with Cammie.

"Just wait till we see the ladies' competition. Sonia will definitely tear everybody apart," Cammie said with determination.

Unfortunately, the girls' competition would only start in two days. Cammie stifled a yawn. She felt really tired. Perhaps it would be better for her to go to bed early. What if Skateland office contacted her early in the morning and invited her to come back to Skateland immediately?

Cammie turned off the light and pulled the covers up to her chin. She slept well that night, dreaming of Skateland's rinks of different colors.

PHYSICAL THERAPY

"Cammie, wake up! Do you hear me?"

Cammie groaned and turned on her back. She didn't want to open her eyes. The door opened, and her mother walked in with a phone in her hand.

"I'm sleeping, Mom." Cammie put her pillow over her head.

"There's a call for you. It's Skateland's office."

"Oh!" Cammie sat up feeling completely awake. Finally, finally, Skateland authorities had contacted her. Cammie had left them a message three days ago, but no one had returned her call. She wondered what had taken them so long.

Cammie snatched the phone from her mother's hand. "Hello!"

"Hello, Cammie. This is Jan Morton from the Admissions Office. You left a message telling us you were ready to come back to Skateland."

"Yes, yes! I'm completely healthy now. I'm ready to practice again," Cammie exclaimed.

"Unfortunately, Cammie, this isn't what your doctor said," Jan said.

Cammie squeezed the phone. "Excuse me?"

"Well, we talked to Dr. Eislaufer. You've got to understand, Cammie, that in situations like yours, we always seek professional opinion before we make final decisions. Dr. Eislaufer contacted your doctor in Clarenceville, and he let us know that at this point, you aren't quite ready for full-time training in Skateland."

"But…but Dr. Gordon told me I could skate." Cammie felt blood pulsating in her temples. They couldn't turn her down. No way!

"Skate, yes, but not full time. I'm sorry, Cammie, but we can't have you back right now. Finish your rehabilitation, and when you're strong enough, we will reevaluate your case."

"Mrs. Morton, wait!" Cammie spoke very fast, fearing that the woman would hang up on her. "Really, I feel great. I can walk normally, and my ankle doesn't hurt at all. I'm sure I could practice full time."

"Cammie, let me remind you that in addition to two practices a day, you would have to skate everywhere. Isn't it too hard for someone who just had an ankle surgery?"

"But it's healed!" Cammie hit her knee with a fist. Why didn't the woman believe her?

"Cammie, let me assure you: we will take you back as soon as you are ready. You're a champion, and we're very proud of you. But I know from my own experience that too much exercise after a serious injury can slow down the rehabilitation process. And we need to respect the doctor's opinion. Anyway, keep doing your physical therapy and perhaps next year—"

"Next year?" Cammie cried out. "But it's impossible! You can't do that to me. Please!"

"I'm sorry, Cammie, but this is the rule. Until you are strong enough to skate to your practices and back, you can't return to Skateland. Our whole staff wishes you all the best, and I hope to talk to your later."

Beep-beep-beep. Gritting her teeth, Cammie pressed the off button and stared at her mother blankly. Her mother didn't say anything.

"Did you know?" Cammie asked softly.

Her mother nodded. "Yes, Mrs. Morton talked to me first. Cammie—"

"No!" Cammie dropped the phone and fell on her pillow, sobbing.

"Cammie!"

"Please, leave me alone!"

"Cammie, I'm on your side."

Cammie raised her wet face from the pillow. "No, you aren't. You did all the best to get me to stay home. You never wanted me to be a skater."

She heard her mother sigh. "Well, perhaps at the beginning I did think you took skating too seriously. But now that I realize how much it means to you, I really admire all the hard work you put into it." Her mother smoothed Cammie's disheveled hair and sat down on the side of her bed. "Look, if you want to go back to Skateland so badly, I won't try to keep you at home. Both your father and I respect your decision."

Cammie wiped her tears with her sleeve. "Honestly?"

"Honestly." Her mother's brown eyes were soft and loving.

Cammie hugged her mother. "I'm sorry I've been acting so nasty."

"I understand. Injuries are never easy to battle. But, Cammie, if you really want to skate, nothing will stop you. You are a champion, remember?"

"But what do you want me to do?" Cammie stared at her Kanga bag sitting quietly in the corner. "Nobody seems to remember anymore that I won Skateland Annual Competition. Now all they see is my broken ankle."

"Well, you've got to prove them wrong. Start your physical therapy, do the best you can, and when you're ready, call the Admissions Office again. You see, sometimes it takes a lot of persistence to reach your goal. Don't give up."

"Okay." Cammie felt encouraged. Her mother was right. Nothing was over yet. She would start her rehabilitation in Clarenceville, and when her foot was completely restored, no one would be able to keep her away from Skateland.

Cammie started her physical therapy the following day, and she found it a nice change from lying in bed. Having spent two months in her room alone, she was now in a place filled with noise and activity. The exercise machines buzzed; people of all ages worked out under the supervision of trainers. In fact, the whole atmosphere reminded Cammie of Skateland Fitness Center. The only difference was that each of the patients had some kind of a problem. Some were recovering from hand and arm injuries; others, like Cammie, were learning how to walk again.

At the beginning of each session, the therapist warmed up Cammie's ankle with a heating pad. After that, Cammie did several exercises involving the rotation of her ankle, rising on her toes, and picking up things with her toes. Then came the most important part of her training: learning to walk.

After twelve years of walking naturally, Cammie had to remind herself to put one foot in front of the other naturally, to shift her weight gradually, to stay balanced over the proper side of her body. In a way it reminded her of learning how to skate. It would probably be fun, if only her right ankle weren't that weak.

Cammie's physical therapist explained to her that during the weeks of not using her leg, she had developed a minor case of muscular atrophy and not just in her ankle, but also in her calves and hamstrings. So now she had to get her muscles back, and the only way it could be done was through hard work. To take some pressure off the injured leg, the therapist gave Cammie a pair of crutches. Even though it was much better than riding in a wheelchair, limping around holding the crutches like an older woman made Cammie extremely self-conscious. When her father suggested that the three of them go out to Olive Garden for dinner, Cammie only shook her head. She knew she wouldn't feel good around people who never thought twice about crossing the room on foot.

After three weeks of physical therapy, Cammie finally managed to cross the room without leaning on her crutches. Everybody congratulated her on her progress, yet she was far from happy. Walking without the crutches was a huge effort; after only five minutes, she was covered with perspiration. *How on earth am I going to skate on this ankle?* she thought miserably.

Cammie wasn't ready to give up, though. When she was back in her room, she practiced walking without crutches until she was exhausted. She told her mom she didn't want lunch, plopped on her bed, and drifted away.

She was awaked by the doorbell. Someone was downstairs talking to her mom. Cammie yawned and looked around. It was already dark; she must have slept the whole day.

There was a sound of someone walking up the steps; then the door opened.

"Cammie, are you still asleep?" her mother asked.

"I just woke up."

"Alex is here."

"Alex?" Cammie sat up, stared at her wrinkled tracksuit, and ran her hand through her disheveled hair. How could she face her friend like that? She should have at least brushed her hair.

There was a click as her mother turned on the light, and Cammie saw Alex's smiling face. His cheeks were red from the cold outside air, and he wore blue jeans and a black sweater.

"Hi there. Your mom says you can walk on your own already," Alex said.

"Kind of," Cammie said. "Wow, Alex, it's so great you're here."

"I'll make tea while you guys talk," Cammie's mother said. "Alex brought some skate pastries."

"You did?" Cammie clapped her hands. Skate pastries were her favorite treat from Sweet Blades.

Alex smiled shyly. "Actually it was Wilhelmina who sent them to you." He moved the chair from the desk and sat down next to Cammie's bed.

Cammie straightened up. "So Wilhelmina knows about my injury?"

Alex's green eyes broadened. "Of course, she does. She is Skateland President after all. She sent for me this morning, right after practice. She asked me to give you this."

Alex handed Cammie a silver envelope. Wilhelmina's name stood over the Skateland logo, and in the middle of the envelope, the words *To Cammie Wester* were written in old-fashioned, slanted handwriting.

"Wow!" Cammie swirled the envelope in her hands.

"I know you called the Admissions and they turned you down. Wilhelmina told me all about it."

Cammie sighed gravely. "Yeah."

She suddenly panicked. What if Wilhelmina's letter was a polite dismissal? What if Skateland President had written her something like, *It was nice having you with us, Cammie. Unfortunately, with an injury as serious as yours…*

"What are you waiting for? Open it up." Alex stared at the letter in Cammie's hand.

Reluctantly, Cammie started ungluing the envelope. "What if it's just a good-bye?" Her hand froze midway.

Alex's eyebrows shot up. "Are you crazy? Wilhelmina would never do that to you. Hey, give it to me!" He snatched the envelope out of Cammie's hand, took out the letter, and began to read.

> Dear Cammie,
>
> I hope this letter will find you in good health. I am sorry about your injury, and my prayers are with you. Let me assure you, I

am perfectly aware of the severity of your condition, yet a day hasn't passed without my thinking of a possible way to speed up your recovery.

Mrs. Morton from the Admissions Office informed me that your doctor wasn't particularly optimistic in his prognosis and opted for a year off from skating. With all due respect, I will still allow myself to disagree with the specialist. My personal experience shows that waiting and resting is not always the most sensible course to take. I believe in more radical rehabilitation techniques, and I am therefore happy to make you an offer.

Mr. Reed, whom you know very well, has come up with an extremely successful method of physical therapy for injured limbs. I have already made an appointment with Mr. Reed, who will be only too happy to explain the details to you. The appointment is in three days, so I suggest that you move back to Skateland immediately. All the paperwork has already been taken care of. I also expect your friend Alex Bernard to be of assistance during your rehabilitation.

I wish you all the best. Please, give my best regards to your family.

Wilhelmina Van Uffeln, president of Skateland.

P.S. Don't you agree that even negative experiences can work out for the good?

"Hey, you're going to skate soon. Isn't that great?" Alex gave Cammie a playful shove on the side.

"Wait. I don't quite get it." Cammie pressed her hands against her burning cheeks. "Does it mean that Wilhelmina wants me to come to Skateland right now?"

"Definitely. That what it says. Hang on … here. 'The appointment is in three days, so I suggest that you move back to Skateland immediately.'"

"But Mrs. Morton, you know, the lady from the Admissions Office just told me—"

"Forget Mrs. Morton. You have the president's permission to move back, and that's it."

"But what if they send me back after I see Mr. Reed?" Cammie's heart sank as she thought how terrible that would be.

"No way," Alex said with determination. "Who in his right mind would even think of crossing Mr. Reed?"

"Well. That's true." Not only was Mr. Reed a tough man, but he also had magical powers. Even the witches were afraid of him.

"Besides, didn't Wilhelmina say that Mr. Reed had some kind of a rehabilitation program for you? I think he'll do some magical trick, and you'll be able to jump right away."

Cammie's heart leaped in her chest as she pictured herself doing a huge double axel. "Do you think it's possible?"

"How can you even doubt it? Don't you remember Mr. Reed's purple ice? And the history book? Healing your ankle would be nothing compared to traveling through time."

"That's right." Cammie beamed. "Alex, can you believe it? I'm going to skate again. Yeah! Woohoo!"

"Cammie, Alex! Tea's ready," Cammie's mother called from downstairs.

"Coming!" Cammie yelled back.

She turned to Alex. "Would you like to watch the nationals on Kanga after tea with me? I think they had the original dance and ladies' short today."

"Sure, that'll be great."

As they walked down the steps to the dining room, with Cammie holding the railing tight, she suddenly stopped and faced Alex. "Hey, do you remember the last sentence in Wilhelmina's letter? The P.S. thing. Something about bad things working together for good."

He nodded. "Sure."

"Any idea what it means?"

Alex shook his head, looking amused. "Cammie, I thought you were bright. If I had placed at Skateland Annual Competition and gone to Junior Nationals, I wouldn't be able to help you with your rehabilitation. As simple as that."

FULL CIRCLE THERAPY

"Here we are!" Cammie exclaimed. From the car window, she could see the familiar statue of the skater in the attitude position coming closer and closer.

Cammie's father slowed down in front of Skateland's main gate. "Here you go, honey. Do you want me to take you to the dorm? I could rent a pair of skates."

With a somewhat nervous grin, Cammie's father waved in the direction of the low brown building with the sign Skate Rentals above the entrance. According to the law, even Skateland visitors were supposed to wear skates. As Sonia had once explained to Cammie, that was the president's way of encouraging skaters' friends and families to get involved in the sport, at least recreationally. However, Cammie knew that her father didn't feel particularly comfortable on ice.

She hugged him. "Thank you, Daddy, but you really don't have to skate. Wilhelmina promised to send an ice mobile for me. There it is … oh, no!"

"Is anything wrong?" her father asked.

"It's Bob Turner. I can't believe it!" Cammie groaned as she watched the young police officer get out of the silvery ice mobile parked at the gate.

Without even bothering to greet Cammie or her father, Lieutenant Turner grabbed Cammie's suitcase and her Kanga bag and threw them unceremoniously to the back of the ice mobile. "You'd better say good-bye fast, loser. My time is precious."

Nasty like always, Cammie thought. Yet Bob Turner was part of Skateland, and for that reason, even his thick lips and the long nose, even his snide remarks, made her feel at home. Now she believed she was really back.

Cammie quickly kissed her father, promised him to behave, to stay in touch, and to take care of herself. When her father's white Honda disappeared around the corner, Cammie grabbed the sides of the ice mobile and slowly lowered herself into the passenger's seat.

"Intermediate Girls' Dorm," Lieutenant Turner barked into the microphone on the dashboard.

The ice mobile jolted forward, gradually picking up speed. Cammie leaned against the soft leather cushion and let out a happy sigh. Finally she was back. There was the Zamboni parking lot on her right. They whooshed by Main Square without slowing down. Cammie only saw that there was some sort of a party—probably, a wedding reception—at the Main Rink.

The ice mobile turned to the left and plunged into a maze of side streets, all of which were named after different skating steps. They sped along a two-way street called Two Foot Glide. Next was Forward Crossovers Street that only allowed people to go forward. If a lost visitor went too far and missed Mohawk Lane going to the right, he had to stay on Forward Crossovers Street all the way down to the Loop Corner.

At its apex, the Loop Corner was connected with Back Crossovers Street that led all the way back to Main Square. Of course, Lieutenant Turner didn't have to worry about making proper turns. The police ice mobile was programmed to navigate around Skateland. They skidded along Lutz Avenue that, Cammie knew, led to the Blue Rink. Halfway along the avenue, the ice mobile turned right into the short Bracket Lane, leading to Axel Avenue. From that point on, everything looked familiar. Cammie's insides felt pleasantly warm when she recognized the roof of the Green Rink in the distance. The ice mobile glided past the Icy Park, and Cammie scowled, trying not to think of her last practice at the pond.

"Oh, I know how disillusionment feels," Bob Turner spoke up.

Cammie turned to him, startled.

"I could have become a champion too if it hadn't been for that darned triple axel," the young man said bitterly. "But who needs the sacrifice? Tell me."

Cammie shrugged. She didn't see the point.

"That buddy of mine—we always practiced together, you know—he ended up in Intensive Care. Triple axel, who needs it?"

"I'm sorry," Cammie said sincerely.

"Oh, you're sorry? Sweetheart, you don't need to be sorry for me. Think of yourself. I was great, you know. I came in second at the regionals; that's not shabby. I would have beaten all of them at the sectionals too, but with only a double axel, I didn't have a chance."

"But double axel is a difficult jump too. I only landed it a day before my competition." Cammie lowered her head. "And then I got injured," she said almost in a whisper.

"Well, it's your fault!" Bob spat out.

"An injury is never a skater's fault. It was Winja who attacked me!" Cammie gritted her teeth. Bob didn't sound sympathetic at all; instead, he was trying to blame her for whatever had happened.

"Oh, really?" Bob turned his reddened face from the road and glared at Cammie. "I saw you practicing in the park without your coach. You brought it upon yourself, and now you're an invalid. Your skating career is over, princess. Bye-bye, skating."

"No, it's not!" Cammie tried to look the young man in the eyes, but he stared at the road intently.

"Well, you may still be able to do forward crossovers, but anything beyond that—"

"Stop it, you jerk!" Cammie shouted at the top of her lungs. She felt tears welling up in her eyes already, but she wasn't going to cry, not in front of the stupid cop.

"You'd better show me some respect. I'm a cop, after all. You figure skating princesses don't like hearing the truth. Yet I'm not going to sugarcoat it for you. Start thinking of a different career, champ. Okay, here's your dorm. Go say good-bye to your buddies."

The ice mobile went to an abrupt stop in front of Cammie's dorm. Bob Turner slouched in the driver's seat, grinning wildly.

Her lips pressed tightly, Cammie slid into the soft, powdery snow and pulled down her Kanga bag. The lieutenant folded his arms on his chest, looking smug. He made no effort to help her. Trying not to step on her injured ankle, Cammie reached for her suitcase and dragged it to the ground. Bob watched her struggling with her heavy baggage, yet he stayed where he was.

Her head down, Cammie headed for the porch, pulling her two bags behind her. The cop's words hurt so deeply that she found it hard not to start bawling like a baby.

Halfway along the ice path, she let go of her bags, turned around, and faced Lieutenant Turner. "You know what, Bob Turner? You may have been a fine skater one day, and perhaps you're a good policeman now. But you're surely not a good person. In fact, you could become a perfect witch."

Bob's dark brown eyes rested on Cammie unblinkingly. "What did you just say?"

"You heard me. You think you're doing a good job protecting Skateland residents, but your heart is cold. And I'm sure you have no friends because no one would want to be around you."

"W-what?"

Cammie swirled around, grimaced as her right ankle twisted, and walked up the steps of the porch. Still fuming, she pressed the doorbell hard.

"Cammie!" Mrs. Page, bright-cheeked and round, enclosed her in a tight hug. "Oh, honey, it's so great to have you back. And look at you. You're back on your feet."

The dorm supervisor pulled Cammie inside then brought her luggage in too. Before closing the door behind her, Cammie looked back, expecting to see the empty street. However, the police ice mobile was still there. Lieutenant Turner sat in the driver's seat staring at Cammie.

The dorm lobby smelt of vanilla and cinnamon.

"They're in the dining room already, waiting for you," Mrs. Page said meaningfully as she helped Cammie slip out of her parka. "You'd better take off your skates too; there's no need to strain your ankle walking in them. I'll take your stuff up to your room and bring you your slippers. Now go to the dining room, and I'll serve you all tea. Then you can talk. By the way, I'm sure you haven't tried my new cookies yet. I've called them Kanga cookies, just like your bag, and they—"

"Hmm, I'm sorry, Mrs. Page, but who do you say is waiting for me in the dining room?" Cammie knew that if she hadn't interrupted Mrs. Page, the woman would have kept going on and on.

Mrs. Page clapped her hands. "Didn't I tell you? Mr. Reed and Alex, of course."

"Oh!" Cammie's fingers shook as she quickly unlaced her boots. She knew Mr. Reed wanted to see her, but she hadn't expected the meeting to happen so soon. Mr. Reed was a nice man. He had tremendous magical powers, but at the same time, he was very strict. Cammie wasn't sure the man wouldn't rebuke her for disobeying her coach. At least Alex would be part of the meeting too.

"Cammie, you're walking on your own!" Alex jumped off from behind the corner table and ran up to her.

"Oh, I don't need the crutches anymore," Cammie said nervously. "Hi, Mr. Reed."

Her eyes traveled to the corner table where Melvin Reed sat, tall and skinny, wearing a black turtleneck over tight black pants.

The older man stood up. "It's a pleasure to see you again, Cammie."

He shook Cammie's hand then pulled in a chair for her and waited for her to sit down. The man's blue eyes rested on Cammie's right ankle. She fidgeted slightly.

Mrs. Page walked in carrying a tray with a teapot, a sugar bowl, three cups, and a tray of cookies. The cookies really looked like Cammie's bag, and they had chocolate chips for eyes and noses.

"Does your leg hurt?" Mr. Reed asked sharply as he added sugar to his tea.

Cammie shrugged. "Not really."

"That's not the answer I want. I need a clear picture of what's going on."

Cammie squirmed. "Well, my ankle does get sore if I walk too much."

"How about skating?"

Cammie sighed. She had actually tried to skate at a public session at her old rink in Clarenceville, but her first attempt hadn't gone too well.

"I do skate, but…but my right foot won't hold the edge. It sort of buckles under me."

"Well, I read your doctor's report, and there's no reason why you shouldn't go back to competitive skating. In fact, with the R.O.F.A., I can guarantee you perfect recovery very soon."

"Rough…what?" Cammie had never heard the word before.

"R.O.F.A. It's a magical device I've invented. Actually, it's an abbreviation that stands for Restoring

Orthopedic Functions Aid. It works well both with common injuries and those caused by curses."

"Oh, great! How fast does your device work? Because the doctor said I'd need at least a year for rehabilitation." Cammie lowered her voice almost to a whisper.

Mr. Reed snorted. "Oh, it would only take a few minutes for the R.O.F.A. to do its job. In fact, the healing will be instantaneous."

"Awesome!" Alex yelled.

"So where is it? Have you brought it with you?" Cammie jumped to her feet, grimaced slightly at the sharp pain in her right ankle, and grabbed the edge of the table to steady herself.

Mr. Reed looked at her askance. "Not so fast. My R.O.F.A. does work miracles. The problem is, I don't have it in my possession."

Cammie blinked. "But—"

"Where is it?" Alex asked quickly.

Mr. Reed spread his arms. "That's it. I don't know."

"What do you mean?" Alex put his cup aside.

"I invented the R.O.F.A. several years ago, and I managed to help quite a few skaters. In fact, Wilhelmina, our honorable president, owes her outstanding spins and footwork to my magical device. Well, don't misunderstand me. Mrs. Van Uffeln was an accomplished skater once. Unfortunately, she developed a bad case of arthritis. Very soon she was confined to a wheelchair." Mr. Reed took a sip of his tea.

"But we saw Mrs. Van Uffeln skate; she's terrific," Alex said.

"She can skate because she used the R.O.F.A. to restore the functions of her limbs," Mr. Reed said. "After only two days of using the R.O.F.A., she no longer needed a wheelchair."

Cammie felt confused. "But she needs one now."

"Because the R.O.F.A. got lost. When Wilhelmina started getting worse again, I couldn't help her," Mr. Reed said gravely.

"What happened to the R.O.F.A.?" Alex asked.

Melvin Reed's shoulders drooped. "My mistake. I should have kept it in my house, of course. There is a lot of magical protection around my cabin. Remember the purple ice? No witch will ever think of coming close."

Cammie and Alex nodded simultaneously. They knew what the man was talking about.

"Instead, I left the R.O.F.A. in the Skating Museum." Mr. Reed slapped himself on the forehead. "It must have been a momentary lapse in judgment. Back then, the Skating Museum was open to the public. How could I assume the glass case would make the R.O.F.A. safe? The witches simply broke the glass and stole the device."

"But how did you know it was the witches?" Cammie asked.

Alex snorted. "It's obvious. Who else?"

Mr. Reed looked at Alex meaningfully. "You're right. Who else? But there's more evidence. Have you ever wondered how Winja manages to get along with about every bone in her body broken?"

Cammie gasped. "You mean—"

"She uses the R.O.F.A!" Alex exclaimed.

Mr. Reed nodded. "Exactly. As you may have already noticed, skating witches are extremely sly and manipulative, but they are hardly smart. They never expected me to find out that they had stolen the R.O.F.A. At the same time, Winja still makes people believe she's really in a lot of pain."

"Isn't she?" Cammie whispered. She had heard Winja whine and moan so many times.

Mr. Reed looked pensive. "Well, perhaps she does feel a certain amount of pain. With so many injuries, there has to be some discomfort. But trust me. She isn't half as sick as she claims to be. For all I know, my R.O.F.A. works wonders."

"So what can we do now?" Cammie asked softly. "Maybe we need to talk to the police?"

Mr. Reed grunted. "Skating witches have no respect for authority."

Alex clenched his fists. "Why can't we just corner them and—"

"And they'll tell us they don't have the R.O.F.A. Then what?" Mr. Reed said soberly.

"I didn't think of that." Alex looked disappointed.

"Of course, we're not giving up," Mr. Reed said. "I know the R.O.F.A. is somewhere in Skateland. So why don't you, Cammie, go after it?"

"Me?" Cammie gasped.

"But Mr. Reed, Cammie is still too weak to skate around," Alex said uncertainly.

Mr. Reed nodded. "I know that. But using the R.O.F.A is only part of the restoration process. As far as I understand, Cammie's injury was caused by Winja's curse."

Cammie nodded sadly.

"See? That's the reason it's taking the ankle so long to heal. On top of that, Cammie was cursed by the Witch of Pride."

Alex almost choked on his cookie. He coughed and put down his cup. "I knew nothing about pride. When did it happen?"

"The day before the competition. The Witch of Pride gave me some roses," Cammie said grimly. "I pricked my finger on a thorn and—"

"But you never told me about it!" There was reproach in Alex's green eyes.

"I wasn't so sure myself. Sonia did suspect something, but I…" Cammie turned to the older man. "Mr. Reed, how did you know?"

Mr. Reed twirled a Kanga cookie in his long fingers. "That was easy to figure out. People around you did notice something peculiar in your behavior."

Cammie felt Alex's intense gaze on her face. She looked down.

"Both Coach Ferguson and Mrs. Page were worried about you. So they called Mrs. Van Uffeln for advice, and she contacted me."

"What exactly did you do?" Instead of the notes of concern, there was a distinct sound of curiosity in Alex's voice.

"Hmm, it's kind of hard to explain." Cammie averted her eyes. Now looking back, she felt really ashamed of herself.

"She put a double axel into her program without her coach's permission. She bragged about her medal and her Charming Skater Prize. Was rude to her coach. Broke a couple of Skateland laws. Is there anything else I missed?" Mr. Reed looked amused.

Cammie wished she could crawl under the table. "I'm really sorry."

"I can see that. It's good, for repentance is the first and most important step to rehabilitation," Mr. Reed said. "Anyway, the reason I mentioned the Witch of Pride's involvement is that before dealing with your injury, you, Cammie, need to be delivered from the curse of pride. The curse of pride preceded the curse of injury anyway."

Alex raised his hand as though he were in a classroom. "How about P.O.P.? It means Pride Obliterating Potion. Wilhelmina...er...Mrs. Van Uffeln gave it to me last year. I was attacked by the Witch of Pride too."

Cammie nodded. Last year, the Witch of Pride had made Alex land a couple of triple jumps at the 1910 World Championships. The audience had been so impressed that they had almost named a jump after him.

Mr. Reed bowed his head. "Unfortunately, P.O.P. isn't going to work in Cammie's case."

"But why not?" Alex reached for another cookie.

"I'm sure Mrs. Van Uffeln explained to you that pride comes in different forms," Mr. Reed said.

"She did say that, yes," Alex said.

"Cammie has been under the influence of the curse of pride too long. Besides, Winja used it as the foundation for casting her own spell. So now it's a double curse. Therefore, what worked for you, Alex, will be ineffective in Cammie's situation. But I know something that will help you, Cammie. There is a rehabilitation technique called F.C.T., which is short for Full Circle Therapy."

Cammie wrinkled her forehead. "What is it?"

"You need to skate at every official practice rink in Skateland, one after another," Mr. Reed said.

Cammie looked at Alex, watched him shrug, and then turned back to Mr. Reed. "But what will that do?"

"Do you know how pride works?" the older man asked. "It robs the skater of her joy. Pure love for skating gets replaced with excessive competitiveness."

Cammie hung her head as she remembered bragging to everybody around her that she was the best skater ever.

"At this stage in your life, you need to go to the beginning, to relive the experience of someone who is learning to skate," Mr. Reed said. "You need to feel the simple, pure joy and love of skating—that's the best cure for pride. And you can do it by starting over again from scratch."

"But how can I do it?" Cammie asked helplessly.

"Your injury has robbed you of advanced skating moves and jumps," Mr. Reed said. "In some way, you have regressed to the beginner's stage.

"Oh, my—"

"Wait, don't get upset. It may actually work in your favor. Start anew. Go back to basic stroking, edges, turns; then move to simple jumps and spins."

"But what does visiting different rinks have to do with getting my joy back?" Cammie asked.

"Skateland rinks are magical," Mr. Reed said simply. "And those different colors of ice aren't random decorations. Each of the colors conveys a certain message. The order of visiting the rinks is particularly important. Start with the Pink Rink, where beginners skate. The pink color stands for joy. This is what you need, Cammie; you don't look like a happy skater to me now."

Cammie let out a deep sigh.

"Go to the Blue Rink afterward. The blue symbolizes innocence. You see, when children learn to skate, they know nothing about jealousy. Skating at the Blue Rink will get the excessive ambition out of your system. The Green Rink is next, and its color stands for freshness. Always remember that there is another day. No matter what happened yesterday, you need to be ready to start afresh tomorrow."

"That's right," Alex mumbled. Cammie knew her friend was thinking about his loss at the Annual Competition.

"The yellow color is symbolic of zeal. You have to be willing to give it all, Cammie. There is nothing wrong with the desire to be the best as long as it doesn't rob you of love and joy. Are you following me?"

Cammie nodded.

"Okay, so the color of the White Rink represents perfect technique. You see, nothing can hurt a flawless skater, neither the witches nor lapses in judgment. And then after technique comes beauty, which brings us to the Silver Rink. See how we have progressed from joy to beauty? Finally, when you're a beautiful skater, you're only a step away from perfection. But … " Mr. Reed made a long pause.

"What?" Cammie whispered.

"Don't you know?" There was a glitter in Mr. Reed's pale blue eyes.

Cammie saw Alex shrug.

"The Black Rink," Mr. Reed said almost triumphantly. "Yes, and don't look at me like that, Alex."

"But there's nothing good about the Black Rink," Alex said, furrowing his eyebrows.

"Unfortunately, beauty and evil often go hand in hand," Mr. Reed said.

"There's no way Cammie's going to the Black Rink," Alex said firmly.

Mr. Reed spread his arms. "It's a requirement."

"Come on!" Alex exclaimed. "You can't make Cammie walk right into the witches' territory."

"And why not?" Mr. Reed asked lightly. "She'll have to face the witches sooner or later. Remember, they are the ones who have stolen the R.O.F.A. So she might as well kill two birds with one stone: get the taste of evil by visiting the Black Rink and retrieve the magical device."

There was a deep silence as Cammie and Alex digested the information.

"And to finish on a high note, the Purple Rink comes last," Mr. Reed said cheerfully. "The purple color symbolizes integrity. A skater with a pure heart will do magic on ice; his performance will far exceed his technical aptitude. He will be able to make the audience cry and laugh, and this will be what we call perfect skating."

Cammie and Alex still didn't say anything.

"You know something, Cammie? Even though the witches have robbed you of your health and joy, you still have that kind of integrity in you. I sensed it the first time you came to my cabin; it's something that cannot be taught. And the day you skated your winning program at Skateland Annual Competition, I could see genuine love of skating shining through every move. This is the reason I gave you my Charming Skater Prize, even thought many skaters were stronger technically."

Cammie blinked and looked away so Mr. Reed wouldn't see her tears.

"You will be able to find the R.O.F.A. after you skate at the Black Rink," Mr. Reed said. "I won't even be surprised to find out that the witches are hiding it somewhere at the Black Rink. Be careful, though; they won't be eager to part with the R.O.F.A. But then after you get the device, come to the Purple Rink. A couple of laps around the purple ice, and you'll be all right, Cammie. This I can guarantee you."

Cammie took a deep breath. "Well...okay. I guess this is the only way. Although—"

Mr. Reed tilted his head. "What's the problem?"

"My leg is too weak." Cammie bent over and rubbed her ankle. "I simply can't see myself skating around Skateland. So I don't know—"

"Alex will be able to help you." Mr. Reed's pale eyes rested on Alex's excited face. "By the way, Alex, I talked to your coach and your teachers. You can take as much time off from school and practices as you need."

"Of...of course!" Alex exclaimed.

"And there's another thing that you'll find helpful," Mr. Reed said.

Cammie raised her head. "What's that?"

"Well, you'll see. In due time. Just remember: no matter how hopeless the situation may appear, there's always a way."

"But—" Alex looked as though he wanted to ask something else, but the older man stopped him with an intense look of his eyes.

"I've told you everything I can," Mr. Reed said.

"When are we supposed to start?" Now that Cammie realized she wouldn't have to visit every practice rink alone, she felt much better.

Mr. Reed gave her a look of surprise. "The sooner the better, of course. I know you can't wait to go back to competitive skating." Mr. Reed winked at Cammie and turned in the direction of the kitchen.

"Mrs. Page, do you think I could have another cup of your delicious tea?"

THE PINK RINK

"So are you ready to hit the Pink Rink?" Alex asked. He stood in front of Cammie's dorm, watching her take off her skate guards. Dressed in black pants and a new black-and-yellow parka, Alex looked trim and polished. Next to him, Cammie felt sluggish and unsteady. To give her injured ankle extra support, she had wrapped it in elastic bandage. Now her right foot was too tight, so Cammie had to loosen her laces. She wiggled her foot. Still, she couldn't say she was particularly comfortable.

"Uh-huh!" With a deep sigh, Cammie unlaced her right boot and then laced it up again.

She wasn't in a particularly good mood. Even though it was great to be back in Skateland, Cammie couldn't help feeling like an outsider. She had spent the previous evening chatting and gossiping with the other girls. They had discussed Sonia and Dana's perspectives at the Nationals.

Sonia was in first place after the short program, but who could expect anything different from her? Dana was in twelfth position—still pretty good for someone who was competing at the Nationals for the first time. The girls had been nice to Cammie; everybody had wished her a speedy recovery, and she had felt almost fine. Almost. Because this morning, when everybody had left for the Green Rink to practice, Cammie had stayed behind.

"Hey, are you all right?" Alex's green eyes looked dark with concern.

"Yeah." Cammie let out a deep sigh and stood up. She pushed herself forward. Well, at least she could still glide.

"Don't worry. We'll get you back in shape in no time. Ready?" Alex winked at her.

"Okay. Pink Rink!" Cammie said to Kanga, who stood faithfully by her side. The animal's yellow eyes flashed, signaling that it was ready.

The bag moved forward, with Cammie and Alex stroking slightly behind. Cammie did her best to appear confident. She tried to steady her right foot, though even the tight bandage couldn't keep it from wobbling. Still it was all right, if only Cammie could last all the way to the Pink Rink. Luckily, the rink was only fifteen minutes away, much closer to her dorm than the Green Rink.

I'll make it. I have to, Cammie said to herself. She felt her back moisten, even though it was cold. How come she had never realized basic stroking required a lot of effort?

Ten minutes later, Cammie felt she couldn't make another stroke. Her right ankle kept buckling under her; she was short of breath, gulping for air. On top of everything else, her right foot felt really tight. It was probably swelling up. Cammie slowed down, shifted her weight to the left side, trying to power pull forward. It helped, but only for a second. At some point she had to put her free foot down. Now her ankle felt sore.

"Do you want to take a break?" Alex skidded to a stop, facing Cammie.

She chewed on her lower lip, fighting tears. "I don't think I can make it. The doctor's probably right. I have to wait for my ankle to heal completely."

"But it'll take a year."

"Well, I have no choice." She pulled off her gloves and unzipped her parka, fighting for breath.

They stood in the middle of Toe Loop Avenue, right at the apex of the three turn. Cammie could see the round building of the Pink Rink. It looked like a huge pink cake decorated with whiffs of white whipped cream. Little skaters ranging from three to about seven years old, most of them accompanied by their parents, could be seen approaching the building from all directions. The rink was so close; if only she could take another step.

"Should we ask for help?" Alex looked around frantically.

The wind picked up. Cammie shivered and zipped up her parka. "I'll rest a little and then skate back to the dorm. And you can still go to your practice, so—"

"Hey, I've got an idea. Kanga!" Alex shouted.

Cammie stared at him. "What?"

"Your bag. Remember how Mr. Reed said that no matter how difficult the situation might be, we would always be able to find help. And I bet he knew why you needed this bag."

"What're you talking about?" Perplexed, Cammie stared at Kanga, who sat comfortably only a couple of feet away from her.

"Grab the handle with both hands."

Cammie put on her gloves and squeezed the handle. The metal surface felt cold.

"Now give Kanga the directions again."

Oh! Now Cammie was beginning to understand. "Pink Rink!" she said loudly.

The bag jolted forward and glided smoothly in the direction of the Pink Rink, pulling Cammie behind.

"It worked!" Alex yelled from behind her. She heard the scratching of his blades against the ice path as he caught up with her.

Cammie felt her lips spread into a smile. Skating behind Kanga felt wonderful. Terrific. All she had to do was keep both feet steady, and the bag pulled her forward really fast. At some point, Kanga picked up speed, leaving Alex behind.

"Woohoo!" Cammie shouted. She looked back at the grinning Alex and gave him a big wave.

He waved back. "Your ride is over, champ."

"What?" She looked around, and at the same moment Kanga skidded to a sharp stop. "Oops!" Cammie slipped but managed to stay on her feet. "I loved it, Alex," Cammie said as she sat down on the step to put on her skate guards.

"Think you could handle a longer trip? Because other rinks are farther away."

"Absolutely. It's so much easier than skating on your own. Wheels!" Cammie told Kanga.

The blades disappeared inside the animal's belly; now that they were inside the building, the bag rode on two sets of plastic wheels.

"Oops!" Alex, who walked slightly ahead of Cammie, stopped as though he had hit an invisible wall.

Forced to stop so suddenly, Cammie tripped and grimaced at the dull pain in her right foot. "Ouch!"

"Security!" a deep male voice barked at them.

Cammie looked around, expecting to see a big menacing-looking man, but there wasn't a living soul in the lobby. Instead, she saw a huge computer monitor with pink letters running across the dark screen: "Please, identify yourself."

"Alex Bernard," Alex said dutifully.

"But my name is probably not on their list," he whispered to Cammie.

"You may come in. Please wear your visitor's pass," the disembodied voice said. There was a click, and a pink badge appeared on the tray in front of the monitor.

Cammie gave her name to the computer and was also given a pink visitor's pass. As she twirled it in her hands, she saw that the pass said, "Cammie Wester." Underneath it was written, "Pinky's Friend."

She grinned. "How cute! But we don't have security at the Green Rink. It's probably because of all the little kids here, right?"

Alex pinned the pass to his black sweater. "We do have security at the Yellow Rink, and I'm sure your rink has it too. It's a new policy. We've only had it for two months."

"Two months?" Cammie grabbed Alex's hands. "Gosh, I think it's because of me. They don't want any more witches' attacks."

Alex looked very serious. "I knew that from the beginning. You see—"

"I want a bear too, Mommy!" a childish voice said from behind Cammie.

As she looked back, she found herself staring in the huge blue eyes of a little girl wearing a pink parka. The girl couldn't be more than five years old, and she pointed to Cammie's skating bag.

"Me too!" Another girl looking exactly like the first appeared from behind a tall, elegantly dressed woman.

"It's not a bear; it's a kangaroo." The woman appeared tired. "And I wouldn't say *no* to a bag like that myself. These wheels give me a hard time."

As the lady pointed to her own skating bag, Cammie remembered seeing the woman and her twin daughters before on the day of Skateland Annual Competition.

"Can I have a bag like this, Mommy?" one of the girls asked.

"It's too expensive. Cammie only has it because she's a champion," the lady said.

Cammie felt her cheeks flush. She hoped the lady wasn't staying for practice. Some champion Cammie was, not even being able to stroke properly. The little girls eyed Cammie with awe.

"Are you skating at our rink now, Cammie?" One of the girls raised her head to look Cammie in the eyes. Her pink hat with pom poms slid off her head and fell on the floor.

"Hmm, just today," Cammie mumbled.

"Why?" the other girl asked.

"Cindy, leave Cammie alone. She's not feeling good."

Cammie caught the woman's quick look at her ankle.

"Sandy, it's time to get on the ice. Coach Greg will be upset if the two of you are late."

"We aren't late!" Cindy and Sandy ran in the direction of the locker rooms, their skate guards clomping against the floor.

The girls' mother smiled. "Have fun, Cammie. And you ... hmm, I don't know your name."

"It's Alex."

"Okay, I'll see the two of you there." The woman followed her daughters to the locker room.

Cammie shook her head. "Great. What will she think of me now? I look like a beginner."

Alex winked at her, looking amused. "She told you to have fun, didn't she?'

They walked through the glass double doors to the arena. The Pink Rink was smaller than the Green Rink but very cozy. The walls were decorated with figures of animals wearing skates. Lamps shaped like flowers hung from the ceiling, casting a soft glow on the light-pink ice.

About fifteen children—ten girls and five boys—skated around the rink. The girls wore pink skating dresses; the boys skated in black pants and pink shirts with black bow ties. Cindy and Sandy were also among the little skaters. They zoomed so fast across the arena that Cammie was afraid the girls would crash with other kids. Yet Cindy and Sandy could maneuver surprisingly well for their age. From time to time there were ripples of applause from the skaters' parents, who were seated comfortably in the bleachers. Even from where she stood, Cammie could see how comfortable the soft burgundy seats looked.

"Welcome to the Pink Rink!"

Cammie and Alex turned around at the same time. A slender man with dark thinning hair eyed them with a kind smile. "I'm head coach at the Pink Rink. My name is Coach Greg. What should I call you guys?"

"Cammie."

"Alex."

"Well, I know who Cammie is, of course. And I saw Alex at the Annual Competition too. Very good jumps." Coach Greg smiled at Alex, and Cammie thought she really liked the man. He appeared to be genuinely happy to see the two of them at his rink.

"All right, pinkies, let's start our practice!" Coach Greg clapped his hands.

The little skaters lined up in the middle of the rink.

"You guys are guests here, so you're free to do whatever you want," the man said to Cammie and Alex.

"I still have problems stroking properly. My ankle is too weak," Cammie said timidly.

"Well, the basic moves we do here may be just what you need." Coach Greg winked at Cammie and skated to the middle of the rink.

Cammie watched the coach lead the little skaters in a series of simple moves, including stroking, one- and two-foot glides, squatting, shoot the duck, beginner spirals, and three turns.

"Come on; let's join them." Alex pulled Cammie by the hand.

"I don't think I'm as good as the pinkies." Cammie laughed apprehensively.

"Sure you are. Come on."

Alex skated to the middle. Cammie had no choice but to follow him. She did her best to concentrate on Coach Greg's instructions. Her right foot refused to hold a clean edge, but as she kept trying, she felt steadier and more secure. Her body probably still remembered the ABCs of skating. Before Cammie knew it, she skated freely along with the tots and even managed to pick up some speed.

"Are you guys ready for bunny hops?" Coach Greg asked.

He demonstrated the jump. "It's very simple. Let's think of ourselves as bunnies jumping over a brook. The important thing is to jump off your toe and land on the other toe."

Alex chuckled next to Cammie. "It surely brings back memories, huh?"

She didn't say anything. There was no way she could pull off a jump, even as simple as the bunny hop. Coach Greg did another bunny hop, this time very slowly, emphasizing each individual move. As he moved forward, he recited a poem.

> Let us do a bunny hop.
> Pick up speed, and do not stop.
> Go fast. You can't be slow.
> Jump and land on your right toe.
> Kick and step on your left blade.
> Go ahead; don't be afraid.
> You are good; the jump is done.
> It's not scary; this is fun.

The excited little skaters chirped like birds as they tried to imitate the coach's moves. Most kids had no problem landing a bunny hop on their first try.

There were a few, however, who leaned forward too much or tripped over their toe picks and fell. Coach Greg moved from one little skater to another, leading them gently through the moves.

"So what are you waiting for?" Alex did a huge bunny hop and waved his arms at Cammie, obviously encouraging her to do the same.

Cammie shook her head weakly. She felt terrified. She couldn't even think of jumping on her injured ankle.

"It's not a triple, you know." Alex stood by her side, his arm stretched toward her.

She hung her head, feeling miserable. Even the five-year-olds were better than her.

"Would you like to try it at the boards?" Alex asked.

She nodded quickly and skated to the edge of the rink. She grabbed the boards hard with both hands. Slowly, tentatively, she walked through the motions, rising on her left toe, swinging her right leg, and gently putting it down. Her body remembered how to do it, but would her ankle handle the impact?

"Now let go of the boards!"

It was easy for Alex to say. Cammie's fingers clutched the boards tight; she couldn't even unclasp her hands. "Maybe next time."

"Having trouble, Cammie? Let me help you." Coach Greg had approached her. "Hold my hand. Go ahead. Now repeat after me. Let us do a bunny hop…"

Cammie couldn't see how reciting the poem could help, but she said the words out loud after the coach. Amazingly, as she heard the sound of her own voice, she wasn't that scared anymore.

"Don't just step; jump. It's easier that way. And don't be afraid. You aren't going to fall. Ready? Let us do a bunny hop…"

Grasping Coach Greg's hand, Cammie leaped forward. She was fine. She grinned widely.

"Good girl. Let's try it again," the coach said.

Cammie didn't even remember at what moment exactly the man had let go of her hand. Her fear was gone. She skimmed over the ice in perfect leaps, feeling as light as a feather.

"Yes!" she shouted without stopping. With the corner of her eye, she could see Alex clapping. The little skaters leaped around her like a flock of robins. Feeling perfectly happy, Cammie lifted her eyes to the last row of seats. She pictured herself skating in front on a big audience.

Well, there was an audience at the rink already, and not just the parents from the front rows. Some people also sat in the back row; who could they be? Skating parents usually sat as close to their kids as possible. But Cammie could clearly see two dark silhouettes in the back row, both tall and skinny. Cammie's eyes glided along the second person's ghost-like face; it had to be a woman. Cammie's eyes slid down to the lady's long limbs. She saw bandages…

"Winja!" Cammie screamed. Her right ankle gave out, and she fell.

"Cammie, are you all right?" Alex knelt next to her, panic written all over his face.

Cammie glanced at her ankle. It was a little sore, but it didn't feel as though Cammie had reinjured it.

"I…I think so."

"Pinkies, I want you to stay in the middle!" Coach Greg's voice came from a distance. "Cammie, do you need help?" The coach now stood next to her.

Cammie got up slowly. "No, no, I'm fine. But there are witches up there. See?" She pointed her trembling hand in the direction of the stands.

Coach Greg's face registered confusion. "What?" He looked up and then back at Cammie and shrugged. "There's nobody there."

Cammie swallowed hard. The coach was right. The stands were empty.

"You must have thought that was a witch!" Alex pointed to the drawing of a skating monkey on the wall.

Somehow, Cammie didn't think it was a laughing matter. Her face turned hot. "No, honestly."

Her words were interrupted by a loud scream.

"What?" Cammie swirled around and yelled too.

The Witch of Fear stood on the ice, her long hair flowing around her wrinkled face. She held little Cindy in her arms. The little girl squealed at the top of her lungs, kicking her legs against the witch's body. Yet the evil woman somehow managed to dodge the blows.

"Let the girl go!" Coach Greg leaped at the witch.

The Witch of Fear didn't even wink, eyeing the man with cold contempt.

"One wrong move, and we will curse the girl." Winja stepped from behind the Witch of Fear. She leaned on one crutch; the other was pointed straight at Cindy.

Coach Greg went into a quick hockey stop. "Do you mean you will really attack a five-year-old?"

Cammie saw that the man's hands were clasped in tight fists.

"Coach Greg!" Cindy whined. The little girl's face was red; tears streamed down her face.

"If you hurt Cindy, you'll have to answer to me," Coach Greg said.

"Oh relax, Greg. It's not the toddler we're after. We want her." The Witch of Fear nodded in Cammie's direction.

"She's almost dead anyway, so what's the big deal?" Winja said lazily.

Cammie could almost feel the witch's cold fingers close around her neck. The pink walls spun around her; she slowly lowered herself onto the ice.

"Oh, that's better. You're giving up, huh?" the Witch of Fear's cold voice said. "Now come here, girl. You have every reason to be afraid."

Now that's it. I really don't have a choice, Cammie thought. *If I don't surrender, the witches will attack Cindy. I can't let that happen.*

"Okay," she said weakly. "I'm coming."

She stood up, feeling how unsteady her legs were. She took two tentative steps in the direction of the witches.

Cindy cried loudly. Somewhere behind her, Cammie heard Sandy join her sister in a loud wail.

Cammie felt a draught behind her, and the next thing she saw was Winja collapse flat on her stomach, screeching wildly. A split second later, Coach Greg snatched the bawling Cindy out of the Witch of Fear's grasp. Alex's face appeared behind the witch's back as he kicked the woman hard on her behind.

Cammie grimaced, expecting the witch to break in half, but nothing happened to the evil woman. Instead, the Witch of Fear dropped herself into a lunge position and glided forward, picking up more and more speed. As she passed the moaning Winja, she reached for the crutch in Winja's hand and pulled hard. With alarming speed, the two witches did a circle around the rink and then headed for the exit. A couple of seconds later, they blended with the darkness behind the door that led to the lobby.

Cindy was still crying as Coach Greg gently put her down. "You're safe now. Don't cry." The man rummaged in his pocket and took out a big candy shaped like a skating dog. "I wonder what this tastes like."

Immediately, the little girl stopped crying.

"I want a candy too, Coach Greg." Sandy was now by the coach's side staring at his pocket.

He grunted good-naturedly. "I'm sure everybody needs one."

He gave all kids, including Cammie and Alex, a candy in the shape of a skating animal. Cammie's was a green crocodile.

Alex gave Cammie a playful nudge on the side. "Because my blades are sharp like a spear, I kicked the witches in the rear."

She almost broke in half with laughter as she thought of the card Alex had sent her. Her trembling had subsided; she could finally breathe.

"Now how about some pairs skating?" Coach Greg shouted. He took Cindy in his arms and glided around the rink, picking up speed. As he bent his knees, getting close to the ice, he swung Cindy wildly. The little girl screamed with, probably, a mixture of delight and fear. After taking the child around the rink twice, the coach repeated the same with Sandy and then everybody else in the group. Only Cammie and Alex were exempt from the thrilling exercise.

"I think you guys are a little heavy for me," Coach Greg told them after the kids left for the locker rooms. "Unless you absolutely want to, of course."

Cammie laughed. "Oh, we're fine. Thank you."

"Good. I'm glad you aren't hurt." The coach frowned a little. "What was that about the witches, though? How did they manage to sneak in? I was sure the new security measures worked."

Cammie hung her head. "It's my fault."

"What're you talking about?" Alex cried out.

Coach Greg looked sober. "Did you let the witches in?"

"Oh, of course not!" Cammie ran her hand across her face. "What I mean is the witches are after me, and now Cindy almost got hurt. I probably shouldn't come to any of the practice rinks. Innocent people can suffer. I guess I just need to give up."

She bit her lower lip, trying not to cry.

"Don't you say that!" Coach Greg said passionately. "It's not your fault that the witches want to destroy skaters' careers. And if you give up now, the witches will win. Is that what you want?"

"No!" Cammie pressed her hands to her chest. She felt slightly better. At least Coach Greg didn't blame the witches' visit on her.

"But I'm still concerned about the lapse in security," the coach said pensively. "How did the witches manage to walk past the security computer? I want to check it out."

The coach walked out of the arena into the lobby, Cammie and Alex following close behind. As they approached the computer at the front door, Coach Greg positioned himself behind the counter and clicked the mouse several times.

"Okay, here you go … Pink Rink Eligibility List updated last night … I see your names on the list, guys … no!"

"What?" Alex stepped behind the counter and peered behind Coach Greg's shoulder. "I can't believe it!"

"What's wrong?" Cammie joined her friend. As she looked at the long list of names, she too couldn't suppress a shriek. At the bottom of the list were three more than familiar names: Winja, the Witch of Fear, and the Witch of Confusion.

"But how is it possible? Who entered the witches' names?" Cammie asked Coach Greg.

"I don't know," he said crossly. "This is something I must find out. But honestly, I think the witches did it themselves. They must have found a way to tamper with the program."

"But why does it say Witch of Confusion?" Alex asked slowly. "She wasn't even at the rink."

Coach Greg looked up. "No, she wasn't in the arena for sure. Hey, you know what? That's the key."

The coach raised his shining black eyes to Alex. "The Witch of Confusion wasn't at the rink because at that moment; she was right here in the lobby tampering with the computer. She must have infected the computer with Babel. It's a really nasty virus that allows you to enter any kind of data in the computer against the program settings."

"I would never think the witches were good with computers." Cammie found herself thinking about the witches with some sort of respect.

Coach Greg smiled sadly. "Unfortunately, they are. The curses not only work on human beings but on computers too. Don't underestimate the witches; they are pretty smart. And almost all of them are decent skaters too. But tell me, what good are excellent brains and strong technical skills if you use them to do evil?"

THE BLUE RINK

Cammie grabbed the handles of her bag and patted Kanga on the furry head. "Ready to go? Blue Rink!"

Kanga flashed its yellow eyes and dashed forward, leaving two perfect tracings on the ice path behind. Cammie glided behind the bag along Lutz Avenue. It was just Kanga and her. Though Alex had suggested coming by Cammie's dorm to pick her up, Cammie had refused. No, she would be fine. Kanga would be with her. She had to learn to move around Skateland on her own, didn't she? Besides, the Blue Rink was really close to the boys' dorm, so why couldn't Alex simply meet Cammie in front of the rink?

Cammie squeezed the handle tighter. Gliding behind Kanga was easy; it was wonderful. Now Cammie didn't have to worry about her ankle giving out. Feeling excited, she began to hum a tune from

The Sound of Music, adjusting the tempo of her song to Kanga's smooth glide. A loud whistle on her left caused Cammie to let her left hand momentarily slip off the handle. She tripped and almost fell. Her right hand still clung to the handle, though, and Kanga pulled her forward at a weird angle. Cammie's body careened to the right, her left foot came off the ice, and she fell. Kanga rumbled loudly and stopped. Cammie could swear the animal was rebuking her.

"What was that?" Slowly, Cammie unclasped her right hand and got up, brushing the snow off her pants.

"Your buddies. Who else?"

A large brown figure blocked Cammie's way. For a split second, Cammie thought that Kanga had somehow grown to the size of a grizzly bear. But then she saw that the huge creature was the Witch of Pride wearing a brown fur coat.

How many fur coats does she have? Cammie thought.

"Oh no, not so fast!" the witch sang as Cammie took a quick step to the left. "Not until we have a little talk."

"We have nothing to talk about!" Cammie glanced in Kanga's direction. The bag was only four feet away, but the Witch of Pride towered between them.

"Look, I'm not here to scare you. I just want to offer you a little deal." The Witch of Pride's voice sounded almost sweet.

"Get out of my way!"

The Witch of Pride looked disappointed. "Well, if you prefer it this way." With a casual shrug, the witch did a quick side hop, and Winja stepped forward. "How about breaking the other ankle? Just for symmetry, huh?"

Winja's gaunt fingers closed around one of her crutches.

"No!" If it weren't for her weak ankle, Cammie could skate around the witches easily, but now ...

Gr-rr-rr! Something leaped at Cammie. Kanga had somehow pushed its way between the witches' legs and now stood right by Cammie's side. There was an unmistakable glint in the animal's eyes, as though the animal was encouraging Cammie to catch the handle.

The minute Cammie's hands squeezed the cold metal, Kanga did a quick U-turn and rushed in the direction of the Blue Rink with speed that equaled only that of an ice mobile.

Behind Cammie, the witches let out a yelp.

"What the heck was that?" Winja's startled voice sounded.

Cammie didn't hear the Witch of Pride's answer, for in a couple of seconds, Kanga had managed to put quite a respectable distance between Cammie and her pursuers. A short glide, a fast turn, and there it was—the rectangular building of the Blue Rink. The whole structure was painted pale blue, and the roof was deep navy.

As Kanga braked in front of the porch, Cammie let go of the handle and rubbed her numb hands.

"Wow, that was some ride. Thank you, Kanga. I'm sorry I didn't like you in the beginning."

The animal didn't say anything, but Cammie somehow knew it understood her.

"Problem is, we're late." Cammie pressed Kanga's button that replaced the blades on its paws with wheels, put on her skate guards, and walked through the double door. A security computer similar to the one she had seen at the Pink Rink greeted her in the lobby. Cammie was allowed to pass without a problem. She looked around at a spacious atrium with a small fountain and two aquariums where small, multicolored fish chased one another.

"Cammie, where were you?" A very concerned-looking Alex ran up to her.

"I met a couple of witches on my way here," Cammie said nonchalantly. She grinned as she saw her friend's face redden.

"What?"

Cammie briefly told Alex what had happened to her. As Alex listened to her story, his face expression changed from panic to surprise and finally to excitement.

"I should have been with you, of course. But Kanga!" He patted the animal appreciatively.

When Cammie and Alex walked into the rink area, the practice session was in full swing. Cammie knew that the Blue Rink was the training ground of pre-pre-liminary and preliminary-level skaters. As she watched about fifteen boys and girls spinning and jumping on the pale blue ice, she admitted sadly that at this point, she wasn't up to their level. Cammie also noticed that most of the skaters were younger than her. There were only two girls who appeared to be about fifteen; the rest of the kids ranged from eight to eleven.

"Welcome to the Blue Rink. My name is Coach Betsy." A short, plump woman skated up to them. Though petite, the lady spoke in a very low voice, and there was a commanding presence in the way the coach carried herself.

"You must be Cammie. And what's your name?" The coach glanced at Alex.

Alex looked a little shy. "It's Alex. Uh, I'm Cammie's friend, just helping her to get around."

Coach Betsy nodded energetically. She had dark curly hair and sharp brown eyes. "Yes, I'm aware of Cammie's condition. Mr. Reed called me and explained everything about your rehabilitation, Cammie. I'll be very happy to help you, and I'm sure Alex will enjoy practicing at our rink too."

"Thank you. I will," Alex said quickly, though Cammie could see he felt slightly out of place at the rink filled with younger kids.

Coach Betsy turned to Cammie. "I saw you at the Annual Competition. You're a very strong skater both technically and artistically. How does your ankle feel now?"

Cammie raised her right foot. "I think it's getting stronger. I even did bunny hops at the Pink Rink yesterday."

Her ankle really did feel better, perhaps because riding behind Kanga had relieved it of some of the strain.

"That's a start," Coach Betsy said. "Well, how about doing some moves in the field first? Alex, I think you can demonstrate for us today."

The corners of Alex's mouth twitched; Cammie could tell that her friend was really pleased. All skaters liked demonstrating difficult moves to their friends. Being singled out by a coach meant that you had mastered a certain element…well, almost to the point of perfection.

As the coach led the group through a series of edges, forward and backward crossovers, three turns, and waltz eights, Cammie felt herself at home right away. Those were the moves she had struggled with so much when she had first started taking skating lessons five years ago. And it was with pre-preliminary moves that Alex and she had managed to destroy the witches' curses three years ago during their first visit to Skateland.

As Cammie looked back at her struggles and victories, she felt more and more confident. Pre-preliminary moves were already part of her; there was no way she could slip off her edge even if her ankle wasn't strong enough.

"Need help?" Alex asked as he skated past Cammie doing backward inside edges.

"I'm fine." Cammie was breathing hard. With her injury, she needed extra effort to stay secure on her edges, yet she had no doubt she was going to succeed.

Halfway through the session, Cammie finally managed to go through every pre-preliminary pattern.

Coach Betsy skated up to Cammie, her eyes sparkling. "I've been watching you, Cammie, and I can tell that you're quite a fighter."

"I slip off the right foot a lot." Panting, Cammie unzipped her warm-up jacket. "I used to do these moves just like him."

Cammie nodded in Alex's direction. Her friend glided across the ice in fast backward crossovers, the eyes of younger girls were glued to his tall figure.

Coach Betsy squeezed Cammie's hand. "Trust me. Everything will come back. Now why don't we take a look at that ankle?"

"Okay." Cammie was grateful for the suggestion. Her right foot was actually beginning to throb in her tight boot.

As Cammie took off her boot, she saw that her injured ankle was really swollen. She prodded it with her finger and grimaced.

"I'll get you an ice pack." Coach Betsy walked away from Cammie.

Cammie wrapped her parka around her shoulders to stay warm and looked around the rink. A tall girl with a long brown braid was warming up with backspins close to the exit. Cammie was sure she had seen the girl before.

"Heather!" Cammie shouted, perhaps louder than she wanted, because everybody at the rink looked in her direction.

"Cammie!" Heather jumped off the ice and ran up the steps to join Cammie in the bleachers.

"I'm so sorry I left the hospital without saying good-bye to you, but—"

Cammie brushed her off. "I know. I know. Dr. Eislaufer told me everything. See, he discharged me the same day."

Heather nodded. "Yeah, I came back a week later asking about you, and you were gone. So how is your ankle?"

Cammie briefly told her about Mr. Reed's rehabilitation technique. As she went on, Heather's eyes grew wider and wider.

"I like it! Wow, Cammie, you're going to skate again!" Heather gave Cammie a big hug.

"Sure. And it's great that you are back at the rink."

"Yeah, I'm done with my physical therapy and working on my axel again. So how about the witches?" Heather asked, keeping her voice low.

"Heather, I'm waiting for you!" Coach Betsy stood on the ice, looking stern.

Heather jumped up. "Uh, it's time for my lesson. Perhaps we could talk later, okay?"

With an excited wave, the girl rushed back and skated up to the coach. Cammie watched her hospital buddy go through waltz jump-loop combinations with a mixture of excitement and jealousy. Apparently, Heather was really serious about landing her axel.

"Come on. You can do it!" Cammie whispered as the girl finished her waltz jump with a backspin.

"Now try an axel. And don't be afraid," Coach Betsy said.

Heather leaped off her left forward outside edge. The beginning looked good, but then the girl landed forward on both feet. Cammie could tell Heather was still afraid of reinjuring her ankle.

Coach Betsy was patient. She led Heather through more preparation exercises. Twice she asked Alex to perform an axel, which he did with strength and ease. As Cammie watched Alex fly across the ice, her whole body longed to do the same. Why couldn't she? She was still a skater.

Cammie looked at her right ankle then slowly removed the ice pack. The swelling had subsided. Cammie smoothed out her sock and pushed the foot into her skating boot. It didn't hurt. Perhaps she could skate some more.

"Yes!" Coach Betsy shouted.

Cammie looked down. Heather stood beside her coach, her cheeks flushing. "Did I land it?"

"What, you aren't sure? Do another, then." The woman nudged Heather forward.

With a shy smile, Heather began to circle the ice in backward crossovers. She bent her left knee, jumped forward, and did a quick one-and-a-half rotation. The landing was a little shaky, but Heather didn't put her free foot down. Though not textbook perfect, it was definitely an axel.

Cammie applauded loudly. Heather glanced in her direction, and Cammie gave the girl an enthusiastic thumbs-up. Unable to sit still any longer, Cammie quickly walked down and stepped onto the ice.

"Cammie, aren't you supposed to rest?" Coach Betsy sounded surprised.

"My ankle isn't swollen anymore. Thank you." Cammie gave the ice pack back to the woman.

"Well, if you want to practice some more, there are still ten minutes left. How about power threes?"

"Uh, could I try an axel? No, please!" From the way the coach's eyes widened, Cammie knew she had a lot of persuading to do.

"Cammie, no! You aren't ready for an axel."

"But it used to be my best jump. I'm sure—"

"Absolutely not. Try it, and you're out of here." Coach Betsy no longer sounded sweet. Her voice became slightly hoarse, and the way the coach's eyes glared at Cammie was strangely familiar. Someone had already talked to Cammie like that. Cammie had ignored it, and…

Cammie let out a quick, "Oh," as she remembered how Coach Ferguson had warned her against trying a triple salchow.

"I'm sorry," Cammie said quickly. "Of course, I…" She swallowed hard, trying not to cry. Feeling her eyes moisten, she turned around and skated in the direction of the exit.

"Wait!" Coach Betsy said.

Cammie looked back. The coach eyed her without a smile.

"Would you like to try a waltz jump?" Coach Betsy asked.

Cammie cringed. "Really?"

"Try it at the boards first. Use your left hand to steady yourself...Good."

Cammie walked through the jump the way she remembered doing it when she had first started skating. Her right ankle was a little stiff, but the feeling of riding out from a jump gliding on the right backward outside edge was familiar, comfortable.

"Alex, do you mind holding Cammie's hand? Cammie, try to jump, but not too high."

Alex squeezed Cammie's right wrist. She bent her left knee and did a small hop. She landed without a problem, even though the heart pounded in her chest as though ready to escape.

"How does it feel?" Coach Betsy asked.

Cammie grinned. "Wonderful."

Heather stared at her, her eyes full of joy.

"Ready to try it on your own?" Coach Betsy asked.

Cammie nodded and moved forward, trying to keep her right foot steady. She did a Mohawk to change direction; it was a little shaky. Never mind. She would work on it. She stepped forward with her left foot and went up. The jump was tiny, and it was still a jump, not a three turn.

"Woohoo!" Alex threw his arms in the air.

The skaters working on axels and double salchows stopped in the middle of their practices and stared at Cammie. She looked down, feeling blood rush to her cheeks. She surely hadn't done anything outstanding, just a very small beginner's waltz jump.

Coach Betsy put her hand on Cammie's shoulder. "That was a terrific jump, Cammie. And I know you will be doing doubles again soon. I enjoyed working with you. Remember that you and Alex are welcome at the Blue Rink anytime. Perhaps working on pre-preliminary moves will be good for your rehabilitation."

"Thank you, Coach Betsy. I really would like to practice here more," Cammie said sincerely. "But now I have to visit every official practice rink in Skateland before I can go back to skating full time."

"I know what you mean." The coach nodded energetically. "Mr. Reed explained the procedure to me. So good luck to you, and I hope to see you in good health."

The woman looked at Alex and smiled warmly. "Thank you for demonstrating for us today, Alex. Now take care of yourself and Cammie."

RAINBOW RINKS

Alex wouldn't take no for an answer. "I'll skate to the Green Rink with you, Cammie, and this is my final word. Don't you realize that the witches want to finish you off?"

He was right, of course, and Cammie chose not to argue any longer. She was excited about going to the Green Rink. It was like coming back home; in fact, she was sure she could find the place with her eyes closed. And yet with Kanga's help, they reached the place in only thirty minutes instead of forty.

Alex was impressed. "Kanga is almost as fast as the ice mobile. Hey, what are we going to do? We're early."

"I wanted to come before everybody else gets here," Cammie said.

"Why?"

Cammie said nothing. She stared at the familiar green carpet in the lobby and at the rows of potted plants on both sides. The light green surface of the ice glittered faintly behind the glass wall. The lights were dimmed.

Cammie looked around. "Alex, go ahead; skate. I want to talk to Coach Ferguson first."

"Are you sure?" Alex opened the door, letting in a draft of cold air.

Cammie nodded. "I need to make it up with her before I go on with my rehabilitation. Remember what Mr. Reed said about the curse of pride?"

As the door closed behind Alex, Cammie pressed her forehead against the glass, watching her friend do strong power pulls. Even in her better days she probably wouldn't have been able to skate with such power.

The entrance door slammed. Cammie looked back abruptly. Coach Ferguson walked in her direction wearing a dark-green jacket and dark pants.

"Cammie?" Coach Ferguson's eyes rested on Cammie's feet. "I thought you weren't ready to skate yet."

"No, I mean I can, but…" Cammie stammered; her voice trailed away. She had been rehearsing her speech for so long. But now that her coach stood so close to her, Cammie had no idea what to say.

Something flickered in the woman's eyes. "Why don't we go to my office and talk? I need a cup of coffee anyway."

Cammie watched Coach Ferguson unlock the door that had her name engraved in silver lettering.

"Would you like something to drink too? Tea or maybe hot chocolate?" the coach suggested.

Cammie shook her head.

"How about candy?"

With a quick, "Thank you," Cammie took a bright green candy from a bowl on the coach's desk. The candy was shaped like a leaf with "Green Rink" written across its surface.

"Coach Ferguson, I…" Cammie desperately looked for the right thing to say.

"I'm listening, Cammie." The woman added milk to her coffee.

"I wanted to apologize to you." Cammie's face turned so hot that tears clouded her eyes, blurring her vision.

Coach Ferguson sipped her coffee. "Why? Because you broke your ankle and now your skating career is in jeopardy? Is that what you're trying to say?"

Cammie swallowed hard, trying not to cry. "I shouldn't have disobeyed you. I know you wanted the best for me. And I was rude. I…" There she was crying again. She hung her head, staring at her boots.

"So how does your leg feel now? Here." Coach Ferguson pushed a box of Kleenex toward Cammie.

Cammie took a tissue and blew her nose. "I'm allowed to skate, though my ankle is still weak. Mr. Reed says I need a special restoration device."

Coach Ferguson nodded. "So I heard. Mr. Reed spoke to me. I do believe in his expertise. So when you're ready, Cammie, I'll be glad to have you back. Although it's not always easy to work with you."

The coach smiled for the first time. Cammie tried to smile back, but her lips shook.

"You're a talented skater, Cammie, but your excessive zeal often gets in the way of your progress. See, if you had obeyed me, we wouldn't be having this conversation now. Instead, you would be out there working on your triples." Coach Ferguson nodded in the direction of the ice.

Cammie followed the woman's look. From the window of the coach's office, she could see Green Rink skaters laughing, taking off their skate guards, and stepping onto the ice.

"But you said I wasn't ready for triples," Cammie said.

A look of annoyance appeared on the coach's face. "I *was* going to start you on triples, but only when you were ready, not when you wanted it. If you want to become a champion, you need to listen to people who know more about skating than you do. Do you understand what I'm saying?"

Cammie quickly nodded.

"Okay, so as far as I understand, your goal at this point is to restore the functions of your injured leg. Is that right?"

"That's right," Cammie said.

"Then go out there and do what you can. Practice stroking, perhaps some crossovers and basic turns. If you feel tired, rest. Don't put too much pressure on yourself. Remember, you have the whole life of skating before you. And good luck with your rehabilitation."

"Thank you." Cammie felt as though a huge weight had been lifted off her chest. Humming, she took off her skate guards and glided forward.

Within the next few days, Cammie visited the Yellow Rink, the White Rink, and the Silver Rink. The Yellow Rink was a huge skating facility that served as a training ground for high-level skaters—novice, junior, and senior.

"Skaters from all over the world come to train here," Alex said as he pointed to several flags hanging from the ceiling. Cammie only recognized the American and the Canadian flags. Alex explained that the rink housed skaters from France, Germany, Italy, Russia, Ukraine, China, and Japan.

Cammie was also impressed to find out that the Yellow Rink had its own fitness center, three ballet rooms, a swimming pool, a Jacuzzi, and a massage room.

"You guys are lucky."

Cammie and her Green Rink friends had to skate to the ballet studio or to the gym when they needed off-ice training.

Alex smiled at her. "Well, you'll probably move up to the novice level pretty soon."

"In my dreams." Cammie didn't feel particularly excited. Her practice hadn't gone too well. The

Yellow Rink skaters were incredible. Almost all of them could land triples without a slightest hesitation. Even before her injury, Cammie wouldn't have been able to measure up to that level. Now she felt like a total beginner. As hard as Cammie tried to focus on her stroking and basic turns, she couldn't help noticing that the other skaters were laughing at her. A man in a camel coat—probably a skater's father—suggested that Cammie take a learn-to-skate class at the Main Rink.

"Ignore them," Alex said.

"They laughed at me!" Cammie whined.

"It's because they're afraid of you. They know that once you're back in shape, you'll beat them easily."

As frustrated as Cammie was, she couldn't help smiling. Alex always had just the right thing to say to her. How lucky she was to have him as a friend!

They visited the White Rink, a training ground for pairs and dancers. Cammie feared there would be more scorn and patronizing looks, but luckily, Alex and she turned out to be alone on the ice.

"Gosh, I'm starving," Alex said as they walked down the steps to the first floor of the Sport Center.

Cammie didn't say anything. She stared at the now empty lobby. Just two months ago she had entered the same building ready for the competition. She had just landed her double axel and—

"Cammie, did you hear what I said? Let's get a sandwich at the Snack Bar."

Cammie looked at the entrance to the Silver Rink. The ice was smooth and clean. "You go ahead. I'd better skate around a couple of times while there's nobody here."

"Are you sure? Because I—"

"Come on, Alex. I'll be fine. There're no witches here for sure."

Cammie did a few laps around the Silver Rink—nothing fancy, just basic stroking. As she watched the silver walls rush past her, she couldn't help thinking that she was at the rink where she had recently won her gold medal. The Silver Rink was the place where she had landed her first double axel in competition; it was the place of her triumph.

Tears fogged her vision, and she wiped them off with a glove. The very thought that only a couple of months ago she could land double-double combinations with ease was unbearable.

"So what? Will I always be like this?" Cammie said out loud. She stopped in the middle of the rink, looking up into the bleachers. No one was watching her.

"I'm still a skater, okay?" Cammie raised her voice. She almost wished the witches were somewhere in the back row. No, she wasn't going to give them the satisfaction of terminating her career. She was going to fight.

Cammie bent her left knee and went into a deep forward outside edge. She held it as long as she could then swung her free leg around. The silver walls whooshed by. He raised her right leg up to her knee then crossed. Her speed increased.

"Yes!" Cammie cried out as she pulled in her arms. Her ride out was wobbly, probably because she had to glide on her injured foot. Yet overall, she had managed to do a decent scratch spin on her first try.

"Did you see me?" Cammie yelled to the empty bleachers.

Silence was the only answer she got, yet she wasn't discouraged anymore. She hadn't lost all of her skills after all.

"So how did it go?" Alex asked as Cammie walked into the lobby.

"Well…I did a few spins." Cammie looked at the poster of Carolina Kostner hanging on the wall across from them, wishing she had the Italian skater's jumps.

"That's great!"

"I only managed forward spins because those are done on the left foot. I didn't even try back ones."

"It's still terrific," Alex said encouragingly.

"But I'm scared of jumps."

"Come on. We're almost finished with your Full Circle Therapy!" Alex said.

"We still have the Black Rink," Cammie said. Somehow, she didn't think their visit to witches' facility would be as smooth as skating in the Sport Center.

"Oh, we'll be fine." Alex winked at her. "Remember the card? 'Just kick the witches in the rear.'"

Cammie grinned. "Sure."

They skated fast in the direction of Cammie's dorm, Cammie holding Kanga's handle tight.

"The sandwich was good, by the way. And you must be starving," Alex teased.

"Well, I'm glad I didn't eat much. Mrs. Page is throwing a big party tonight in honor of Sonia and Dana's coming home from Junior Nationals."

Alex slapped himself on the forehead. "Gosh, I completely forgot. Mr. Randell is doing the same for Jeff and Kyle. And of course, Peter and Kevin are back too."

"You can go to your dorm, then. I'll be fine with Kanga," Cammie said.

Alex looked at his watch. "Nay, there's still time. Besides, I'd better not take any chances with the witches."

"I don't think they are watching us tonight." Cammie peered into the thicket of the Icy Park on their left but didn't see any movement.

"And what makes you so sure?"

"Stop!" Cammie said to Kanga.

The animal grunted and froze in its spot. Cammie let go of the handle. "I'm sure the witches know we're going after them. So why bother looking for us?"

"Hmm. You may have a point. Still I'd better walk you to your dorm," Alex said.

"So are you ready to hit the Black Rink tomorrow?" Alex asked Cammie as Kanga stopped in front of Cammie's dorm building.

"Sure. The sooner the better." She sat down on the steps to put on her skate guards.

"Don't forget to wear something wild. Remember what kind of people hang out there. Hey, wait, I have something here!" Alex put his hand into his pants pocket and took out a flyer. Running across the dark contour of the Black Rink were bright red letters: *Rap Night at the Black Rink. Rebels and Outcasts Welcome.*

"Rebels and outcasts, how about that?" Cammie flipped the flyer in her hands. "Is that where we're going?"

"Why not? We'll blend in with the crowd. That's why I'm telling you to wear something hip-hop, you know."

"Like what?" Cammie cried out. "I don't have anything in that style."

"Well, you girls can always think of something. Yeah, and by the way, the party starts at ten. So you'll have the whole day to yourself." Alex winked at Cammie.

"Oh, all right." Still thinking about what would be appropriate to wear to a rap party, Cammie pressed the doorbell.

RAP NIGHT AT THE BLACK RINK

The door opened immediately, and a very excited Sonia grabbed Cammie by the hand. "Cammie! I can't believe you're skating already!"

Cammie smiled wryly. "I spent enough time in bed; thank you."

"So how is your ankle? Mrs. Page says you're in some kind of rehabilitation program." Sonia's blue eyes traveled down Cammie's legs.

"Well, Mr. Reed says he can restore my ankle completely." As the two of them walked up to their room on the third floor, Cammie told Sonia everything about the R.O.F.A. and about her trips to Skateland practice rinks. Knowing how emotional Sonia was,

Cammie deliberately left out the fact that the magical device was still in the hands of the witches.

Sonia nodded energetically. "I believe each of the rinks will add something to your progress. Besides, I'm sure you're almost up to your level now."

Cammie groaned. "I can't even do decent crossovers."

"Oh!" Sonia's eyes darkened.

"But I did several spins today."

"Well, spins are definitely more challenging than crossovers. So when will you be able to use the R.O.F.A.?"

"Soon, I guess."

"Good. Because I can't wait to see you do your jumps again. And this time—"

Before Sonia could finish her sentence, someone knocked on the door, and a split second later Liz's excited face appeared in the doorframe.

"Come on, you guys. Dinner's ready."

They walked down to the dining room, where all the girls already sat at their tables. Most of them wore tracksuits and bathrobes, looking relaxed. The only person who was dressed up was Dana. In her black sweater dress and black leggings, her long blonde hair down, Dana looked absolutely gorgeous.

Trying not to limp, Cammie approached the table where Sonia and she usually sat. "Hi, Dana."

Dana tossed the thick mane of hair to her back. "So you're skating again, then."

"I think so." Cammie moved her glass closer and took a sip. It was peach iced tea, her favorite.

"I bet it's hard to be back on the ice with an injury like yours."

Probably not much more difficult than being back in Skateland after coming in seventeenth at Junior Nationals, Cammie almost said. Almost. Perhaps two months ago, she would have done just that. But somehow, in the last few weeks something had changed inside her, and now she had absolutely no desire to tease Dana.

She could almost sense the girl's pain and disappointment. Going to your first national competition and doing poorly was hard enough to take. Cammie knew exactly what was going on in Dana's mind. She probably blamed herself for not having skated up to her potential. Perhaps she dreamed of another chance, maybe next year. But that other chance might never come. Life was too hard, too unpredictable. Cammie understood it now, and the least thing she wanted was to add to Dana's grief.

"Dana, I think it's great that you beat eight other girls," Cammie said sincerely. "And next time it'll be even easier for you. I'm sure you'll medal next year."

Dana's blue eyes rounded with surprise; she put her spoon down, staring at Cammie without blinking. Next to Dana, Liz twisted her face in an expression of bewilderment.

Sonia reached for a slice of garlic bread. "Dana, Cammie is right. If you had landed that double axel, you'd definitely be in the top five. And you did it in practice. I saw you."

Dana's lower lip twitched. "I tried to work extra hard to get it consistent."

"You will," Cammie said. She saw Dana's facial muscles relax a little as the girl glanced in her direction.

They spent the rest of the evening laughing and talking about all kinds of things, enjoying extra portions of Mrs. Page's competition cake. With a thick layer of whipped cream and several chocolate medals on top, the cake practically melted in their mouths. After their third cup of tea, Mrs. Page finally told them to go to bed.

Cammie slept so well that she didn't even hear Sonia leave for her morning practice. Her Kanga bag no longer woke her up at five o'clock. Cammie often wondered how the animal knew that she could sleep in. One day, when she saw Mr. Reed, she would ask him that question. For now, she just accepted Kanga's grace.

For nothing better to do, Cammie spent the day working out in the gym, exercising her ankle. She also read two chapters from her history book, wrote a book report for her English class, and solved seven math problems.

It's amazing how much you can do when you don't have to go to practices, Cammie thought as she put her pencil down.

The sky outside was dark blue with burgundy streaks. A sound of laughter came from downstairs followed by several excited voices. Cammie didn't have to look out of the window to know that her friends were coming back from their afternoon practices. It was almost time for dinner, and then Cammie and Alex would go to the Black Rink. Perhaps, if they were lucky enough, they would even find the R.O.F.A. tonight. Cammie shivered with anticipation. But boy, what was she going to wear to the rap party?

Cammie opened her closet and looked through her clothes. She dismissed the skating dresses right away; anybody dressed in elastic and sequins would look like an outsider at the Black Rink. How about jeans and a sweatshirt? Casual clothes would probably be okay.

Cammie put on her best pair of jeans. Oh no, they barely reached her ankles; she must have grown in the last couple of months. Besides, the pants looked almost too casual. But what choice did she have? The jeans she wore every day were even worse. Perhaps she needed to ask her mother to take her out shopping. Cammie took her best light-blue sweatshirt off the rack and pulled it on. The sweatshirt had been given to her by Isabelle two years ago, and Cammie only wore it for special occasions.

There came a knock on the door.

"Come in!" Cammie closed the closet.

Dana walked in. "Hi."

"Hi!" Cammie was slightly surprised. Even though Dana and Liz's room was right across from Cammie and Sonia's, Dana had never visited Cammie before.

"I went to Sweet Blades before the afternoon practice, and I thought you could use some sugar boost." Dana handed Cammie a bag of hard candy shaped like snowflakes.

"Wow. Thanks." Cammie put a candy in her mouth and smiled at the rich peach flavor. "Want some?" She handed the bag to Dana.

The girl shook her head. "I've eaten enough already. Hey, are you going anywhere?"

Cammie nodded. "To the Black Rink."

Dana stepped back, her mouth wide open. "What?"

Cammie chuckled at the girl's open expression of horror. "Got to."

"But why?"

For some reason, Cammie didn't mind confiding to Dana. The girl wasn't her close friend, but Cammie knew she wasn't as sensitive as Sonia. And it would probably be good for someone to know where Cammie was in case something happened.

"Would you like to sit down?" Cammie asked.

"Uh, okay." Dana plopped on the carpet and hugged her knees. The bright green sweater made Dana's pale blue eyes look almost turquoise.

Cammie told Dana about the witches, her injury, and Mr. Reed's rehabilitation program.

"So Alex and I are going to the Black Rink tonight. I only hope we'll be able to blend with the crowd. Do you think I look all right?" Cammie tugged on her sweatshirt.

Dana looked at her critically. "Absolutely not. Girl, you'll be spotted as an outsider right away. This isn't what people wear to rap clubs."

"How do you know?"

"My older sister is into hip hop. Tell you what. I've got something for you." Dana stretched like a cat, jumped to her feet, and disappeared behind the closed door. Fine minutes later, she was back carrying a bundle of clothes.

"Put these on," Dana said in a very determined voice.

Cammie got into a pair of tight dark-blue jeans with gold trimmings. "They fit."

"I knew they would. Here's the top."

Cammie put on a white T-shirt with a picture of an exotic-looking singer.

"It's Tupac, my sister's favorite rapper," Dana said. "Now this comes next."

Cammie grimaced uncertainly as she studied a short black leather jacket. "This is too expensive. What if it gets ripped or something?"

"What are you going to do, play hockey in it?" Dana threw the jacket at Cammie.

"You never know with the witches." Cammie put on the jacket and looked at herself in the mirror. "I like it."

"We're not done yet." Dana helped Cammie to put on long silver hoop earrings and matching bracelets. A thick silver pendant shaped like an intricate symbol completed the ensemble.

"What does this mean?" Cammie ran her finger across the pendant.

"Just my name in Chinese. My sister's friends' grandfather makes these. Okay, let's work on your makeup."

Cammie laughed. "It's not a competition."

"It's more important than a competition. Although…" Dana looked at the door. "How about after dinner? You don't want Mrs. Page to see you like this. She'd be worried sick."

"True." Cammie took off Dana's clothes and put on her bathrobe. "What if Sonia sees me? She may come in any minute."

"Sonia has a ballet class after dinner," Dana said.

"Oh, that's right. Aren't you going there too?" Cammie put on a pair of thick wool socks.

"Give me a break. I just got back from the nationals for crying out loud."

They had dinner downstairs, and after Sonia left for her ballet class, Dana helped Cammie to get ready for her trip to the Black Rink.

"Maybe I can come too?" Dana asked.

Cammie almost dropped her boot. Had Dana really suggested that? The girl who had always been so competitive; she had hardly talked to Cammie after her victory at Skateland Annual Competition. So what had changed? Was Dana being nice to Cammie because, with her injury, Cammie no longer posed a threat to her? Or because Dana hadn't done too well at the nationals herself? Or perhaps the two of them were finally becoming friends?

Cammie looked at Dana's determined face. "No, Dana. I'll be safe with Alex. But thanks. If I don't come back tonight, let Mrs. Van Uffeln and Mr. Reed know." Dana shook her head so hard that her long blonde locks almost covered her face. "Nothing will happen to you, Cammie. You'll be fine."

"Wow, Cammie, you look hot!" Alex's green eyes widened as Cammie skated down the ramp leading from her dorm entrance to the sidewalk.

"Do you like it?" Cammie tugged on her jacket, enjoying the smoothness of the leather.

"You bet. I think you should wear this stuff at Saturday public sessions."

"It's Dana's." Cammie twirled the silver pendant between her fingers. "Hey, you don't look too bad yourself!"

In a long, oversized sweatshirt that almost reached his knees Alex looked like a typical hip-hop singer.

"Are you sure you'll be able to skate in these?" Cammie studied Alex's pants. They were so wide that she could probably squeeze her whole body into one leg.

"Are you doubting my abilities, champion?" He soared up in a delayed waltz jump and landed smoothly.

"That was awesome!" She clapped her hands. "I wouldn't try any triples, though. Oh, yes, and spinning too may be a problem."

"Well, we're not going to a competition."

"Where did you get these clothes anyway?"

He grinned. "Remember George, Jeff's roommate? The one who joined a hockey team? That's what he wears when he's not at the Yellow Rink. Okay, we'd better go."

With Kanga pulling Cammie ahead, they reached the Black Rink in record time.

"Last time I was here with Isabelle, I barely had time to look around," Cammie said as she eyed the black marble floor of the lobby. "So what—"

Ya-ang! The floor moved under her feet, and the next second she was falling forward. She was about to crash on the hard surface and then … whoosh! She landed on something soft and resistant; the floor sank under her, throwing her up again. Cammie bounced once, twice …

"What the—?"

"Hi!"

Cammie raised her head and shrieked. Staring at her was the smiling face of a skeleton. Yes, she could clearly see the white protruding bones and the sharp teeth.

"Welcome to the Black Rink, and I apologize for the little prank." The skeleton's face shrank then vanished, and a boy of about sixteen appeared in front of Cammie. The boy was grinning openly.

"You just stepped on a trampoline. Cool, huh?"

"Yes, very cool." Alex grabbed the boy by the hand and shook it hard. "What do you think you're doing?"

"Hey, don't get too crabby, man. It was nothing but a warm welcome. Black Rink security." The boy winked at Cammie.

"Aha, and … the skull?" She swallowed hard.

"I told you. It's not real. See?" The boy showed her a plastic mask.

"She's recuperating from an injury," Alex barked. "Don't you realize she could get hurt?"

"Look, buddy, it's all right. You're at the Black Rink. And speaking of injuries, you might want to talk to Winja's victims. They'll cheer you up."

"Winja's victims?" Cammie's head began to spin.

"We'll think of that." Alex took Cammie firmly by the hand, and together they crossed the dark, cavernous lobby. "What a jerk, huh? Anyway, we can't be too careful here."

The area seemed endless, probably because it was dark. The lobby was lit by three circular lamps that hung low from the ceiling. Or was there a ceiling at all? As Cammie looked up, she could see nothing but sheer blackness.

"Hey, are you the crippled ones?" An overweight, rosy-cheeked girl blocked Cammie and Alex's way. Cammie saw that the girl walked with a noticeable limp.

"What?" Cammie felt confused.

"No," Alex said quickly.

The girl's small eyes narrowed. "Well, okay. Even if you're healthy, would you mind making a contribution to Winja's Victims' Fund?"

"What's that?" Cammie asked.

"Come and meet our club members." The girl motioned for Cammie and Alex to follow her.

Cammie obeyed automatically.

"Cammie, don't listen to her!" Alex hissed.

Cammie shrugged. "Why not?"

They walked into an enclosed area occupied by about a dozen of teenagers. Cammie saw a couple of bandaged limbs, and one boy had a set of crutches sitting next to him. The rest of the kids, however, seemed perfectly healthy.

"I brought you two more victims!" the girl who had invited Cammie and Alex exclaimed. "My name is Wendy, by the way."

"Lisa!"

"Eric!"

"Jill!"

Cammie's head spun as she tried to remember the kids' names. She introduced herself too, and Alex joined her, though with obvious reluctance.

"So what's bothering you?" Wendy asked.

"It's my ankle," Cammie said before Alex pulled her by the sleeve.

"And the doctors say you'll never skate again." The boy whose name was Eric sounded as though he already knew the answer.

"Yes, but—" Cammie was about to tell her new friends about the R.O.F.A., but this time, Alex put his hand over her mouth and pulled her aside.

"Hey, what're you doing, man?" the victims shouted in protest, though no one made an effort to stand up.

"She needs to see a doctor!" Alex snapped.

"Winja'll be here in about an hour. She has all the medical supplies you need," Wendy said.

Cammie gasped. "Winja?" She almost choked as Alex's hand pressed hard against her mouth.

"See you guys later. Thanks." Alex pulled Cammie around the corner where there were two doors leading to restrooms. It was only there that he finally released her.

"What's wrong with you?" Cammie asked angrily. She jerked the bathroom door open.

"Where're you going?"

"Are you following me to the bathroom too?" She slammed the door behind her and quickly exhaled. She took a tube of Dana's lipstick from her pocket and added some to her lips. Stupid Alex had really ruined her makeup. Wondering what had gotten into her friend, Cammie put the lipstick back into her pocket. She hadn't brought a purse, and at Alex's insistence, she had left Kanga outside.

"You don't want it to be stolen, do you?" Alex had said.

Cammie took a deep breath and walked out of the bathroom.

Alex looked livid. "We'd better do what we've come here for and get out. Did you hear what the victims said? The witches will be here soon."

Cammie sighed. "Let's skate."

They crossed the lobby that was now crowded with noisy teenagers and pushed the door leading to the arena.

The familiar cold draft hit Cammie in the face as she walked along the rubber path. The glossy black surface shimmered in the light of about a dozen lamps. She bent down to remove her skate guards. Alex already stood on the ice, shuffling his feet.

"This ice is really fast. Be careful, Cammie. Take your time."

Before Cammie could say a word, there came a hissing sound followed by a tap, and a male voice said, "Welcome to the Rap Night at the Black Rink."

The rolling of drums almost silenced the young man. As Cammie raised her head, she saw a skinny African-American boy with a Mohawk haircut. Even though it was dark, he wore sunglasses, and several silver chains hung from his neck, making a striking contrast with his black T-shirt. There was a cordless microphone in the boy's hand, and behind him several musicians tuned their instruments. Cammie noticed four guitar players, a saxophone player, and a keyboard player.

"I'm Sam Diener, and I'm a skater." The young man swung his arms and began to move. He glided forward faster and faster then soared in the air in a perfect split jump. The sounds of the drums reverberated against the black ice as Sam went into a complicated footwork, including several toe hops and half jumps. Grabbing the boards tight, Cammie watched the young man with awe.

"So the sucker sucks again," a drooling voice said behind Cammie.

"He's not a sucker!" The second voice undoubtedly belonged to a girl, and it sounded familiar.

Cammie fought an urge to look back. For some reason, she thought she'd better not get recognized.

"Oh yeah?" The first voice now sounded sarcastic. "Nobody likes him except weirdoes who practice ballet moves in the basement."

"Do me a favor and shut up!" the girl's voice grunted.

Cammie felt someone brush past her, and she looked sideways. She saw a tall girl with waist-length black hair. She wore tight low-cut jeans and a pink tank top.

But it's so cold here! Cammie thought.

The girl turned and looked straight at Cammie.

Cammie gasped. "Isabelle!"

Yes, it was really her old friend, or rather the girl whom Cammie had considered a friend until she had delivered her to the witches. Isabelle would probably do the same now. Cammie and Alex had better get out. But how? Without trying the black ice first? No, that would be silly.

"Do you know this kid?" A Hispanic guy with dark curly hair stepped from behind Isabelle.

"Do you expect me to know every toddler in Skateland?" Isabelle asked haughtily. Without waiting for her friend's answer, she stepped onto the ice and glided forward.

"Uh-huh, that's not good. Isabelle can't be trusted." Alex sounded concerned. "Let's do a couple of laps and leave, okay?"

Cammie nodded. Holding on to the boards, she put a foot on the ice, then another. Boy, she had already forgotten how incredibly smooth the black ice was. It seemed to bounce slightly under her blades, pushing her forward, giving her tremendous speed. It would have been fine under different circumstances, but now that Cammie's ankle was unsteady, she didn't feel like moving particularly fast. She tried to brake, but the ice carried her forward.

"Cammie, be careful!" The wind whistled in her ears and carried Alex's message away.

To help her balance, Cammie spread her arms and bent her knees, making sure her torso was properly aligned over her blades. So far so good.

The rink filled up with skaters. The drummers went into another combination of taps, beats, and bangs. Cammie saw flying hair and black T-shirts as tall figures whooshed by her. A guy with long dreadlocks almost knocked her over and rushed forward without bothering to apologize. A tall girl tap danced across the arena then went into a huge axel. The crowd applauded loudly.

A stocky guy wearing a baseball cap positioned himself in the front row of the bleachers, squeezed into a tight ball, and suddenly jumped onto the ice within ten feet from Cammie. She lost balance, flounced her arms, and sat down on the cold ice.

"Urgh!" She tried to push against the ice with her hands, but the black surface was too slippery.

"Alex!" She looked around helplessly, but her friend was too far away. A tight group of twizzling girls separated them.

"Still taking a learn-to-skate class, huh?" a familiar voice whispered in her ear.

Cammie rose on her knees and stared at Isabelle.

"I know you're hurt beyond repair. Serves you right." Isabelle dashed forward, her long hair bouncing against her back.

"No, I'm not!" Cammie said angrily and brought herself up.

"Skating sucks!" the guy in a baseball cap shouted.

His words were followed by an avalanche of catcalls and whistles. Two girls in high-cut shorts with pink streaks in their dark hair squealed and clapped violently.

"Give it all, people!"

The drums shouted, and the guy began to sing.

Who would want to be a skater
On the ice that's white or pink?
Who would think of jumping, spinning,
Doing steps around the rink?
Who would like to get up early,

To practice at the crack of dawn?
If you do it, then one morning,
You will see that your life is gone.
That's why we all hate jumping, stomping,
Kicking, picking, gliding, sliding,
Ain't it surprising?
Falling, stalling, trailing, failing,
Until we hit the end,
Which is nothing!

"Nothing!" the crowd boomed.

The singer lowered himself into a fast sit spin. The rest of the skaters joined him.

"Get out of the way!" a broad-faced boy yelled at Cammie.

She stepped backward, just to be pushed on the side by a sour-looking girl. "Hey, easy now!"

"Gosh!" Cammie looked around and screamed as a sharp blade of a skater doing a camel spin whizzed by, missing her by inches.

"Cammie!" Alex called from somewhere on the right.

Cammie strained her eyes, hoping to see her friend, but all she could discern was a quick interchange of light and shadows as the skaters spun around her.

Someone cussed at her loudly. Cammie cringed.

"Hey, baby, you either do what everybody else does or get out of the way."

The light from the swinging lamps hurt Cammie's eyes; she squinted. "Alex!" Her voice got drowned out in another pattern of the drums.

> Skipping, hopping, never stopping,
> Soaring, roaring, this is boring.
> Training, flying, always trying,
> And then you realize: you're a loser!

Everybody around Cammie shot up in the air; it looked like a jumping contest. Cammie had to hand it to the Black Rink skaters. A lot of them were really good jumpers.

Cammie watched a tall guy perform a gorgeous triple toe loop; then she felt a strong push in the back.

"Ah!" Before Cammie could even think, she lay prostrate on the ice, gasping for breath.

"Are you really trying to get yourself killed, or are you just an idiot?" an angry voice said above Cammie.

"No, I … " Cammie coughed.

She felt herself pulled up to her feet; she looked up. A heavyset blonde girl stood next to her, and the expressioin of her gray eyes wasn't friendly.

"It's Cammie, right?" The girl didn't sound as though she was asking a question.

"Do you know me?" Cammie smiled. "You must have read the article in *Skateland Sensations*."

The girl snorted. "Oh, who needs that junk? No, you and your friend stopped by our house three years ago, remember?"

Cammie studied the girl's bloated face. Yes, it did look familiar. And then it came back to her—a small pink house and four fat kids serving Alex and her junk food. And then the kids had taken Cammie and Alex to the Witch of Pride's rink and—

"You're Lucy!" Cammie said.

The girl smirked. "Actually, I'm Annie."

"Oops, sorry."

Whether she's Lucy or Annie, I'd better get out of here, Cammie thought. She surely didn't want the girl to summon the Witch of Pride.

"Scared, huh?" Annie's lipstick was bright pink, just like Cammie's.

"No, I…" Cammie didn't know what to say.

"Relax. I'm not going to take you to the witches." Annie tucked a stray lock behind her ear, and Cammie saw that the girl was wearing black fingerless gloves.

"Care for a drink? You surely look like you need one," Annie said.

Why not? Cammie thought. She had spent enough time on the black ice already, and she was sure it would count toward her rehabilitation. And staying at the arena much longer was dangerous.

"Come on." Annie grabbed Cammie by the hand and led her to the exit. Cammie felt herself relax. Holding on to someone made skating around the Black Rink much easier.

"Cammie!" Alex's voice called; her friend sounded worried.

Cammie looked around. Alex looked as though he was trying to get to her, but he was pressed from all sides by two rows of girls swinging to the music.

"I'll take care of her, daddy!" With a giggle, Annie led Cammie upstairs to the second floor.

"This is our snack bar. Cool, huh?"

Cammie looked around the cold room lit up by a few candles perched on the tables. Maybe the place was cool, but it definitely wasn't cozy. She flinched.

"Yeah, it's freezing." Annie approached the counter. "Zack, why on earth isn't the fireplace on?"

"Energy preservation. Witches' order," a young man in a black sweater said curtly.

"Oh, screw the witches. Turn the fireplace on, and then bring me a gin and tonic and a can of Coke for the child." Annie nodded in Cammie's direction.

"I'm not—"

Annie narrowed her eyes. "So you want a gin and tonic too?"

"No!" Gosh, Annie had to be crazy.

"Coke, then." Annie sat down at one of the tables and signaled for Cammie to take the chair across from her. The glass door looking out to the arena was right next to them. Cammie could see the skaters holding hands, kicking their feet wildly.

"So what's your story?" Annie asked.

"What do you mean?" Cammie accepted a can of Coke from the bartender and muttered a quick, "Thank you."

"What are you doing at the Black Rink?"

"Just recuperating from an injury." Cammie knew she should be quiet about the R.O.F.A.

"And the doctors aren't optimistic about your skating career." Annie didn't look surprised.

Cammie clenched her teeth. "And why do you say that?"

"There's nothing new under the sun." Annie sipped her drink and took a pack of cigarettes out of her jeans pocket. She clicked a silver lighter.

Cammie watched the girl, mesmerized. "Do you smoke?"

Annie smirked. "Don't you see for yourself?"

"But smoking is bad for skaters."

"Who cares what's good and what's bad anymore?" Annie inhaled deeply, staring at the crackling fire in the fireplace.

"I lied to you, you know?" Annie said. "Of course, I saw the article about you in *Skateland Sensations*. I even saw the highlights of Skateland Annual Competition on television in Sweet Blades. Normally we aren't allowed to watch skating events, but this time—"

"*Who* won't allow you to watch skating events?" Cammie felt shocked. How could a girl living in Skateland not have access to competition broadcasts?

Annie exhaled slowly. "Never mind that. Anyway, I saw you, and you were good. Very good."

The girl's gray eyes stared at the bar stand with rows of bottles. "At least you were recognized for your efforts. I wasn't. Do you know I went to nationals once? The novice division."

Cammie almost spilled her Coke. "You did?"

"I came in third," Annie said bitterly.

"But that's terrific!"

The girl's eyes darkened. "What do you know? I didn't deserve to be third. I should have won. Sandra Lamberg, the girl who came in second, couldn't even jump. And Leslie Dubois, the winner, well, she wasn't bad. But hey, she had been skating since she was four. What do you expect? I started at seven. Don't you think they should have taken that into consideration? I mean, my overall progress?"

"I don't know." What Annie was saying didn't make sense to Cammie. Nobody ever cared when a person had started to skate. It was the end result that mattered.

"Anyway, it wasn't fair," Annie said angrily. Her hands shook as she lit another cigarette.

Cammie felt sorry for the girl. She looked as though she was really hurting.

"Look, I think you still did well, and maybe, next year—"

"Ha ha ha!" Annie's laughter sounded forced. "I quit four years ago. That's it." Annie squeezed her cigarette violently against the black glass of the ashtray.

"Oh!" Now Cammie understood. Annie had been so disappointed that she had decided to give up skating for good. And then she had gotten out of shape.

"But you can always start over again," Cammie said encouragingly.

"I'm eighteen!" Annie snapped.

Desperately looking for something positive to say, Cammie raised her eyes to the ceiling, where stuffed bats and spiders floated suspended by ropes. "You aren't that old yet. And hey, look at Wilhelmina."

"Oh, don't you ever mention that name to me! I hate the old brat." Annie covered her ears.

Cammie shrugged surreptitiously. What could Annie possibly have against Skateland President? Though strict, Wilhelmina was the nicest person Cammie had ever met.

"So now we're in the same boat, I guess." Annie's eyes slid down toward Cammie's ankle.

Cammie shook her head. "No, we're not. I'm on my way to complete rehabilitation. And once I get the R.O.F.A.—"

Annie puckered her forehead. "R.O.F.A.?"

Before Cammie knew it, she told Annie everything. As she went on and on, she watched the girl's harsh expression soften.

"That's great. Good luck, then!" Annie shook her head, looking amazed, and ordered herself another gin and tonic.

"But listen; it's sort of a secret. The witches aren't supposed to know anything. I still don't know which of them has the magical device, so…" Cammie spoke very fast.

"Sure thing." Annie emptied her glass, looking much more cheerful.

The loud music downstairs suddenly stopped; there was a deep silence.

"What's going on?" Cammie asked.

Before Annie could say a word, a cold voice spoke up. "Attention, Black Rink skaters. Your presence is required at the arena now. I repeat…"

Annie jumped off her chair. "Gotta go."

"Why? Who was that?" Cammie stood up too.

Annie nudged her on the back. "The witches are here, and they need us. You'd better stay here; they won't see you. And once the witches start working on group numbers with us, you'll be able to leave quietly."

"Ah, okay." Cammie lowered herself to her seat again.

Annie was on her way to the door when it swung open and a very harassed-looking Alex ran inside.

"Cammie, the witches are at the rink. We need to get out."

"Don't worry. I'll make sure they won't see you," Annie said.

Alex looked at the girl with genuine surprise. "Hey, thanks."

"Sure. You know what? The two of you'd better get under the table in case the witches look up."

Yes, that was a good idea. Alex helped Cammie to crawl under the small table and then joined her.

"Annie, when do you think will be the best time to leave?" Alex asked.

The girl seemed to be thinking. "I'd say in about fifteen minutes. Good luck!" She winked at Cammie and ran out of the snack bar.

"I told you, fat kids aren't that bad," Alex said as he leaned against a leg of the table.

"Yes, Annie is really nice."

As Cammie told Alex about Annie's disappointment over the third place, her friend stared at her, looking bewildered.

"Is she crazy? If everybody who missed the gold quit, who would we be left with?"

Before Cammie could say something, the door cracked.

The two of them froze under the table, trying not to breathe. From her position, Cammie could see the lower part of the torsos and the legs of the people who had just walked in. There were about four or five of them, and they were definitely women dressed in black robes. But it meant … no, it couldn't be true.

"They're right here, Winja," Annie's voice said.

"Alex, she lied to us!" Cammie shrieked, but at the same moment she felt herself being pulled out from under the table. There was a click, and the bar lit up. In the bright light, the witches' faces looked even uglier.

As Cammie looked into the pale eyes of the Witch of Fear, she felt as though her limbs were filling up with ice. A cold cloud enveloped her; she couldn't breathe anymore. She drifted away.

WINJA'S CABIN

*W*ake up right now, sleepy head!

Hey, what was that? Cammie sat up and rubbed her tired eyes. Thick darkness hung around her; she couldn't even see the white outline of the window frame. It had to be the middle of the night, so why had Kanga decided to wake her up? Besides, Cammie didn't even go to early morning practices anymore.

The practice is about to start . . .

"Stop it, Kanga!" Cammie protested.

A loud bang came from the room nearby, followed by a scream. "Ah, you stupid . . . no!"

Cammie strained her eyes, but everything was dark. She groped around, looking for something familiar. Her bed felt hard; there were no sheets, only a thin mattress. Hey, there wasn't even a bed. The mattress sat right on the floor.

"Where am I?"

"Hush!" Someone said next to her; then a warm hand squeezed her arm.

"Alex! Is that you?"

"Yeah, where are we?"

"I don't know. But it's not my dorm room for sure."

There was a sound of something hard falling on the floor; then another blood-curdling scream came from behind the wall. "Somebody help me. I'm dying!"

Still wondering where she was, Cammie jumped up from the mattress and ran to the sound of the voice. The footsteps behind her meant that Alex had joined her. Cammie's hand felt a handle; she turned it, pressed the door hard, and almost fell forward.

"No!" Cammie looked around.

She stood in a very untidy bedroom with pale-gray wallpaper peeling off the walls. An old-fashioned metal bed stood in the middle of the room. Winja sat in bed, tangled in a thick black-and-blue quilt, one of her bony legs with protruding veins sticking out from under the quilt. The woman swayed from left to right, her hands clasped tightly around her head.

"O-o-o, a-a-ah!" Winja moaned.

"What's wrong?" Alex's husky voice asked from behind Cammie.

"Stupid animal!" Winja's teary eyes darted to the corner of the room, where Kanga sat, its eyes aglow.

"Reciting stupid poems at five in the morning—just great! It scared the beejebees out of me." Winja shook her head, causing gray tangled locks to spill all across her face.

Cammie and Alex exchanged mischievous glances. So it was Kanga who had startled Winja. How cool!

"And then this stupid bag mentioned winning or losing. I thought I had to compete today," Winja whimpered. "Nothing could be more stupid. I haven't competed in thirty years. Anyway, I bolted up, jumped forward, and ... how about that?"

As the witch unclasped her fingers, Cammie saw a huge red bump the size of a golf ball sitting right in the middle of the woman's forehead. The bump was the color of a plum, and the swelling seemed to be increasing. Okay, so the witch had jumped forward and hit her head against the bed rest. Next to Cammie, Alex chuckled. In spite of all the confusion, Cammie too found the situation hilarious. She giggled.

"Go ahead. Laugh at me!" Winja griped. "Guffawing at a living soul who's in pain—that's all you youngsters are capable of."

Alex stopped laughing immediately. "Oh, I'm sorry."

Strangely, Cammie also felt compassion for the injured witch. "We didn't mean to be nasty," Cammie said apologetically. "You probably didn't know about Kanga's special functions, so—"

"Now blabbing isn't going to help!" Winja snapped. "Don't you see I'm in excruciating pain? Go ahead; do something!"

Cammie looked at Alex helplessly.

"What can we do?" Alex asked.

"Oh, I probably have a concussion. I may need to get admitted to the hospital."

"It's not a concussion," Alex said angrily. "With a concussion, you'd be throwing up all over the place. See, my roommate once—"

"Uh, I don't know," Winja muttered. "Now don't just stand here. Give me an ice pack at least."

Cammie looked around. "Where is it?"

"Where can ice packs be? In the refrigerator in the kitchen, of course." Winja snarled. "Hey, don't touch anything there!" she yelled as Cammie walked out of the bedroom.

Cammie flipped the light switch. A lonely bulb hanging from the ceiling on a cord and a light socket brought into focus a large round table, a scratched stove, and a big refrigerator. Two fat mice scurried across the filthy floor.

"Ah!" Cammie screamed. She hated mice.

"Are you all right?" Alex appeared at her side immediately.

"M-mice!"

He looked relieved. "I thought you saw another witch or something."

"Well, I hate mice." Cammie opened the freezer door. "Alex, what're we doing in Winja's house?"

Alex looked confused. "All I remember is the witches coming at us, and then I woke up here."

"Weird!" Cammie noticed that the refrigerator was filled with all kinds of pills and strange-looking solutions. She picked a dark-blue ice pack and closed the door.

Back in the bedroom, Winja snatched the ice pack from Cammie and pressed it against her forehead. "Oh, ahh, it hurts! Now go back to the other room. I'm going to sleep some more. Only nutty skating fanatics get out of bed before dawn."

From her nightstand, Winja grabbed a small bottle and shook out two yellow pills. She quickly swallowed them and patted her flat stomach. Cammie noticed that the witch's brown pajamas were torn in three places and half of the buttons were missing.

"Don't you want water?" Cammie asked. She couldn't imagine taking medications without water.

Winja grimaced and shook her head. "Go sleep. We'll talk in the morning."

She clicked her lamp off; the room was dark again. Cammie and Alex had no choice but to go back to the adjoining room where they had woken up. They looked for the light switch, but the walls felt bare.

"Shall we try to get out of here now?" Cammie's hand finally found the window. The shutters were closed, but Cammie was sure they would be able to force them open somehow.

Something clanged next to her.

"The shutters are locked; I've found the lock," Alex said angrily. "And we would have to walk by

Winja to escape through the front door. Besides, I feel sleepy. I can hardly keep my eyes open."

Only now did Cammie realize how weak and tired she was. "Yeah, let's wait till the morning."

Feeling that her legs would give way any minute, Cammie reached for the mattress strewn on the floor where they had slept before. She didn't even remember her head touch the thin cotton pillow.

"Now get out of bed, you brats! How come the beast didn't wake you up?"

Cammie opened her eyes. For a moment, she didn't know where she was, but when she saw Winja leaning on her crutches next to the mattress, she remembered everything. Alex and she had been kidnapped.

Alex sat up and let out a yawn.

"What do you want?" he asked Winja.

"I wish I could get what I wanted," the witch grumbled.

Cammie saw that the bump on the woman's forehead was still bright purple.

"However, it's not up to me to decide. The Witch of Pride is calling a special meeting this morning, and that's where your destiny will be determined. Until then, you'll stay here. But I don't want you snooping around. Is that understood?"

Okay, so Winja was leaving. That was good. With the evil woman out of the way, Cammie and Alex would have plenty of time to plan their escape.

"I asked the two of you a question. Did you understand me or not?" Winja raised one of her crutches menacingly.

"Yes," Cammie said quickly.

"Yes what?" Winja's puckered face glowed with obvious delight.

"We got the message," Alex said calmly.

"That's better." Winja's crutch squeaked as she proceeded toward the exit. "Maybe, if you behave, the Witch of Fear won't be too harsh on you."

The door slammed; then there was the sound of a key turning in the lock.

Cammie looked at Alex nervously. "Anything but the Witch of Fear."

"Let's cross that bridge when we get to it, okay? First of all, we're looking for the R.O.F.A., right? And chances are, the device is in Winja's house. Remember all the medicines she has? Now where do you think she could hide the R.O.F.A.?"

"Probably in the bedroom," Cammie said.

Winja's bed was unmade; her brown pajamas lay in a heap on top of the quilt. Cammie quickly looked under the pillow, threw off the quilt, and even stripped the sheets off the mattress.

"There's nothing here."

"I'm not finding anything either," Alex said, rummaging through Winja's closet.

"How does she even skate in all these long skirts?" Alex turned out the pockets of a long quilted skirt. "No R.O.F.A. here either."

"By the way." Cammie raised her head from the nightstand littered with medical bottles. "Has anyone told us what the R.O.F.A. looks like?"

Alex turned away from the closet. "Hey, no!"

"So how are we going to find it?"

"Hmm." Alex walked away from the closet. "I'm sure we'll recognize it when we see it. Okay, there's nothing in the bedroom. Let's search the kitchen."

"Ugh!" Cammie didn't want to go to the kitchen.

"What's wrong?"

"The mice," Cammie whispered. Of course, the little rodents weren't as terrifying as the Witch of Fear, but she didn't want to look at them either.

Alex looked amused. "Relax, I'll go in first and scare all the predators away."

Winja's kitchen looked as messy as last night. An unfinished bottle of milk sat on the table strewn with breadcrumbs. Next to the bottle was a half-eaten onion. The kitchen smelled of burnt oatmeal.

"We haven't had any breakfast, by the way," Alex said.

"I'm not hungry," Cammie said quickly as she saw a small skillet with the remains of what looked like vegetable soup. The soup was covered with a thin layer of mildew.

"Come on. We've got to eat something." Alex opened the refrigerator. "Okay, there are a couple of raw potatoes, three onions … hey, a jar of sauerkraut. Want some?"

Cammie pretended to be gagging.

"Yeah, this is exactly what I feel. Okay, no R.O.F.A. here either." Alex closed the refrigerator. "We've got to find the device fast, and then we'll go to Skater's Finest Food. I want an omelet with hash browns."

Cammie opened one of the kitchen cabinets. "Look, skating animal crackers!"

"Good." Alex accepted the bag and took out three crackers shaped like rabbits wearing skates.

Cammie helped herself to a skating fox. After throwing the empty bag in the trashcan, they did a thorough search of all the cabinets, but there still was no sign of the R.O.F.A. Cammie felt disappointed. Perhaps the magical device wasn't even in Winja's house.

"I found it!" Alex exclaimed triumphantly and raised a big cardboard box. The picture on the box showed a strange-looking device with several metal clasps.

"Yes, that's it!" Cammie clapped her hands. "Give it to me. I'm going to put it around my ankle right away."

"Wait, I want to see it myself first." Alex opened the box and put his hand inside.

"Ouch!" Alex dropped the box.

"What's wrong?" Cammie looked at Alex's hand and screamed. Alex's index finger was trapped between the metal clasps of the device.

"It hurts! Oh, it hurts so much!" Alex shook his hand, but the clasps held his finger tight.

"Come here!" Cammie forced Alex to sit down on one of the wood stools at the kitchen table. She studied the metal construction.

"Cammie, I think my finger is broken," Alex moaned.

That was exactly what Cammie thought, but she didn't want to get her friend upset.

"Wait; maybe it's just a bruise." Slowly, she pressed on one of the clutches, and Alex's finger slid out. The upper part of the finger up to the middle joint was slowly turning purple.

"Oh, no!" Alex bit his lip hard.

"Where's that ice pack?" Cammie opened the freezer door and scanned the shelves filled with ice packs of different sizes and colors. She handed Alex a small black ice pack. Squinting with obvious pain, Alex wrapped it around his finger.

"It's not the R.O.F.A. But what is it?" Trying to keep a safe distance, Cammie looked at the metal structure that now lay discarded on the floor.

Alex moaned. "Silly me. It's a mouse trap."

"A mouse trap?" Yes, now Cammie understood. Winja's house swarmed with mice, so of course the witch needed something to keep them away.

"That was so stupid. I've seen them before." Alex slapped his knee with his healthy hand and grimaced. Apparently, the impact was too much for his broken finger.

"We need to stabilize your finger. Wait. I'm sure Winja has plenty of splints," Cammie said.

She turned out to be right. The witch's cabinet was filled with all kinds of medical supplies. Cammie chose a small metal splint with soft padding and helped Alex slide his finger inside. Then she gently wrapped an elastic band around it and secured the splint with Velcro.

"Feeling better?"

"I guess so." Alex's face looked ashen. "It still hurts, though."

"A pain killer, that's what you need." Cammie rummaged through Winja's cabinets again. "Here you go. Advil."

Alex swallowed the pill. About ten minutes later, Cammie could tell her friend was feeling better. At least, his face had returned to its normal color.

"Alex, you know what I just thought? The R.O.F.A. isn't in Winja's house," Cammie said.

He frowned. "What makes you so sure?"

"Winja's bump," Cammie said. "She was in a lot of pain; we saw that. Don't you think she would have used the R.O.F.A. to cure it if the device was in her house?"

Alex's lips rounded. "How stupid! Gosh, we weren't thinking. We've just been wasting our time. Plus this stupid finger."

"It's okay," Cammie said reassuringly. "At least it's not your leg. You'll be able to practice in a couple of days. I know. Sonia told me once how she had skated with a fractured wrist. So don't worry! Let's just get out of here."

They left the witch's house without problems. Cammie had expected Winja to play some tricks on them, like hiding their skates, but everything seemed to be all right. The cabin door was locked, but the lock on the shutters in Winja's room was broken, so they got outside easily.

"Great!" Cammie breathed in the fresh air and looked happily at the snow-covered oak trees around the cabin. "Which way is the exit from the park?"

"Hey, what's that?" Alex shouted.

Cammie looked in the direction he was pointing and let out a loud, "Oh!" The trees surrounding Winja's house stood close to one another, looking like a natural fence around the cabin. Even one of the mice living in the witch's kitchen would have a hard time squeezing itself between the thick trunks. The only way to get outside Winja's property would be along an ice path that started at the front door of the cabin and disappeared in the thicket.

Yet when Cammie skated closer, she saw that the path was far from straight. It curled and turned. It changed shapes. At some point, it twisted like a spiral or split into two barely connected strips of ice. As Cammie thought about it, she realized that a skater stepping on the ice wouldn't be able to merely glide forward; he or she would have to perform complicated footwork. Cammie groaned. Leaving Winja's property might be a problem.

"What's this?" Alex asked.

Cammie turned to him. He stared at a piece of yellowish paper clipped to one of the trees.

"'Instructions on leaving Winja's property. Visitors, please read!'" Cammie read out loud.

"'A rocker, a loop, four backward power pulls'—hey is that what we're supposed to do?" Alex sounded dumbfounded.

"'Five twizzles on the left foot…' Gosh, I'd never be able to do them. Boy, look at that, 'ten twizzles on the right foot.' Who would be able to do that? And 'three brackets,' no way!" Cammie's knees gave away; she lowered herself into the snow.

"Well, if that's what we have to do…" Alex looked determined.

"You're nuts. I mean, when I was healthy I could probably do a few twizzles on my right foot, but on my left foot I could barely do two in a row. But now that my ankle is weak, I wouldn't even try."

"Yeah, it sure looks scary." Alex scratched his head.

"It is scary. And…oh, no!" Only now did Cammie notice that the ice path they were supposed to skate on was about fifteen feet above a ravine. It meant that if they slipped and fell, they would get injured for sure.

"Winja has surely thought of everything," Alex said through his teeth. "You know what? I bet there's another way out. Don't tell me Winja does those advanced steps each time she leaves her cabin or comes back."

"Maybe she has done it so many times that now it's easy for her," Cammie said.

Alex grunted. "She can barely walk without her crutches."

They searched the whole property but found no other exit. Winja had really thought of everything. For several minutes, Cammie and Alex stood staring at the path that coiled at weird angles ahead of them. A hawk landed on a low branch of an oak tree, studying them with obvious displeasure.

"Tell you what; you wait here. I'll cross the pass and go to Mr. Reed. He'll come for you," Alex said.

Cammie shivered. She hated the idea of staying alone at Winja's property. "What if Winja returns before you and Mr. Reed are here?"

"Well, I'll have to hurry."

"But you can't do that footwork. The steps are too advanced for you."

"Well, it looks like there's no choice." Alex stepped on the ice.

"Alex, please!" Cammie put her hand over her mouth. What if Alex fell and broke something? She knew how much time it took for a broken bone to heal. She absolutely had to stop her friend.

"Alex, when Coach Ferguson told me I wasn't ready for triples, I disobeyed her. And—"

Alex went into a tentative rocker; his body swayed slightly, but he managed to stay vertical.

"And I broke my ankle," Cammie said nervously. "And … Alex, come back. Please!"

She saw Alex's jaw tighten as he did power pulls.

"Alex, it's not worth it. Maybe … maybe there's a phone somewhere in Winja's house. Yes, sure, we can call Mr. Reed. Okay, Alex?" Gosh, why hadn't they thought of it earlier?

Alex completely ignored her. Now he was facing twizzles on his left foot. Cammie's head began to spin.

"Alex!" she called again. "Alex, please!"

He bent his knee, raised his right foot. One, two, three… *Oh please, let him be all right!* Cammie prayed. *If only Alex stays alive, I'll do anything. Please, just let him finish the pattern without getting himself killed!*

"All right!" Alex shouted excitedly.

Cammie opened her eyes. Alex stood on the other side, waving both hands at her.

"Wow, Alex, you're a genius!" Cammie clapped her hands.

"Hey, I haven't been taking dancing lessons for nothing!" he yelled back.

"I'm going to practice those steps too when I get better. I—"

"So you did leave the house after all!"

Cammie let out a quick, "Ouch!" and fell backward. Luckily, she landed on her behind. Unable to believe her eyes, Cammie stared at the grim-looking Winja, who was brandishing one of her crutches at Alex.

"I told you to stay in the house, didn't I? That's it. Now—" Winja raised her crutch.

"Stop it!" Cammie shouted. "You can't hurt Alex. He completed the step sequence perfectly."

Winja turned her reddened face toward Cammie. "So what? I didn't ask him to do the footwork. Don't think you can just twizzle your way out of here, kiddies!"

Winja bent her knees and jumped on the coiling path, blocking Alex's way. Alex, who was about to skate back in the direction of Winja's cabin, stopped short.

"Leave me alone, stupid witch!" he yelled.

Next thing Cammie saw was Alex grabbing a hold of Winja's crutch and snatching it from the woman's grasp. The witch, who had definitely not expected the counter attack, lost balance and sat down on the hard-pressed snow.

"Don't you dare touch my crutch!" Winja screamed.

The witch's sharp blade connected with Alex's calf.

"Ouch!" Alex grabbed his leg. The heavy crutch slid from his hand and fell on the ice path. A high-pitched sound came from the ice, and the multiple twists and turns straightened out instantly. Unable to believe what had happened, Cammie stared at the perfectly straight ice path.

"Oh, no!" Winja groaned.

Without giving the whole thing another thought, Cammie crossed the path in five quick steps and dropped herself on the ground next to Alex. Her friend sat clutching his leg.

"The crutch!" Alex shouted to Cammie. "Get the crutch."

Cammie reached sideways and picked up the metal clutch.

"Give it back! It's mine!" Winja roared.

Cammie jumped to her feet and raised the crutch above her head, watching Winja recoil.

"You have no right to do it. The crutch belongs to me!" the witch screeched.

Cammie took a step forward.

"No!" The witch grabbed the hem of her long skirt and dashed into the thicket. The branches cracked loudly under her blades.

"Good job, Cammie!" Alex smiled at her.

Cammie swirled the crutch in her hands. "So that's how the ice path gets activated. Winja turns it off when she has to get to the other side herself. But to keep unwanted guests away, she turns it on. Wow."

"Yup. It's an easy path for her and a trap for intruders. Or prisoners, whatever." Alex quickly exhaled and unclasped his fingers.

"How is your leg?" Cammie bent over.

Alex's pants were ripped. As he rolled up the right pant leg, Cammie squeaked at the sight of blood oozing from the wound.

"Now relax, Cammie. It's nothing but a small cut. The important thing is we just escaped Winja and didn't get hurt." Alex took off his scarf and wrapped it around his calf.

"Think you can skate?" Cammie asked.

"Of course." Alex hopped on his leg. "No problem."

"You need to see a doctor anyway. Let's go home now, okay?"

"Sure. We both deserve a good rest. We'll visit the other witches tomorrow."

"And the crutch?" Cammie still held the scratched metal thing in her hand.

"We'll hide it somewhere. Let Winja learn to skate without extra support."

Cammie laughed. "Did you see her run away from us? She isn't as sick as she looks."

"Well, that's what Mr. Reed told us."

Still talking about Winja's deceptive nature, they skated toward the exit from the Icy Park. When they finally reached the statue of a skater in the attitude position, they stopped for a short break. From where they stood, they could see a long row of houses on Axel Avenue and, farther away, the outline of the clock tower on Main Square.

"Look. I have an idea. Give me that crutch," Alex said.

He knelt in front of the statue and dug a deep hole in the snow.

"What're you doing?"

"Hiding Winja's crutch." Alex scraped several layers of snow over the crutch then smoothed it with his hand. "Winja will never think of this place, and we can easily access the crutch if we ever need it again. It has magical powers."

After burying the crutch, they approached Axel Avenue.

"I can get to the dorm myself. You go home and rest," Cammie said.

Alex looked hesitant. "Are you sure?"

"I'm positive. Go ahead."

"Hey, where's your Kanga bag?" Alex looked around.

Cammie slapped herself on the forehead. "Oh my gosh, we left it in Winja's house. Should we go back for it?"

Alex shook his head. "Let's find the R.O.F.A. first. Then when you're stronger, we'll get the bag back. Don't you worry."

Cammie sighed. She missed her Kanga already.

"All right, so I'll see you tomorrow and—"

Before Cammie could say another word, a shade fell on the two of them, blocking the sun, and a raspy voice said, "We meet again, kiddies. I don't think we need to wait till tomorrow."

THE WITCH OF PRIDE'S MANSION

As the witches carried Cammie and Alex to the Witch of Pride's ice mobile, Cammie did her best at kicking the evil women on the sides. She even bit Winja, who had been trying hard to restrain her.

"She injured me!" Winja moaned as she raised her wrist with traces of Cammie's teeth.

Apparently, Winja expected sympathy, but that wasn't what she got. The Witch of Fear merely burst out laughing. "I thought *you* were supposed to inflict injuries on skaters."

"I did! Not only is the girl handicapped now, but I broke the boy's finger. And I cut his leg too. I deserve at least a modicum of respect from you, Fear."

The Witch of Fear rolled her eyes. "Because the brats escaped from your property and we had to run around the park looking for them, right?"

"It's because they stole my crutch!" Winja took a small tube and a white roll out of her pocket. She squeezed out some cream on her hand and wrapped her wrist in elastic band.

"A good witch would never let her magical object get stolen," the Witch of Pride said haughtily as she opened the ice mobile door.

"Where is my crutch?" Winja barked at Cammie and Alex.

Alex appeared completely innocent. "We buried it in the snow."

"Where?" Winja snarled as she advanced on him.

"Somewhere there, under a tree." Alex waved in the direction of Winja's house.

"Did you mark the spot?" Winja's voice dropped; she coughed hard.

"No," Alex said. "Should we have?"

"Idiots, oh idiots!" Winja tugged on her long tresses of grayish hair. "What am I supposed to do now? Oh, I'm going to kill you brats. You wait!"

Winja's long fingers scratched Cammie's hand.

"Ouch!" Cammie pulled her hand away, staring at the red marks.

"Enough! You'd better comply with the decision of the witches' board," the Witch of Pride said sharply. "Cammie and Alex are going to my house."

To the Witch of Pride's house? That wasn't too bad. Cammie and Alex needed to visit it anyway. Cammie cast a quick glance in Alex's direction. He winked at her, signaling that he understood.

"Okay, the Witch of Fear will sit next to me, and you, Winja, will join Cammie and Alex in the back seat," the Witch of Pride said.

"Next to the brats? No way. I already played host to them last night." Winja looked at Cammie and Alex, her eyes flashing with hatred.

"Quiet!" the Witch of Fear slapped the silvery side of the ice mobile.

The Witch of Pride grimaced.

"You, Winja, have already messed up everything. So now you'll do what we say or else … " The Witch of Fear brought her wrinkled face close to Winja's. The Witch of Injuries took a quick step back, muttering that she was sorry.

Winja sat in the back seat between Cammie and Alex, which made talking impossible. As the ice mobile moved across the Icy Park, Cammie wondered what the Witch of Pride's home would be like. She hoped it would be cleaner than Winja's cabin and that there would be no mice. Perhaps it wouldn't be particularly big and they would find the R.O.F.A. fast.

The ice squeaked under the ice mobile blades as it took a sharp turn to the right and glided along a straight path. Tall pine trees stood on both sides almost blocking the sky. It looked like an early evening, though Cammie knew it was still daytime.

"Welcome to the mansion of Pride!" The Witch of Pride turned to Cammie and Alex, and her smooth teeth sparkled white against scarlet lipstick.

As Cammie looked straight ahead, she couldn't suppress an excited, "Wow." Towering in front if her was a huge stone mansion with a gabled roof. Through a tall front window, Cammie could see a huge crystal chandelier whose lights were lit, even though it was daytime. The ice mobile slowed down and stopped.

"Here we are!" The Witch of Pride slid from behind the driver's seat and opened the back door of the vehicle.

"Come on. Don't be shy!" She gave Alex a playful tap on the arm.

Alex pulled away from her.

"I'm not going to curse you, you know," the Witch of Pride said lightly.

"Really?" Cammie found the Witch of Pride's behavior a little suspicious. So far the witch was being nice to them, but who knew what was coming next?

"I just want you guys to have fun in my house; that's all. Come on." The Witch of Pride skated up to the front door and put on her skate guards.

Cammie and Alex did the same. They couldn't run away even if they wanted to. Winja and the Witch of Fear were right behind them. The spacious lobby felt warm from the fireplace in the far corner. The parquet floor was so smooth that Cammie wondered if her skate guards might scratch it.

"Let me show you your rooms, and then you'll have lunch with me," the Witch of Pride said.

"I'm not eating with *them*," Winja said grimly.

"I don't remember inviting you," the Witch of Pride sang.

Winja's eyes bulged. "Ah, that's what you're like now! Treating two skating freaks better than your best friends? Witch of Fear, what are you waiting for? Talk some sense into her."

"Well, I believe Pride deserves a chance," the Witch of Fear said coldly. "She may actually end up with more success than you. Come on."

She took Winja firmly by the arm and let her out of the mansion. Their guards clomped against the hard floor; then there was a sound of the door being slammed, and the two witches were gone.

"Good!" The Witch of Pride clapped her hands. "Up to the fifth floor, then."

"Where are you going?" the witch called as Cammie and Alex automatically moved in the direction of a marble staircase.

"Here's the elevator." The witch pressed a gold button, and two sliding doors parted, revealing a roomy elevator with two red leather couches inside.

"Wow!" Cammie took a step forward, studying the carved wood walls and a flower-shaped chandelier inside the elevator.

"Sit down on the couch; let your tired legs rest." The witch's voice sounded friendly.

Cammie and Alex shrugged simultaneously and obeyed, enjoying the feeling of expensive leather embracing their thighs. The elevator glided up smoothly, the door opened, and the three of them stepped out into a long hallway.

"Your room is here, Cammie." The Witch of Pride opened a wood door decorated with a gold figure of a spinning skater.

"And you, Alex, will stay right across from Cammie."

The minute Cammie crossed the threshold she knew it was the best room she had ever seen. The walls were painted pale gold, the floor was covered with a thick gold-and-brown carpet, and a four-post bed with a headboard in the corner was furnished with a stack of pillows of different sizes.

"The bathroom is here." The Witch of Pride pushed the door on the left. "You can also help yourself to the clothes in the closet."

"I can't believe it!" Cammie exclaimed as she stared at the huge closet filled with pants, sweaters, skirts, and dresses of all styles and colors. A special section was reserved for skating dresses. Cammie's hands shook as she pushed the hangers around. Oh, how she wished she could wear this purple dress for her short program! And for her long program, she would try this white-and-yellow dress with a polka dot skirt. Oh, no, she'd look better in this black-and-white dress. The sequins would go well with her hair.

"May I?" Cammie took the dress out of the closet and gave the Witch of Pride a questioning look.

The witch smiled warmly. "That's what these clothes are for. Tell you what. Why don't you choose something to wear for lunch, and you'll wear this dress to a skating practice."

"At the Black Rink?" Cammie wasn't sure she loved the idea of visiting the witches' rink again. Besides, the gorgeous dress would look out of place at a rap party.

The Witch of Pride brushed a piece of lint off her blue velour tracksuit. "Of course not. My guests practice at the Rink of Pride. You'll like it. Go ahead; change."

She left the room, and Cammie rummaged through the nonskating clothes. There were so many outfits to choose from! Finally, Cammie settled on tight dark-blue jeans and a white long-sleeved T-shirt with "A fun deed is pride's creed" displayed in the front.

To complete her look, she put a silvery leather jacket over the T-shirt and replaced her skating boots with a pair of silver high-heeled shoes. She also helped herself to some makeup on the vanity table and took the scrunch out of her hair. She studied her reflection in the mirror and liked her new look. The heels had added a couple of inches to Cammie's height, and the makeup made her appear older and more sophisticated.

Perhaps the Witch of Pride isn't that bad after all, Cammie thought. *Why would an evil person let me use her beautiful things?*

Somebody knocked on the door.

"Come in!" Cammie shouted as she fastened a silver pendant with an emerald lizard around her neck.

Alex walked in wearing black designer jeans and a purple pullover over a white turtleneck.

"Hey, you look cool!" Cammie exclaimed.

"So do you." For some reason, Alex looked a little worried.

"Have you looked around for the R.O.F.A. yet?" Alex asked.

"I searched the closet." Cammie felt ashamed as she realized that she had completely forgotten why they were in the Witch of Pride's mansion in the first place.

"See, I told the witch about my broken finger, and she put it in a cast." Alex raised his finger, demonstrating a black-and-gold cast. It looked more like an expensive accessory than a medical device.

"I know what you mean. The Witch of Pride isn't that bad after all."

Alex shook his head. "That's not the point. Why didn't she use the R.O.F.A. on me? I'm afraid the magical device isn't here."

Cammie thought for a moment. "Well, you can't be sure. Perhaps the witch doesn't want us to know the R.O.F.A. is in her house. She's probably afraid we'll steal it. She knows I need it badly."

"Do you think the Witch of Pride knows about Mr. Reed's rehabilitation technique?" Alex asked.

"She probably does. Winja uses the R.O.F.A. all the time, remember?"

"How on earth are we going to search this huge place?" Alex scratched his head. "It may take weeks. Besides, the witch won't want us snooping around too much."

Cammie waved her hand. "Ah, let's not worry about it now. We'll think of something."

Secretely, Cammie almost wished it would take them a while to find the R.O.F.A. So far she liked the Witch of Pride's mansion. She didn't want to leave until she had a chance to try on all of her knew outfits.

The door swung open, and the Witch of Pride appeared, wearing loose black pants and a red blouse.

"I hope you guys have worked up a good appetite looking through your new clothes," the witch said. "Oh, you both look so chic. Come on. Let's have lunch."

Lunch was served in an airy dining room, and there were just the three of them.

"To you!" The Witch of Pride raised a tall glass with something sparkling red inside. "Fierté, that's the name of it. Best wine to serve with lunch. Do you want some?"

Cammie gasped and shook her head violently. Next to her, Alex did the same thing.

"Well, I'm not going to put pressure on you. Skate shake for you two, then." The witch pointed to several multicolored bottles. "Take your pick: cherry flavored or lemon, orange, strawberry, watermelon, or mango. Sorry, I didn't order any blueberry or papaya shakes; those aren't my favorite."

Cammie and Alex thanked the witch and helped themselves to cherry skate shakes. A maid in a white-and-blue uniform brought in trays with cold cuts, cheeses, and salads. Cammie saw two braids wrapped around the young woman's head and a pair of very pale blue eyes.

"Nurse Vicki!" Cammie exclaimed. She recognized the evil nurse from the hospital.

Vicki eyed Cammie with obvious annoyance but didn't say anything.

"Well, she used to be a nurse. Now she works for me," the Witch of Pride said. "And she doesn't mind the change at all. Is that right, Vicki?"

From where Cammie sat, she could see the young woman's nasty grimace. However, Vicki obviously pulled herself together, for her voice sounded meek. "Of course not, Witch of Pride."

"People like being around me," the Witch of Pride said. "I'm not mean like the Witch of Fear or miserable like Winja. Neither do I control or destroy people. And of course, I'm very organized, unlike the Witch of Confusion. Just wait, you guys. We'll have a lot of fun together."

Cammie caught Alex's worried look. She too felt uneasy. Really, what was the witch going to do to them? On the other hand, Cammie couldn't help agreeing that the Witch of Pride's mansion was definitely a step up from Winja's cabin.

"Aren't you hungry? Dig in. The food isn't poisoned." The witch took a sip of her wine and piled some Caesar salad on her plate.

Staying hungry won't help us, Cammie thought and reached for a roll. Alex was already chewing a mozzarella stick.

Everything tasted great, but just as Cammie thought she was full, Vicki brought in another tray, this time with bowls of soup.

"Personally, I like French onion soup." The witch smiled at Vicki, who had deposited a bowl in front of her. "But chicken corn chowder and clam chowder are also good, so take your pick."

Cammie chose chicken corn chowder. The soup was hot and delicious.

Cammie pushed her bowl away and said, "Thank you," to Vicky, who had just returned with a tray of hot sandwiches.

"More food?" Alex stared at a big cheese steak sandwich, apparently not sure if he had room for it.

"And why not?" The Witch of Pride took a bite of an Italian sub. "Food is one of the chief pleasures of life."

Feeling that they would hurt the witch's feelings if they said no, Cammie accepted a spicy chicken sandwich. She swallowed the last bite and patted her stomach.

"Uh, that was really good. Thank you!"

"Feeling full, huh?" The witch grinned at Alex, who squinted like a cat.

"Yeah!" Alex beamed back.

"Time for dessert, then." The witch snapped her fingers, and Vicki reappeared in the room carrying a tray with ice cream sundaes and plates of cakes.

"It's too much!" Cammie shook her head, but Vicki was already loading her plate with slices of cheesecake, carrot cake, and Boston cream pie.

"Don't forget the ice cream!" the witch said.

"But I can't!" Still Cammie picked on her sundae, at least to find out what it tasted like. Boy, it was good! But it probably wasn't a good idea to eat so much. *Athletes have to watch their diets*, Cammie said to herself. *Well, you don't eat like that all the time*, someone whispered in her ear. Perhaps the witch had said those words, but too busy with her dessert, Cammie didn't really care. *I'll skip dinner tonight*, Cammie thought and bit into her carrot cake.

When Vicki finally cleared the table, Cammie felt so full that she could hardly breathe. On top of that, she suddenly remembered that she hadn't gotten enough rest last night. Winja's cabin wasn't a comfortable place to sleep in. Cammie put her hand against her mouth to suppress a yawn, but she couldn't keep her eyes open.

"Ready for a nap? Personally, I always rest after lunch. Beauty sleep, they call it, and they're right. Look at me, kids. I won't tell you my age, of course, but believe me. I don't look any different than thirty years ago, when I was still a competitive skater."

Cammie looked at the woman's double chin and rolls of fat around her midriff and doubted that the witch had had the same figure in her competitive days. But she wasn't going to criticize the woman who had been treating Alex and her so well.

"Go to your rooms and take it easy for a while. See you later." The Witch of Pride stood up.

Cammie and Alex did the same. As Cammie waited for the elevator, her head spun. All she wanted to do was sleep.

"I'm so tired." Alex yawned widely. "The witch isn't too bad after all, is she?"

"I guess not." Cammie rubbed her eyes. "I'll see you later, okay?"

"Sure. Sleep well."

Back in her room, Cammie got out of her nice clothes and pulled on a lace nightgown that she had found in the closet. She was asleep even before her head touched the pillow.

When Cammie woke up, the room bathed in bright sunlight.

Cammie looked around at her four-poster bed and her blue silk sheets. And then she remembered; she was in the Witch of Pride's mansion.

"But we got here in the afternoon!" she exclaimed. She frowned as she looked at her watch again. Ten after ten. Did it mean she had slept through the day and through the night? Amazing.

Shaking her head, Cammie got out of bed and headed for the shower. Then she studied the contents of her closet again and put on white jeans and a black long-sleeved T-shirt. A black-and-white jacket completed the ensemble.

"Cammie, are you awake?" Alex's voice came from the hallway followed by a loud rap on the door.

"Sure, come on in!"

Today, Alex wore gray cargo pants and a dark-green sweater. "Did you just wake up too?"

"Yes, can you believe it? Where is the witch?"

"I don't think she's at home. I called for her, but nobody answered. Do you want to look for the R.O.F.A. while she's out?" Alex asked.

"Sure."

They left Cammie's room and walked along the hallway.

"I'd search the witch's quarters first," Alex said. "Let's go down to the fourth floor. I saw her go there yesterday."

They walked down one flight of steps. Just like on the fifth floor, there were doors on both sides. Alex pulled the first door open. "Look, it's an exercise room. Think she'd keep the R.O.F.A. here?"

"Why not? People get injured when they exercise."

They looked underneath every exercise machine, but there was nothing that could be used as a restorative device. Slightly disappointed, they moved to the adjoining room.

"It's a music room!" Cammie exclaimed as she stared at a baby grand piano and four guitars. A flute sat on a pulpit next to a tenor saxophone.

"Does the witch know how to play?" Cammie ran through the piano keys.

"No idea," Alex said absentmindedly. He was looking through a stack of CDs in the corner. "Boy, she has hours and hours of skating music. Look: "Night on Bald Mountain" by Mussorgski—cool piece. I wish I could skate to it."

"But still no R.O.F.A." Cammie closed the music book she had been studying. "Let's move on."

They looked for the magical device in the library filled with romance novels and mysteries. Cammie couldn't help noticing that there were no skating books of any kind. They passed a snack room stocked with candy, cookies, cashews, peanuts, and potato chips. Alex helped himself to a jar of peanuts. Cammie put a bag of hard candy in her pocket, but they still didn't find the R.O.F.A.

Finally, they opened the door that led to a richly furnished bedroom. It looked a lot like Cammie's only bigger and even more luxurious. There was a fireplace at the far end of the room, and a dark-brown velour couch sat next to a tall window. Cammie thought that the witch probably enjoyed sitting on the couch and admiring the view of the snow-covered park outside. A half-finished bottle of wine and an empty glass sat on the carpet next to the couch. On the windowsill was a big box of chocolate blades. Cammie reached for a candy and put it in her mouth.

The king-size bed was unmade, and a red robe sat on top of the pillow.

"Check the nightstand!" Alex said as he looked under the pillow.

"There's nothing there." Cammie opened the closet door. There were even more clothes than in her room.

"Wow, Alex, I was wondering how many fur coats the witch had. One, two…seven, eight. Can you believe it? No, there are probably nine because she must be wearing one now, so—"

"Ah, Cammie, we need to get out!"

"Why?"

And then Cammie heart it too: loud music from downstairs.

"The witch must be back!" Cammie closed the closet and ran out of the room after Alex. Together they leaned against the banister, watching the lobby. The Witch of Pride stood in the middle wearing a light-gray fur coat. Music poured out from the loudspeakers in the corners, and a very sour-looking Vicki sang along, "I'm glad to greet you, Witch of Pride. To be with you is sheer delight!"

Alex shook his head. "That's crazy!"

"Ah, my dear guests!" The witch must have seen them. "So are you enjoying your stay? Did you have a good rest? And how about your clothes?"

Cammie and Alex assured her they were fine. Yes, and they loved their new clothes too.

"Well, are you ready to eat?" The Witch of Pride shook off her coat; the delicate fur slid down to the floor. Vicki picked up the coat and walked out of the lobby. Cammie was about to say that she had eaten too much yesterday, but the minute she thought of food she realized she could actually eat something.

"I thought so." The Witch of Pride looked fresh in her bright-red sweater and black pants.

They had a big lunch. At the beginning, Cammie thought she wouldn't let herself overeat, but the colossal burgers with French fries tasted so good that she ended up as stuffed as the day before.

This is getting out of control, Cammie thought as she watched Alex giggle at one of the witch's jokes.

How on earth are we going to skate feeling so bloated? Cammie asked herself. Her jeans felt tight; she shifted in her chair.

"So are we going to your rink now, Witch of Pride?" Alex asked as they were enjoying large servings of apricot cobbler with vanilla ice cream.

"Uh, perhaps." The witch sipped her Irish cream liquor. "Do you guys feel like practicing now?"

Cammie and Alex stared at each other. Cammie wasn't even sure she could walk steadily; her stomach seemed to be pulling her down.

The witch tossed her long hair behind her back. "Neither do I. Therefore, I have a suggestion. How about watching a movie?"

"Okay!" Cammie and Alex exclaimed. That was an excellent idea. Perhaps it would be good for them to take their minds off their quest for a short time. Besides, they couldn't look for the R.O.F.A. when the witch was home anyway.

They followed the Witch of Pride to the television room equipped with comfortable armchairs and a huge plasma TV. The witch rummaged through a stack of DVDs. "How about *The Matrix*? I haven't seen it, but I heard it's a good movie."

"Oh sure," Alex said excitedly.

Cammie felt a little surprised. Somehow, she had thought they would watch a skating movie. But probably an action movie would be good for a change. They made themselves comfortable in soft armchairs, with their feet on footrests. Vicki had put bags of cashews and peanuts and cans of Coke on trays next to them so they could enjoy their snacks without getting up. As the maid brought in bags of popcorn, Cammie breathed in the rich buttery smell and smiled happily.

After the movie, Cammie and Alex felt drowsy again, and the witch recommended another nap. They slept till dinner and then feasted on Mexican food. This time, Cammie didn't feel very bloated; her stomach must have stretched a little. After dinner, they watched the sequel to the first movie called *The Matrix Reloaded*. And then it was nine o'clock, and Vicki served them hot chocolate and cookies. Cammie thought they would watch something else, but everybody was too tired, so they made it an early night.

Their second day in the Witch of Pride's mansion was very much like the first; the third appeared to be a carbon copy of the second. They finished *The Matrix* series and moved on to *Twilight* and then to *The Da*

Vinci Code. Once Cammie suggested watching a skating competition, but the witch was dead set against it.

"Don't you guys have enough skating in your life already? Actually, scientists have proven that taking some time off from your favorite activity boosts your creative potential. Yes, and in case you don't know, skating videos are forbidden in my house."

The longer Cammie stayed in the Witch of Pride's mansion, the more she enjoyed sleeping late in the morning and eating good food. Vicki was an excellent cook, and she served them something different every day. Alex enjoyed Eastern cuisine the most, while Cammie preferred Italian cooking. The Witch of Pride said everything tasted so good that she couldn't really decide what she would rather eat.

"Variety is the spice of life. This is something I know for sure," the witch always said.

Days rolled by. Cammie and Alex were happy, and sometimes Cammie wished they would stay in the Witch of Pride's mansion forever.

THE EYE OPENER

On a Saturday afternoon a week after arriving at the mansion, Cammie sat on a white leather couch in the living room, lazily flipping through the pages of *Seventeen* magazine. Except for *Vogue*, *Good Housekeeping*, and *People*, that was the only magazine Cammie could find in the Witch of Pride's mansion. The witch had told them that she would rather have no skating literature in her house, and honestly, Cammie didn't even miss skating that much.

Cammie took two cashews from the jar that sat on the couch next to her and turned a page. It was after noon, and the Witch of Pride still hadn't returned.

She'd better come back home soon. Cammie was getting really hungry.

The doorbell chimed in the lobby downstairs. Cammie didn't move, thinking that answering the door was Vicki's job. But the visitor kept ringing the bell; apparently, Vicki had gone out too. Slowly, reluctantly, Cammie put the can on the floor and strolled to the lobby. As she lifted the latch and turned the handle, the door opened, letting in a cloud of frosty air. A tall, overweight girl in a plaid coat and knit cap stood on a porch with a big package in her hand.

Cammie let out a quick, "ouch," and stepped back. "Annie! Is that you?"

Annie sneered. "And who else do you think it is? Santa Claus? Nay, it's just the little old me, and the package isn't for you. Where is the witch?"

"She isn't home. Give me the package and leave," Cammie said firmly. She didn't want to let Annie in, not after the girl had given her and Alex over to the witches.

With just a casual push on the shoulder, Annie moved Cammie away and crossed the threshold.

"You can't come in!"

Ignoring Cammie's clenched fists, the girl unwrapped her scarf and took off her coat. "I guess I'll wait for the witch in the living room. Are you going to offer me a drink or not? As far as I remember, I showed you more hospitality at the Black Rink."

"You…how can you? You betrayed me, and now you expect a treat from me?" The flames of the fireplace danced in front of Cammie, and her forehead was moist with perspiration.

"You stupid idiot!" Annie chortled. "What I did was nothing but a survivor instinct. And if you want to be a witch, you'll have to understand it sooner or later."

"What?" Cammie stepped back, thinking that she had misunderstood Annie. "I don't want to be a witch."

The girl rolled her eyes. "Then what the heck are you doing here? And don't give me that R.O.F.A. junk again. Your skating career is over, and you know it."

"Out!" Cammie shouted. "Get out now!"

Annie didn't move; she looked amused. "You aren't my boss, little Cammie. And in case you still have some delusions, let me tell you the truth. The witch is doting all over you for a reason. Has it ever occurred to you?"

Cammie unclenched her fists and let out a deep sigh. "What do you mean?"

"The witch serves you good food; she shows you movies; she showers you with gifts. Am I right?"

"Perhaps." Cammie folded her arms. "So?"

"She wants you to start enjoying this life without skating. Now tell me the truth. You don't even practice anymore. Is it true? Tell me."

The front door slammed, and the Witch of Pride walked in. Today she wore a floor-length black fur coat and a white fur hat. When the witch saw Annie, her puffy face reddened. "What are you doing here?"

The girl looked defiant. "The Witch of Destruction sent you a package."

"Fine. Give me the package and get out." The witch stretched her hand.

Cammie saw the girl's jaw tighten as she handed the package to the witch. Before turning the handle, Annie lingered for a second.

"I told you *out*!" The Witch of Pride's voice sounded shrilly.

Annie's shoulders stiffened. "Fine. I'll leave."

Then without a pause, the girl began to scream. "Witch of Pride, it's not fair. I'm not any worse than these … these losers. And yet you give them stuff and treat them like Olympic champions and—"

"I don't remember asking for your opinion," the witch said calmly.

Annie stomped her foot. "They won't stay with you anyway. Especially the boy. His dream is to become a champion, so—"

"Now I've had enough of this." The witch crossed the lobby and grabbed Annie by the shoulder. A huge ruby glittered on the woman's middle finger.

"They'll betray you. You'll see!" Annie spat and hissed.

Before the door slammed shut after the girl, Cammie heard her last statement: "You aren't even a skater anymore, Cammie. And once you join the witches' program, she'll be as nasty to you as she is to me."

The Witch of Pride locked the door. "Sloppy pig! Did you see her? She isn't even wearing skates anymore. What's wrong?" the witch asked Cammie, who stood rooted to her spot.

"Uh, nothing." Cammie felt her head spin. Could Annie be telling the truth and the witch really had some evil agenda? And Cammie and Alex really didn't skate anymore.

"Are you up for another movie? I went out and bought *A Night in the Museum*." The witch waved a DVD at Cammie.

"Uh, sure." Cammie decided she'd better not make the witch upset. Alex and she would figure out what to do later.

"Okay, so I'll go change and meet you guys in the TV room." The Witch of Pride blew a kiss at Cammie and headed for the elevator.

Cammie took the elevator up to the fifth floor. When she reached Alex's room, she was completely out of breath. Really, not skating around was finally getting to her.

Alex lay in his bed deep in sleep.

"Alex, wake up now! We're in trouble." Cammie shook her friend by the shoulder.

Alex opened one eye, looked at her, and closed it again.

"Alex, come on!"

He turned to the other side and pulled the covers up to his chin.

I wish Kanga were here, Cammie thought sadly. "Alex, open your eyes!" She shoved him on the side.

"Um-murr-purr!" Alex smacked his lips and was still again.

Well, if Cammie didn't have Kanga with her, she would have to act like the alarm clock.

"Wake up right now, sleepy head!" Cammie shouted so loudly that her ears began to ache. Ignoring the unpleasant feeling, Cammie recited the lines of Kanga's wakeup poem. "But if you stay in bed and snooze, you'll never win; instead you'll lose!"

"I thought I already won." Alex opened his eyes. "Cammie? Where's my medal?"

He patted himself on the chest, looking glazed. "I just stood on the podium at the Olympics. Did you see me? I won. I did two quads in my free program, and—"

Cammie didn't think the situation was funny, but she laughed anyway. "Alex, you've been sleeping. We're in the Witch of Pride's mansion, remember?"

"Ah!" Alex sat up in bed and looked around at the closed drapes and the pile of clothes next to his bed. His eyes darkened. "So I didn't win the Olympic gold?"

Cammie rolled her eyes. "No, you didn't."

"I'll be darned!" Alex slapped himself on the knee and grimaced slightly. His finger was probably still bothering him.

"So are we going to watch a movie or what?" Alex yawned and reached for his T-shirt. "You'd better wait outside while I get dressed."

"Alex, wait! There's something you need to know." Cammie told him about Annie's visit and what the girl had told her. "Do you see what's going on? The Witch of Pride wants us to join the witches' school. That's why she's been so nice to us."

Alex looked skeptical. "So what? We won't apply to that stupid school, and that'll be it."

"Of course we won't, but the witch has something on her mind. She's smart, you know. That's the reason she's been treating us so well."

Alex grinned. "Don't worry about it."

"You'd better hurry up, kids. I can't wait to watch that movie with you!" The Witch of Pride's voice sounded right next to Alex's door.

"See? She watches our every step," Cammie whispered.

Alex curved his lips. "Baloney. Are you going to let me get dressed or not?"

Feeling worried, Cammie waited for her friend in the hallway. When the two of them reached the TV room, they found the witch slouched in an armchair in a yellow silk robe. She twirled a glass of Fierté in her hand.

"Look, guys, I want to tell you something before we start watching the movie. Today you, Cammie, overheard a nasty exchange between Annie and me. Let me assure you: things aren't as bad as they seem. Annie is a pathological liar, and she only said those things because she's jealous of you guys. She's not a talented skater, nor does she have your good looks." The witch's eyes focused on Alex, causing him to blush.

"And Annie doesn't have the true star quality, and this it what it takes to become an Olympic champion." This time, the witch glanced at Cammie.

Though Cammie enjoyed the compliment, she thought she'd better ask for an explanation.

"What's star quality?"

"Well, there are many good skaters, but few of them really make it to the top. To win the Olympics, you need to become almost like a beast believing that you're superior to everybody else. And you need to be willing to do anything—do you hear me?—*anything* to reach your goal. Remember: everything is okay as soon as you're the best. Even cheating and lying are acceptable because if you're on top of others, people will never notice. And if they do, well, they'll ignore it."

Cammie cringed. Cheating, lying?

"Believe me. It may come to that, though it doesn't have to." The witch gave Cammie a charming smile. "You're a good enough skater to make it on pure talent. Yes, and another thing—don't sweat too much. Skaters who work too hard never win."

"Really?" Alex shot a puzzled look at the Witch of Pride.

Cammie too was surprised. How could you become an Olympic champion without working hard?

"Having fun—that's what matters the most." The witch raised her index finger. Today she had orange nail polish on. There was a pause, during which Cammie thought hard about what she had just heard.

"So speak up. What's bothering you?" the witch asked.

"Hmm, we don't skate anymore," Cammie said gingerly.

"Oh!" The witch took a sip of her wine and gently put the glass on the carpet. "Well, did I ever tell the two of you not to skate?"

Alex rubbed his forehead and shrugged.

"I did ask you several times if you wanted to skate, but you said you were too tired. So I let you rest. Does that make me evil?" The witch's dark eyes lingered on Cammie.

Cammie shrugged awkwardly. "Of course not. It's just... you never told us to go to practice."

"Aha!" The Witch of Pride jumped to her feet. "A very common mistake. Coaches tell their skaters what to do all the time. They nag them. They put too much pressure on their students, and then they wonder why the skaters miss their jumps in competitions."

"And why do they?" Alex asked eagerly. Cammie knew he was thinking about his own fiasco at Skateland Annual Competition.

"Too much strain, for all I know." The witch sat down again, looking delighted. "Trust the Witch of Pride, kids. Don't ever work too hard; it will turn you into nervous wrecks. If you don't feel like going to practice, stay home and rest. Believe me. It'll do you lots of good. Let me put it this way: only skate when you feel like it."

"Hmm." Cammie was trying hard to digest what she had just heard. Perhaps the witch was right after all. For all Cammie knew, skaters who had won big competitions didn't work any more than the athletes who had come in closer to the bottom. Even Alex…

"So are you ready for a movie?" The Witch of Pride asked Cammie.

Cammie took a deep sigh and nodded.

Days rolled by, and Cammie and Alex still hadn't skated once. They didn't miss practices on purpose. Every night before going to bed, Cammie told herself that tomorrow everything would be different. She would get up early and go to the the Witch of Pride's rink. After all, it was so close.

"Just walk around the building, and there it is," the witch had told them.

But morning came and went, and Cammie was still in bed. And when she did get up, there were always things to do. Taking a nice hot bath, looking through the closet for a new outfit to wear for lunch. Eating, watching movies, trying different snacks— all those pleasant things kept Cammie and Alex busy.

The Witch of Pride had six shelves filled with DVDs. And if that wasn't enough, she brought something new for them to watch every day. And after enjoying a movie, all of them were ready for a nap, of course, for they needed strength to watch another in the evening.

Sometimes Cammie worried about her ankle. It didn't hurt anymore; yet the muscles didn't seem to be getting any stronger. She remembered what her doctors had said about the importance of daily exercises. Yet she never went to the witch's exercise room and she always used the elevator to get from one floor to another.

"It's okay," she would say to herself. "Once we're out of here, I'll be back to my old schedule. I'll be working very, very hard."

The Witch of Pride left the house every morning, taking Vicki with her. That gave Cammie and Alex plenty of opportunities to look for the R.O.F.A. They searched the mansion with a fine-tooth comb, but they never found the magical device.

"Do you think we need to leave?" Cammie asked Alex once. "The R.O.F.A. must be in the Witch of Fear's house."

Alex looked uncertain. "You may be right, but I kind of like it here. How about staying a couple of more days? I think both of us deserve a little break."

Cammie nodded. "Okay. Just a couple of days, all right?"

But days became weeks, and still Cammie and Alex didn't feel like leaving. The Witch of Pride was sweet and friendly. She never ran out of compliments, telling both Cammie and Alex that they had great futures ahead of them.

"I'll come to cheer for you when you compete at the Olympics," the witch said one day during dinner.

"Oh please do!" Alex exclaimed.

Cammie didn't say anything.

"Don't you need my support, Cammie?" the Witch of Pride asked.

Cammie cleared her throat. "Of course, I do. It's just…I think we really need to go back to practices."

The witch spread her arms. "Of course! Go ahead. It's only two o'clock now. However…" She took a DVD out of her pocket book. "Would you guys rather skate or watch *Jurassic Park* with me?"

Jurassic Park was supposed to be really scary. Cammie had once overheard Dana tell Liz about it.

"I'd rather watch the movie," Alex said firmly.

"How about you, Cammie?" the Witch of Pride asked.

"Hmm…we can always skate tomorrow," Cammie mumbled.

"Good thinking!" The Witch of Pride picked up her glass and walked to the TV room, motioning for them to follow her.

One day, when Cammie sat in the living room polishing her fingernails, the doorbell rang. Cammie ignored it until she heard loud screams in the lobby followed by the Witch of Pride's cussing. Wondering what was wrong, Cammie walked to the lobby and stopped abruptly.

Lieutenant Turner stood in the middle of the foyer, his nose appearing even longer on his reddened face. He waved his hand at the Witch of Pride, who eyed the young man with obvious annoyance.

"Yes, that's what I'm telling you, Witch of Pride. The young ladies are your responsibility. So if you don't want them to be sent away from Skateland, you'll have to sign a consent form."

"What's that?" The Witch of Pride's face twisted in disgust as though she were chewing on a lemon.

"It says here that Vicki and Annie are being released into your supervision."

"And what if I don't sign this stupid form?" The witch raised her left foot and balanced a bright-red slipper on her big toe.

"I already told you: we'll have to send Vicki and Annie away. SUI is a serious offense. In case you don't remember, it's *skating under influence*. Your young witches got smashed on beer."

"I'm perfectly aware what SUI is," the witch snapped. "But I don't think you have any proof."

"We sure do. Four witnesses saw the young ladies drink beer and then skate at the Main Rink."

The witch's slipper fell on the floor. "Do you mean the Black Rink?"

"No, they went to the Main Rink, and there were a lot of people there, so—"

The witch picked up her slipper and tossed it at the policeman. He ducked just in time. "Idiots, what idiots!" the witch roared. "Isn't there enough room at the Black Rink? Now give me that silly form. I'll sign it and then…"

Muttering something under her breath, the Witch of Pride took a red pen out of her pocketbook and quickly put her signature on the piece of paper that the lieutenant had handed her.

"I'll change and meet you at the police station," the witch said to Lieutenant Turner.

"I can take you there myself," the young man said.

"I have my own ice mobile. Thank you," the witch said icily and walked out of the lobby, ignoring Cammie. Or perhaps she simply hadn't seen Cammie watching the scene.

The moment the Witch of Pride was gone, Lieutenant Turner turned to Cammie. "Cammie, I'm here to give you a message from Mrs. Van Uffeln."

"What?" That was the last thing Cammie expected. "Does Wilhelmina know where we are?"

The young man smirked. "Wasn't it Mrs. Van Uffeln who came up with that whole idea of Full-Circle Therapy? Only it doesn't look like you're working hard on your rehabilitation."

Cammie felt blood rush to her cheek as the policeman looked at her bathrobe and slippers.

"Anyway, the president told me you might need this." Lieutenant Turner opened the front door, and Cammie saw her Kanga bag sitting on the porch.

"You'd better take it to your room, for I don't think the witch will let you keep Kanga in the house," the policeman said softly.

Cammie shrugged. "The Witch of Pride lets us do anything we want."

"I'm only giving you Mrs. Van Uffeln's message." The lieutenant stiffened up, saluted, and walked out of the lobby, closing the door behind him.

Cammie stared at the bag. So Wilhelmina wanted her to have it. And the Witch of Pride wasn't supposed to know about Kanga. That was interesting. Cammie didn't think the witch would object Kanga's presence in the house. She was really a nice person. On the other hand, Wilhelmina Van Uffeln had never given Cammie wrong advice.

Cammie quickly replaced Kanga's blades with wheels and pulled the bag up to her room. She waited for the Witch of Pride to leave the house. When it became clear the woman was gone, Cammie sat down on the carpet next to Kanga, deep in thought. Why was it important for her to have the bag back? What exactly were Cammie and Alex missing? They no longer went to practices, so Cammie didn't need a bag for her stuff. The navigator was of little use too. And of course, they slept till ten or eleven o'clock every morning, so the alarm clock wouldn't do them any good. So the only other function Kanga had was…

"The media player!" Cammie exclaimed. Sure, that was it. Even though Cammie and Alex watched movies every day, none of the films were skating related. And they hadn't seen a skating competition in weeks. So did Wilhelmina think it was important for them to see one?

Cammie went to Alex's room, found him asleep, and returned to her bedroom. She positioned herself on the floor next to Kanga and pressed the media player button. The animal's paws dived inside the belly pocket and returned with a monitor. Cammie looked through a long list of skating competitions taking place all over the world. Junior Worlds. Yes, that was the competition Cammie really wanted to watch. Junior Ladies' Free Skate, live. Cool. It meant Cammie could cheer for Sonia.

Cammie positioned Kanga on a chair next to her bed and plopped on the soft mattress. The girls' standings after the short program appeared on the screen. Cammie was shocked to see that Sonia was in third place after a Japanese girl and a Russian skater. That was unusual. As far as Cammie knew, Sonia had won every competition she had ever entered.

Cammie sat through the first three groups of competitors, each consisting of six skaters. Sonia was in the last, strongest group. At the beginning, Cammie thought it would be boring to watch less-advanced skaters. And yet when the first competitor froze in the middle of the ice in her beginning posture, Cammie found herself wishing the girl would do her best.

"Oh!" Cammie groaned when the girl fell on her initial triple flip. "Come on!" She slapped her knee when the skater two-footed her triple loop. "I could do it once, you know!" Cammie said angrily as the harassed girl did a single axel instead of a double. "If you keep making all those mistakes, I'll beat you in a couple of years!" Cammie announced, leaning back onto her pillow. She felt warm and comfortable.

The girl's score was abysmally low. The rest of the skaters performed with different degrees of brilliance. Some glided through their programs; others struggled even with simple moves. Several girls looked so nervous that they didn't seem to be enjoying themselves.

"But I did great last time I competed. Did you see me, Kanga?" Cammie reached for a lollypop shaped like a snowman on her nightstand. "Of course, I was the best." Cammie made a funny face and chanted with exaggerated flare. "North or South, East or West, Cammie Wester is the best!"

Finally, the announcer invited the last group of skaters to take the ice for their warm-up. Cammie watched the girls take off their skate guards and shoot across the ice in high speed. Yes, there was Sonia wearing a very cute green-and-silver dress. Her curly hair was fastened with a matching scrunch.

Boy, she must be nervous, Cammie thought. She closed her eyes for a second, remembering what skating in a warm-up was like. She thought of the last-minute rush through the program; of the shaking legs; of the ice, either too hard or too soft; of the buzz in the ears; and then she thought how terrible it would be to forget her program midway.

"Really, it wasn't that much fun!" Cammie shivered and pulled the covers on top of her legs. "Let

Sonia sweat out there, and I'll relax in this comfort-able bed. Right, Kanga?"

Cammie felt wonderful, except for an unpleasant tickling that was forming somewhere in her chest. She rubbed her chest and her stomach to get rid of it.

"Ladies, your warm-up is now ended. Please leave the ice," the announcer said.

The girls rushed to the exit, all except the Japanese competitor, who was supposed to skate first.

"I always liked skating last." Cammie opened a can of Coke and took a swig. "See, Kanga, you already know what the rest of the girls did, so ... wow!"

The Japanese girl had just landed a triple toe-triple toe combination.

Will Sonia be able to top that? Cammie wondered. Surely she had aced her triple-triple combination at the nationals, but as far as Cammie knew, it still wasn't consistent.

The Japanese skater fell from her double axel.

"Hey, how about that? I can do it, and I'm only an intermediate skater."

Can you really? a voice whispered inside of her.

"Sure!" Cammie reached for another lollypop, but her hand froze in the air. Honestly, could she even land a single axel now?

"But I'm still recuperating!" Cammie told the nagging voice.

I thought you sat in your bed eating candy, the voice said nastily.

"Hey, give me a break! I've been through a lot," Cammie shouted. She couldn't hear the voice anymore, but the uncomfortable feeling was still there.

When the Japanese girl's scores appeared, she was in first place. Cammie sat through the next three girls' performances. The girls were actually better than the Japanese girl, but because the Japanese skater had a huge lead after the short program, no one managed to move up.

Sonia skated next to last. When Cammie saw her roommate, small and fragile, she doubted Sonia could beat the Japanese skater. She wondered if Sonia would even attempt her triple-triple combination.

"I probably wouldn't," Cammie said to Kanga. "I'd play it safe. Because it's better to win any medal than to lose the competition altogether."

You didn't play it safe last time. There was that voice again.

"And I ended up getting injured. Gosh!" Cammie threw the empty can across the room and watched it bounce against the wall. Whether Sonia tried her combination or not, she was competing at the Junior Worlds. And Cammie sat in the Witch of Pride's mansion; she didn't even skate anymore.

Sonia picked up speed, did a quick three turn…Cammie clasped her hands as she watched her friend do a secure triple flip.

"Yes!" Cammie exclaimed, and at the same moment, Sonia soared up in the air again, this time in a triple toe loop. It was a beautiful, perfect combination.

Mesmerized, Cammie watched her roommate skate the rest of her program. Sonia performed the most difficult moves easily. When the girl glided across the rink in a spiral, Cammie could see her perfectly happy face.

Cammie felt her eyes moisten. *What am I doing here?* she thought. Sonia went into her final combination spin, picking up speed. *I used to be a good spinner*, Cammie thought. She rose on her elbow. *Was a good spinner? So what does that mean? I can't spin anymore? Gosh, I can't skate anymore!*

Feeling panic rise within her, Cammie jumped off her bed and approached the mirror. "No!"

Cammie closed her eyes, hoping that the overweight girl she stared at was a product of her imagination. She looked in the mirror again and began to cry. Cammie Wester had never had those puffy cheeks, and her thighs had never been so wide. She had always been slim and trim, and now her jeans felt tight, and she felt lazy and sleepy. *What am I doing here?* Cammie thought again.

Ignoring the weakness in her right ankle, Cammie ran out of the room and knocked on Alex's door. Nobody answered. She pushed the door open. The drapes were drawn. Alex was asleep. A half-finished can of cashews sat on his nightstand next to three empty cans of Coke.

Cammie lowered herself on the floor, thinking hard. So they had been stuffing themselves with junk food and watching movies for over three weeks, sleeping their lives away and wasting their time. Was everything over for them now?

Cammie buried her head in her hands and began to cry.

Alex stirred in his bed then sat up, looking confused. "Cammie, are you all right?"

She shook her head, her ponytail brushing her face. "We're not skaters anymore."

"Sure we are." Alex threw the covers away and stood up, yawning. As he raised his arms, Cammie saw how wide his midriff was.

"You've gained weight," Cammie said flatly.

Alex looked at his protruding belly. "Hmm, you're right. I'll have to lose it before the next competition."

"Alex, you're nuts!" Cammie cried out. "There'll never be another competition. Do you understand it?"

His eyes were wide open. "Why not?"

"Do you feel like practicing now?"

"Hmm, not really."

"Alex, there's something I want you to see. Now." Before Alex could say something, Cammie ran to her bedroom.

Alex followed her, although she heard him mutter something like, "You're acting weird today, you know?"

Kanga still sat where Cammie had left it, and the monitor was dark blue. Cammie went back to the list of competitions and chose the title Junior Worlds: Junior Men's Free Skate.

"Oh, is it live?" Alex pulled an armchair closer.

"No, the boys competed two days ago. But it doesn't matter."

They both watched Jeff skate to his first Junior Worlds' silver medal.

When the camera focused on Jeff's happy face, Alex sighed. "I know what you mean. We're slightly out of shape."

"Slightly?" Cammie cried out.

"Okay, we're really out of shape. What difference does it make?"

"It makes a huge difference. Because, Alex, the truth is, that we need to get out of here. And the sooner the better. Because if we stay longer, we'll never be able to skate again."

THE RINK OF FEAR

As they closed the heavy front door behind them, Cammie shivered at the feeling of cold air on her face. "It's freezing out here!" Alex grunted something undistinguishable. He didn't look particularly happy. Cammie knew he'd rather be in his soft, comfortable bed. She cast a longing look at the dark window of her bedroom on the fifth floor. Gosh, why did everything in the Witch of Pride's mansion have to be so cozy?

It's not too late to come back, a nasty thought crossed Cammie's mind. Perhaps they could really stay with the witch a little longer. Cammie would take a hot bath and then have a cup of hot chocolate with a slice of cheesecake and nestle under her down comforter ... *Yes, but how about skating?*

A gust of wind slapped Cammie on the face. She cringed and put her hands into her pockets.

"You know what? Let's go to the dorm now. I don't think it's a good idea to visit the Witch of Fear at night. Her castle is scary enough even in the daytime."

Alex wrapped his scarf tighter around his neck. "Hmm, you may be right, but we'll be easier to spot during the day. We can't just walk in the castle and ask for the R.O.F.A."

"True." Cammie looked around. Tall trees swayed in the wind; except for the snow around the ice path, everything was dark.

"We'll be fine," Alex said. "The Witch of Fear will never catch us. I'm sure she's asleep now. All of those witches like taking it easy. We'll find the R.O.F.A. and get straight out."

Cammie shuddered at the idea of running away from the witch. "You can definitely outskate the Witch of Fear. But what am I going to do with my weak ankle?"

"You have Kanga. Come on."

The cold wind must have awaked Alex; he surely looked much more alert, even excited at the idea of going to the white castle. Cammie only wished she could share her friend's enthusiasm. She sighed and moved forward. Alex skated fast on deep secure edges. Cammie trailed behind, her hands clasped around Kanga's handle. She felt sluggish and bloated. Even her skating boots felt too tight.

"Alex, wait for me!"

He turned around, his face sweaty. "I just want to get it over with. I'm exhausted."

"I wouldn't tell by the way you skate. Do you have to be so fast?"

"Do you call that fast?" Alex grabbed a handful of snow and put it in his mouth. "My legs are killing me. Besides, I'm thirsty and hungry, and I want to go to bed."

"Do you want to spend another night at the mansion?" Cammie looked at the black silhouttes of trees behind them. The Witch of Pride's mansion wasn't that far away.

Alex moaned. "Stop it, Cammie! If we go back now, we'll never be able to leave again. Come on, let's move."

The bright silhouette of the white castle appeared from around the corner.

"Stop!" Cammie breathed out. Kanga screeched to a halt.

Alex looked back. "Are you okay?"

"What exactly are we going to do when we're inside? We don't even have a plan."

"We'll play it by ear. Come on. Let's go."

Cammie nodded, but she couldn't move. Her feet were glued to the ice.

"Cammie, the longer we wait, the scarier it will be."

Cammie waved her hand. "All right."

The glass building seemed to be lit from the inside. Tall and poised, the castle would look beautiful if it were not for the figurines of dragons, bats, and gargoyles running along the façades. Just looking at the interplay of light and shadows on the walls of the building gave Cammie the creeps.

To get to the entrance, Cammie and Alex had to cross the witch's private rink. The ice looked beautiful, perfectly smooth, and the color was pale pink.

Cammie raised her foot and then lowered it. "Alex, I can't."

"Cammie, relax. There's nothing to worry about."

"Oh really? What makes you so sure the witch hasn't jinxed the ice? Remember what happened last time?"

"Hmm."

Cammie knew Alex too thought of their experience three years ago. The Witch of Fear had bewitched her rink so nobody could skate there without performing a series of outside and inside waltz eights. Fortunately, by that time, Cammie and Alex had practiced compulsory moves long enough, so they had managed to complete the assignment. Yet if something similar happened now, Cammie didn't have a chance. Not with her weak ankle, anyway.

"But she doesn't even know we're here," Alex said. "You know what? I'll step on the ice first, and we'll see what happens."

"I don't want anything bad to happen to you either."

"Oh, I'll be fine. Let me—"

"No!" Cammie grabbed Alex's hand. "You know what? We'll step onto the ice together at the same time."

They joined hands. Cammie closed her eyes and jumped. The ice responded with a soft thud.

"See, it's okay," Alex's voice said next to her. "Ah-h-ah!"

Before Cammie realized something wasn't right, Alex's hand slipped away; then she felt herself being lifted in the air. Instinctively, she let go of Kanga's handle. For the last time, the white castle flashed before her; then everything plunged into darkness. Cammie tried to scream, but the wind grabbed her by the throat, choking her. She coughed and closed her mouth. With the corner of an eye, she saw a sneering gargoyle rush past her; then she was pulled inside the castle.

Cammie fell on hard ice, but fortunately, nothing seemed to hurt. She took a deep breath and sat up, looking around. She was in a dark circular room with several long corridors stretching in different directions ahead of her. The only bright spot was a moon-cast reflection of the window frame.

"Alex!" Cammie called.

Dead silence was the only answer she got.

"Alex!" Cammie raised her voice and strained her eyes to see something in the depth of the passage closest to her. *He must be in one of those corridors*, she thought. Yet she felt too scared to get up. Perhaps Alex would hear her and come to her rescue.

"Alex, where are you? Are you all right?"

"Oh, he's fine, though he can't hear you." The cold, husky voice had come from somewhere behind Cammie.

"Who's that?" Cammie looked back and shrieked.

The Witch of Fear shook her head at her, looking amused. The witch's long gray hair looked stringy and unkempt. Cammie also saw that the woman was wearing a nightgown.

"Sneaking into my house in the middle of the night. That's a felony. I should probably report you to the authorities."

Oh please, call the cops now! Cammie silently prayed. She'd much rather face Captain Greenfield or even Lieutenant Turner than the Witch of Fear. It was that particular witch Cammie hated the most.

Even though it was Winja who had broken Cammie's ankle, Cammie never felt completely helpless in the presence of the Witch of Injuries. There was always something Cammie could do. The evil woman could be fooled. Cammie could run away, hide, scream—whatever.

The Witch of Fear was much worse; there was something sinister about her. When the witch looked straight at Cammie, her eyes acquired a terrible glint that robbed Cammie of all hope. It paralyzed her, turned her into a nervous wreck, and gave her the desire to give up. Cammie knew she wouldn't be able to stand up to the evil woman, not on her own.

"Although I don't think it's a good idea. Why should I rob the good, hard-working policemen of their long-deserved night's rest?" The witch scratched her long nose. "I'm sure we can handle this little problem ourselves."

"Where's Alex?" Cammie whispered. Her hands were getting numb; she rubbed them hard.

The witch bared her sharp teeth in a smile. "Oh, you'd better think about yourself, girl. Anyway, why did you decide to pay me a visit? Is it the R.O.F.A. you're after?"

Cammie couldn't suppress a gasp.

"You're way too trustworthy, young lady." The witch's gray eyes were slowly turning pink then crimson.

Cammie tried to look away; she could hardly breathe.

"Sharing your plans with someone like Annie. What can be more stupid than that? Didn't you realize that the girl would run straight to me?"

Annie. Of course! So she had told every witch about Cammie and Alex's plans, not just the Witch of Pride. And Cammie had thought the girl wasn't that bad, that she wanted to change, to go back to skating. She lowered her head, swallowing tears. So that was the end of their quest. Now the Witch of Fear would destroy the two of them for sure.

"What're you worried about? I'll let you have the R.O.F.A. if that's what you want."

What? Cammie's eyes dried up immediately; she stared at the witch, dumbstruck. The witch's eyes were back to their normal pale-gray color.

"That's right. I'm not playing games with you. Here. Take it." The Witch of Fear waved her hand. It looked as though a black curtain had been raised, and Cammie saw a passage of about fifty feet long stretching in front of her. The corridor led into a circular room with a podium covered with a black velvet cloth. Something bright and silvery sat on top of the podium.

"Is that really the R.O.F.A.?" Cammie's head spun. Could it be true, and they had finally located the healing device? The silvery object did look like it had magical powers. It pulsated and shimmered. But would the witch really let Cammie use the R.O.F.A.? She would definitely want something in return.

"It's the R.O.F.A., all right. I've used it myself a couple times, and Winja practically lives on it." The Witch of Fear grinned.

"So … so what do you want me to do?" Cammie's voice became husky; she cleared her throat.

"Nothing. Just take it."

"But … but … " Cammie didn't know what to say. Things were too good to be true. Could the witch be trusted? Cammie wished she could talk to Alex.

"Now you'd better take it before I change my mind. First you break into my home, and then you sit on the floor and mope. So you don't want the

R.O.F.A.? Then get out!" The witch's index finger with a long nail pointed somewhere behind Cammie.

"No!" Cammie cried out. Gosh, what was she thinking? Who cared if the witch was going to make Cammie do some moves in the field? After Cammie got healed, it wouldn't matter. If only her ankle got strong again, Cammie could handle anything.

Without waiting another second, Cammie pushed off the ice, heading for the corridor. Her eyes were fixed on the object on the podium, so when her foot gave way, she could still see its silvery side.

"What's wrong?" She was falling, falling, and there was nothing she could do about it. Cammie waved her arms, trying to stay upright, but it seemed as though she had no control over her body. She flew into the darkness headfirst. She buried her head in her arms, expecting a hard blow. She didn't hit the ice for what seemed like eternity; it felt as though an invisible hand pulled her through the darkness.

Bang! A dull blow was followed by a feeling of coldness against her thigh. The lights went on. Cammie looked around and yelped. The only thing she saw was ice. She sat on very smooth surface, and the ceiling above her appeared to be covered with the same grayish substance. The rink seemed to stretch for miles and miles ahead. Cammie couldn't tell how far it went.

Cammie squinted and looked straight ahead of her. There was a slightly overweight, scared-looking girl about a hundred yards away. Oh, good. At least, she wasn't alone. Perhaps that fatty would tell her where the exit was.

Cammie stood up clumsily; the plump girl did exactly the same. Slowly, Cammie moved in the girl's direction. The girl appeared to be approaching Cammie.

"Hello!" Cammie shouted.

Hello,–ello, ello! The sound came back to her, loud and intimidating.

"I'm Cammie. Who're you?" Cammie yelled.

I'm Cammie. Who're you? the walls responded.

"Oh, no!" Cammie slapped herself on the knee. What she had heard was her voice multiplied several times. She took another step forward and saw that there was another girl behind the first, and it looked exactly the same. Cammie glanced back. Another girl faced Cammie with her back, and there also were girls on her both sides, all looking identical.

"Those are my reflections!" Cammie exclaimed, realizing that the walls of the rink were covered with mirrors.

Reflections-ections! the echo answered.

"Weird!" Cammie spat out and grimaced at the sound coming back to her. "I can't be so fat!" Cammie exclaimed.

Fat, fat, fat, the echo teased her.

I need to get out of here, she thought. But how could she do it? All she saw was the pale-gray ice and her own reflections. Still there couldn't be a rink without an exit. All those girls had somehow gotten inside. Well, of course, there weren't many girls, just Cammie, but what difference did it make?

Cammie looked right and then left. Everything looked the same. She skated forward, determined to move as far as the surface allowed her. At some point, she would hit the mirror, and then she would definitely find some door. Her reflections skated toward her, and as Cammie looked at the girl in the green parka closely, she realized how clumsy her stroking was.

Cammie gritted her teeth and straightened up. "Shoulders down; chin up; bend your knees!" Cammie remembered Coach Ferguson's instructions too well, and she shouted them at herself, ignoring the nagging echo. If she had to skate around the rink with mirrored walls, at least she was going to do it right.

Cammie was getting tired, but there seemed to be no end to the rink. Cammie clenched her teeth and picked up speed. Now she was flying toward her own reflection, and to her great joy, she saw that it was getting bigger. It meant she was getting closer.

Bang! Cammie's body bounced against the hard surface. She fell backward. The room spun once, twice …

"No!" Cammie closed her eyes, trying to fight dizziness. The ice shook under her, and then all motion stopped. Cammie slowly unglued her eyelids. She was in the same mirrored room.

"Now that's enough." Cammie rubbed her eyes, determined not to panic. If she wanted to get out of this stupid place, she needed to concentrate. Okay, what direction was she supposed to take?

"There!" Cammie said loudly, pointing at her reflection ahead. She stood up and took two tentative strokes.

Whoosh! The rink spun again. Cammie lost balance and fell.

She lay on her back, and her elbow was sore. Her reflection stared at her from the ceiling, the mouth wide open, the legs bent at awkward angles.

What if the exit is on the ceiling? Cammie thought. She stood up and made a weak attempt at a jump. Immediately the rink began to spin, and Cammie fell again, this time on her side. Fighting tears, she forced herself to sit up.

What was she going to do? The evil rink wouldn't let her skate anywhere. So that was the witch's trick. How on earth could Cammie believe that the nasty woman would simply hand her over the R.O.F.A.? She took a deep sigh then exhaled slowly. *Calm down,* she told herself. *It's nothing but a mind game. The exit has to be somewhere. I just need to try every direction.* She skated to the left; the rink spun and threw her down. She tried to move right, and the result was the same. The rink held her captive.

After several hard splats, Cammie didn't even remember where the floor ended and the ceiling began. No matter where she looked, she could see nothing but pale ice and her own wretched figure. The pitiful reflection never stayed in the same spot.

Sometimes Cammie saw it right in front of her; she would stretch her hand to reach it, but her fingers would touch nothing but air. Sometimes the miserable-looking girl would be far away. Cammie wished the reflection would disappear so she could concentrate. But minutes went by, and nothing changed.

Cammie shivered in the cold rink. She felt thirsty, hungry, and tired. Every inch of her body hurt. What time was it? She had no idea. Alex and she had left the Witch of Pride's mansion around midnight. Now it was probably late morning. Or maybe it was evening already. Or perhaps the next day. What if several days had already passed, and Cammie hadn't even noticed? What if she had been bouncing against the spinning ice for a week? And how much longer was she going to stay in this scary place? A month? Two months? A year? What if the witch kept her at her rink for the rest of Cammie's life? Cammie would grow old and pass away, staring at her own dying reflection.

The rink spun twice. Cammie swallowed, fearing she might get sick. "Help!"

Help-help-help! the echo answered.

Cammie closed her eyes, refusing to fight any longer. So that was it. She would never get out of the evil place. She was going to die.

"So what are you waiting for?"

Fighting dizziness, Cammie opened her eyes. The room didn't spin anymore. Instead, the Witch of Fear stood right next to Cammie, a nasty smile playing on her gaunt face.

Cammie looked in the direction the witch was pointing. The silvery R.O.F.A. sat right on the podium, and the podium was really close. It couldn't be more than twenty feet away. Somehow Cammie had managed to enter the circular room. As she glanced up at the walls, she saw that they were made of snow. Small snowflakes swirled in the air.

"Aren't you going to take the R.O.F.A.?"

Feeling too disoriented to question the evil woman's intentions, Cammie made a weak attempt to lift herself from the ice. But the moment she straightened up and saw the cold surface of the ice under her feet, her body stiffened. How was she going to skate across the room? What if the rink started spinning again? What if she slipped and fell? If it happened, she would definitely get injured again. She would break the other leg and probably both hands too. Hey, she could even fall on her head, get a concussion, and even die. Yes, people could die from concussions. Cammie had heard it somewhere.

"Why aren't you getting up?" The Witch of Fear did three twizzles on her right foot then switched to the other side.

"I…I'm scared," Cammie whispered. Her legs shook; she sank down again.

"Scared, huh?" The witch was all joy. "So you're no longer the cool Cammie Wester, the newly crowned intermediate champion of Skateland. Is that true?"

"What?" Cammie rubbed her forehead.

The Witch of Fear folded her arms on her chest. "So here you are, Cammie, injured, proud, and scared. Congratulations, girl, there goes your skating career."

"Fine." Cammie closed her eyes. She didn't care about being a champion anymore. All she wanted to do was to get out of the witch's castle. But she couldn't even move. And the very thought of skating to the dorm made her sick. Gosh, why on earth had she taken up skating five years ago? It was such a dangerous sport. She should have tried something safer, like a sewing class.

"And you, Alex Bernard?"

Cammie lifted her heavy eyelids and saw her friend lying on the ice directly across from her. Alex's face was almost as white as the snow on the walls.

"You know, my buddy, the Witch of Pride didn't want me to attack you. 'Such a charming young man and so delightfully proud'—that's what she said. She wanted to keep you all for herself, young man. Yet you didn't appreciate her generosity. You chose to escape with this stupid brat Cammie. Well, now you're paying for your wrong decision. You'll share Cammie's destiny, Alex. Look at you. You're injured too. Proud like the Witch of Pride herself and now scared. Awesome!"

The Witch of Fear wrapped her nightgown tighter around her skeletal body and did a series of waltz threes around the room, humming a creepy tune. Then the witch blew a kiss at the two of them and disappeared around the corner.

"Alex!" Cammie called faintly.

His eyes looked especially bright against his pale face. His hair was disheveled.

"Cammie, I can't skate anymore. It's over." Alex's voice trailed away. He coughed and covered his face with his hands.

"It's all right. Who needs this stupid skating anyway?" Cammie exhaled and lowered herself on the ice. The cold feeling was strangely pleasant. She no longer shivered; the ice was part of her. She knew in a moment she would blend in with its gray nothingness.

And then comes the end, which is nothing, a line from one of the Black Rink songs popped in Cammie's mind. The rapper was right. Skating took you nowhere. Perhaps you enjoyed it for a short time, but then you got injured. Or you became too full of yourself, and you were no longer excited about practices. Skating took everything out of you until there was nothing but cold fear left. And the only way to deal with that fear was to give up, to become one with the gray ice…

"R-r-r-r! Wake up right now, sleepy head."

What was that? Cammie's head felt heavy. She opened her eyes and squinted at something brown and furry that sat on the ice two feet from her.

"Kanga," Cammie whispered, surprised. Kanga had never woken her up in the Witch of Pride's mansion. The last time Cammie had heard the bag's wakeup call was in Winja's cabin. Now the animal had obviously decided to talk to her again. Mr. Reed must have reprogrammed the device again, restoring the alarm function.

"For it is later than you think. Wake up and hurry to the rink."

"I'm at the rink already." Cammie sighed and closed her eyes again.

"But if you stay in bed and snooze, you'll never win; instead you'll lose."

"We have lost," Cammie murmured. "We have both lost."

"Cammie, the R.O.F.A.! Kanga can get it for us."

"What?" Cammie looked up.

Alex pointed to his neck then to her. "The pendant, Cammie."

Automatically, Cammie ran her hand against her neck. Her fingers brushed against the smooth surface of the skate hanging on a silver chain.

"Throw the pendant at the R.O.F.A.!" Alex shouted.

"Why?"

"Look at Kanga!"

Cammie glanced at her bag. The animal's yellow eyes glowed menacingly. Cammie knew what it meant. It was probably five in the morning, and Kanga was reciting its usual wakeup poem. Because Cammie hadn't responded to the call, Kanga's next step would be pulling the blanket off of Cammie. Of course, Cammie had no blanket, yet there was a cloth draped around the podium with the R.O.F.A. on it. So if Kanga took the cloth for a blanket…

"Cammie, quick!"

Kanga rose on its paws, ready to pounce. Summoning all her strength, Cammie ripped the skate pendant off her neck and tossed it in the direction of the podium. It fell right on top of the R.O.F.A.

With a loud snarl, Kanga rushed to the podium. Mesmerized, Cammie watched the animal's front paws go up; then Kanga's sharp claws grabbed a hold of the black cloth and pulled. The R.O.F.A. slid down onto the ice and rolled in Alex's direction. He stretched his hand and picked it up. "Yes!"

Cammie clapped her hands. "Kanga, you rock! Give it to me, Alex. I want to try it."

"Let's get out of here first. We don't want the witch to know we got the R.O.F.A." Alex put the silvery roll into the pocket of his parka and stood up. Cammie expected her friend to skate up to her, but he waited, biting his lip. Alex no longer looked excited; instead there was sadness all over his face.

"Cammie, I…I'm too scared to skate."

The witch's curse! Cammie too shuddered at the idea of stepping on the ice. Still…

"We need to get out of here. Let's skate one more time, okay?" Cammie did her best to sound encouraging, though she freaked at the very sight of the ice around her.

"I can't. My legs won't hold me. I know I'll slip and break my neck." Alex's face was covered with perspiration. He shook his head and sat down on the ice.

"What're we going to do?" Cammie looked around the room at the powdery snow and the swirling flakes. The only thing she hated looking at was the ice, but it was impossible. Except for the podium, the room had nothing but ice. Cammie tried to concentrate on the podium. The black velvet cloth was now on the ice, and something glistened on top of it. It was a piece of jewelry. Cammie's pendant.

"I know what to do!" Cammie exclaimed. If only she could reach the pendant, she would bring Kanga to her side and ask the bag to take them home. But was she brave enough to cover the twenty feet that separated her from the pendant?

Of course, she could do it. She wouldn't even have to get up; she'd crawl on her stomach. Even if she slipped, she wouldn't get hurt too much.

Cammie clenched her teeth and rolled on her stomach. Even lying on the ice felt scary. Cammie could physically sense menace emanating from the cold surface. The ice was her deadly enemy. It was there to destroy her. *I won't think about it*, Cammie told herself. Her legs barely moved, but she pushed herself forward, rising on her elbows. She could do it. As long as she kept her eyes on the pendant and not on the ice, she didn't have to think about the dangers of skating. Cammie's back hurt; she wasn't used to crawling like that. But she was getting closer. One more push … There! Her fingers closed around the sparkling skate. Cammie's hand shook as she slipped the chain over her head.

"Kanga!" Cammie shouted.

"R-r-r!" The bag skated up to her.

Cammie squeezed the handle hard. Alex raised his head, looking at her wearily.

"Alex!" Cammie said to Kanga.

The bag glided across the room to where Alex sat.

"Alex, grab the handle. Quick!"

He rose on his knees and reached for the handle.

"Okay, let's get out of here." She gave Alex a questioning look. "So where are we going?"

"Home," Alex groaned.

Cammie nodded. "Kanga? Boys' dorm."

TRIBUTE TO THE WITCHES

"**A**ren't you going to try the R.O.F.A.?" Alex tapped his pocket where Cammie knew he had put the magical device.

She shook her head. "Maybe later." *I don't need any magical devices anymore,* she thought. *Even if my ankle does get stronger, I don't want to skate ever again. This sport is too dangerous. No, I'm going back home to Clarenceville.*

Kanga glided forward fast. The wind pushed Cammie and Alex in the back. As they got closer to the exit, the trails of the Icy Park looked more groomed. The thickets had been replaced by nicely trimmed fir trees. Instead of gnarled roots and ugly stumps, the trails were lined with ice sculptures portraying skating animals. They passed a circular pond with light blue ice; they were already close to the exit from the park. Okay, there was the statuette of a skater holding a flower with multicolored petals. Axel Avenue was right behind the tall trees. Kanga slowed down to take a sharp turn around the statue.

"Cammie, look!" Alex exclaimed.

"What?"

"The statue. Look at it."

"Kanga, stop!" Cammie shouted.

The bag froze in its spot, and Cammie slowly unclasped her numb fingers. Next to her, Alex stood staring at the stone figure, his mouth agape.

"It looks like a witch," Alex said in a flat voice.

Wondering what he was talking about, Cammie shifted her eyes to the statue and shrieked. It was unbelievable. No longer did the figure holding the Skateland logo look like a graceful skater. Gone were the long limbs, the perky ponytail, and the sweet smile. Instead, a drab old woman with long, matted hair and a puckered face stared gloomily at them. Even the flower that the statue clutched in its wrinkled hand looked different, its petals wilted.

"It's a witch," Cammie whispered. "But why?"

"Maybe we're in a wrong place?" Alex turned around, scanning the area. "Perhaps it's something the witches have built, something we haven't seen before."

Cammie shook her head. "No, it is the entrance to the Icy Park. Don't you see the street sign? Here is Axel Avenue."

"True." Alex massaged his injured finger. "But I still think it's the witches' job."

"Of course," Cammie said. "But why? Why did they destroy the beautiful statue?"

Because the witches always destroy things. Just like they destroyed us, Cammie thought bitterly. For that was the end of Cammie and Alex's skating careers. They would return home and forget everything about Skateland.

Cammie sighed deeply to drive away tears and put her hand on Kanga's handle again. "We'd better get to the dorm, Alex."

"Not so fast, kiddies, not so fast!" several familiar voices shouted in unison.

Cammie groaned and looked back at the three witches staring at them. "Haven't you done enough? Leave us alone!"

Before any of the evil women could say anything, Winja shuddered and began to scream. "Look at the statue! Something happened to it."

The Witch of Fear approached the grim figure with a flower and touched the gray stone. "Hmm, the statue does look different. Is it your job, Pride? Now don't lie to me!"

The Witch of Pride snorted. "Yeah, right, like I have nothing better to do than giving statues a makeover. I bet it was you, Winja. Didn't you tell me once how back in junior high you drew beards and mustaches on the portraits of famous people in your school books?"

"Yes, but that was years ago!" Winja looked intimidated. Cammie actually saw her shrink under the Witch of Fear's heavy look. "I didn't do anything to this statue, I swear…Hang on! I think I know what happened."

Winja studied the stony witch, looked down at her bandaged knees, and finally fixed her beady eyes on Cammie and Alex. "Yes, that's the only explanation. It's them."

"What?" Cammie cried out. It was unbelievable. To suggest that Alex and she had turned a beautiful statue into a witch—how could Winja even think that? Besides, even if Alex and she wanted to pull a prank like that, how on earth would they do it? None of them had ever taken a sculpting class.

Meanwhile Winja knelt on the snow and started digging a hole. Next to Cammie, Alex yelped.

The crutch! Cammie remembered. That was the place Alex and she had hidden Winja's crutch. But how on earth had the witch figured it out?

"Going to plant a tree in your honor, Winja?" the Witch of Fear asked sarcastically. "I would rather expect Pride to do it."

"There it is!" With a shout of triumph, Winja raised her crutch above her head. "Now which of the three of us is the smartest, huh? When I saw the deformed statue, I knew the transformation had something to do with magic. And I've been looking for my crutch everywhere. Cool!"

"Uh, not bad." The Witch of Fear actually looked impressed.

The Witch of Pride snickered. "What do you mean *deformed statue*? Actually, I like it better this way. It's a tribute to us witches. A witch holding Skateland's logo … doesn't it suggest that we are the elite residents here?"

The Witch of Fear nodded appreciatively. "Absolutely. So justice has triumphed after all, huh? Okay, back to business. I think you have something that doesn't belong to you, kiddies."

"Just leave us alone," Cammie said wearily.

"Oh really?" The Witch of Fear said with mocking surprise. Cammie noticed that she had replaced her nightgown with a black robe. "I hope you don't expect us to let you get off so easily."

"Is that what you call getting away easily?" Alex sounded exhausted. "We're injured, fat, and scared. What else do you want?"

The Witch of Pride smacked her bright-red lips. "Oh, my cute champion, so you're still looking for justice. Let me tell you: this is exactly what we're after. Give us the R.O.F.A. and we'll let you go."

"Okay," Cammie said quickly. They didn't need the magical device anymore. They were never going to skate again.

"I'll take it." Winja stepped out from behind the Witch of Fear and stretched her long hand in a torn gray glove. The lump on her forehead looked greenish.

"Give it to her, Alex," Cammie whispered.

Alex's eyebrows shot up. "Now wait a minute."

"Just do it, Alex," Cammie said.

"But your ankle!"

"I'll never skate again anyway."

"But you'll still need your leg to walk normally. Look!" Now Alex spoke to the witches. "We need the R.O.F.A. to restore Cammie's ankle. You can have it afterward. Oh yes, and I wouldn't mind using the device on my finger either."

"Now you hand it over," the Witch of Fear said firmly.

Alex shook his head. "Then we aren't giving you the R.O.F.A. at all."

"Look, young man, you're not in the position to negotiate with us," the Witch of Fear said angrily.

"By the way, we could use the Kanga bag too." The Witch of Pride cast a greedy look at the furry animal, who still sat by Cammie's side.

Cammie's heart skipped a beat. "You want the bag? My Kanga?"

"And why not? You aren't a skater anymore." The Witch of Pride did a series of smooth choctaws and clicked her tongue. "Man, I'm still a brilliant skater. So give me the pendant, Cammie."

"No way!" Cammie squeezed the silver skate.

The Witch of Pride gave her a look of disgust. "Then we'll have to resort to violence, though I'm reluctant to do that."

Cammie sat down on the ice and hugged the animal by the neck. She wasn't going to let the witches take away her faithful Kanga.

Winja advanced on Cammie, her crooked teeth bared, the crutch shaking menacingly in her hand. The Witch of Fear took a step toward Cammie, her sharp fingernails pointed at Cammie's neck.

It's over, Cammie thought. *We can't fight the three strongest witches. We have to give up.*

Yes, you can, a small voice said inside her head. *You're a skater, remember?*

Not anymore, Cammie thought bitterly.

No one can take skating away from you unless you choose to give it up.

Cammie took a deep breath. The witches' tall figures bent over her. The Witch of Fear stretched her clawed hand toward Kanga.

"No!" Cammie shouted. "I'm not giving up."

The Witch of Fear's hand jerked back. "What was that?"

"Get away from me, witches! I'm a skater."

"You'd better tell the young lassie to behave, champion!" the Witch of Pride patted Alex on the shoulder.

Alex jumped backward. "Leave us alone."

The Witch of Pride's twisted mouth looked like a smashed tomato. "Oh, how about that? The losers have some guts."

"We aren't losers; you are!" Alex cried out.

"Do you want to see who is a real loser?" the Witch of Fear approached Cammie.

Cammie closed her eyes. "Help! Somebody help us!"

Next to her, the three witches guffawed. "No one is coming to your rescue, brats."

"Please!" Cammie squeezed her pendant and wrapped her other arm around Kanga's soft torso. "Mr. Reed, help us! Please!"

Next to her, Alex raised his voice too.

"How silly is that? The skate sharpener's cabin is too far away," Winja croaked.

Someone pulled on Kanga's bag, but Cammie held on tight. She kept her eyes closed not to look at the Witch of Fear. Cammie didn't care about Winja; after all, she was already injured. And as for the Witch of Pride...well, Cammie couldn't imagine how anyone in her position could be proud anymore.

The witches screamed around them. Next to Cammie, Alex too prayed for help.

And then everything became quiet, so quiet that Cammie could hear the wind shuffling the snow off the tops of the trees. What did it mean? Had the witches left? Cammie was too scared to open her eyes. Perhaps she was merely dreaming, and if she woke up she would find herself surrounded by the evil witches again. No, she'd better stay asleep.

"Mr. Reed!" Alex's voice called somewhere close to Cammie.

"Greetings," a very familiar voice said.

No, Cammie was definitely in the middle of a dream, for it couldn't be...

"Cammie, look who is here!" Alex exclaimed.

She couldn't keep her eyes closed anymore; they popped open. Still unable to believe what she saw, Cammie stared at Mr. Reed towering over the three witches, who lay sprawled on the ice in awkward postures. Winja's left leg was wrapped around her crutch, her right toe pick scraping the ice. The Witch of Pride's legs were spread in almost a spreadeagle position, her mouth opening and closing like a fish's. The Witch of Fear lay still, her face twisted in the expression of annoyance.

"Mr. Reed, you've come. You heard us!" Cammie blurted out.

The man's eyebrows shot up. "Of course I heard you. What's so surprising about that?"

Cammie caught Alex's confused look.

"But your cabin is miles away from here. Or did you just happen to be somewhere close to this place?" Alex asked.

Mr. Reed shook his finger at the two of them. "That's what happens when kids don't read instruction books."

"What?"

"Cammie, have you ever bothered to study Kanga's instruction book? It lists all the functions of the bag," Mr. Reed said.

"What instruction book?" Cammie had never seen any instruction book.

Mr. Reed spread his arms. "That's what I thought."

He approached Kanga and stroked the animal's right side. To Cammie's utter amazement, the fur on Kanga's side spread, revealing a hidden pocket. Mr. Reed took a thin booklet out of the pocket and handed it to Cammie. "Page three. Read chapter five from the Table of Contents."

"'Kanga's Special Functions,'" Cammie read. "'A. Alarm clock; B. Navigator; C. Bottle Carrier ...' Well, I know about those. 'D. Skate Guard Reminder ...' What's that?"

"If you forget your skate guards, Kanga will rebuke you," Mr. Reed said calmly. "Do you want to see?"

Without waiting for Cammie's answer, the man shook Cammie's skate guards out of the bag and zipped it back up.

Kanga let out a loud squeal and shouted, "Hey, you forgot your guards again. Get them before I count to ten."

"Wow, I never knew it could do that!" Cammie felt very impressed.

"Well, the reason you didn't must be because you never leave your skate guards behind. That's good," Mr. Reed said. "Okay, keep reading."

"'E. Help,'" Cammie read. "Help?"

"Exactly. It means that when you're in trouble, Kanga will send a signal to me. I'm perfectly aware that skating witches won't stop short of hurting a promising skater. And we're looking at two very promising young skaters here." Mr. Reed's blue eyes studied Cammie for a second and then lingered on Alex's flushed face.

"We aren't promising skaters," Alex said morosely.

Cammie nodded. "He's right. Not anymore."

"I know you were severely attacked." Mr. Reed's gaze moved to the witches, who still sat on the ice.

Cammie saw the evil women cringe.

"Just let us go, Reed. What do you expect from us anyway? Repentance? You're not getting it," the Witch of Pride snarled.

"Oh, of course not. You're hardly in the position to renounce your wrongdoings," the old man said lightly.

"Then what on earth do you want?" The Witch of Fear raised her head, wincing as though she were in pain.

Mr. Reed lowered his head. "Nothing whatsoever."

"Then could we please go?" Winja whined.

"I'm not keeping you here." The corners of Mr. Reed's lips twitched.

The three witches got on their feet hastily. "Do you mean it? We can go now?" the Witch of Fear asked quickly.

Cammie followed the interaction with amazement. She had never seen the witches so intimidated by anyone's presence.

"Witches, you may leave now," Mr. Reed said simply.

The ice scraped hard under the witches' blades. The branches creaked as the women dashed into the thicket. Mr. Reed stood quiet for a moment, his eyes following the witches' escape. Then he turned his calm face to Cammie and Alex. "Now, my dear friends, I think it's time for a short ride."

Tough Decision

A ride? Cammie wondered what Mr. Reed meant by that. As far as she remembered, the man didn't own an ice mobile, and she knew she would never handle a long skate to Mr. Reed's cabin.

Mr. Reed raised his hand, and a silver ice mobile wearing the sign Skateland Police emerged from one of the side trails. A young dark-haired policeman rose from the driver's seat.

Oh no, not Lieutenant Turner! Cammie thought. The last thing she wanted now was to be reprimanded for breaking the law. Perhaps if Captain Greenfield had showed up, they might have a chance at convincing him that they had been skating around the Icy Park to get the R.O.F.A., not to have fun.

But Cammie knew negotiating with overzealous Lieutenant Turner would be a lost cause.

Mr. Reed chuckled. "No need to worry, my dear friends. Lieutenant Turner is here at my request."

Yeah, right, Cammie thought. Well, of course the older man probably meant the best, but perhaps he didn't realize how much Lieutenant Turner hated Cammie, especially after she rebuked him sharply when she had returned to Skateland from home. Then again, Bob Turner had brought Cammie's Kanga bag to the Witch of Pride's castle. That was a nice thing to do, but he had merely been acting on Wilhelmina's orders.

"Hi, Cammie, how is your ankle?" Lieutenant Turner was slightly out of breath.

What? The stickler had actually asked her how she felt. Cammie stared at the young man and shrugged.

"Mr. Reed told me everything about your rehabilitation. I hope you're feeling better. Uh, how are you, Alex?"

Now it was Alex's turn to be surprised, though Cammie thought her friend did a better job at acting cool. "I don't remember you reading us our rights, Lieutenant. Still, I think it would be better for us to remain silent."

Bob Turner's face turned hot pink and then crimson. "I…I thought…"

"It's good you decided to use your mind for a change," Alex said.

"Alex, stop!" Cammie whispered loudly. Nasty as he was, Lieutenant Turner was a cop. Talking back to a policeman would surely put them in trouble.

"What do we have to lose now?" Alex said bitterly. "Go ahead, Lieutenant; tell us what a great skater you are. And then you may laugh at us."

"Now wait a minute!" Mr. Reed stepped between Alex, who was clenching his fists, and Bob Turner, who had his head down.

"Lieutenant Turner has been a great help to me. Without him, my trip to the Icy Park would have been much longer. And I do believe Bob is genuinely concerned about your well-being, Alex," Mr. Reed said.

Alex stared at his boots. Cammie stroked Kanga's head absentmindedly.

"Do you mind taking Cammie's Kanga bag, Bob? You can put it on the back seat," Mr. Reed said.

As Lieutenant Turner pulled the bag away, Mr. Reed winked at Cammie. "Bob is a different person now. Never before did I hear him worry about anyone other than himself. And now he's been calling and asking about you for weeks. You must have told him exactly what he needed to hear, Cammie."

"When did you talk to this baboon?" Alex whispered when Mr. Reed looked away.

"He gave me a ride to the dorm when I returned from home," Cammie whispered back.

"And what did you say?"

"Well…" Cammie felt hot in spite of the chilly wind. "The truth, I guess. 'You think you're so cool and all, but you have a cold heart.'"

Alex whistled. "And that changed him?"

"I don't understand it myself," Cammie said sincerely.

"We all need to know the truth about ourselves," Mr. Reed said. He must have overheard Cammie and Alex's conversation. "Illusions can be destructive, but the same is true about self-deprecation. The important thing is to be aware of your strengths and weaknesses and then move on from there. Anyway, don't be harsh on Bob, my friends. Four years ago he had his share of witches' attacks, and I'm afraid he didn't handle them wisely. Now he's willing to change. Don't take this chance away from him."

So Lieutenant Turner had been attacked too. No wonder he had given up skating. Cammie felt a wave of hatred toward the wicked witches rise within her. How could they go around like that hurting people, robbing them of their dreams? Why couldn't anyone do anything about it?

"Let me help you to get into the ice mobile, Cammie." Bob Turner stood next to her, his hand outstretched.

"I'm fine. Thank you," she said automatically. She raised her right foot but froze at the very sight of the rough ice under her feet. What if the ice threw her off again? "I mean…" Cammie raised her eyes at Mr. Reed. Perhaps the older man could give her a hand?

"I would take advantage of Lieutenant Turner's offer," Mr. Reed said calmly.

With a heavy sigh, Cammie leaned on Bob's arm and let him lead her into the ice mobile.

"Thank you," she said stiffly as she sank onto the soft cushion.

"No problem." Bob stepped away to let Alex, who was being assisted by Mr. Reed, slide into the seat next to Cammie. The two men sat down in the front.

"Your cabin, Mr. Reed?" Bob Turner asked.

"Naturally." The older man fastened his seat belt.

The ice mobile dashed forward, leaving two perfect tracings on the ice behind it. The sight of the statue with a flower disappearing around the corner reminded Cammie of something that had been bothering her.

"Mr. Reed, the statue at the entrance to the park looks like a witch now."

"It does indeed," the old man said without looking back.

"But why?" Alex asked.

Mr. Reed turned to face them, his face pink from the cold wind. "Can't either of you think of a reason?

"Well, we hid Winja's crutch under the statue." The moment Cammie said those words, she wondered if Mr. Reed would reprove them for ruining the statue. Really, why would Skateland residents want a witch as the symbol of their village?

"You got it," Mr. Reed said. "Winja's crutch is a magical object, so it has evil powers. Its close proximity to the statue of a skater couldn't leave the statue intact. Actually, this kind of transformation is quite common. Looking at the witches, would you believe that at some point in their lives they were beautiful women?"

Cammie shook her head. "They are ugly now."

Alex made a nasty face.

"Well, if you had a chance to look at their younger pictures, you'd be surprised. See, it's important what kind of desires and intentions a person harbors in his heart. If there is nothing but negative thoughts and emotions, then even the most perfect facial features will be distorted, and the individual will look hideous. Evil is destructive."

"Will the statue go back to normal once the crutch is gone?" Cammie asked. "I'm sorry, Mr. Reed. We shouldn't have hidden it there. But we didn't know."

Mr. Reed shook his head. "It's hard to tell what will happen to the statue. But in my opinion, it's most unlikely that it'll ever look beautiful again."

"So they'll have to build another statue," Alex said. "Gosh, I wish they won't make us pay for it. My dad will kill me."

"It's not your fault." Mr. Reed said. "Actually, I started noticing certain changes in the statue long ago. It surely couldn't stay immune to all the curses and jinxes of the park. Of course, Winja's crutch planted right under the statue has sped up the process. But don't worry. Sooner or later, the image of the skater would have turned into a witch anyway."

Cammie stared at him. "But what changes are you talking about, Mr. Reed? I didn't notice anything."

"Me either. I thought the statue looked the same," Alex said.

"You could only notice it if you took a really good look at the statue." Mr. Reed thought for a moment. "Well, the skater's smile looked less and less sincere. Her fingernails got more pointed with every coming day. I also saw wrinkles forming in the corners of the girl's mouth and on her forehead … There's too much evil in the Icy Park. The witches are getting more and more restless. See, negative thoughts and feelings can't be kept inside for a long time. Sooner or later, they will spill out and destroy everything around."

The old man looked away. They rode in silence for another ten minutes. Then the ice mobile took a quick shortcut through the thicket. The blades hit a mogul; the vehicle careened to the right and slid back unto an ice path straight ahead of them. Cammie could already see the fir trees surrounding Mr. Reed's rink. Now in broad daylight, the purple ice looked even brighter.

"Here we are," Mr. Reed said. "No, Bob, we aren't going to the house at this point. Will you please drop us off at the rink?"

At the rink? Cammie squeezed the leather seat. Skating was the last thing she wanted. Why couldn't Mr. Reed invite them to the house and let them rest a little?

"Mr. Reed, uh, we're not up to skating now," Alex said softly as the ice mobile stopped next to a wood bench about fifteen feet away from the ice. Mr. Reed's cabin stood directly across from them on the other side of the pond.

"But you must," the older man said simply. "Whatever problem a skater may suffer from, skating it away is the best cure."

"But…" Alex's face contorted as though in pain; he blinked and looked away.

Cammie knew her friend was too embarrassed to admit he was afraid of skating. Alex Bernard, one of the best athletes in Skateland, too scared to step onto the ice? It was unbelievable. He would much rather leave Skateland for good than try to explain to other people what he was going through.

Cammie cleared her throat. "Mr. Reed, er…"

"Go on," the older man said as he helped Alex out of the ice mobile and led him toward the bench.

She couldn't think of anything to say. Bob Turner held Cammie's hand as she lowered herself on the bench next to Alex.

"Thank you, Bob. I won't keep you any longer. Have a nice day," Mr. Reed said.

Lieutenant Turner saluted to the older man and walked away, his blades sinking deep into the snow. Before getting into the ice mobile, Bob turned around and looked at Cammie. For some reason, she felt sorry for the young man.

She waved at him. "Thank you for your help, Bob. It was really very nice of you."

Alex grinned. "You aren't a bad cop, after all, Lieutenant Turner."

The young man's face lit up instantly. "I know you'll skate again, Cammie. You too, Alex."

He saluted to the two of them, jumped into the ice mobile, and drove away.

"Well, I'm glad there's no misunderstanding between you and Skateland police," Mr. Reed said. "Bob Turner is hardly perfect. He may appear insensitive, but deep inside there is a tender, loving heart. Okay, back to business. You don't have to tell me anything. I know what's going on. You have been severely attacked by three witches. The curses are powerful, so we'll deal with them one at a time. Let's take care of your fear of ice. First thing I want you to do, my friends, is to look at the ice for a while."

Obediently, Cammie stared at the purple ice that stretched out in front of her. She didn't think of the rink as an arena to skate on; she merely enjoyed the way the sunlight spilled onto the bright surface, making the pond sparkle. She breathed in the smell of the pine trees that looked especially dark against the pristine snow. The longer Cammie studied the purple ice, the more she realized that the color of the rink wasn't solid. It seemed to shimmer and vibrate; tiny currents swirled underneath the surface. At some point, the ice would become deep purple, almost black. And then the undercurrent would ebb away, making the sheet of ice appear violet, almost lavender.

"It's beautiful!" The words came out of Cammie's mouth before she could even think.

"It looks…almost alive!" Alex breathed out next to her.

Mr. Reed nodded. "Good observation. The purple ice is alive…in a way. What I mean is that is has restorative powers. And this is exactly what the two of you need."

The old man removed his skate guards and stepped onto the ice. He pushed off his left outside edge and drew a big circle. He switched sides and repeated the move. Now Cammie and Alex were looking at a perfect figure eight.

"Good ice," Mr. Reed said approvingly. "Now who goes first? Cammie? Alex?"

Cammie glanced at her friend nervously and saw his green eyes narrow in concern. Sure, it was easy for Mr. Reed to talk. What if the ice played a trick on them? What if it knocked them down? What if it started spinning? Cammie shuddered, remembering the feeling of nausea.

"No one is ready, huh? Same time, then," Mr. Reed said lightly. "Stand up, both of you!"

Cammie saw Alex's body stiffen as he slowly got on his feet. Well, no matter what Alex did, Cammie wasn't going to take another risk.

"Nothing bad will happen to you, Cammie," Mr. Reed said.

She stared at her boots stubbornly, noticing how scuffed up the toes looked. She would have to polish them once she got to the dorm. Why, though? She wasn't going to skate again.

"Cammie, I promise you'll be fine. The purple ice would never hurt an honest skater," Mr. Reed said.

Cammie took a couple of deep breaths, telling herself to relax. Of course, she wasn't at the Witch of Fear's mirrored rink. And besides, she believed that Mr. Reed would never give her bad advice. The man wanted the best for Alex and her, so she had to do exactly what Mr. Reed had told her. Yes, she knew all those things, but the fear was too strong, and it robbed her of her strength. Cammie closed her eyes; she couldn't even look at the ice.

"Here you go. Good job, Alex!" Mr. Reed shouted.

Cammie opened her eyes. Alex stood on the edge of the rink, looking very much like a beginner, with his feet turned in, his arms raised stiffly above his head.

"Go forward; stroke the way you used too," Mr. Reed said warmly.

Alex stared at his feet as though uncertain in what direction they were supposed to move. Then he pushed off his left foot, lost his balance, swung his arms wildly, but miraculously managed to stay erect.

"Don't you worry; don't you worry!" Mr. Reed boomed encouragingly. "I told you. You aren't going to fall. The purple ice will hold you. Do some stroking again."

Alex nodded but didn't move.

"Bend your knees; it's the ABCs of skating," Mr. Reed said.

Alex bent his knees and pushed off his left foot again. This time, he managed to glide forward about ten feet.

"Don't raise your shoulders!" Mr. Reed shouted.

Now Alex appeared more relaxed as he did a wobbly circle around the rink. Cammie noticed that with each stroke, her friend looked stronger, more polished, more confident. She felt a twinge of excitement.

"I'm not dragging you onto the ice, Cammie," Mr. Reed said without looking at her.

She stood up, feeling determined. If Alex could skate, she was going to try it too. She felt her body shake as she stepped onto the purple ice. Mr. Reed appeared too busy coaching Alex to look at her.

Ah, whatever! Cammie clenched her teeth and pushed off the hard surface. The feeling was wonderful. The purple ice welcomed her; she felt strong, secure. She spread her arms and glided forward faster and faster.

"Yes!" the wind whistled in her ears.

"All right!" Alex waved at her from the side.

She saw him picking up speed too; now he was ahead of her. Of course, Cammie's ankle wouldn't let her move too fast, but whatever she could do at this point could be considered a definite improvement.

"That's enough!" Mr. Reed called after Cammie and Alex did three laps around the rink. "Feeling any better?"

Alex rubbed his red cheeks. "I feel great. Thank you, Mr. Reed."

"No more fear of ice?" The man's pale blue eyes rested on Cammie's face.

Fear of ice? The very idea seemed ludicrous. How could somebody be afraid of ice? Ice was a skater's friend. It threw you up in the air on your jumps; it gently hugged you on your landings; it pushed you around on your spins. Yes, ice was beautiful, and there was absolutely nothing to be afraid of.

Cammie opened her mouth to explain all those things to Mr. Reed, but the older man was the first to speak up. "I know what you want to say, Cammie. You love skating too much to let fear ruin your joy. That's what the purple ice is about. It takes the skater back to his or her first love of skating. And perfect love casts out fear."

"The only problem is … " Cammie felt her voice trail away. "My ankle!"

Mr. Reed nodded. "I know. And it brings us to the next step. You have found the R.O.F.A., I presume."

"Here it is." Alex reached into his pocket and took out the silvery roll.

Mr. Reed accepted the magical device with gentleness bordering on reverence. "Restoring Orthopedic Functions Aid. R.O.F.A. Do you guys know how it works?"

He didn't wait for their answer; instead, he unwrapped the silvery roll. The inside surface of the R.O.F.A. was pure gold. Strewn across it was a splatter of multicolored gems. The patterns formed by the gems looked like ice school figures: eights, brackets, loops, threes. There also were some special figures: grapevines, paragraphs, spectacles, and some figures Cammie couldn't name.

"Do you recognize the colors?" Mr. Reed asked.

Cammie came up closer and stared at the pink, blue, green, yellow, white, silver, and purple gems. The colors definitely looked familiar.

"Skateland colors," Alex said next to Cammie.

Mr. Reed nodded. "You got it. Each of the colors represents an official Skateland rink. Do you remember having to attend every rink as part of your rehabilitation, Cammie?"

"I did skate at every rink," Cammie said.

"As I already told you, practicing at those rinks helped you to recreate your experiences as a beginner skater. Now that you have gone through the whole cycle, the R.O.F.A. will complete the restoration process. By the way, did you notice that the black color is missing in the R.O.F.A. patterns?"

Cammie studied the arrangements again. Yes, Mr. Reed was right.

"When you skated at different rinks, you experienced everything the life of a skater can offer. Unfortunately, evil is a big part of it. Yet the R.O.F.A. has the power to heal; it is pure and perfect. Therefore, there is no room for evil in it."

Cammie looked at the beautiful decorations on the gold background, wishing the life of a skater would also be free of evil.

"Okay, Cammie, take off your right boot. I will wrap the R.O.F.A. around your ankle, and then you'll skate some more," Mr. Reed said. "Then after you're done, we'll let Alex use the device for his broken finger."

The fabric of the magical device was soft. As Mr. Reed secured the Velcro around Cammie's ankle, a pleasant feeling of warmth shot through her body. Right away she felt her leg getting stronger.

"I'm sure it feels good." Mr. Reed must have noticed her happy smile. "Ready to show us what you can do?"

As ready as ever, Cammie wanted to say. Suddenly she felt as though there had never been an injury in her life. She had never left her practice rink; she could still do double jumps. She was almost ready to start working on her triples. She had never been afraid of ice. No, she loved skating more than anything else in the world.

"Take it easy, though," Mr. Reed said, and again Cammie wondered if the old man could read her thoughts.

She started stroking around the rink, and this time her right ankle felt as strong as the other foot. Cammie stopped, raised her right foot, and gave it a critical look.

"How is it?" Alex shouted from the bench.

"It's … it's good. I can't believe it. I can skate normally again!"

"Great!" Alex yelled and started clapping.

Mr. Reed nodded appreciatively and brought his hands together too.

Cammie did a fast three turn first on her left foot and then switched sides. If felt easy; it felt wonderful. She tried a backspin, no problem. She went into a tentative waltz jump and landed it. Well, perhaps she didn't feel as light as before, but at least her injured ankle could hold jump landings. "Yes, yes!"

"Cammie!"

She looked up into Mr. Reed's calm face. "I have to warn you. The R.O.F.A. has restored your ankle tissues, but the healing has nothing to do with your skating skills. Magic or not, you have missed more than three months of skating. You have gained weight, and your body has grown. It means you have lost some of your technique. Therefore, you need to get that muscle memory back before you even attempt any double jumps. Those extra pounds will have to come off too. You are facing a lot of hard work, Cammie, a lot of hours on ice. There will be moments when you will feel disappointed, angry at yourself. Not everything will happen at once.

"A lot of skaters get discouraged after an injury; some of them even decide to give up skating for good. Think of it, Cammie. Are you ready to practice hard like never before? Are you prepared to take lots of falls before you can do things that once were so easy for you? Do you think all the effort is worth it if there is absolutely no guarantee that you will be an advanced skater again?"

As Cammie listened to Mr. Reed, flashes of her life in Skateland went through her mind: long hours of practice, bumps and bruises, the injury, tests, competitions, and the witches who had never left her alone. She swallowed hard.

"At this point, some people think it would be better to move on." Mr. Reed spread his arms. "You never know."

The sun smiled at Cammie from the sky, and the purple ice gleamed under her feet, as though inviting her to keep skating. She looked at Mr. Reed pleadingly. "Can I skate a little more? Please."

The older man rubbed his face, but Cammie saw that he was trying to hide a grin. "How come I knew exactly what your answer would be?"

But I didn't give you any answer, Cammie wanted to say but decided against it. Instead, she smiled at Mr. Reed and glided to the middle of the rink. She went into a three turn, swung her leg around, and swirled in a perfectly centered spin. She raised her right leg behind her and arched her back, looking up into the sky. The fir trees and the snow moved so fast around her that she could no longer discern any individual objects. But the sky stayed blue and calm, and Cammie felt calm too.

Now she knew she could take everything. Hard work, tough falls, tests, and competitions—everything would be fine as long as she was able to skate. She was a skater, and no one, not even the witches, could take that away from her. Cammie spun and spun. She was back on the ice, and that was the only thing that mattered.